Sign up for our newsletter to hear
about new and upcoming releases.

www.ylva-publishing.com

OTHER BOOKS BY AMBER JACOBS

Nights of Silk and Sapphire

PRIMAL TOUCH

AMBER JACOBS

CHAPTER 1

Tyger! Tyger! burning bright
In the forests of the night;
What immortal hand or eye
Could frame thy fearful symmetry?

—"The Tyger" by William Blake

JAGGED SHADOWS TWISTED WRAITHLIKE THROUGH the jungle undergrowth, flickered between the trees and grasses, and formed a body for a pair of ice-blue eyes that gleamed in the darkness with feral intensity. She moved soundlessly along invisible trails, avoiding twigs and surface roots with uncanny ease, leaving not a trace of passage in the moist earth. From time to time she would pause, lift her face, and take several rapid breaths through her nose. The air was thick and humid. So little breeze stirred the dense undergrowth, she was able to detect distinct scents of sweat, leather, and gun oil lingering in the heavy air. Dappled shafts of sunlight filtering through the canopy reflected off pearly white teeth as her upper lip curled back in a snarl, the rumbling purr that followed almost subliminal.

She had stalked her prey for many hours, and the stress was starting to wear on her aching muscles. She would need to select a good striking position soon, before her energy flagged, but she had learned the merits of caution and patience a long time ago.

Prowling carefully around a shallow gully, body held close to the ground, she listened to the unaccustomed sounds of the men who had foolishly wandered into her hunting grounds. There were three of them, moving through the jungle in a loose single file. The high-caliber guns they carried and the weathered clothes they wore marked them as her enemy: poachers.

She picked her way forward, realizing the men were following an old, well-worn animal trail. Leaping over the broad, moss-covered trunk of a fallen tree, she risked a burst of speed to take up a position ahead of their path. There she crouched, studying the approaching trio through narrowed eyes, sharpening her focus as the moment approached.

With three-to-one odds, she would need to strike hard and fast before the poachers could recover and move to defend themselves. There wouldn't be a second chance.

David Tow swatted fiercely at a fly and scowled at his companions. "How much farther, Jaz? We've been walking for hours."

The man in the lead glanced back with a smirk, taking a greater amount of pleasure in his irritation than Dave felt was polite. "What's the matter, Dave? A few insects too much for you?"

"Damn straight. I can't breathe in this place without swallowing a bloody bug."

"Be another hour, at least, until we reach Corbin's camp," said Jaz, swinging his machete in lazy strokes to help clear the thicker branches from their path. "And that's if he hasn't moved on."

"Moved on?" The third hunter, Tae, wiped his sweating brow angrily. Where Jaz was tall and rangy, Tae was short and wiry, his skin gleaming like burnished brass in the humid air. He had left his home in China—a country where it was growing increasingly difficult to make a living in the poaching game—to join this expedition, and Dave could see he didn't like to think he'd come all this way for nothing. "What d'ya mean, 'moved on,' Jaz? He knows we're coming, right? Why would he clear out?"

Jaz shrugged. "Jack Corbin don't like to wait around. If he finds a trail, he's gonna take after it, whether we're there or not. So pick your feet up, boys, and hope we aren't too late."

Leaving off their grumbling, the two men followed in silence for long minutes. Dave eyed the jungle nervously, listening to the strange, alien cries of unseen animals. Even in the still air, the dense foliage seemed to be constantly in motion, giving the eerie impression that invisible creatures lurked behind every shadow. "This place gives me the creeps, Tae," he muttered.

Tae shrugged, unconcerned. "You never hunted in India before, huh?"

"Nope, mostly in Africa. You know, elephants and stuff. Bigger game, bigger target. It's a lot more open than this. You can see what's coming."

Tae grinned. "Hunting tigers and leopards ain't like that," he said. "You just gotta be real careful and hope they don't find you before you find them."

Dave shivered and clutched his rifle tighter, his eyes wide as he scanned the jungle undergrowth. "I got a bad feeling about this gig," he said in a loud whisper. "I've been hearing things about India the last few years."

"Me too." Tae's expression hardened. "But I'm not gonna let a few rumors and ghost stories keep me from hunting the white gold that's out here."

"Damn straight," Jaz put in, dropping back to listen to the conversation. "You know how much we stand to make from this hunt, Dave? Hell, the money's spicy enough for Jack to get involved, and he don't waste his time on bullshit." He grinned wolfishly. "When we walk out of this jungle, we're gonna be rich men."

"That's *if* we walk out of here, Jaz," Dave said. "From what I hear, lots of guys like us aren't getting to be that lucky." He slapped at another flying insect, feeling sweat trickle down his spine. "You hear about the team that came out here three years back? Right in this same park, too, and hunting the same damn thing as we are."

Tae's face grew very still, and he nodded. "I heard the bodies were so ripped apart the rangers didn't even know for sure if they were human. Had to get some medical guy out from Delhi just to figure out all the pieces."

"Bah." Jaz waved his hand dismissively. "Amateurs. So they made a mistake and got shredded, big deal. All I know is, there's a helluva good chance there's a white tiger out here, and I want a piece of it. If you babies want to back out, go ahead. But remember, a chance like this only comes along once in a lifetime." So saying, the tall hunter stalked off, taking the forward position and eventually vanishing behind a curtain of lush greenery.

Tae and Dave exchanged glances. "He's right, you know," Tae said after a moment. "Poaching's a dangerous game, any way you cut it. Word hasn't got out about this yet, but when it does, every idiot out there is gonna want to take his shot. We got here first. We got Jack frickin' Corbin leading the hunt. This is too good to pass up."

3

"Yeah, I guess. Still…" Dave pulled the butt of his rifle into his shoulder. "I'm not letting some freaky tiger-ghost take me out."

"That's the spirit." Tae grinned and slapped his companion heartily on the back. "Now, you guard the rear, and I'll run the flanks, okay?"

Dave nodded. "Be careful," he warned. "There's rangers out here too, don't forget."

"I won't." Tae waved and then disappeared off the practically nonexistent trail, leaving Dave alone.

He scanned the jungle nervously, remembering some of the horror stories he'd heard before coming here. India wasn't the same hunting ground it had once been, he'd heard. Since the government had implemented the so-called "Project Tiger" back in '73, things had started getting tougher, but in recent years, they had gotten worse still. The Chinese were now almost militant about clamping down on poaching and were urging their neighbors to do the same. But the lure of hunting the great white tiger had called Dave away from the African savanna. He could only hope that the wild rumors of mysterious jungle terrors—the so-called "Indian Menace"—were nothing more than exaggerations intended to scare away the gullible. Patting his rifle reassuringly, he managed a weak smile.

"You won't be sneaking up on me, whatever you—"

It happened so suddenly, Dave didn't even have time to squeak. A tremendous force crashed into him from behind, knocking him to the forest floor and pinning him down. Dave struggled, winded from the impact, trying to flip himself over and call a warning even as the adrenaline surged through his blood. He felt a large, warm body pressing him down, smelled the strong animal musk of sweat, then something crushed his head into the moist earth, and stars flashed behind his eyes as his air supply was cut off. He desperately scrambled about for a weapon, but he'd lost his rifle in the fall. He tried to yell, then felt something burn across his shoulder. Panic engulfed him, and his struggles grew more frantic as the burning flared into searing agony.

Something was clawing at his back and shoulders!

With supreme effort, Dave managed to turn his head a fraction, just enough to dimly make out the light-orange stripes with shadowy dark lines that colored his attacker. Before he could draw breath to scream, however, something curved and sharp hooked itself under his throat and tore upward.

Dave managed a strangled croak, which turned into a shallow gurgle. His vision dimmed, then faded into black.

"Dave?"

Cold eyes framed by darkness and death snapped up at the sound of someone crashing through the jungle. A low growl rumbled from deep within her throat as the one they'd called Tae appeared, his rifle shouldered. He stopped, frozen, when his wide hazel eyes settled on her.

"Dear God!"

Her upper lip curled back in a snarl, baring her teeth as she crouched low over her kill. She watched the tip of his rifle waver, then dip, as the poacher stood in hypnotized shock, too dazed to fire. She sprang before he had a chance to recover his senses, rushing forward with a feral growl. Only when her bloodied claws lashed out with the speed of a striking cobra did his finger clench desperately at the trigger.

The gunshot startled the birds in the canopy above, its sharp report echoed by quickly silenced screams.

"Jesus Christ!"

Ashley Richards covered her mouth, her dark eyes wide as she stared at the two mauled bodies lying on the forest floor. Grady Neilson, her friend and colleague, offered a comforting pat on the back and tried to urge her away from the grisly scene. Ashley shook off his hand and took a step closer. She spared a quick glance behind her to where Simon Reynolds was comforting his shocked assistant, before turning back to study their bloody discovery.

One man's body lay face down on the forest floor, his rifle a few feet away. Great tears in the back of his shirt revealed a series of deep, bloody gouges. From the amount of blood soaking the earth around his neck, it was obvious his throat had been torn out, and the churned dirt around him gave testimony to his desperate struggles before death. A second body lay nearby, similarly mauled.

Ashley studied the two bodies and the bloodstained ground around them, taking a careful step closer. "What the hell happened here?"

Despite the gory scene, Ashley felt only a flutter of queasiness, as she knelt to get a better angle to study the closest body. Her work often took her to remote and wild regions of the world, and she'd seen her share of animal attacks. It took a lot to turn her stomach.

"Uh…Ash?"

Ashley glanced over her shoulder to where Grady stood. "Hmm?"

Grady lifted an eyebrow and looked pointedly to the camera she held— the camera which was somehow focusing on the dead man's torn throat.

"Not a good time," Grady said quietly.

"Oh…right." Ashley blushed, regarding her hands with a stern, slightly puzzled look; they had an unfortunate habit of doing this.

Grady did a bad job of hiding his smile as she lowered the camera. Ashley's first instinct upon encountering anything new or interesting had always been to take a photograph, and it took a conscious effort on her part to restrain the compulsion. Sometimes taking a photo crossed cultural boundaries, sometimes it was simply inappropriate, and other times it could be hazardous. Grady still liked to remind her of the time she'd stood in the path of an oncoming elephant stampede, oblivious to the danger while snapping away merrily. Though he rarely argued with her about how reckless she could sometimes be, Grady had had some choice words for her after he'd rushed in and pulled her back to safety.

That fearlessness, driven by her innate and insatiable curiosity, made Ashley a difficult, yet colorful, friend to have around.

It also made her one of the best wildlife photographers in the business.

The two of them had been in India for eight weeks now, and were about to wrap up their assignment, when rumors filtered down from the Parks department that a white tiger was sighted in the Bandhavgarh National Park. Unwilling to pass up such a remarkable opportunity, Ashley had used her considerable charm to convince a reluctant Grady to delay their return to the United States. Joining Simon and his assistant Grace—two scientists who were tagging and monitoring the Bengal tiger population in the area— the group had set out into the jungle, accompanied by their Indian guide and tracker, Tarun.

No sooner had base camp been established than the sound of a gunshot echoed from the forest depths. Tarun had rushed to investigate. Though he warned the group to remain at camp, Ashley insisted on going with him, and the others had joined her, their curiosity piqued.

None of them had expected the carnage they found.

Ashley looked up from her study of the dead man as Tarun appeared from the undergrowth. The guide was a tall, muscular man, given to wearing open-necked shirts and cargo pants.

Ashley raised a blonde eyebrow questioningly at his dark expression.

"There's another one not far down the track," Tarun reported calmly in his heavy Hindi accent. "Looks like he tried to make a run for it. Made it about thirty paces before he was taken down." Hands on his hips, Tarun scowled at the torn bodies, then at the ground around them.

"What killed them?" asked Grady, the slight quaver in his voice giving lie to his outward calm.

"A tiger?" Ashley guessed.

Tarun shook his head. "I doubt it. Tigers don't kill like this, and they typically avoid humans."

"Looks like a big cat of some kind. I mean, look at those claw marks." Ashley pointed at the bodies. "What else could it be?"

"Tigers don't slit their prey's throat," Tarun argued, "not so cleanly. And they leave tracks. I can't find a single trace of whatever did this—no scent markings, no prints, nothing." He shook his head, clearly more upset by the lack of tracks than by the bodies themselves.

"What should we do?" asked Simon timidly. The prematurely balding, middle-aged zoologist looked at the bloody remains for a second, then hastily averted his gaze. "We can't just leave them here, can we?"

"No." Tarun sighed. "Ashley, could you and Grady go find some good-sized branches? I'll get the rope from the packs and we can make a set of litters. We'll drag them back to camp, call the rangers, and get them to come deal with this."

Ashley frowned. "Are you sure we should move them? Won't someone want to investigate the scene of the crime? Look for evidence?"

Tarun gestured to the ground. "No one will find anything here," he said. "Look around. There's no evidence, no tracks, and frankly, I doubt the rangers or the police will bother investigating this at all. They've got better things to do with their time."

"What do you mean?" asked Grady.

"Look at these guys." Tarun pointed to the rifle one man still clutched in his bloody hand. "What do you think they were doing out here with guns like that? They're poachers. Probably here to kill the same tiger you people came for." He shook his head and spat angrily on the ground. "We take them back to camp and turn them over to the authorities. Where it goes from there is none of our business."

Ashley glared at the dark man for long moments, not entirely happy with how casually he was treating the incident. Then she smiled a little coldly and said, "Fine," grabbed Grady by the arm, and pulled him away to look for suitably strong branches to make a litter.

Nearly five hours later, Ashley watched from her fallen-log seat as Tarun shook hands with a uniformed ranger and exchanged a few quiet words. It had taken over two hours to drag the bodies back to their base, even with all five of them putting in an effort, and it was now dark. A quick radio call had alerted the proper authorities, who immediately sent out a Jeep team to relieve them of their charges. Although Ashley didn't speak Hindi, from the tone of the conversation shared by Tarun and the head ranger, it seemed the uniformed man wanted to deal with everything as quickly and quietly as possible.

As their visitors left, Tarun strode over to the others. Taking his seat beside the small campfire, he offered the group a grim smile.

"Well, that's that," he said simply.

Ashley struggled to keep her expression neutral. "So they'll look into it, right?"

Tarun shrugged. "Maybe. But like I said, a couple of poachers won't warrant much interest." He paused a long time, then continued in an ominous-sounding tone. "Besides, they know they won't find anything. From what the head ranger told me, they've been seeing this sort of thing a lot the past few years."

Grady leaned closer. "What sort of thing?"

"Poachers turning up dead in the jungle, ripped to pieces." Tarun pulled a toothpick from his pocket and chewed it thoughtfully. The look on his face was the same one Ashley remembered seeing her father wear when he told ghost stories during family camping trips. "Not just here, either. Up in the Himalayan mountains, and on the grasslands, something's hunting them down, then disappearing. It leaves no trace except the dead."

8

Grace's eyes were as wide as saucers, and she stared at him in terror. "What is it?"

Tarun shrugged and sighed dramatically. "No one can tell for sure. But some of the more superstitious elders are spreading rumors about a spirit at work." He eyed his attentive audience. "They say the goddess Durga has sent the great tiger she rides down here to protect its children."

Ashley snorted. "You don't believe that, do you?"

He smiled and shook his head. "Whatever killed those men was flesh and blood," he said quietly. "I don't know what it was. But I've seen tiger attacks, and that wasn't like any tiger attack I've ever heard of."

Simon cleared his throat. "Could it have been..." He hesitated. "Well, could it have been a man?"

"Humans leave more tracks than any cat." Tarun fixed each member of the group with a hard stare, finally settling his gaze on Ashley. "I think it would be for the best if we take extra care when we go out there. I'd like the chance to spend my commission."

Each of them nodded, their expressions serious and somber.

"Good." Tarun clapped his hands and stood up. "Anyone hungry? I know I am, after all that excitement."

Somewhat unenthusiastic murmurs of agreement met his change of subject; Ashley could see that Grace and Simon were still a little queasy with the memory of the slashed bodies so fresh in their minds. While Grady helped Tarun with the supplies, Ashley took out her camera and a soft felt cloth, beginning the familiar routine of cleaning her equipment. She paused, repressing a sudden shiver as she felt the hairs at the nape of her neck prickle. Glancing over her shoulder into the pitch-dark jungle, she frowned thoughtfully a moment, then turned back to her task with a shrug.

She had the eerie sensation that someone—or something—was watching her.

Perched in the branches of a giant tree, she watched the campfire illuminate the faces of the group below. These people were not here to hunt, she could tell. Poachers liked to stay mobile and inconspicuous, and this group was carrying far too much equipment to qualify as either. Still, she intended to keep an eye on them all the same.

As she looked on, her eyes slightly narrowed at the obvious spirit of camaraderie displayed by the group, she found her attention settling more and more on the shorter of the two women. Something about the blonde stranger fascinated her. Called by a rare curiosity she couldn't explain, the shadowy figure abandoned her lofty post and crept slowly closer to the camp, nostrils twitching at the dimly remembered scents of civilization. Eventually, she settled down in the thick undergrowth, perfectly camouflaged by the dark stripes across her form. Her shimmering blue eyes held an expression of fascination as she watched the young woman pick at her food.

The woman was small of frame, almost elfin, yet even her simplest movements bespoke a natural grace and strength. Her features were beautiful, but not uncommonly so. Still, the flash of her smile when one of her companions said something funny lit up her face and made her stand out from the others. Merriment and life sparkled in her mahogany brown eyes. There was something strange about her, something unusual. For the first time in years, the watcher felt a tingle of interest grip her, making her want to move closer to the woman.

For over an hour, she lay hidden in the shadows, body pressed against the dewy earth, watching, unable to tear herself away from the clearing. She knew she needed to leave, knew she would need to hunt soon if she wanted to eat that night. But she couldn't convince her limbs to move. Even when the various people in the camp bade one another goodnight and retired to their individual tents, she couldn't shake off the stranger's lure. For another hour, she lay there in silence, frozen, wrestling against the inexplicable desire to actually enter the camp and see the woman again. Eventually, realizing she wasn't going to get anywhere if she didn't satisfy this interest and move on, the dark figure rose and prowled forward, leaving the shadows behind.

Wary, alert, ready to bolt at the least sound or scent that was out of place, she ventured slowly toward the small, domed tent into which the blonde had disappeared. Pausing outside, she sniffed the air cautiously, uncertain whether to proceed or retreat. After a minute, she eased down the tent zipper, pushed her head through the gap, and stepped inside.

It was dark in the tent, but years of hunting at night allowed her to make out the softly snoring form wrapped in a sleeping bag. Head cocked to the side, she moved closer, only barely resisting the urge to brush aside a lock of honey-colored hair that obscured her view. The stranger looked peaceful in slumber, her lips bowed slightly as though smiling at a pleasant dream. The dark figure bent forward, memorizing the woman's scent, mesmerized, unable to prevent the low, rumbling purr that rose from deep in her belly. So caught up was she in watching the sleeping woman, it took her several seconds to acknowledge when the pale lashes flickered and parted, revealing sleepy brown eyes that quickly widened.

A flurry of movement startled her as the wakened blonde surged backward, tangled in the sleeping bag, frantic to escape. A heartbeat later, the still night was shattered by a piercing scream. Stunned, she stood frozen for a long moment; sapphire eyes locked with woodland brown, both of them breathing hard in shock. Finally, the sounds of alarm coming from the other tents managed to penetrate her momentary shock, and she snapped into motion.

Before the panicked blonde could draw breath for another scream, she whirled around and fled back outside, barely sparing a glance for the beams of torchlight already scanning the darkness. Diving back into the safety of the dense undergrowth, she scolded herself for ever indulging such a foolish curiosity.

Ashley struggled to regain control of her rapidly beating heart, still trying to get her mind caught up with what was going on. The strange creature was gone. She stared wide-eyed at the tent doorway, shaking, her breath coming in hard gasps. A moment later, Grady and Tarun appeared, the guide holding a rifle and sweeping the surrounding area with a torch.

"What happened?" Grady demanded, moving forward to check on her.

"I saw it!"

"What? What did you see?" Tarun stood guard at the doorway, still scanning the jungle.

Ashley stammered, confused. "I-I don't...really know. It was gone so quickly." Her eyes narrowed as she tried to remember exactly what she'd seen in the indistinct light. "It had light eyes...and stripes."

"A tiger?" Tarun eyed her nervously. "Are you saying a tiger was in the camp?"

Ashley shook her head. "No, it wasn't a tiger. It looked almost...human."

"What?"

"I'm not sure." Ashley shrugged helplessly, recovering her nerve quickly now that the intruder was gone. "I couldn't see it very well. But it stood upright like a human. And its eyes seemed more human than feline." She put a hand to her forehead, wishing she'd gotten a better look. "I'm sorry. I just woke up and there it was, right in front of me." She chuckled shortly, willing herself to calm down. "It scared the shit out of me."

"Hey, it's okay. You're safe now." Grady gave her a quick hug and a reassuring pat on the shoulder.

Tarun had moved away from her tent, shining the beam of his torch over the ground and kneeling to inspect something. When he looked back up, he was scowling. "There are no prints, human or otherwise."

Ashley eyed him a little defensively. "Are you saying I imagined it?"

"No, I'm saying that what you saw was probably the same thing that killed those men."

"Oh. Sorry."

He smiled at her. "That's okay."

"Why did it come here?" Simon asked, shining his own flashlight over the surrounding jungle with a jittery hand. The timid man looked somewhat ridiculous standing there in his flannel pajamas, and Ashley stifled the urge to giggle at him.

Tarun shouldered his rifle and glared toward the jungle. "Maybe it was curious about us," he guessed. "Perhaps it wanted to get a closer look. Let's just hope it doesn't decide we're some kind of threat."

"Maybe." Ashley gave her friends a slightly embarrassed smile. "I'm sorry I woke you all."

"Don't mention it," said Grady. "But you still look pretty shook up. Sure you don't want some company for the night?" he offered. "I'll be a gentleman."

"Hah!" Ashley punched him softly on the arm. "I'll be fine. Whatever it was, I think I scared it as much as it scared me." Her eyes softened. "But thanks for the offer."

"Okay. You call if you need anything."

"I will."

Grady and the others trailed back to their own tents, leaving Ashley to herself. She could hear them whispering among themselves and felt a bit sheepish. She hadn't been that frightened in a long time. The shock of waking up to those piercing eyes still made her tremble.

Acknowledging that her keyed up nerves had chased away the prospect of sleep, Ashley lit a kerosene lamp and reached for the pile of books that lay next to her backpack. Grabbing one, she flipped it open and began to read about the great cats she was there to shoot.

Not so far away, a dark, striped figure used sharp claws to pull herself up into a tree. Settling down, still breathing hard from the encounter, she rested long moments in silence, wrestling with the desire to return and see again those mesmerizing eyes that seemed to call to her with a song stronger than any she'd heard before.

The next morning, Ashley slept in. She had finally drifted off early in the morning, her eyes strained from reading by lamplight. By the time she emerged from her tent, tousled and blinking in the light, all the rest of her companions were already up and about. She joined them around the cold ashes of the fire, and noticed that Tarun was absent. She guessed he was off checking for signs of their midnight intruder.

"Sleep okay?" Grady inquired as she sat beside him, his sincerity ruined only by the amusement in his eyes.

Ashley scowled. She usually had to kick him in the ribs to get him moving in the morning. "Fine, from about three o'clock onwards. After that thing woke me up, I had so much adrenaline in me I could have run a marathon. I stayed up and did a bit of reading."

"Mmm, I saw the light. I'm afraid the coffee's cold, but I saved you some breakfast." He handed her a bowl of porridge, and she rewarded his consideration with a charming smile.

"Thanks." She ate the sweetened oats eagerly, humming as the sugar helped kick-start her recalcitrant body. "Are we going to get the hide set up today?"

Grady nodded. "Yep. Tarun already found us a spot down by the river. Said there were a number of tracks and markings there, so you should get some good shots if you're lucky. Once we've got you all set up, I was thinking I'd head over to the east ridge." He gestured with a stick toward a ridge of rocky, treacherous-looking mountain that rose from the plains some distance away. "The view should be terrific."

"Great. Maybe I'll go up there with you tomorrow."

"Sure, if you'd like."

Ashley finished her breakfast and turned her attention to Simon and Grace. "Will you guys be staying with me in the hide?"

Simon nodded. "If a tiger shows up, we'll let you get your shots, then tranquilize and tag it. It's pretty routine stuff. If we can provide evidence to back up the reports of a white tiger, we'll probably call in a team to come out and collect it." He shook his head ruefully. "The zoos will go wild if we find it."

Ashley had done her research, and knew the potential benefits that could be derived from the discovery of a white tiger in the wild. In the last hundred years, only a dozen or so white tigers had been reported, and with the rapid decline in the population of Bengal tigers—the only species to produce the white strain—that number was likely to drop a good deal farther, very quickly. The few specimens in captivity in the United States all owed their ancestry to Mohan, a white male who had been captured by a maharaja in 1951, and who had then been mated with his daughter to produce more white tiger cubs. This inbreeding was the only way of securing the color strain, unless another tiger could be captured that had the double recessive allele that produced the white pigmentation. As a result of inbreeding, the possibility of genetic defects, miscarriages, and early death rose with every new generation.

Ashley recalled the white tiger pictures she'd seen, taken of captive specimens in the National Zoo in Washington, D.C. Feline eyes that would normally be a tawny gold were instead a clear, piercing blue, and chocolate-colored stripes patterned snow-white coats. She shivered in anticipation. If she could bring home photos of a white tiger from the wild, her already impressive reputation would soar. Not to mention the sheer challenge of such an endeavor. It was an opportunity few ever saw, and Ashley didn't intend to screw it up.

"Well," she said, as she slapped her thighs and stood up, "sitting around here won't get the hide built. Grady, why don't you get the gear and meet me down by the river?" She scooped up the dirty dishes. "I'll go on ahead. I can get these washed up and look for a good place to set up."

"Fine. Simon, would you give me a hand with the heavy stuff?"

"Sure."

Leaving the others to organize the aluminum poles and camouflage netting that formed their traveling hide, Ashley made her way to the river with the dishes.

She and Grady made a good team, and the magazine they worked for took advantage of their dynamic by sending them out together as often as possible. Though only twenty-six years old, Ashley possessed an innate talent for photographing wildlife, and it hadn't taken long for her to impress her peers with a seemingly endless run of breathtaking shots. Not wanting to rely on talent alone, Ashley believed in always being prepared. Even now, with her arms cradling a load of dirty dishes, her camera was strapped around her neck and ready in case an opportunity presented itself.

Grady, on the other hand, was a scenic photographer. He never failed to find beauty and majesty in whatever landscape presented itself, whether deserts and grass plains or oceans and cityscapes. Ashley enjoyed having him as her partner largely because of his adaptability and patience; his work often required him to wait hours for just the right lighting, and some of the prep-work setting up his shots could get pretty elaborate. It also didn't hurt that he rarely tried to discourage her when she wanted to do something a little "out there."

Since they'd started going on expeditions together, three years ago, their body of work had attracted national acclaim and earned them a string of prestigious and ever-more-challenging assignments. Ashley knew she had particularly impressed her superiors with her work capturing dangerous wildlife in spectacular settings, and it showed in the fact that in the last year or so, more and more assignments took her and Grady into potentially hazardous regions of the world. Ashley had enough professional ambition that she was willing to take greater risks to find the perfect images she wanted, and this had earned her a reputation for fearlessness and tenacity.

They had set up camp some distance from the water source, not wanting to scare the wildlife away from their drinking spot, and the hike served to wake Ashley more thoroughly. By the time she reached the edge of the sluggish river, she was sweating lightly in the humid heat, but feeling quite happy. Ashley liked the jungle, and the Bandhavgarh National Park was one of the nicest she had ever visited. Located in the Vindhya Mountains of Madhya Pradesh, the small park boasted the highest population density of tigers in the country. Furthermore, it was known for its white tigers, sometimes going by the name of "White Tiger Territory."

Of course, tigers weren't the only thing worthy of note. In any direction were insects of every type and birds of every color. It was never truly quiet here; the jungle creatures constantly communicated in a myriad of fascinating ways—the stuttering chatter of monkeys, screeches and cries of parrots and hornbills, and more ominous sounds less easily identified.

This was Ashley's first trip to India, and what she had seen so far was enough to make her want a return visit. While she didn't much care for the crowded cities—she had never liked the feeling of being crushed against so many other people—the rural areas were fascinating. There was a general atmosphere of respect for the animals of the land that was rare in most developed countries. Ashley had seen monkeys, peacocks, and even the deadly cobra living in apparent harmony with the people, who tolerated, and even paid tribute to their company. In one of the larger towns, Ashley had seen street performers dress up like monkeys and mimic the actions of the mischievous creatures. An English-speaking tourist had told her the performers were paying homage to Hanuman, one of the Hindu gods.

As someone who had always loved animals, and who now made a living from photographing them, Ashley could appreciate the kind of relationship the people of India had with their native wildlife. Outside of tribal cultures, it was rare to find such deification. Wandering along the course of the river now, stepping over a downed tree that crossed her path, Ashley started looking around for a safe place to wash the empty bowls.

Distracted by the sights and sounds of the jungle around her, Ashley's attention was brought back to sudden focus when she rounded a bend in the river and found she had company. A large, burly man stood not thirty feet from her. Crouched low against a tree, dressed in army fatigues and camouflage shirt, he was studying the edge of the water. Ashley first thought he was a ranger, and she very nearly called a greeting. Then she noticed the menacing-looking hunting rifle he held. Rangers didn't carry such formidable equipment. Ashley's eyes widened. She gave a silent prayer of thanks that the man, whom she now realized must be a poacher, had his back to her.

Very slowly and carefully, Ashley edged a few steps backward, considering her options. This man might have friends out there somewhere—she knew poachers generally worked in groups—and she scanned the dense jungle cautiously for any sign that she had been spotted. Nothing seemed amiss, but that didn't count for much. There was enough cover to hide an army of poachers. She needed to get back to Tarun so he could alert the park rangers. They'd know how to deal with this. Decision made, Ashley continued backing slowly away from the man.

Her luck held for a few more paces, before her heel snagged a treacherous root. Ashley might have been able to keep her balance, but for the dirty dishes still clasped in her hands. She toppled backward.

The fall to the soft ground was quiet enough, but the tin plates clattered loudly, despite her best efforts to cushion them. She saw the man's head turn toward her, and she quickly rolled off the trail and into the jungle.

Lying in the dense undergrowth, she held her breath as she heard the man coming closer. He was taking his time, and Ashley held herself perfectly still as he passed by her position. *Please, don't let him see me,* she thought. *Just for a few more minutes, until Tarun and Grady get here with the hide, please let him not notice me.*

Ashley wasn't the type to get scared needlessly, but she breathed a sigh of relief when the poacher moved past her without incident. Unfortunately, she also shifted her body a little against the ground. Her elbow was pinned against a branch, and the movement caused a noticeable rustle.

The poacher froze in his tracks. He turned. Through the undergrowth, Ashley saw his eyes home in on her hiding spot and knew she'd been found.

She took half a second to mentally compare her chances if she stayed put against her chances if she ran. The man was large and thick-bodied, with tangled red hair and a bushy beard. He looked tough, but probably not too fast. Ashley concluded she was better off making a run for it. She got her legs under her and broke from her cover.

Head down, she sprinted toward camp. She heard a shout, then a string of curses and the sound of pursuit. Chancing a quick glance behind her, she caught another moment of bad luck—a downed tree blocked her path.

She hit the obstacle at full speed and went down hard, the wind knocked from her body. Pain flared in her legs, and she tumbled into a headlong roll.

The poacher was on her before she could recover. Red-faced and sweating, the man grinned cruelly at her "Not so fast now, huh, blondie?"

Ashley's dark eyes were wide, and she held up her hands in surrender. "Please, don't hurt me. I promise I won't tell anyone you're here."

The man shook his head. "Sorry, lady," he said gruffly. "Can't trust no one in my line of work. Guess this is what you get for straying off from the tour group, huh?"

"I'm not a tourist. I'm a photographer," Ashley explained, holding up the camera around her neck as evidence. "I have friends, and they're not far away. If you kill me, they'll call in help and this whole place will be swarming with rangers."

The poacher's eyes narrowed. "That true?"

"Uh huh." She nodded frantically. "Let me go, and I swear I won't tell them about you. You can just go your way, and I'll go mine. What do you say?"

He considered for a long moment, obviously wondering whether to believe her or not. Eventually, he shook his head again. "Sorry, lady, but I ain't in the market of taking chances. Only one way to make sure you stay quiet, so don't make this harder than it has to be." He worked the bolt on his rifle and pulled the butt into his shoulder.

Ashley started backpedaling furiously away from the man, her eyes glued to the barrel of the gun as it swung up and fixed on her with unavoidable precision. She was drawing breath for a final scream, when a chilling, terrible sound stopped her. The low, rumbling growl, so primal and fierce, drained the blood from the poacher's face in a heartbeat. The man turned away very slowly, and Ashley was able to see behind him.

Two sets of eyes widened. Ashley's jaw dropped. She wanted to finish her scream, but could only stare past the man to the strange figure crouched on the mossy trunk of a fallen tree.

It was a woman. A woman unlike any Ashley had ever seen before. Even though she was bent in a crouching, feline position, the woman was clearly tall and powerfully built. She wore a brief outfit consisting of a halter top and a short skirt, both made from what Ashley was certain was genuine tiger fur. The outfit was almost invisible, however, for the woman's entire body was painted in ochre and pale ivory tones patterned with tawny brown stripes. Even her classic, angular face was done up to mimic the mask of a tiger, the stripes framing cold, clear blue eyes that were fixed firmly on the frightened poacher. A mass of dirty black hair tumbled over the woman's shoulders, much of it woven into a chaotic tangle of thin braids. Ashley noticed the woman's right hand tapping against the bole of the tree, four hooked talons jutting from between long, powerful fingers. Though the claws were primitive, Ashley had no doubt that they were as effective a weapon for the woman as they would be for a real tiger.

Hearing a hoarse, strangled gurgle from the poacher, Ashley tore her gaze from the strange woman and glanced at her former adversary. The man's face was extremely pale behind his thick beard, his eyes bulging from their sockets in abject terror. The hands that gripped the rifle were shaking so badly that Ashley thought for a moment he was about to have a heart attack. Frantic eyes darted left and right, searching for an escape. When the tiger-woman's rumbling growl rose an octave and her lips parted to reveal pearly white teeth, the man apparently decided to take his chances. He dropped the rifle, turned, and ran into the jungle as fast as his trembling legs could carry him, leaving Ashley behind with the strange intruder.

Ashley found herself caught in the penetrating gaze of sapphire eyes.

Uh oh!

Ashley swallowed hard as the tiger-woman gave a feral smile, revealing what seemed to be uncommonly large canine teeth. The full force of those unsettlingly clear cobalt eyes settled on her, the growl still rumbling, but softer now. Ashley wanted to follow the poacher's example and run away, but her legs refused to obey her.

When she heard a quiet *snick* sound, she looked down and was appalled to realize her hands had lifted the camera about her neck and—entirely of their own volition—snapped a quick shot of the predatory figure on the log.

The striped woman rose from her crouch and stalked closer. Ashley held perfectly still, hardly daring to breathe. "Shit! What the hell have you gotten yourself into this time?" she muttered under her breath, her eyes trained with fatalistic fascination on the sharp, claw-like weapons held in each of the woman's hands. The tiger-lady approached along a zigzag path, her expression intense and curious. Ashley remembered watching her niece's two-year-old cat move the same way when she was stalking a mouse. The comparison was not particularly comforting.

The woman closed the distance between them, pausing when she got to within a few feet. She leaned forward, her head cocked to the side as she sniffed interestedly, then stepped nearer still, until Ashley could see the grainy texture of the paint that covered her body and make out the highlights in her ebony, tangled hair. The woman circled, sniffing, her eyes roaming up and down. Ashley held herself stiffly under the scrutiny, following the stranger with wide eyes.

"I really hope I don't smell like dinner," she breathed quietly to herself. Then she noticed that the woman was no longer growling. Instead of that low, ominous rumbling, the stranger made a series of short, sharp, barking coughs that Ashley wasn't quite sure how to interpret. When the tiger-lady finished her inspection and stopped in front of her, Ashley gave her a tremulous smile. It was met with a slight softening of stern features, and she noticed for the first time an expression of wary intrigue and reluctant fascination on the stranger's face. The woman made the strange coughing bark again, the sound completely inhuman and beyond Ashley's ability to replicate.

"You're not planning to eat me...are you?" Ashley asked.

The dark head cocked to one side and a crooked smile tugged at painted lips. Before Ashley had time to wonder whether her words had been understood, the sound of crunching footsteps and echoing conversation came from around the river-bend. Blue eyes widened instantly, darting to the forest. The woman gave Ashley a last, curious look, then whirled around and fled back into the jungle, wild hair whipping about her face as she ran. Ashley noticed that her running style was quite unique, shifting unpredictably between short, swift steps and long, leaping strides that carried her swiftly through the dense, unpredictable undergrowth. Within heartbeats, she had disappeared as though she'd never been there.

A moment later, Grady and Tarun rounded the bend in the river, lugging between them the heavier components of the hide. Behind them trailed Simon, carrying coils of rope. "Hey, Ash," called Grady. "Are you done there? Give us a hand."

Ashley shook her head dazedly, still rooted to the spot. It took Grady a moment to realize something was wrong. Then his eyes fell on the poacher's abandoned rifle, and he dropped his load and rushed to her side.

"Ash! What happened? Are you okay?"

Ashley pointed a shaking finger to the jungle. "Did you see her?"

"See who?"

"The tiger-woman." Ashley finally snapped out of her dazed state and gestured wildly at the jungle. "She ran off when she heard you guys coming. She saved me from a poacher I found here. He was going to kill me, and then she was there, and she scared him off. She had claws, and she was all stripy—"

Grady grabbed her by the shoulders and forced her to stop jumping around. "Hey, slow down," he said, glancing worriedly at Tarun, who had picked up the rifle. "Tell us what happened from the beginning."

Ashley began describing the strange encounter, her excitement building. While she talked, Tarun carefully inspected the rocky ground, then moved over to the fallen log. When Ashley had finished, the tracker pointed to something.

"There are scratch marks here on the wood," he said. "No tracks of the woman, but the poacher left a trail so obvious a blind elephant could follow him. He was running from something."

"Of course he was running," Ashley said, planting her hands on her hips. "I just told you about the woman."

"And I believe you. I'm just saying she didn't leave any footprints, only those scratch marks. Did she threaten you at all?"

Ashley considered. "I don't think so. She growled a bit, but she didn't seem to want to hurt me. It was more like... I don't know. Like she was curious about me."

"Did she say anything?"

Ashley shook her head. "I don't know if she knew how to talk. She looked like some freaky, female version of Tarzan, only with tigers instead of gorillas." She sighed, wishing now that she'd had more time with the bizarre woman. "I wonder what she's doing out here."

"Killing poachers," Tarun stated. He scowled. "Let's just hope she doesn't think we're here to harm anything. Come on, let's get this hide set up."

"Wait a minute!" Ashley glared at the man. "Aren't we going to report this? She's out here all alone. Shouldn't we tell someone?"

"And what would we report? That there's a jungle-woman out here who thinks she's a tiger? Bah! No one would believe us for a minute. We've got no proof, no evidence, and no tracks."

"We do so!" Ashley held up her camera. "I took a picture of her. If we show it, they'll have to believe us."

"She has a point," Simon chimed in, catching her excitement. "Imagine it, a woman living out here alone in the jungle! Without any sort of contact with outsiders! She could have been living in the park for years! If we could find her..."

Tarun considered, but again shook his head. "I'm not calling out the rangers for this. She could be anywhere, and there are too many places she could hide. We'd never track her down."

"So we just forget about her?" Ashley spluttered, furious. "How can you be so cavalier about this?"

"Because there's nothing we can do," Tarun said. "You're here to photograph and tag tigers, not some crazy woman who thinks she's a tiger. I'm not being paid to track down someone who doesn't want to be found."

Ashley glared at him, about to argue further when Grady stopped her. "He's right, Ash. We've got a job to do. Let's not get sidetracked. If we try to hunt her down, she might turn nasty. Let's just do what we came here to do and get out before she decides we're a threat."

Ashley looked at the others, but now even Simon shrugged helplessly. It was clear she was on her own. "Fine. We'll let it go." Folding her arms across her chest, she frowned at her companions and gave every indication that she was not pleased.

Grady sighed. "Should we at least report the poacher?"

"I suppose. But the rangers are aware there's been increased activity." Tarun hefted the poacher's rifle. "Without his gun, at least this one shouldn't be able to do much damage."

The four spent the next hour setting up the hide, with Ashley giving her companions the silent treatment and occasionally complementing that with cold glares, aimed mostly at Tarun. How could the man have so little reaction to her bizarre encounter? Where was his curiosity? Ashley, who never failed to let curiosity guide her course, found his ambivalence infuriating.

By midday most of her frustration had burned off; the familiar task of tying down the plastic camo netting was a good distraction, allowing her thoughts to settle so she could consider them clearly. Perhaps in his role as a guide, Tarun had simply seen too much of the death and cruelty wrought by heartless poachers for him to feel much compassion when they were being slaughtered in kind. Perhaps that accounted for why he, like the rangers, seemed to hold so little interest in tracking down whoever was killing them. It didn't change Ashley's opinion that they should investigate further, but she decided there was no point staying mad at Tarun.

Although the conventional way to deal with tigers was to track them on elephant back, Grady had insisted a hide would work better. Though she didn't say anything, Ashley suspected her partner was afraid of riding the great beasts. He'd refused to ride camels before, too. Still, she didn't mind. The lumbering, awkward gait of the elephant made it difficult to focus her camera, and Ashley thought the added danger of being on the ground would be more than compensated for by the increased quality of the pictures she could take.

Once the hide was up, the group decided to take a hike along the river to where Tarun knew a waterfall was located. Grady spent over an hour setting up shots and capturing the beauty of the scene, while Ashley wandered around looking at the various birds and the group of curious monkeys that had decided to investigate their presence.

All through the day, however, her mind kept returning to the strange woman. Who was she? What was she doing out here? By the time they finished and returned to camp for dinner, she had worked herself into a nice little obsession, and she knew without a doubt that she had to learn more of the stranger. Fortunately, she considered, the woman seemed very interested in them. Ashley suspected that in time, she would return. Perhaps she was watching them even now.

After the others had gone to bed, Ashley stayed awake beside the dying campfire, hoping the tiger-lady would pay another visit now that she was alone. She waited nearly an hour, concentrating carefully, trying to sense the woman's presence. Eventually, she reluctantly accepted that the stranger wasn't going to be stopping by tonight. Rising from her solitary vigil, she rubbed sleepy eyes with the back of her wrist. She had barely taken two steps toward her tent, when something in the distance drew her attention. Squinting a little, Ashley smiled to herself.

About halfway up the side of a nearby ridge, a faint speck of orange light glimmered in the darkness like a lonely star.

"There you are," Ashley whispered, grinning as she marked the location in her mind. "Well, well, well. It seems you're not so much an animal that you don't know how to light a fire."

Ashley hummed to herself as she went to bed, already planning a hike out to the mountains in the morning.

Ashley wolfed down her breakfast the next morning, asking Simon and Grace to mind the hide without her. She was going on a hike. Grady watched her with a frown, as she stuffed a rubber poncho into her backpack and slung it over her shoulder.

"Where are you going?"

Ashley glanced back at him with a smile she knew he would recognize from years of experience working with her.

"Shit, Ashley. Please tell me you're not going off hunting that damn woman."

Her smile grew a fraction wider.

Grady threw his hands up in the air in disbelief. "Jesus! What the hell is wrong with you? Why do you have to go looking for trouble all the time?"

"I'm not looking for trouble," she said calmly. "I'm going on a little hike out to the ridge, just like you suggested."

"Then at least wait for me to get my gear so I can come with you. Or wait for Tarun to get back." Their guide had gone off to search the forest for fresh tracks; Ashley had deliberately timed her departure so she could avoid an argument with him.

"Sorry, Grady, I'm going alone. I don't want to spook her off by bringing an entourage. Besides, you have your own work to do, remember?" She smiled fondly at his exasperated expression. Grady was always trying to look out for her, and while Ashley knew she didn't need his help, it was nice to know someone cared. "Relax, I'll be fine."

"Ashley, this woman almost certainly killed those poachers. I doubt she wants people just dropping by," Grady argued. "You saw the bodies. She's a murderer. Do you want to end up like those hunters?"

Ashley paused as she remembered the shredded, mauled bodies and the blood-soaked ground. Then she shook away the memories. "She's had two opportunities to hurt me, and so far all she's done is growl a bit. I don't think she sees us as a threat."

"Then can't you just leave things be? Please?" He clasped her gently by the shoulders and caught her gaze. "For me? You know I try to stay out of your way when you want to go off and do something dangerous, but this is just plain foolish. I'm asking as a friend, Ash. Just leave the woman alone."

The sincere, pleading tone of voice very nearly worked. Ashley could tell Grady was genuinely concerned, but she couldn't let a mystery this intriguing go without investigating. Her curiosity simply wouldn't permit it. "I can't," she said softly. "If I don't do this, it'll eat me up from the inside out. I have to try to find her."

"But why?"

Ashley shrugged. "I just do." Standing on tiptoes, she planted a quick, soft kiss on Grady's cheek. "It looks like about a two-hour hike out to the mountain. If I'm not back by nightfall, don't come looking for me." She held up a hand to forestall his next words. "I mean it. You'll only get lost in the dark. Wait until morning, at least. Okay?"

He nodded reluctantly. "Just be sure that doesn't happen." He ran his fingers through his hair in what Ashley knew was a gesture of frustrated acceptance. "What makes you think she's over near that mountain anyway?"

Ashley winked. "Just women's intuition, I guess." Adjusting the straps on her backpack a final time, she waved back at Grady and made her way out of camp.

The hike was as long as she had anticipated, so Ashley took her time and enjoyed the journey. At a few places along the way, she stopped to take photographs, capturing occasional shots of young monkeys as they played among the short, twiggy bushes under which their parents sat. By the time she reached the ridge, Ashley was breathing hard and the front of her loose cotton shirt was damp with sweat. Her active lifestyle kept her extremely fit, but that didn't count for much in the Indian heat. Thick, ominous clouds had moved in from the north, turning the air more humid. Taking a rest and refilling her water bag at a fast-running stream near the base of the mountain, Ashley studied the slope before her, searching for the most likely site for a camp.

Half an hour of exploring later, she found a broad-entranced cave that tunneled into the side of the rocky mountain, about halfway up. Ashley examined the dusty ground at the mouth of the cave, smiling when she saw scuff marks that might have been footprints. Pulling out a flashlight, she hesitated only long enough to flick it on before creeping into the cave.

The artificial light quickly revealed the signs of occupation Ashley had hoped to find. Several small boulders were positioned around a modest fire pit in the center of the spacious cave, and a blackened, cast-iron pot sat in the cold ashes. There was no sign of the mysterious woman, and Ashley didn't know whether she felt disappointed or relieved. She shone the light on a simple sleeping mat, then spotted several wooden crates stacked at the rear of the cave. Investigating, she found cans of fruit, burlap sacks filled with rice, a fully stocked first-aid kit, as well as toiletries and hygiene products. The discovery prompted a full grin.

"Not enough of a ghost that you don't need to eat, I see."

The cave narrowed toward the rear but continued on about ten feet and opened up again beyond that. Ashley was just about to continue her explorations when a familiar rumbling growl stopped her, raising gooseflesh on her arms. Her eyes widened in alarm as she felt the dark presence behind her, and she slowly turned around toward the mouth of the cave.

Sure enough, there stood the tiger-lady, watching her with eyes that gleamed with a feral intensity in the dim light. Remembering the torn bodies in the jungle, Ashley wished she'd listened to Grady's pleas. There was little doubt the claw weapons the woman held had produced the bloody carnage.

"Um…" Ashley held up her empty hands. "I-I didn't mean to intrude," she stammered. "I saw the firelight last night, and I just wanted to, um… say thank you. In person. You know, for yesterday, when you saved me from that guy by the river? My name's Ashley. Ashley Richards."

The glittering sapphire eyes held her for a long moment, then the growl died away to silence. The painted woman glanced around the cave and, apparently deciding everything was as it should be, strode toward her visitor.

Ashley swallowed, her hands trembling nervously, but the tiger-woman ignored her completely and simply scooped a wooden dipperful of rice from one of the sacks of supplies. She then went back to the fire pit and emptied it into the pot, stirring in water dipped from a cask before she began to build a fire over the dead ashes. From time to time, she glanced at Ashley, but for the most part seemed to ignore her presence.

Ashley stood frozen as she watched the strange woman light the fire using sparks struck by hitting an old knife against a shard of flint. When the light grew sufficient, she shut off her flashlight and slowly moved closer to the crouched figure.

"Listen, I really didn't mean to just barge in on you like this," she said in a low voice. The strange woman glanced up, her expression blank. Ashley studied her curiously with narrowed eyes. "I don't suppose you speak English by any chance?"

No reaction.

"Hindi?"

Nothing.

Ashley sighed. "Great. I guess you're not going to be much of a conversationalist then, huh?" She ran her fingers through her hair and watched as the woman stirred the rice with the dipper, then added a handful of raw, finely chopped vegetables from a nearby pouch. "Well, I came out here to thank you, but you can't even understand me, so I guess that's going to be tough. I should probably just be thankful you haven't decided to add me to your dinner menu." Ashley shrugged helplessly. She wanted to sit down and study the woman further, but the silence was getting oppressive. Nervously, she started backing toward the mouth of the cave. "Look, I think I should probably head back to my friends. They'll get worried if I don't return by sundown. You know how it is. But it was really nice to meet you, and I really appreciate you scaring that poacher off yesterday." She paused. "Well, I guess I'll see you later." Turning, she took a step away.

"Stay."

The single word, spoken in a raspy, hoarse whisper, stopped her instantly. Ashley spun back around to find the tiger-woman studying her.

"What did you say?"

There was a long silence as the woman turned her attention back to her cooking. "There's a storm coming down from the north," she said in a low, ragged tone. "You'll never make it back to your friends before it hits. If you like, you can stay here until it passes."

Stunned, Ashley stared at the crouched figure. "You can talk!"

27

The woman glanced up again, a hint of humor touching her eyes and a smile twitching her lips. "So can you."

Ashley moved closer, amazed. "I mean, you speak English. Why didn't you say something instead of letting me prattle on like an idiot?"

The woman's smile widened, teeth gleaming in the firelight. "I enjoyed listening to you talk," she said, coughing to clear her throat when her voice broke. "It's been a long time since I last spoke."

Ashley shook her head in wonder, then remembering she'd been invited to stay, quickly claimed the boulder opposite the painted woman. "I'm Ashley," she said, holding out her hand.

The woman studied her hand for a moment, but made no move to shake it. "I know. I heard you the first time."

Unperturbed, Ashley grinned and took her hand back. "Do you have a name?"

The woman hesitated, and Ashley had the impression she was taking a moment to remember something. "Leandra," she said after a long moment. "My name is Leandra Thornton."

"Well, it's nice to meet you, Leandra Thornton," Ashley said politely. Outside, a sudden clap of thunder exploded in the distance. The wind began to pick up, and Ashley recognized that her companion was right. A storm was about to break. "Thanks for letting me stay here. I'd hate to be walking back in that."

"You hungry?" Leandra held up the still simmering rice. "It's not much, but it's quite edible. There's enough for both of us."

"Yeah, that'd be great." Ashley then realized something familiar about Leandra's accent. "You're an American, aren't you?"

"I suppose I was, before I came here." Leandra hesitated, then added, "I moved around a lot."

"I see." While the striped woman stirred their meal, Ashley found herself contemplating her situation. Here she was, in the wilds of India, sitting in a cave opposite a woman painted up as a tiger, who was cooking them lunch. The scenario was so bizarre it felt surreal. Still, Ashley wasn't going to complain. She let herself study her companion more openly.

Leandra was long and lean, but her body rippled with powerful muscles beneath the paint. Ashley guessed she was at least six feet tall, positively dwarfing her own five-foot-four stature. Her motions were graceful and elegant, yet Ashley detected a slight stiffness in the way she used her right arm. She had high cheekbones that made her vivid blue eyes stand out all the more, and angular features reminiscent of those found on ancient Greek sculptures. Her hair, which looked as though it hadn't been introduced to a brush in a long while, framed her face in a wild mass of braids and tangles. Her feet were bare, and she smelled pleasantly of musk and earth. In all, Ashley thought the strange woman was probably quite beautiful under all the paint and hair.

She glanced to the side and saw the two sets of handheld claws and reminded herself that this woman was a killer. Each set consisted of four hooked talons, made from what looked like bone lashed to a wooden grip. Simple tools, Ashley thought, but obviously capable of extremely lethal acts of violence.

"Something wrong?"

"What?" Ashley looked up to find Leandra regarding her curiously. "No, nothing's wrong. I was just..." She gestured to the claws. "I mean..." She studied the woman with what she hoped was a non-judgmental expression. "We found the bodies in the jungle. You killed those men, didn't you?"

Leandra reached for the claws and held them up to the firelight. "They came to hunt the tigers," she said. "I hunted them."

"You murdered them," Ashley corrected.

Leandra's eyes hardened. "They were scum," she hissed. A growl rumbled in the back of her throat, and her lip curled into a snarl. "They deserved what they got."

"Deserved to be slashed to pieces?"

"Yes." Leandra settled down, and the growl vanished. "Have you ever seen what poachers do to the animals they kill?"

Ashley shook her head.

"They butcher them completely. Not a single part of a tiger is wasted. The bones are ground up and used in medicines that claim to cure muscle pain and arthritis. The tails are made into soaps to cure skin diseases. The flesh is cooked and made into Tiger Soup, the brain into a cure for acne. Even the whiskers are made into charms for courage and protection. Those men hunt tigers without a care for the fact that they're almost wiped out. All they care about is their own greed."

Ashley swallowed, made nervous by the intensity of Leandra's description. "So you pass judgment and execute them?"

"Yes." Leandra scowled, anger gleaming in the depths of her eyes like fiery coals. "They deserve to die. I know. I used to be one of them."

"Oh." Ashley blinked in surprise. "You were a poacher?"

Leandra looked away, her expression impossible to read. "A long time ago, in another life...yes."

Ashley considered the dark-haired woman carefully. "And now you're...what?"

A slight shrug. "Something else. Something better, I hope."

"Seems like quite a dramatic change," Ashley commented, her eyes roaming meaningfully over the painted skin. "What was the reason?"

Leandra's smile was wistful. She stretched her right arm stiffly and spoke in a hoarse whisper. "Let's just say someone sat me down and gave me a stern talking to."

An awkward silence reigned for long minutes, and Ashley barely repressed the urge to fidget. "How long have you been out here?"

"Not sure. What year is it?"

"You mean you don't know?"

Blue eyes scanned the Spartan cave. "No calendar. Out here, there's only day and night, not month and year."

Ashley considered that, then said, "It's April 14, 1998."

Leandra seemed to take a long moment to absorb her words, dark brows drawing low over her eyes as she reflected on the news. "In that case, I've been out here nearly four years." She shook her head, adding almost to herself, "It feels like so much longer."

"Four years?" Ashley stared at her in wonder. "All alone in the jungle for four years?"

"Not alone. The tigers keep me company."

There was silence, except for the sounds of the storm that had settled in outside, until Leandra decided the rice was properly cooked. "I don't have any bowls or spoons," she apologized, dishing the meal out onto two huge palm-type leaves and handing one to Ashley.

"That's okay. I'm sure I'll manage." Hungry enough not to care, Ashley used her fingers to shovel the rice and vegetable mix into her mouth.

After a moment, her eyes widened in surprised pleasure. "This is pretty darned good."

Leandra shrugged. "Hunting's been poor the last few days. These are my emergency staples."

As she ate, Ashley noticed the clear blue eyes would frequently dart up to study her, then quickly look away. Leandra seemed every bit as curious about her as she was about Leandra. She couldn't help but find the tall woman's nervous, shy interest a little bemusing. She was also surprised to hear the low, rumbling sound of a feline purr coming from her companion as she enjoyed her meal, and she smiled. "I guess you don't get many visitors out here, huh?"

Leandra shook her head, eating her meal slowly and carefully. "None that are welcome."

"And I guess, from all the stories of poachers being killed in other parts of the country, you must travel around some, right?"

"Wherever they go, I go." Silence for a moment. "I like it here," Leandra continued quietly in her deep, raspy voice. "Sometimes, I camp near the Himalayas. It gets cold up there."

Ashley gestured to the wooden crates. "Where do you get the supplies?"

"Sometimes from the poachers. Sometimes from the villages. I take what I need."

Ashley gave the carefully painted body a meaningful once over. "Why do you paint yourself like that?"

The way Leandra's eyes instantly avoided Ashley's indicated her discomfort with the subject. "It helps me to hunt...to blend in, like camouflage. Out here, being human is a disadvantage, so I learned to live the way they live."

"They?"

"The tigers." Leandra pointed at Ashley's camera. "You're a photographer?"

Ashley recognized that Leandra was changing the topic of conversation, and chose not to press her interest further. For now. "One of the best," she said proudly.

"Here to photograph the tigers?"

"Yep, among other things."

Leandra grinned fractionally. "I could smell the plastic sheeting from your hide at fifty paces. A tiger could smell it from a hundred." She gave Ashley a knowing look. "I think you're after the same thing those poachers were hoping to find."

"The white tiger?"

Leandra nodded.

"Well, sure, I heard rumors about one…and I can't deny it'd be a dream come true to see a white tiger in the wild. But I only want to take pictures of it. The poachers want to kill it. There's a big difference."

"Is there?" Leandra chewed thoughtfully, her expression difficult to read. "Sometimes people come here hoping to find a particular thing, but find something much different than what they expected." She smiled coldly. "Those three men came to hunt a white tiger. They weren't prepared for what they found instead."

Something about the strange look in Leandra's eyes clicked in Ashley's mind, which raised and then confirmed her suspicions. She stared at the woman. "There isn't any white tiger, is there?"

Leandra's expression didn't change. "Out here," she said quietly, "things get mixed up so easily. The jungle is all shadows and light, constantly in motion. It doesn't take much for your eyes to play tricks on you. Sometimes in the jungle, what you see isn't what you see at all."

"It was you all along, wasn't it? Some idiot tourist or something got a quick look at you, and thought you were a white tiger."

"Maybe."

"That's just great. You know, I'm supposed to have already finished this assignment and been back on a plane for home. I only delayed it because I wanted a shot of that damn cat." She snorted ruefully as she finished the last of her rice. She and Grady had tickets to fly out in a fortnight, and they couldn't change them. Still, ever willing to look at the positive side of life, Ashley decided not to let the delay bother her. "I guess I should make the best use of my time, though, as long as I'm stuck here."

Leandra licked her fingers as she studied her companion. "So you're disappointed?" she asked. "About not finding what you came for?"

"Well, yeah. Like I said, it's a once in a lifetime thing, you know? But I'm glad I tried. And on the bright side, I got to meet you." She grinned.

"It's not every day I run across a unique individual like you. So, I guess the trip out here was worth the hassle I'm going to get when I return to work."

After licking the last hint of flavor from her palm leaf, Leandra stood and wandered over to the cave mouth. Outside, the rain began to ease. The thunder moved into the distance, as the storm slowly passed over them.

Fascinated, Ashley watched the strange woman. Her feet seemed to flow over the ground rather than touch it. "How do you do that?"

"Do what?"

She gestured to the ground, which was almost barren of footprints. "You don't make any noise when you walk, and you don't leave footprints. How?"

Leandra's smile was mysterious. "When you spend enough time in the jungle, you learn to hide your movements. It's simple, really, once you get the hang of it. See?" She demonstrated how she placed her feet when she walked, the weight evenly distributed, then rolling with the heel as she lifted up. Ashley shook her head in amazement.

"That's pretty cool. You know, you've got half the people out there thinking you're some kind of vigilante ghost. I'll bet the poachers are terrified."

"They are, and with good reason."

Ashley joined Leandra at the cave entrance, and they watched in companionable silence as the rain pushed farther south, eventually diminishing to a light drizzle. It was after midday, and Ashley knew she had to get back to camp before Tarun decided to come after her, but she was reluctant to part from her new acquaintance. Leandra may have felt the same way, given the curious glances she kept throwing her way.

Still...

"I really should get going, I suppose," she said quietly.

"Mmm."

"You know, if you'd like to come down and join us at the camp, I'm sure you'd be more than welcome."

"Thanks, but I don't think I'd fit in. I'm, um...not really dressed for company." Leandra held up a painted hand and wiggled her striped fingers.

"Yeah, I guess you're right." Ashley was disappointed. "Well, it was really nice meeting you, Leandra. And I really do appreciate you saving me yesterday."

"You're welcome."

Ashley had turned to leave when a hand grabbed her arm and stopped her. She glanced back, an eyebrow raised, and saw Leandra obviously struggling with something. She waited patiently for her to sort through her thoughts.

"I know a place not too far from here," Leandra said very quietly. "It's a favorite roosting spot for peacocks. If you wanted to, maybe I could take you out there before you leave? I'm sure you could get some good pictures of them."

Ashley's smile lit her face. "Sure, that sounds great. How about we go there tomorrow?"

Leandra smiled too, her expression relieved but still shy. "Okay. I'll come get you in the morning, all right? Just take a walk out of the camp and I'll find you."

"Absolutely." Ashley brushed a lock of hair behind her ear. "I don't suppose you want the others knowing about you, huh?"

"Tell them what you want," Leandra said, her voice starting to crack from the unaccustomed use. "As long as they don't mention me to the rangers, it's okay."

"Great. So, I'll see you tomorrow?"

"Tomorrow."

With a smile and a happy wave over her shoulder, Ashley started making her way down the slope, back to her friends.

Leandra watched from the mouth of the cave as Ashley carefully picked a path down the rain-soaked terrain, feeling a residual smile still curving her lips. She hadn't had much to smile about in a long time, and it was a nice feeling. Only when her visitor was out of sight did she return to the cave and seat herself on one of the boulders by the fire.

It was strange, she mused. She had been alone a long time now; four years seemed like too short a figure to measure the length of her self-imposed exile. It had been so long since she'd last spoken that the sound of her voice had surprised her when she'd used it today. It seemed deeper than she remembered it. Even her own name had taken a moment to dig up from where it had lain for so long, unused, in the back of her mind.

If she took a deep breath, Leandra could still detect the last traces of the young woman's scent in the air. Deodorant, perfume, cotton. Things she hadn't thought of in a long time. Ashley hadn't just brought herself into the cave; she'd brought a glimpse into a world Leandra had turned away from years ago. She now remembered what it felt like to hear another person talk and to have company. She recalled other things, as well. Flashes of various images and remembrances returned to her: the tall, monolithic skyscrapers of the city, the softness of clean, down-filled quilts, the simple luxury of being able to eat without having to hunt first.

The faces of loved ones lost before she came here.

Leandra sat quietly, remembering things she had thought forgotten, looking forward to hearing more of the sound of Ashley's voice in the morning.

Returning to the camp, Ashley endured Tarun's frustrated scolding with a patient smile, content to ignore his reminders that he had been hired to guide them and keep them safe, and that he couldn't very well do that if she was constantly running off alone.

When his words had no visible effect, Tarun threw his hands in the air and stormed off, muttering about how he'd never get work again if one of his clients got killed while under his care. Ashley watched him go with an amused smile, then settled herself comfortably on the ground by the fire. Grady immediately joined her.

"I'm guessing from the satisfied look on your face that you found what you were looking for?"

"Indeed, I did." Ashley folded her hands behind her head and leaned back against a tree branch, teasing Grady with the simple reply.

"And?"

"And her name is Leandra, and she's very nice."

Grady made an impressed sound and raised an eyebrow. "You spoke with her?"

"Yep. Just so happens she's an American. We had quite a nice little chat. She even cooked us lunch."

"Leave it to you to find an adventure wherever you go," he said, shaking his head a little. "So, what's her story? Why is she out here?"

Ashley's smile faltered. "Actually, she didn't say exactly why she's out here," she admitted after a moment of reflection on her meeting with Leandra. "I got the impression she follows the poachers around and...well—"

"And kills them," Grady finished.

Ashley shrugged. "There are militant groups all over the world that track down and exterminate poachers," she argued in Leandra's defense. "We saw some of that in Africa." The situation with the African elephants was so dire, the government had been forced to take drastic action to stem the trade in black market ivory. "Leandra's not any worse than the men who are hunting the tigers to extinction."

Grady merely grunted. "Did she mention why she dresses up like a tiger?"

"I think she wants to live like they do, and it helps her to look the part," Ashley explained. "She's strange. Even when she talks normally, her voice sounds like it comes from deep in her chest. She actually purrs when she's relaxed. And I mean real purring too, not fake stuff...like she has no control over it." She shook her head, remembering. "She really does behave a lot like a cat."

"So I take it she's going to leave us in peace?"

"She knows why we're here, and she doesn't mind." Ashley considered whether to tell Grady there was no white tiger, but decided against it. While Grady probably wouldn't care, Simon and Grace would be very disappointed. Ashley thought it would do the scientists good to have the hope of finding the rare creature. "I think she was just curious about us before, and that's why she came snooping around the other night."

"Uh huh. So, I guess she wants to be left alone now, right?"

Ashley grinned, knowing Grady was hoping that with her questions about the tiger-woman answered, she would let the matter go. "Actually, she invited me out for a walk tomorrow morning. There's a place she knows where I can get some good shots of peacocks, and she offered to show me."

Grady eyed her intently. "Are you certain that's a good idea? Is she safe?"

"Oh, for crying out loud, Grady," Ashley said with a snort. "She's not going to hurt me. She's been out here a long time with no one to talk to. I think she just wants a little company, and I'm more than happy to give it to her." She glared at her partner until he looked away. "She's interesting and unusual, and she's probably very lonely. It doesn't do any harm to be nice to her. Especially if she can get me closer to the animals."

"All right." Grady held up his hands in defeat. "Do what you want. You always do, anyway. I'm just trying to watch out for you, that's all."

"I know that. But you haven't even met her, so don't judge her by the fact that she's a little different. I'll be fine."

Grady let the matter rest and turned the conversation to work-related issues. Ashley spent the afternoon seeing to her equipment, then wandered down to the river to join Simon and Grace at the hide. When night fell, the group came together around the campfire for dinner. Tarun was still upset at Ashley, but it was clear Grady had spoken with him about her and he didn't argue further about her actions.

Retiring to her tent, Ashley lit the kerosene lamp and began leafing through her texts on the great cats again, this time looking at the descriptions therein with her thoughts on her new acquaintance. She already knew tigers were solitary animals: their only contact with others of their species occurring during breeding times, or the long period a cub would spend with its mother. Their habitat was widespread. The great cats seemed able to survive in any terrain that provided cover, large prey animals, and water. She read a few passages about their hunting methods, not surprised to find they relied mainly on stealth and camouflage to capture prey. Tigers could charge with tremendous speed and power, but only in short bursts. Tigers took their prey from behind, if possible, using their weight to bring the quarry to the ground, then biting the neck while holding the animal down with a forelimb. Sometimes they would break the neck, or sometimes bite down on the throat and strangle their prey (a technique that had given rise to the legend of blood-sucking tigers, which Ashley thought was ridiculous since cats didn't have lips and therefore weren't able to suck anything).

Reading that passage, Ashley remembered the bodies of the poachers they'd found: the deep, slashing claw marks across their backs and the way their throats had been torn open. She shuddered, certain Leandra had learned her killing style from the creatures she protected and imitated.

Ashley wondered what Leandra must have experienced in her four years in the jungle. She didn't need to be a psychologist to realize that such an extensive period without social contact must have taken a toll on Leandra's mind.

"Four years," she mused quietly. "Four years of living like an animal, of trying to be an animal. I wonder how much a person could forget about being human in that length of time."

After putting aside her books and shutting down the lamp, Ashley lay in her sleeping bag, deep in thought. She pictured Leandra's behavior today. She had seemed okay. While her voice had been raspy from lack of use, she had spoken clearly and thoughtfully. She was polite. She probably relied more on her sense of smell than a regular person would, but that was understandable.

So, you said you used to be a poacher, Ashley thought, trying to piece together her history from the sparse information Leandra had given her. *I can picture that. It would probably be the sort of thing that would teach good survival skills. But then, one day, someone says something that maybe gives you an attack of conscience, so you decide to turn over a new leaf and do something to help the animals you used to hunt. And so you...*

Unfortunately, that was where Ashley's pondering ran into a brick wall. There were safer, smarter, and more effective ways to fight poaching than to come out here alone, dress up funny, and start killing off the hunters one by one.

"There's something else," she whispered. "I'm betting it takes a lot for someone to turn away from the rest of the world and decide to live with wild animals."

Ashley recalled the strange, almost desperate look in Leandra's eyes as she'd been about to leave. The yearning expression that had crossed Leandra's face just before she'd offered to show Ashley the peacocks.

"You've been out here a long time," she whispered to the absent woman. "No one to talk to. No human contact except the men you hunt. You probably feel more kinship with the tigers than with your own species. And yet today, you not only talked to me, but you wanted to see me again." Ashley felt privileged that Leandra had opened up to her, even if only a little. "I bet you've forgotten what it's like to have a friend who can actually talk with you." She smiled to herself. "Perhaps I should remind you."

Closing her eyes, Ashley snuggled into a pillow of folded clothes and let herself drift off, the image of piercing blue eyes and a powerful, tawny-gold figure the last thing she remembered before sleep claimed her.

Ashley grinned with delight as she finished off another roll of film and changed the cartridge with an automatic ease gained only after years of practice. A group of four peacocks and perhaps a dozen peafowl ranged before her, the males displaying their magnificent, shimmering tail-fans in the early morning light. She gave her unusual companion a radiant smile before focusing for more shots.

"This is fantastic!" she exclaimed for the fifth time. "I can't believe how close they let us get."

They had come out here just after first light, hiking the short distance to the clearing in relative silence. Upon arriving, Leandra surprised her by folding her hands over her mouth and giving a piercing, very authentic-sounding peacock call. The sound attracted a host of preening and excited birds, much to Ashley's delight. Now the sun was well into the sky, and Ashley was almost out of film. Leandra hadn't spoken much, so Ashley talked a little about her family and her work just to fill the quiet. The peculiarity of the scene, with Leandra sitting back on her haunches listening to her with a slight smile playing about her lips, made for a slightly awkward atmosphere. Still, it was worth a little awkwardness to be here.

Finally finishing off the last role of film she'd brought, Ashley fiddled with her camera a few moments before settling down next to her companion, trying not to be too obvious about sneaking sidelong glances at Leandra's unusual appearance.

"Wow! I can't believe how many pictures I got. I mean, I already had a few shots of peacocks, but nothing like these. I only wish I'd brought more film." Grady was always trying to get her to update her equipment, raving about the superiority of the new digital cameras over the older models, but Ashley refused to listen. She preferred the comforting reliability and simplicity of using real film. Now, she smiled at her striped companion, noting that even Leandra's sitting style was vaguely feline. She could also hear the sound of quiet purring, and from that she surmised her companion was in a good mood. "Thank you for bringing me out here."

"You're welcome."

They watched the magnificent birds continue their antics, enjoying the display. Though she tended to judge her own work with a strict eye, Ashley felt confident she had captured at least a few terrific shots this morning. Photographing in the wild was a tricky game, and getting that perfect image relied on luck every bit as much as planning, equipment, or setting.

"You know," Leandra said quietly after a long period of silent contemplation, "if you wanted me to, I could show you some other places. There's a spot, upriver a few miles, where the elephants usually water. And there are lots of other birds and animals you could photograph. I wouldn't mind taking you to see them."

"That'd be great." Ashley could sense again that her companion was very nervous, and she actually found the strong, predatory woman's uncertainty rather cute. "But you know, Leandra, if you want to spend time with me, you don't have to go to all this trouble."

Leandra's expression grew even more nervous, and she started fidgeting with one of the cords of hair hanging over her chest. "What do you mean?"

"I mean it's okay if you want company," Ashley said gently, her expression soft and open. "I guess you haven't had a friend for a while, right?"

Shy, timid blue eyes glanced up, then quickly away. "Well, maybe not in the people sense, no. But I do have friends out here." She nodded at the peacocks.

Ashley chuckled. "I probably don't want to meet some of your other friends, huh?"

"Probably not."

Ashley studied the painted woman for a moment. "I'd really like to be your friend, too, Leandra," she said quietly. "If you want some company, you can just say so; I'm more than happy to spend time with you. Even if it's for no particular reason. You don't have to take me to see animals. You can just ask." She paused, uncertain. "You know, I read that tigers are solitary. They spend almost all their time alone. But you're not a tiger, you're a human being." From the guarded look that dropped immediately over Leandra's face, Ashley realized she'd hit a nerve. "It's not such a good thing for a human to be alone for too long."

Leandra's posture stiffened, her expression guarded. "I know that." The purring was replaced by a threatening growl.

Ashley raised her hands in a calming gesture. "I'm not trying to make you angry," she said. "I'm sure you have a reason to be out here like this, and I'm not saying you shouldn't be here if it's what you want. I'm just saying that, maybe, it would be good for you to be around another person. Like me, for example." She smiled, reassured when Leandra realized the unfriendly noises she was making and stopped them, looking embarrassed. "When was the last time you spoke actual words? I mean, before we met?"

"About three years ago, I guess."

"Does anyone in the outside world know you're here?" Ashley probed gently. "Family? Friends?"

Leandra shook her head. "Anyone who knew me probably assumes I'm dead," she whispered. "I doubt they miss me much, anyway."

Ashley scooted closer, amused to see Leandra's nostrils twitch as she sniffed the air. There were a thousand and one questions burning on the tip of her tongue—a thousand things she wanted to ask Leandra about her life and what had brought her here—but she resisted the desire to give them voice. Working with animals all her life had taught her that you couldn't get close to a wild animal if you moved in too quickly. Calm and patience worked best. She decided to employ those same tactics with Leandra. "I think you need to be reminded that you're not an animal," Ashley said, very slowly reaching out and pushing back the mass of hair. "Under all this paint and hair, there's a beautiful woman, not a giant cat. You don't want to forget that."

Leandra sat frozen, trembling slightly, and it seemed for a long moment she had forgotten to breathe. She stared back at Ashley with wide eyes, visibly struggling not to retreat from her more intimate proximity. Ashley held her position until she saw the wild, instinctive urge diminish, and Leandra relaxed.

"I haven't forgotten," Leandra whispered in a hesitant voice. "But it's nice to be reminded, sometimes. And I'd like to show you the animals anyway, if you want to see them."

"Okay, then." Ashley backed away and resumed her seat. "I'd like that."

"Good."

A long period of silence followed, and then Leandra glanced shyly at Ashley. "You know," she said quietly, "I'm not crazy or anything."

Ashley chuckled. "I never thought you were."

"Good." Leandra offered a slight smile. "I was just confirming it."

Ashley cast her eyes over the tall woman's striped body. "I'm not going to lie and say I think you're exactly 'normal,' but I've been around long enough to tell the difference between eccentricity and madness. I wouldn't be here with you now if I thought you were insane."

Leandra considered that before giving her a grateful smile. Ashley could read Leandra's body language well enough to recognize her longing for company after such a long period of isolation. Utterly intrigued by the strange woman, Ashley was more than happy to provide some human contact; she couldn't even begin to imagine what it would be like to endure four years alone in the wild. How lonely it must be.

The two women sat quietly and watched the peacocks finish their preening and wander off. They lingered even after the birds had left, exchanging a few words now and then but mostly just enjoying the sounds of the jungle creatures at play all around them.

Dressed in camouflage fatigues, a tall, well-built man watched through a pair of binoculars as the group of five gathered around a small fire to share their evening meal and talk as the sun went down. With a rifle slung over his shoulder and basic essentials like a water flask, a compass, and a broad-bladed hunting knife belted around his waist, the six-foot-tall man cut an impressive, confident figure. His dark-blond hair was held back in a loose ponytail, a few strands pulling loose in the humidity and clinging to his sweat-streaked face. His skin was deeply tanned, and wrinkles had formed at the corners of his eyes from years of squinting into the sunlight. Intense, green eyes burned from deep-set sockets as he observed the gathering.

Behind him, another man watched in similar fashion, this one sporting bright red hair and a thick beard. A deep scowl pulled the corners of his mouth down when he spotted a familiar figure sitting on a fallen log, laughing with her friends.

"That's her," he said. "The little blonde bitch on the right." He shook his head. "Told me she was a photographer or something. Guess it's lucky fer me I didn't kill her, right, Jack?"

Jack Corbin grunted, as his shrewd eyes took in the details of the camp and its inhabitants. "That balding guy's no photographer," he decided quickly. "From the looks of the gear they're toting, him and that brunette sitting next to him are scientists or some such. Probably doing research. The Indian guy must be their guide, getting paid to babysit, make sure nothing bad happens." He worked the binocular focus wheel and brought the petite blonde into sharper detail. She didn't look like much, he thought, wondering whether he should believe the man behind him. "Blondie's no worse for wear after your little encounter with the 'Indian Menace'," he observed.

The grizzly redhead scowled. "Maybe she ran away like I did. Or maybe that thing only kills guys like us. How should I know what happened?"

Corbin replaced his binoculars in a case attached to the belt around his waist. "Tell me again what it looked like."

"It was a woman," the man explained for the dozenth time. "Only she was like a tiger. She had claws, her skin was stripy, and she moved like a cat. I swear it's the truth."

"And you ran away."

"Damn right I ran. If you saw that thing, you'd have run away too."

Corbin just grunted, still unsure what to make of this report. "I had three other men coming in for this hunt," he said quietly. "They're two days late now. I guess that means they didn't make it."

"If they got caught by the ghost, they sure as hell didn't make it."

Jack Corbin was not prone to flights of fancy. He had traveled every continent on Earth, had tracked and hunted almost every creature capable of killing a man, and had never encountered any beast that couldn't be overcome with caution and a loaded gun. His reputation was widespread among those who lived in the shadowy world of the black market animal trade, and though he could have lived a soft life of luxury from the money he'd made in his dealings, Jack preferred the excitement and danger of his work.

Three years ago, he'd heard the reports of a poaching expedition that had been massacred in the Indian forests, the details of which had been enough to make even a ruthless hunter like him a little nervous. At the time, he'd assumed it was some kind of scare tactic the rangers were using to frighten away poachers. The stories told of some mystical, tiger-like spirit stalking the jungle, ravaging those who dared to hunt the great cats. He'd scoffed at the lunacy of it, even as many of his comrades started avoiding the Indian territory.

In the years that followed, more rumors had filtered down to him of men lost in the jungle—some never found; some discovered by rangers, their bodies mauled and shredded with fearful savagery. Now, lured here by the chance to hunt the rare white tiger, Jack wasn't sure what to make of the story brought to him by his companion, but he intended to tread carefully. He hadn't become successful as a poacher and smuggler by being rash.

Having never hunted with Shaun Duggan before, Jack trusted his bizarre story just enough not to discount it. The man seemed a touch too eager to believe in a superstitious explanation, but he'd obviously seen something. Jack could hear the nervousness in his voice.

"So what're we gonna do?" Shaun asked.

Jack considered long and hard. Eventually, he nodded toward the distant campfire. "We'll watch them closely," he stated. "If they're here for the tiger as well, maybe we won't have to work so hard to find it. We can let them do the work for us."

"And what about the ghost?"

"We find it, and we kill it." Jack turned away, unslung his rifle, and headed back to his camp, some two miles to the west. "If it's real enough that it can kill a man, it's real enough that we can kill it."

"But how?"

"Simple." Jack shot him a withering glance. "First, we lure it out of hiding. Once I get a good look at it, I'll decide the best way to take it down."

Shaun's expression suggested he still had reservations, but he was smart enough to keep them to himself. On the way back to camp, Jack pondered the safest way to lure out the strange menace, rather enjoying the first true challenge he'd had in a long while.

CHAPTER 2

In what distant deeps or skies
Burnt the fire of thine eyes?
On what wings dare he aspire?
What the hand, dare seize the fire?

—"The Tyger" by William Blake

FOR THE LAST FOUR DAYS, Ashley had thoroughly enjoyed herself, having seen more of Leandra than she had any of her other companions. She'd quickly developed a routine: after breakfast each morning, she would walk out into the forest around the camp and along the river, knowing that the enigmatic woman would join her once she was alone. Once, Tarun had tried to follow. Leandra hadn't shown up, and Ashley had lectured the protective guide sternly that she was quite capable of taking care of herself. Tarun grudgingly accepted that he couldn't discourage Ashley from befriending Leandra, and turned his attention to helping the others.

The two women had settled into a comfortable rhythm, spending their days in peaceful companionship in the wilderness. Sometimes, Leandra would take Ashley out to places she knew were favorite haunts of various animals, other times to scenic locations she thought Ashley might enjoy seeing. Leandra's voice grew stronger as she became accustomed to speaking again, and soon she was talking more, explaining the habits of the creatures with whom she shared the jungle. Occasionally, she would even relate amusing stories of their antics, such as the time a group of mischievous young monkeys had found a sleeping bear and decided to wake it up with a pelting of pebbles, then scampered away unharmed as the drowsily irritated beast struggled to catch them.

Ashley was continually amazed by Leandra as she learned more of her life these past four years. She was fascinated most of all by her strange, symbiotic relationship with the great cats who dominated everything out here—a relationship Leandra spoke of rarely, and one which was clearly her strongest link to the forest.

In turn, Ashley talked about her life in America; about her older sister, Evelyn, who had married young to a childhood sweetheart who had since become a successful physician; and about their daughter, Casey, who was now seventeen and seemingly intent on following in her aunt's footsteps as a troublemaker. She described her house and the quiet town that lay a short drive away from it.

When she spoke of the outside world, Ashley noticed Leandra's expression would become even more intense and focused than usual, as though she wanted to absorb every word and description that was offered. Seeing Leandra's obvious fascination with the world she'd left behind, Ashley talked more and more about her life and the places she'd visited.

Today, Ashley had risen earlier than usual, wanting to get in a quick bath before she went looking for Leandra. The high humidity was making her feel decidedly sticky. When the others gathered for breakfast, she was humming a happy tune. She smiled cheerfully at Grady's early morning scowl and handed out mugs of strong coffee to Simon and Grace, who exchanged amused glances at her merriment. She was in a very good mood this morning, already looking forward to another day spent in the company of her new friend.

She grinned at Grady as he settled himself on his tree-branch seat with a groan, rubbing the sleep from his eyes.

"Good morning, Grady," she greeted him in a singsong voice. "Urgh." He accepted the coffee she offered and sipped the bitter brew slowly for a few minutes before meeting her sunny smile. "Why are you in such a good mood? Last I heard, you weren't any closer to getting pictures of that damn cat. Let me guess: You're going off with tiger-woman again today, right?"

"I told you, her name is Leandra. And yes, I'm spending the day with her." Ashley gave her partner a grin. "I don't see why you're so down in the dumps about it, Grady. For one thing, she's helping me get some unbelievable shots. For another, she's keeping me out of trouble, so you can get your own work done in peace without having to worry that I'm about to get run down by a herd of elephants or something." That earned her a wry grin from her partner, who never missed an opportunity to remind her of the time he'd had to rescue her from a stampede in Kenya because she'd been too busy taking photos to get out of the way. "Leandra's a wonderful person, so don't be so grumpy about me spending time with her."

"And when are we going to be introduced to your mysterious friend?" asked Simon. The scientist had made no secret of his eagerness to meet Leandra, and had already probed Ashley for every scrap of information she had about her. "Did you ask about letting us talk to her?"

Ashley took a sip of coffee while she composed a polite rejection. While she knew Simon had only the best intentions, she also knew Leandra would not welcome his questions about her life. "I'm sorry, Simon, but I don't think she'd be interested," she said, watching his expression drop. "She's just a very private person, I'm afraid, as you can probably understand. I don't think she wants a bunch of people staring at her and asking lots of questions."

"But I wouldn't be at all intrusive," Simon argued. "I'd just like to see her, that's all. Maybe ask her a few questions—nothing too personal, of course. It's just that she could offer incredible insights into how the tigers spend their time out here...there's still so much we don't really know."

"I understand, and I'll mention it to her. If she's interested in meeting you, she'll tell me when she's ready. Okay?"

Simon nodded reluctantly. "Okay."

Finishing off her breakfast and grabbing a change of clothes and her bathing accessories, Ashley headed off to the river for a quick wash. The humidity in the jungle was high, and even though she was accustomed to roughing it in the wilderness, she didn't like feeling sticky and smelly. Finding what looked like a safe, fairly sheltered part of the river, Ashley laid out her gear and stripped down, rather enjoying the guilty little thrill that came from being so exposed outdoors.

Just as she was reaching back to unhook her bra, a familiar throaty voice called a cheerful greeting from behind her. "Morning, Ashley. You taking a bath?"

Ashley gave a startled squeak and grabbed for her towel, covering herself as she spun around to glare at Leandra. The striped woman was perched on a boulder nearby, head cocked to the side as she regarded Ashley curiously.

"Damn it, Leandra! What the hell are you doing here?"

Leandra looked confused. "What do you think I'm doing? I came to see you, of course."

Ashley blushed a deep crimson. "You shouldn't sneak up on people like that," she scolded, pulling the towel around her body more securely. "I was just about to..." She gestured to the pile of clothes, the soap and washcloth, and then the river.

"Bathe?"

"Yes."

Leandra settled down on the rock more comfortably. "That's okay. I'll just wait until you're done."

Ashley laughed out loud, then realized Leandra was serious. Frank, startlingly clear, blue eyes continued to watch her openly, and Ashley's blush deepened. *I guess her sense of modesty was one of the first things to go when she came out here.*

"Um...would you mind...you know, turning around or something?" Ashley asked.

"Why?"

"Well, I could use a little privacy, you know."

Dark brows contracted in puzzlement, then shot up as Leandra grinned in sudden understanding. "Oh, you're embarrassed to be naked around me?"

"No, but..." Ashley fidgeted with the edge of the towel uncertainly.

"You don't need to be shy, Ashley. I doubt you have anything there I don't already own myself."

"I know that, but still..."

"Would you be more comfortable if I joined you?" Leandra asked, reaching for the leather cord that held her top closed.

"No!" Ashley quickly stopped that line of thought, shaking her head in amusement. "That's a very nice offer, but I don't think it'll be necessary, thank you."

Leandra shrugged and settled down again. "As you wish."

Ashley sighed. "Do you even remember the meaning of the word modesty?"

"I understand the concept," Leandra said dismissively, inspecting one of her claw weapons. "It doesn't have any place out here. I lived naked for probably three months before I realized it was more comfortable to have at least some support." She spread her arms to display her brief outfit. "Modesty is constructed from the concept of shame. Beyond comfort and the need for warmth, clothing is entirely dispensable." Seeing that Ashley didn't seem likely to take her bath if she didn't get some privacy, Leandra turned away. "I won't watch you, if it makes you uncomfortable."

Ashley groaned. *This is what I get for making friends with Jungle Jane,* she thought. "Fine." Deciding to make it quick and get it over with, she turned back to the river and pulled the towel from her body. Quickly stripping off her undergarments, she grabbed the soap and washcloth and waded out into the surprisingly cold, mountain-fed water.

Lounging easily on the boulder, Leandra used the rock to touch up one of her claws, gently rubbing the bone weapon against the stone and blowing away the shavings. She inspected each of the hooked talons carefully, sharpening those that needed it before she felt her eyes start to drift curiously back to the river. Not wanting to do anything that might make Ashley uncomfortable around her, Leandra subtly observed the naked woman scrub herself vigorously.

Ashley's outdoor lifestyle had given her a fairly even tan, and her body was lithe and firm from a physically demanding career. She was slender without being bony, delicate without being weak, and her observer found her entirely enchanting. High, firm breasts quickly captured Leandra's attention, and she enjoyed the sight of a naked female form for the first time in many years. Ashley was a beautiful woman, and having learned from experience not to fight her instincts, Leandra didn't bother arguing with her attraction. She realized it would not be wise to act on it, however.

After four years of social denial, the company Ashley gave so easily to Leandra was like water to a woman dying of thirst. She craved it with a deep passion, hungered for every scrap that was offered, and hoarded in her memory each precious moment spent in the young woman's presence. She knew Ashley would be leaving sooner or later, and didn't want to do anything to hurry that departure. She might frighten her away by expressing her not-so-platonic interest.

Tearing her gaze away from the nymph-like figure in the water, Leandra turned her attention back to the jungle, trying to recall the faces of some of the women she'd bedded before coming out here. There had been many, she remembered, and not one of them had ever meant more to her than a simple night of pleasure. She had seduced them, taken them, and then left them as soon as something more interesting came along. Of course, it had been a long time since Leandra had thought more than fleetingly of sexual pleasure. The struggle for survival consumed most of her thoughts these days. Still, sneaking a peek at her new friend as she finished her bath, Leandra found that the myriad faces in her memory had now dissolved into Ashley's soft, gentle features, and she was glad the paint hid her blush as she wondered how the young woman might look in the throes of ecstasy.

"Okay, I'm ready."

Leandra looked back to find Ashley had finished her bath and was now dressed and waiting. She had changed into an army green, cut-off tank top and cargo shorts, her blonde hair still wet and tousled about her face.

"You want to wait here while I take this stuff back to camp?" Ashley asked, holding up her bundle of dirty clothes and the towel.

"Sure."

"Great. I'll be quick." Ashley hastened away, and Leandra watched her departure with a wry smile. She happily allowed her eyes to wander over the photographer's backside until she disappeared back into the forest, enjoying the way the brief outfit displayed Ashley's slender curves. An unconscious rumble stirred in Leandra's throat, and she settled down on the rock to sun herself, purring contentedly as she looked forward to the day ahead.

"So, have your friends had any luck finding tigers?" Leandra asked, offering her arm to Ashley so she could keep her balance as they navigated a treacherous stretch of nearly dry riverbed. Ashley accepted the assistance gratefully, having already slipped twice on the slimy rocks.

"Some," she replied. "Apparently, they bagged a young male yesterday morning after I left. Hit him with a tranq gun then collared him, no problems." They made it past the slippery rocks. She had watched Leandra spring barefoot from one rock to another and envied the unbelievable agility she could never hope to match. "It would have been nice to see him. Simon thinks he's probably the dominant tiger in this territory."

"Actually, he's a rogue male, just passing through."

"How do you—" Ashley stopped, seeing the knowing grin on the Leandra's face, and rolled her eyes. "Right. Forgot who I was talking to."

"That you did."

As they made their way farther along the edge of the river bank, Ashley cast her friend a curious look. "So… Just how close can you actually get to a tiger? Seriously, I mean."

"Seriously?" Leandra considered. "It depends."

"On what?"

"Lots of things. Like, for example, how well the tiger knows me, and what kind of mood it's in. Plus, some species are more aggressive than others. And I wouldn't get within a hundred feet of a male during mating season."

Ashley absorbed this slowly. "Well, what's the closest you've ever got? Have you ever petted one? Like, a real wild one?"

A slightly uneasy expression crossed Leandra's features for a moment, and Ashley noted the way she rubbed at her right shoulder as though it pained her.

"Let's just say I've been closer than you'd ever want to get."

Hearing from Leandra's tone that she was getting uncomfortable, Ashley smoothly moved the conversation on. "Do you always keep your body painted like that?"

"Pretty much. The paint makes it easier to blend in and helps to mask my scent."

"What do you use for paint?"

"Crushed ochre and other kinds of clay or mud." Leandra displayed her patterned arm. "I mix it with fat I take from my kills so it doesn't wash away so easily in the rain."

Ashley studied the grainy, rough texture of the paint, running a finger along Leandra's arm and feeling the slightly greasy finish.

"How long does it last?"

"Depends on how active I am. Usually a week or two, and then I take a bath and wash it off. It takes a few hours to apply again."

Ashley admired the intricacy and detail of Leandra's design. "Must be tough doing your back, huh?"

"At first, but I got used to it. Now it's just another routine for me. I could do it blindfolded, if I had to."

"Well, I think it looks nice." Ashley grinned at the self-conscious smile she received for the compliment. "Although," she added, "you scared the shit out of me the first time I saw you."

Leandra nodded. "Yeah, that's another good thing about it. If poachers do see me, they're usually so shocked they don't react quickly enough to save themselves."

"Right." Ashley's smile faltered at the reminder that her companion was a killer. It was difficult to reconcile the memory of Leandra's bloody handiwork with the considerate, sometimes charming woman she was coming to like more and more with each passing day. Despite the constant predatory air that seemed to hang around Leandra like a shroud, Ashley recognized that an oddly vulnerable woman lived beneath the primal markings and tangled hair. While there was no doubt in Ashley's mind that Leandra was capable of extremely savage acts of violence, it was easy to forget that as she enjoyed the other woman's company.

Leandra was watching her awkwardly, seeming to intuitively sense where her thoughts had wandered. Before she could open her mouth to offer any kind of reassurance, the sharp report of a distant rifle shot echoed through the jungle. The startled birds in the canopy took to the wing, filling the air with their raucous cries.

The change in Leandra's demeanor was immediate: her muscles snapped taut like cords of wire beneath her skin, and she dropped into a low crouch. She cocked her head to the side, eyes ablaze with feral fire. Ashley met her gaze for a moment, paling as she heard an ominous growl rumble from her striped companion.

"That was too far away to be Tarun."

"Poachers," Leandra hissed, her eyes alight with a fire Ashley hadn't seen before.

"It could be rangers—"

"No. That's a large-caliber hunting rifle. Only a poacher would have use for one out here." For a moment, Leandra's expression appeared conflicted, then she offered an apologetic, regretful smile. "I'm sorry. I have to check it out."

"I understand," Ashley said quietly, cursing the interruption to their day.

"There's a bend in the creek up ahead," Leandra said, clearly every bit as disappointed as she was. "It's not too far, just watch your step on the rocks. If you want to, you can wait there for me, and I'll be back as soon as I can."

"Okay."

Just as Leandra turned to leave, a moment of gut-level concern made Ashley reach out and grab her arm, pulling her back. The feeling wasn't something she could place or explain—after all, Leandra seemed more than capable of dealing with danger, and when Leandra met her gaze, questioning, she released her grip with an embarrassed smile.

"Just...be careful, okay?"

Leandra flashed her a quick, toothy grin. "Always." She patted Ashley's hand, turned away, and ran off into the jungle, her body blending quickly with the shifting shadows and dense undergrowth.

Ashley watched her vanish, then sighed and continued making her way along the creek bed alone.

Leandra moved quickly and stealthily along barely visible forest trails, every sense open and alert to the slightest sound or presence. She knew this part of India better than any other, having spent so much of her time here, and she moved with confidence over the familiar ground.

It wasn't long before her pace slowed, and she started stalking with greater care as she neared the place she guessed was the origin of the gunshot. Sniffing the air and listening attentively, she found nothing out of place. A quick but thorough search failed to turn up any blood or tracks, and she snarled in frustration.

This *had* to be the place. From the echo, Leandra was certain the shot had been fired from here, or somewhere very close by. And she knew from experience that poachers didn't take idle shots. They fired only to kill, knowing every shot meant the possibility of attracting the attention of any rangers in the area. Leandra didn't have anything to fear from the patrols, since she could avoid them if they came snooping around, but as she continued searching for some signs of the shooter, she felt a growing sense that something here was wrong. It was nothing she could put her finger on, just a gut feeling of disquiet that made her even more cautious than usual.

Eventually, her patience was rewarded. A single spent shell, nestled among the leaf litter, caught Leandra's attention. She swooped on it immediately, cold eyes searching for and finding faint tracks leading away. There was no sign of a kill, however. In fact, there was no sign of a target at all. Certainly, no animal had been in this area for some time. That thought made her all the more curious about why the shot had been fired. She moved into the deeper cover of the shadows and began hunting her quarry.

After several minutes of pursuit, the tracks left the comforting shelter of the jungle and moved into more open ground, near a steeply cascading river. Leandra hesitated, not liking to leave her cover and venture into the open while she was hunting. Pacing a few strides back and forth, growling without realizing she was doing so, she felt her anger rise with her frustration. This was her territory. Her hunting ground. Having spent so much time modeling herself and her behavior after the great jungle cats, Leandra had picked up their same territorial possessiveness. This was an invasion, and she didn't like letting it go unpunished. Besides, if she let this poacher get away, he might actually find what he was almost certainly looking for.

Unwilling to give up the hunt, she studied the surrounding wilderness carefully, then cautiously left the shelter of the undergrowth, every nerve ending alert and ready to warn her of the slightest danger.

The tracks followed the course of the river for another hundred-odd paces. For a while, Leandra had little trouble reading them, then all of a sudden they disappeared into the rock-strewn waters. Crisscrossing the swift-flowing but shallow river with remarkable agility, she searched both banks for any continued sign.

Nothing. The poacher seemed to have vanished.

Leandra's senses picked up on something out of place. The instincts that had kept her alive out here through four long years screamed a silent warning, and her striped figure crouched behind a bush and froze for a split second as she searched the surrounding wilderness. There was nothing visible, but the openness of her position made her feel exposed and vulnerable. Trusting her instincts, she leapt up and ran as fast as she could back into the jungle. She wasn't going to jeopardize her safety for this hunt. She had learned long ago when to give up the chase and wait for a better opportunity.

Within a heartbeat, Leandra's figure was just another set of shadows cast by the canopy above, and she started making her way back to Ashley, wondering at the sense of peril that still disturbed her.

"Amazing!"

Jack Corbin breathed a quiet, impressed whistle as he watched the distant figure melt back into the underbrush. Even with his powerful binoculars, Jack couldn't find the woman again once she'd escaped his scrutiny.

His plan had worked perfectly, however. As he had predicted, the single shot had attracted the attention of the strange tiger-woman, and he'd had little trouble laying a trail for her to follow. Luring the stranger into the open allowed him to watch from a safe distance, where he could verify the threat she posed. And from what he'd seen, Jack had not been disappointed. His only regret was that their ruse might have alerted the woman to danger.

He turned to his companion with a thin-lipped smile. "It seems I owe you an apology, Shaun," he said. "As difficult as your story was to believe, I can't deny the evidence of my own eyes." He chuckled. "Not quite a ghost, however. She's as much flesh and blood as you or me."

Shaun grunted, his arms folded across his chest. "So why didn't you just shoot her?"

Jack shook his head. "She wasn't still long enough for me to get a clear shot. She sensed us watching and ran," he said, still marveling at the strange woman's apparent hyper-awareness. "She's quick and wary. We'll need to set an ambush, which means finding her usual haunts and then figuring out the pattern of her movements."

"Who is she?" Shaun wondered aloud.

"Probably some half-crazed vigilante," Jack guessed. "Some activist who took a bad trip and went nuts. Looks like she's been living out here awhile, which means she must have developed good survival instincts. More animal than human, I'll bet. Still..." He offered a confident grin. "We'll be doing the hunting now, and while she may be fast, I doubt she can dodge a bullet."

"That's *if* she's human," Shaun said. "She's the one who killed all the other guys. I bet they were careful too, but it didn't do 'em any good, did it?"

Jack scowled. "They were taken by surprise. We can do the same to her. She won't be expecting us to attack her." The doubtful expression lingered on Shaun's face, so Jack spoke in a firmer tone. "That woman is all that stands between us and a fortune. We kill her, then we start the hunt for the white tiger. If those scientist people find it before we do, we'll just go in and take it, nice and simple. Are you gonna let your idiotic superstitions stop you from getting a big fat paycheck?"

Shaun shook his head reluctantly. "Of course not. But—"

"But nothing! She's just some whacked-out loon who's gone psycho and started killing poachers. We put her down, and then when we get out of here, everyone else'll thank us for getting rid of the 'tiger-ghost.'" Jack clapped his brawny companion on the shoulder and turned him back toward their camp. "This is the sort of thing that'll make for a powerful reputation," he continued. "We'll both be legends."

Shaun's eyes lit up. "Really?"

"Absolutely."

"And you're sure we can get her?"

Jack snorted. "I've hunted everything on this planet that walks or crawls. Trust me, humans are a lot easier to kill than big cats."

Shaun considered this in silence for a long moment, and Jack didn't interrupt his thought process. Finally he nodded. "Okay, I'm in. What do we do first?"

Jack smiled. He knew Shaun couldn't resist the tempting possibility of bragging that he'd helped kill the "Indian Menace." Smacking Shaun heartily on the back, he began to outline his plan.

"Hey!"

Ashley was sitting on a fallen log, trying not to fidget with concern, when the familiar throaty voice startled her. Jumping up, she breathed a sigh of relief when Leandra's striped form emerged from the forest. "Jeez, Leandra, what did I tell you about sneaking up on me?" she scolded.

"Sorry." Leandra grinned teasingly, not making much of an effort to appear repentant. "I'll try to remember to make noise next time."

"Thanks." Ashley sat back down and gestured for Leandra to join her. "So, what did you find?"

"Nothing much. No blood or signs of a kill, only a single set of tracks that died in a river. But there was something strange about it...something wrong."

"Like what?"

"I'm not...really sure." A distant, confused expression flittered across her features, and Ashley realized it was probably difficult for Leandra to translate her instincts into words. "It wasn't really something I could hear, or smell, or even see. But I could feel something out there, like I was being watched."

"I know what you're talking about," Ashley said. "I seem to recall experiencing the same thing the first night you paid me a visit."

"Can't blame me for being interested," Leandra said with a wry smile. "You did set up camp in my hunting ground, remember."

"I know." Ashley considered Leandra's report. "Maybe the shot was just a signal or something," she suggested. "It's pretty easy to get lost out here if you don't know what you're doing. Maybe two groups were just using the sound of the gunshot to find each other."

"Maybe." Leandra shook away the memory of the hunt, and Ashley had a feeling she was more interested in turning the conversation back to lighter, more pleasant topics. "Would you like to keep going? There's a nice little clearing not too far up ahead. We can take a break there and have something to eat."

"Sure."

The two stood and continued on down the creek bed, while Ashley told a story of her niece's last escapade, which had resulted in a suspension from school. Leandra listened attentively to every word, the easy smile on her face making Ashley more than happy to fill the silence.

The next day, Ashley took her walk down by the river, and as usual, Leandra quickly joined her. As soon as the striped figure emerged from the jungle, Ashley noticed a mysterious smile on her friend's face and quirked an eyebrow at her. "What are you smiling about?"

"Nothing big," Leandra replied. "There's a small herd of chital feeding a few miles east of here in the grasslands. I found them last night, but there wasn't time to hunt, so I left it for today. I haven't been bringing in much prey lately, so this is good."

"Why haven't you been hunting?" Ashley asked, then realized the only possible reason. "Oh." She smiled self-consciously. "You know, you don't have to keep me entertained, Leandra. If you need to hunt, that's fine. I don't want to cause you problems."

"It's no problem." Leandra started guiding their footsteps along the riverbank, heading east. "I'd rather spend the time with you. It's been a nice change for me to have another person around. But still, I could use the meat. I've been draining my rice supplies too quickly."

"So I guess you can't do much today, huh?"

"Actually," Leandra said, giving her a shy smile in return. "I was going to ask if you'd like to come with me. As long as you stay quiet, you shouldn't frighten them away."

Ashley's face lit up with pleasure at the invitation. She was delighted at the opportunity to see more of how Leandra lived. "I'd love to come. Are you sure you don't mind?"

"Very sure."

"Well, okay then. Great!"

It took an hour to reach the place where the spotted deer were grazing; by the time they arrived, Ashley's tank top was dark with sweat and clinging to her lithe figure. She noted with envy that Leandra wasn't even breathing hard, despite the intense humidity. The striped woman raised a hand to signal a halt just before the end of the dense jungle cover, her eyes intense and alive as she surveyed the open grasslands beyond. Ashley shivered with excitement and watched with interest as her friend sniffed the air.

"All right," Leandra murmured, licking her lips. "Can you see them?" She pointed.

Ashley squinted, standing on tiptoes to see over the high grass, and shook her head. "Nope."

"Let's see if we can get a little closer."

The two moved very slowly along the edge of the forest, Leandra making less noise than a ghost. Ashley winced every time she stepped on a dry twig or crinkly leaf, feeling clumsy next to the stealth of her friend. When they found a better position, Leandra pointed again and Ashley was delighted to see the small group of chital grazing no more than fifty feet away.

It was difficult to count how many deer there were, since some were sitting and resting, while others cropped at the dry grasses or stood on hind legs to reach the sweeter leaves of the trees above. Also, several of them seemed to be standing lookout. They were well accustomed to being prey for the great jungle cats or packs of scrawny wolves, and were suitably wary of any hunters. Ashley bit her lower lip.

"Can you get close enough without them seeing you?"

"Seeing me? Yes. Smelling me is trickier. But they're not the biggest problem. Look in the tree branches just above where they're feeding."

Ashley looked, her eyes narrowing in confusion. "Monkeys?"

"Uh huh. They might be able to spot me easier, and if they do, they'll warn the chital. The two groups often form alliances for mutual protection—it always helps to have friends out here, especially when you're on the bottom of the food chain."

Ashley didn't see any way Leandra could get near the skittish deer. It was clear she hunted in the same manner as the great cats she mimicked, and without a gun, or at least a bow or a spear, it seemed a hopeless task. "Maybe you could wait for a better opportunity."

"No need for that. Here, I'll help you into this tree so you can get a better view."

"You mean you can still do this?"

"Sure. I've stalked harder prey than this."

Ashley looked between Leandra and the chital, confused. "But how can you—" Painted fingers pressed against her lips and stopped her questions.

"Watch and learn."

With a helpful boost from Leandra, Ashley climbed into the lower branches of the stout tree and settled comfortably to watch. The extra height gave her a much better view of the grassland.

"I'll be moving into the wind," Leandra explained softly. "Just keep your eyes on that stretch of grass over there," she said, indicating it with her hand, "and you should be able to see me okay."

"All right, but I don't see how you're going to do this."

Leandra's eyes were predatory, yet playful. "You will." Then she turned and vanished silently into the jungle.

Ashley settled herself into a better position and waited, busying herself with checking her camera and getting ready to take photos, should the opportunity present itself. Recalling what she'd read of the hunting techniques of tigers, she thought it would be a miracle if Leandra could bring down one of the deer. The dark-haired woman was agile, and certainly stealthy, but she was trying to use the same methods as a creature that must outweigh her by at least a hundred pounds. A tiger could use its weight and strength to bring down prey, but Leandra had no such advantage. Also, tigers had teeth. Leandra had only a set of claws, which, while they were long and sharp, couldn't compete with the gifts nature had provided the predator cats. According to Ashley's reading, only about one in twenty tiger attacks were successful. How could Leandra match them? Full of questions, Ashley looked through the viewfinder on her camera and waited for her companion to reappear.

After a time, Leandra's tawny form emerged from the undergrowth. On all fours, she held her body only a few inches off the ground as she stalked the unsuspecting deer. Seeing her friend in action for the first time, Ashley now understood the merits of the body paint. The stripes blended in with the golden hue of the grasses, camouflaging Leandra very effectively. It took a while for Leandra to gain ground on her wary prey, and she paused often to lie flat in the grass, making sure the vigilant monkeys didn't spy her. Ashley could only marvel at Leandra's endurance. She was sure she couldn't have held her own body up like that for more than a few minutes, yet Leandra seemed capable of maintaining her position indefinitely.

Damn, she's good, Ashley thought, snapping a few quick shots and admiring the display of primal cunning before her. Through the camera, she could see the muscles along Leandra's thighs and arms stand out beneath the paint like steel cords, and she admired her in amazement. She's certainly got the body for this stuff—all muscle and sinew, barely a hint of fat on her whole frame. Tough, lean...sexy as hell.

Wait a minute. Sexy?

Ashley blinked in confusion at the unusual assessment that came unbidden to her mind. Then her eyes narrowed in honest speculation as she reviewed the distant, crouched figure of her friend.

Well, she is sexy, she admitted frankly. *She's got a body to die for and absolutely gorgeous eyes. If her hair was introduced to a comb once in a while, I bet it would look really great. And that husky, throaty voice... God, if she were one of those phone sex women, she'd make a fortune!*

Ashley let her eyes roam a little more personally over Leandra, her lips pursing in serious contemplation. *Plus,* she added mentally, *she's got that whole animal magnetism thing going on, even if she's not aware of it. And in her case, it's pretty much the most literal version of animal magnetism you could ask for. I don't think she has any idea of how sexy she is when she purrs, or stretches herself.*

God, I didn't think I went for the "bad-girl" type. Still, she couldn't deny the simple truth: Leandra was an intriguingly sensual creature, and Ashley could admit to feeling more than a little attracted to her.

As Ashley was pondering these uncharacteristic thoughts, Leandra had moved to within striking distance of the deer. Crouched in the tall grass on her haunches, she was visibly gathering her energy before she pounced. Ashley thought she seemed particularly cat-like at that moment, and was certain that if Leandra had possessed whiskers and a tail, they would both have been twitching in anticipation. She furiously snapped away with her camera, tense with excitement and awe.

In a sudden burst of movement, Leandra pounced. Her attack was brief and incredibly swift. She threw herself bodily at a small doe with enough power to knock the startled creature off its feet and onto its side. Even before Leandra had wrestled for a grip on her victim's neck, the rest of the herd leapt away and sprinted desperately from the scene. In the trees above, the monkeys raised a chorus of protest and indignation at the intruder, as they sought cover among the higher branches of their roost. The doe was stronger and tougher than Leandra and quickly tried to regain its balance to flee. But a moment later, Leandra attacked with a devastating, almost frenzied, series of slashing swipes. Her hands clenched tight on the grip of her claws, their wickedly sharp talons extending between her fingers, she tore out the throat of the terrified deer and held it against the ground until it stopped thrashing.

Ashley's mouth hung open at the savage display, images of the mauled poachers rising again in her mind. She shuddered, now seeing a more graphic display of Leandra's killing technique and imagining how she must have used it against the human intruders. Ashley lowered the camera with shaking hands. The attack had lasted only seconds and had taken the deer completely by surprise. They'd never seen it coming.

Swift, brutal, and frightfully effective, Leandra's hunting style was every bit as awesome a spectacle as a real tiger attack.

Ashley hadn't been a wildlife photographer for so many years without witnessing up close just how savage and untamed the animal kingdom could be. It was, she reminded herself, simply the way the natural world often worked. Leandra had lived in the wild for four years, making her home among some of the most effective predators on Earth. She'd had to learn to endure the harsh environment and to hunt and survive, just as the tigers did.

The only difference was that Leandra could defend herself against the one threat the great cats were helpless against: man.

Quickly placing the roll of exposed film in a plastic case, Ashley scampered down the tree and dashed over to her friend. When she reached Leandra, she was surprised to find the woman's painted skin shimmering under a light sweat and her breath coming hard—almost panting. Trying to ignore the spattered blood that marked her body and her crimson-stained hands, Ashley beamed a brilliant smile.

"That was incredible," she said, crouching down next to her friend. "I've never seen anything like it."

Leandra rubbed her side where the thrashing hooves of her prey had struck a glancing blow. "Thanks," she panted, wiping her bloody hands in the grass and proudly admiring her kill. "It took a lot of practice to get the hang of hunting like this, but..." She shrugged. "It's how I was taught."

Ashley studied the slain doe and grimaced slightly at the horribly torn throat. "What now? I mean, you're not going to start ripping it apart with your teeth, right?"

"Of course not." Leandra chuckled, the throaty sound rumbling deep in her chest. "I'll butcher it here, take the best parts with me, and leave the rest for the wolves and the carrion feeders. I can dry and salt some of the meat and eat the rest tonight."

Ashley looked dubiously at Leandra's claws. "You can't carve a carcass with those, can you?"

"No." Leandra reached into a hidden pocket stitched into the folds of her brief skirt and pulled out a piece of flint. She held it up, displaying a wickedly sharp edge. "When I first came out here, I had a steel knife, but it's worn down now. I use this instead."

"Oh."

Ashley watched Leandra cut away the skin of the doe and begin to harvest the best parts: the haunches, flanks, and chest. Having spent time among tribal people both in Africa and Australia, Ashley wasn't at all squeamish about the butchering process. She took the slices of bloody meat from Leandra and laid them on a bed of grasses she had made. As Leandra worked, her eyes constantly flicked about them, and Ashley watched her curiously. "You expecting someone?"

"A kill doesn't go unnoticed out here for long," Leandra explained. "In a few minutes, something's bound to find us, and we have to be gone before that happens. I don't want to have to fight off a pack of hungry wolves."

Ashley understood and started eyeing the surrounding grasslands with more trepidation. "Has that ever happened before?"

"A few times," Leandra said. "During the first months I was out here, I didn't have much luck catching food for myself. I had to scavenge what I could from the kills of others."

Ashley didn't want to think about what Leandra must have eaten to survive. "Good thing you got better, huh?"

"Yeah."

Finishing in a hurry, the two friends gathered the bundles of meat and hastened away from the open grasslands. Both felt much better as soon as they were once more in the shadows of the jungle. Leandra led the way to her cave, where she invited a very willing Ashley to stay for lunch. They enjoyed a simple meal of venison and some kind of root vegetable that was sweet and nutty. Ashley noticed Leandra's appetite was somewhat voracious.

"You remind me of my niece's cat," she said. "Every time you offer her food, she just can't resist, even if she's already full."

"It's a survival trait," Leandra said around a mouthful of charred venison. "You eat as much as you can, as quick as you can, before something bigger and stronger comes along and takes over."

"Will the meat attract anything to the cave? I mean, the animals must be able to smell it from a mile away."

"They won't come here," Leandra said confidently. "A wolf won't get too close to a tiger or a leopard unless it's starving, and they treat me the same." She gave a feral grin. "I have the privilege of being near the top of the food chain."

"Oh. Right."

After they ate, Ashley helped her friend start curing the rest of the meat, first cutting it into thin strips and then laying it out on a rock by the fire to dry.

Ashley watched Leandra surreptitiously as she used a rag to clean the blood from her hands and forearms. Curious, Ashley let her dark eyes wander along the tall woman's body with subtle stealth. She quickly became lost in the effect the rippling muscles had on the patterned skin, dark stripes flexing with every movement. She tried to imagine what Leandra might look like without the paint, and was surprised to find the image difficult to conjure. She was so accustomed to the stripes that she barely noticed them anymore. They were as much a part of Leandra as the claws, or the purring, or the aura of primal power she projected. With a roguish smile, Ashley allowed herself the guilty delight of enjoying the fact that her friend's outfit left so very little to the imagination, and she was soon trying to mentally fill in the few blanks that remained.

"Ashley?"

"Hmm?" Glassy eyes snapped into guilty focus, and Ashley blushed, realizing her mind had been about to take a happy little jaunt down Fantasy Lane. Fortunately, Leandra was apparently intent on her task of preparing the meat.

"Could you get me the salt? It's in that small crate on the top of that stack over there."

"Oh, sure. No problem." Ashley cleared her throat and retrieved the small paper bag filled with white salt. After handing it to Leandra, she settled down on her rock seat and continued to watch as her friend proceeded to salt the meat, working quickly and easily. Ashley smiled to herself, and tried not to notice just how well-formed Leandra's hands and fingers were.

She succeeded, but only because her eyes quickly found other, even more interesting, parts of the tiger-woman to study.

It was nearly dark by the time Ashley made it back to camp, and Grady and Tarun were obviously starting to get nervous about her prolonged absence. At first, they greeted her return with relief, but that quickly dissolved into another lecture.

"If you're going to go traipsing through the jungle with that woman, the least you can do is come back at a reasonable hour," Grady fumed, towering over her diminutive figure in an unusually insistent stance.

Ashley, however, refused to be intimidated. "I was perfectly all right," Ashley returned sharply, glaring up at him. "If I want to stay out there all night with Leandra, that's my business, not yours."

"Oh really? So you'll just forget about your friends who are back here, worried sick about you, is that it?" Grady took a deep breath and tried to calm himself. "Look, Ashley, just try to remember that when you're gone for that long, and we have no idea where you are—"

"You did know where I was," Ashley interrupted. "I was with Leandra, and that means I'm safe. She'd never let anything hurt me."

Grady scowled, then pointed to flecks of dark crimson staining Ashley's arms and clothing. "So what's this? Blood?"

Ashley flushed. "It's not mine," she explained. "She took me hunting. I got a little dirty, that's all."

"Hunting? Are you going to try telling me that's not potentially dangerous?"

"No," she said, her irritation turning to anger. "But it's certainly no more dangerous than any of the other things I've done. Why is it pissing you off so much that I'm spending time with this woman?"

"I just don't like you taking risks when you don't need to, that's all." Grady sat down next to the fire near Simon and Grace who sat quietly, merely observing. "We're here to do a job, Ashley, not spend time with the locals."

"And Leandra's helping me do my job."

"Is she? Have you asked her about the white tiger?"

Ashley hesitated, unsure how best to answer without admitting they were on a snipe hunt. "I don't...I mean, she uh..." She swallowed nervously. "She doesn't really like to talk about the tigers much. I don't want to push her about it."

Grady slapped his thighs, but he looked calmer. "Well, maybe you should. Remember, we're only here for another week and a bit. Then, we're flying out, and if you haven't got the pictures by then, that's it. You don't get a second chance at this sort of thing."

"I know. But I'm not going to do anything to make Leandra uncomfortable."

"And that's another thing," Grady continued. "I think maybe you're getting too attached to this woman. What happens when we leave? How's Leandra going to take that?"

"She knows when I'm leaving. It's good for her to have some company. Some *human* company."

"So you're telling me you're not getting attached?"

Ashley lowered her eyes, recalling the thoughts she'd had today. "There's nothing wrong with making friends with her," she said softly. "I like her, and I fully intend to spend as much time as I can with her before I have to go back home."

Their argument continued even after the sun had disappeared, and eventually Ashley, already tired from her busy day and in no mood to deal with her partner's tantrum, announced she was retiring to her tent. Grady backed down and let her go without comment, but his expression was less than happy.

Inside her tent, Ashley breathed a sigh of relief and let go of her tension. She rarely argued with her partner like this. If she didn't know better, she would suspect Grady was jealous of the time she'd been spending with Leandra. As partners, they spent so much time together, both in the field and at work, that rumors of a romantic or sexual affair between them made the occasional circuit around the offices. Ashley and Grady both found the whispered suspicions rather amusing and often teased each other with campy propositions. Ashley knew her partner well, however; Grady enjoyed his bachelor lifestyle far too much to want a relationship with someone as troublesome and headstrong as herself. The two were friends and nothing more.

It was unusual for Grady to be this protective, Ashley mused as she stripped off her clothes and crawled into her sleeping bag. Lying back with a quiet groan, she relaxed aching muscles, closed her eyes, and hoped that with a little time, Grady would get over whatever was bothering him.

After a few moments of quiet peace, Ashley reflected on an entirely pleasant—and very active—day. Fit as she was, her calves and lower back were killing her. She wasn't used to hiking so far all at once. The throbbing heat in her muscles spread almost pleasantly through her body, and she let her attention turn to the more surprising thoughts that had cropped up in her mind that day.

Long ago, Ashley had admitted to herself a more than passing interest in other women. As a teenager, being intimate with another female had seemed quite an enticing prospect. However, while she might be adventurous and bold in most aspects of her life, those characteristics hadn't ventured into her personal relationships. In fact, her love life could best be described as chaste and boring. She hadn't had a boyfriend in almost three years, and even though Ashley had considered romantic liaisons with a few women, she'd never been able to summon the courage to actually make the first move. The one time another woman made a polite overture, Ashley was so shocked and tongue-tied that she'd declined in a panic and spent an entire week slapping herself on the forehead in regret.

Of course, the blame for most of her relationship problems lay squarely in her own lap. She was heavily involved in her work, which often required her to travel overseas for months at a time. When she was home she preferred spending time with her family rather than dating, and none of her romantic interests ever seemed worth sacrificing her independence over. Ashley had pretty much resigned herself to the fact that she wasn't likely to ever meet that "special someone" and found ways to deal with her natural wants and needs by herself. Though her sex life was less than inspiring, she still had a vivid imagination and a healthy appetite, and she quite often found her fantasies drifting into contemplations of the female gender.

Still, Leandra was unlike any of her previous fantasy lovers. Ashley analyzed her feelings critically, as she recalled the images of Leandra stalking her prey. Her visions of the perfect woman ran along fairly simple lines: short enough to kiss properly, cultured, sophisticated, and confident. She would be athletic rather than muscular, with a stable, preferably unadventurous, job. Oh, and she would have long, silky, fine hair through which Ashley could comb her fingers. These characteristics were noticeably absent in her new friend.

Barefoot, Leandra was at least six feet tall—too tall to make a comfortable kisser. She was certainly confident, but the jungle-woman was the polar opposite of cultured or refined. She painted her body and mimicked giant cats, had no sense of modesty whatsoever, and had a tendency to growl when upset. Leandra's body was tough and hard from her difficult lifestyle, and her "job" was best not even analyzed. Finally, Ashley had serious doubts she could ever comb her fingers through that tangled mane of thin braids. All in all, Leandra was a far cry from Ashley's ideal woman.

Well, maybe I've been barking up the wrong tree, Ashley thought. *Maybe, the problem is that I've always gone for the stable, steady type to balance out my impulsive tendencies. Maybe, I should have been looking for someone more like…*

She paused. More like what? A woman who's been living in the Indian jungle for four years and likes to kill poachers with her clawed hands?

It was, Ashley noted, a faintly ridiculous situation.

Of course, she does have some interesting qualities. I mean, just because she doesn't fit my perfect ideal doesn't change the fact that she's one hot looking lady. And she has no inhibitions whatsoever. That would certainly be a change. Thus far, Ashley's sexual experiences had explored only two positions, neither of which had greatly impressed her. *I bet Leandra would be willing to try new things…experiment and stuff.* Ashley grinned rakishly as she considered the possibilities of having such an open, unreserved lover.

God, I bet she'd be a wild one between the sheets.

Ashley hugged her makeshift pillow and hummed happily. She knew she was too chicken shit to even consider making a move on Leandra. There were far too many blindingly obvious reasons to steer clear of the whole messy idea. For one thing, she would be leaving soon. For another, Leandra's freedom from inhibitions might not extend to this kind of situation.

Most compelling of all, Ashley liked Leandra. She enjoyed spending time with her, enjoyed their increased camaraderie and the way Leandra was gradually talking more about herself and her life. Ashley could see the almost desperate way Leandra clung to every word she spoke, and she didn't want to do anything that might make her retreat back into her primal, animalistic world.

Leandra made a fine subject for her fantasies, but Ashley knew she wasn't the most suitable target for a meaningful—or even a meaningless—relationship.

Sighing, Ashley rolled over and let herself drift away, imagining possible scenarios of what could never be.

The next morning, Leandra woke just as the sun lit the distant horizon with a golden hue. The early morning chill didn't bother her. In fact, it felt refreshing. She took a deep breath and uncurled her long, supple form, wincing at the familiar stiffness in her right shoulder. Rising from the thin sleeping mat that served as her bed, she spent a few moments stretching her body before beginning her morning routine.

Over a small fire, she cooked a few slivers of venison from yesterday's kill. Leandra had never been good at cooking, so she had gotten used to the taste of burned food. Tearing the charred meat apart with her teeth, she finished her meal and licked the grease from her fingers before wandering outside to meet the new day.

Usually, Leandra spent her mornings hunting the animals that often watered at the nearby creek. She would then patrol her hunting grounds, keeping an eye out for rangers and searching for any signs of more sinister intruders. Sometimes she visited with her animal friends, reminding them of her presence in the jungle lest they forget and mistake her for just another human tourist. But not today. The promise of Ashley's company was more than enough to make her forget about her usual activities.

After watering at the creek, noting that she would need to take a bath soon and redo her body paint, Leandra made her way to Ashley's camp. What would have been a respectable hike for most people was, for Leandra, a relatively short walk. As the sun rose fully into the sky, she was perched among the branches of a tree, watching Ashley and her companions eat breakfast and talk.

Just watching the vibrant blonde, even from a distance, started a low, rumbling purr deep in Leandra's chest. She had learned to make such feline noises during her first year in the wilderness; although tigers and other great cats weren't capable of purring, they certainly seemed to understand the meaning of the sound just as well as their smaller kin. Because feline communications encompassed so many subtle dynamics, Leandra found it useful to be able to articulate as many sounds as possible when living among the unpredictable, often savage, jungle predators. The way she moved, even the way she held her eyes, had similarly been adapted to mimic feline behavior. After all these years, the purring came without conscious thought, as intrinsic a part of her as her heightened senses and agility.

As she watched the group and noted their interactions, Leandra wondered how they might react if she were to wander into their camp. Ashley had told her that the two scientists wanted to meet her, but Leandra was cautious about exposing herself to questions. Would these people accept her? Would they be shocked by her appearance and mannerisms? Ashley had grown accustomed to her peculiarities during their time together, but it might not be so easy for others. Looking at the nearby gathering and watching her friend as she chatted with the other people made Leandra wish she had the courage to enter their group and be a part of their apparent camaraderie. She wondered at the unusual impulse to join them, and realized it stemmed from a desire to be closer to Ashley.

She wanted to be a part of Ashley's world, the world she had turned her back on a very long time ago.

Shaking her head to clear away the strange longings, Leandra noticed for the first time a subtle tension in the group below. Though she was too far away to hear their words, she recognized that some conflict had arisen between Ashley and the man sitting next to her. Leandra's eyes narrowed as she watched, seeing for the first time signs of displeasure in her friend's face. From her sharp gestures and angry expression, Leandra could tell that Ashley was upset with her colleague.

Ashley stood up from her tree-stump seat and glared at the man, saying something that was obviously meant to put an end to their argument. Then she turned and stalked off, heading down toward the river. Leandra smiled, knowing her friend was going to their normal meeting place. Her smile disappeared when the man threw down his plate and followed. Her eyes narrowed in frustration, and Leandra quickly leapt to the ground and moved after the two figures.

She caught up to them at the river and watched from the cover of the jungle undergrowth as the heated conversation continued. Now, however, she was close enough to hear the nature of the conflict, and she was surprised to find it was about her.

"For the last time, I'm not staying at the hide with Simon," Ashley fumed. "Now go away. Leandra won't come if you're here."

The words pleased Leandra. *She accepts me so easily,* she marveled. *She doesn't ask questions when she knows I don't want to answer. She just lets me be who I am around her.*

Unfortunately, the tall, dark-haired man didn't back down. "Then maybe I should just stay with you," he snapped, folding his arms over his chest. "You shouldn't be going off with that woman."

Leandra growled under her breath, not liking this man at all.

"I can do what I want, Grady. It's none of your business."

"It is when you're not doing your job," Grady returned. "You need to ask her about the white tiger. If she knows anything about it, you need to find out."

Ashley's face was flushed with anger. "I am *not* going to use Leandra just to get a few photos!" she shouted. "She's my friend, not some hired tiger-tracker like Tarun. If you want the damn cat found, why not go shout at him to do it? It's what we're paying him for, isn't it?" She turned from the man, clearly intending to walk away.

"Wait a minute, Ashley!" Grady reached out and grabbed her shoulder, forcefully spinning her around and pushing her against a tree.

Leandra's instincts had her moving before she could take a moment to reconsider: she broke from the shadowy undergrowth and cleared the ground between them in two bounding strides. Before Grady could get another word out—and before Ashley had a chance to retaliate herself—Leandra yanked him away and hurled him against the bole of a fallen tree. His eyes shot wide in surprise, then panic, as he met her cold gaze, and he gasped when she crouched over him and pressed razor-sharp claws against his neck. Leandra felt a low, ominous growl vibrating in her chest, and she bared her teeth in a feral snarl.

"Leandra." Ashley had quickly recovered from the surprise appearance, laying a calming hand upon her shoulder. "It's okay, he wasn't going to hurt me."

Leandra glanced back at her, instantly calmed by the luminous dark eyes and reassuring expression. Still, her growl turned deeper, and she leaned closer to Grady's motionless face, sniffing at him, knowing he was terrified by the primitive gesture. With an effort, she resisted the urge to lick his cheek and see if she could get him to wet himself. Instead, she slowly retracted her claws and stepped off the petrified man.

Ashley flashed her a quick, decidedly wicked, little grin as she helped Grady stand. The man was still staring at her in awed fear, and Leandra watched him through slitted eyes, still growling low in her throat.

"Grady, I think you should go back to camp now, don't you?" Ashley suggested. "We can talk more this evening."

Grady looked at her in shock and gestured at the painted woman. "*This* is the woman you keep saying is harmless?"

Leandra bared her teeth and gave a feline hiss.

"She was just protecting me," Ashley explained, giving Leandra a scolding look that she chose to ignore. Ashley gave her partner a little push in the direction of their camp. "I'm perfectly safe with Leandra, so go back to camp and leave us alone."

Grady gave Leandra a last baleful glare, but eventually he nodded. "Fine, but we're going to have a talk about this later on." He turned and headed down the riverbank.

Once he was out of sight, Ashley turned to Leandra. "You didn't need to frighten him like that," she rebuked her, but laughing eyes revealed that she wasn't at all angry. "I thought he was going to pee his pants."

"Sorry. I saw him grab you, and I just reacted."

"Grady's a little frustrated," Ashley explained. "I'm not sure why, but he's got a bug up his butt about me spending so much time with you."

Leandra shuffled her feet and looked uncomfortable. "I don't want to be causing you problems," she muttered. "You know, if you have a job to do—"

"Hey…" Ashley took the Leandra's arm and gave it a gentle shake before releasing it. "I'm doing my job just fine. Believe me, Leandra, you're not hindering my work at all."

"Okay then." Leandra smiled sheepishly. "I guess he's not going to like me any better for attacking him."

Ashley snorted. "I don't care what Grady thinks. He should know better than to try to push me around like that. If you hadn't put him in his place, I'd have done it myself." She patted her friend on the shoulder. "Still, thank you for jumping in. It was a very nice gesture."

"No problem." Leandra toyed with a lock of her hair as they began strolling along the riverbank. "I didn't really think about it," she admitted after a moment. "I just didn't like seeing him get rough with you. I mean, you're my friend, so…"

"I understand. Guess you're a little territorial, huh?" Ashley joked.

Leandra took the question seriously, however. "Maybe I am. I don't like it when…" She hesitated, recalling faces from the past she had fled, faces almost forgotten. "I don't like it when someone tries to hurt my friends."

Ashley gave her a warm smile. "Well, I don't mind if you're a bit overprotective. It's not something I usually like, people butting in and trying to fight my battles for me, but I'm willing to make an exception for you." She chuckled, and added, "Just as long as you don't get it into your head to start marking your territory."

Leandra laughed too. "I promise I'll resist the urge, no matter how tempting it might be."

"Good."

Laughing and joking, the two women continued off into the jungle together, eager to spend another day in pleasant companionship.

A few hours later, seated on a low cliff and looking down at a herd of elephants splashing about in the shallow river below, Leandra recalled the conversation she'd overheard between Ashley and her partner. She glanced at the photographer who was snapping away at the giant animals with her camera.

"Your friend seemed pretty upset about you not finding what you came here for," she observed casually.

Ashley shrugged. "I haven't told him there is no white tiger," she said. "I think it would probably just make him angrier now."

"It meant a lot to you, though, didn't it?" Leandra said gently.

"What? Seeing the cat? Well, sure. I mean, it's a once in a lifetime opportunity. And for someone in my career…" Ashley set her camera down and just sat with Leandra, watching the elephants. "It would have been something very special."

Leandra cocked her head to the side, thinking. "Coming here looking for a wild tiger, wanting to get close to one… That's a pretty dangerous job."

"I know. But it's no more dangerous than other assignments I've had."

"Oh?"

"Yeah." Ashley drew her feet under her and sat cross-legged on the rocky ridge. "Two years ago, I spent three months in a little village in Alaska, shooting the polar bears. I got a lot closer to them than I really wanted to, let me tell you. Those things are faster than they look. And last year, we were in Australia photographing crocodiles, and I had the brilliant idea of setting up an underwater hide right where the damn things were swimming." She slapped at an insect foolish enough to crawl up her leg. "I was lucky to get out of there with all my bits and pieces still attached, although I did get some amazing shots."

"So you're used to taking risks?"

"Sure. It's part of the job."

"Does it ever scare you?"

"I guess, sometimes. But usually only afterwards, when the bad stuff has already happened. I've been bitten three times by snakes, at least a dozen times by spiders, and I can't tell you how many times by other things. One of the snakebites was pretty scary. It hurt like hell, and my breathing went all funny—I started seeing spots and stuff. I was in the hospital for a while." She held out her left leg and displayed the faint white scars of the fang marks. "One time, I went into the water with a few great white sharks, and it freaked me out a little even though I was in a cage. The guys in the boat were throwing chum into the water, trying to get them thrashing around so it would look more impressive on camera, and I was pretty nervous. Usually though, I'm too busy taking pictures to worry about the danger until it's too late. I get scared afterwards."

"So tigers are just another routine job for you, I suppose."

"Well, yeah." Ashley considered. "It's my first time here, of course, and a white tiger's pretty unusual."

"You weren't even supposed to come out here, were you?" Leandra asked, recalling what Ashley had said about delaying her return to the States for the chance to shoot the rare cat.

"No, but I'm glad I did. Maybe that's part of the reason why Grady's upset. We've been away from home quite a while now on this shoot. When I heard the rumors about the white tiger, Grady didn't really want to come here, but I charmed him into it, and now all I'm doing is spending time with you."

"You have a boss back home?"

"Yeah."

"Will you get in trouble when you return empty-handed?"

"Who's empty-handed?" Ashley gestured toward the elephants. "Thanks to you, I've got some of the best stuff I've ever taken. A few people might bitch for a while, but no one can complain about the quality of my work." She paused for a moment. "Besides, I have a very good reputation. My boss won't yell at me too much, or I might take my talent elsewhere."

Leandra absorbed that, pleased that her friend wasn't going to get into any trouble on her account. "You must have been doing this stuff for a while then, right?"

"Since I was a girl. I started out as an assistant photographer when I was nineteen and progressed from there."

"And you like the work?"

"I love it," Ashley said with enthusiasm. "I get paid well, I get to see the world, and I'm doing something to help bring attention to the problems of endangered species everywhere. My work helps generate interest and support for environmental protection groups. Plus," she added with a grin, "on occasion, I get to meet some very interesting people. Like you."

"Sometimes," Leandra whispered, almost to herself, "I wonder what might have happened if I'd found a good job that made me happy like that. Sometimes I look back on everything I did, on all the mistakes I made, and I try to picture where I'd be now if things had worked out differently."

She regretted saying the words when Ashley's expression turned cautious; Leandra hadn't spoken much about her life before she came here, only alluding to her time as a poacher. The fact that Ashley hadn't pushed her for details despite her obvious curiosity was something Leandra appreciated; the memories were painful to recall.

"We all make mistakes," Ashley offered hesitantly. "Even the best of us aren't perfect. It's part of being human."

"Maybe." Tears sparkled in the corners of Leandra's eyes, but she wiped them away before they had a chance to fall. "Still, that doesn't make it any easier."

"You know what I think? I think sometimes the hardest part about making a mistake is being able to accept it, and then move on." Ashley paused. "If you let something drag you down and let it fester inside you without confronting it, you never really learn from what you've done wrong. Do you understand what I mean?"

"I do." Leandra pinned Ashley with an intense gaze; she felt exposed, vulnerable...but forced herself to continue. "Have you ever made a mistake," she asked in a low, husky whisper, "that was so bad, so unforgivable, that you wished you could just curl up into a ball and die, rather than face the pain of dealing with the consequences?"

Ashley was silent for a long moment, then she shook her head. She shifted a little closer, eyes brimming with sympathy and understanding "No," she whispered, "I can't say that I have. But whatever happened, Leandra, it's in the past. You shouldn't let it hurt you anymore."

"Maybe." Leandra looked away, but Ashley gently lifted her chin up, forcing the blue eyes to meet her own.

"No matter what you did wrong, no matter how bad it was, it doesn't change who you are today."

"You don't know what you're talking about," Leandra protested. "You have no idea what I was like before I came here. I was a heartless monster. I hurt anyone who was stupid enough to get close to me. I slaughtered hundreds of animals just because I liked the sense of power it gave me." She covered her face and turned away. "If you had met me back then, you wouldn't have wasted the time to spit in my direction."

Ashley remained silent a long while, then Leandra felt the cautious touch of her hand on her shoulder. "I don't care what you were like before you came here, Leandra," her voice whispered. "That's not who you are now. If it were, do you think I'd be here with you now? That I'd want to be your friend?"

Leandra was still for a moment. Slowly, she turned and looked up. "I guess not."

"Exactly." Ashley closed the distance between them and pushed the dark cords of hair out of Leandra's face. "Whatever you were in the past, when I look at you now, I see a good person, Leandra. A person I've grown to like very much, in only a few short days."

"Still…"

"Still, nothing. I'm sure you've done things you regret, things that you wish you could take back. But you can't let them keep you from trying to make a better life for yourself. If you made a mistake, no matter how bad it was, you should learn from it, and then put it behind you."

Leandra smiled faintly, accepting the comfort for a moment before pulling away. "Some mistakes need to be punished before they can be forgiven," she said softly. Drawing her knees up under her chin, she turned away and fixed her gaze deliberately on the bathing elephants. Although she could feel Ashley still studying her, obviously curious, Leandra was grateful she seemed to understand the conversation was over.

Ashley was subdued and thoughtful when she returned to an empty camp that evening. A quick look around confirmed that the others were still working, probably down at the hide or searching the jungle, and Ashley couldn't help but feel a little grateful for their absence. She wanted some time to herself to do some serious thinking.

Leandra had remained pensive through the rest of the day, and the two had parted company much earlier than usual. Though Ashley wanted to ask more about Leandra's past, she restrained her desires, knowing the questions would do more harm than good. She had accepted her companion's somber mood and let the silence continue to build. Eventually, she had taken her leave.

Not wanting to sit still, Ashley decided to make herself useful by gathering firewood. As she wandered the perimeter of the camp, collecting a bundle of dry, fallen limbs, she continued to reflect on her friend's melancholy spirit. While she was concerned for Leandra, Ashley couldn't help but let her thoughts focus on her own reactions to the revealing conversation of that morning. For some inexplicable reason, she had found herself growing even more attracted to Leandra after hearing more about her troubled past. Somehow, the whole thing had served to make her all the more intriguing. Ashley now had to deal with the fact that she had developed an entirely frustrating and illogical—but nonetheless incredibly powerful—crush on the strange woman.

"Way to go, Ashley," she mocked herself as she absently picked up more sticks. "Come out here on a simple assignment, and you go and get the hots for some freaky tiger-woman with enough emotional and psychological baggage to sink a battle cruiser. Argh!" She rubbed her forehead. "Why can't you just have a normal life? You know, like your sister. Find some guy, settle down, and start making a few babies. But no, you have to be adventurous. You have to go to In-dee-a," she sang sarcastically.

"Leandra is not my type, even if she is drop-dead gorgeous." She stopped and closed her eyes. "I am *not* attracted to disturbed people, even if they do have that whole sexy angst thing going on." She shook her head determinedly. "And I am *not* interested in getting naked and sweaty with some jungle-woman...even though I bet she could get me screaming like a steam engine." Ashley's vivid imagination decided to kick in with a few decidedly naughty scenarios, and she slapped herself on the forehead, trying to dislodge them.

For all the impracticality of her thoughts, Ashley couldn't help but be a little amused at herself. It had been a long time since she'd felt this way about someone, and it was kind of nice to finally have such a strong focus for her lustful thoughts. Leandra's distracted melancholy had allowed Ashley a chance to let her eyes roam with less fear of being caught (although, she admitted, half the fun of looking was knowing it was a little risky), and she'd spent most of her day sneaking peeks and trying not to giggle like a schoolgirl. Remembering that now, she grinned fully, her eyes alight with devilish fires. "God, I'd forgotten what it feels like to have a serious crush," she thought aloud. "I just hope she doesn't catch on. I don't want to scare her off, now that she's opening up."

To be honest, Ashley didn't really think Leandra would be offended by another woman being attracted to her. From what she'd learned of the woman's personality, Leandra didn't place any importance on trivial preferences like sexuality. Her life out here had apparently taught her to think in much more basic terms: good or bad, safe or dangerous, like or hate. Less consequential things didn't seem to bother her. Still, Ashley didn't want to disturb their current relationship.

Besides, I wouldn't even know how to tell her I like her. I mean, that I really like her. I can't just come right out and say it. I've never had the guts to say it to a man before, and I sure as hell wouldn't be able to say it to a woman.

Ashley paused, going over her mental ramblings. "What am I doing? I can't believe I'm actually trying to justify this thing, let alone wondering how to tell her I've got the hots for her. That's enough!" Arms laden with a stack of wood, she made her way back to camp. "From now on, I'll just stick to the fantasy and leave it at that. She can be my bad-girl dream-lover, but that's it." Dumping the wood by the fire, Ashley sat down and started checking over her equipment, effectively occupying her mind with the routine chore.

Sometime later, the sound of approaching footsteps made her look up, and she met Grady's somewhat cautious expression with a neutral face. He was alone. He settled himself on the log opposite her.

"Hey."

Ashley regarded him coolly. "If you're planning on another shouting match, save your breath," she said quietly, turning her attention back to her work. "Nothing you say will make me stop spending time with Leandra, or convince me she's of any danger to me."

Grady ran his fingers through his neatly cropped hair. "I know," he said in a soft voice. "And I'm sorry I lost my cool this morning. I didn't mean to grab you like that."

"You're just lucky Leandra was there," Ashley said with a slight smile. "If she hadn't jumped in like that, you'd be nursing a swollen crotch."

Grady grinned crookedly. "Yeah, well, as it was she scared the shit out of me."

"She was protecting me."

"Mmm." Grady was silent for long moments. "You know, until I saw her with my own eyes, I thought you were exaggerating. But she's just as you described her, right down to the growling and snarling."

"She's nice once you get to know her." Ashley stopped her careful work and set her equipment aside. "I don't understand what you have against her."

"She's an unnecessary distraction…and a killer," Grady said. "Nothing you can say in her defense can change that fact. And having met her, I'm sorry, Ash, but I like her even less."

Ashley's expression hardened. "She's still my friend, and I *do* like her. So just accept it."

"I know," Grady said, holding his hands up in a peaceful gesture. "You've made it quite clear you're going to go your own way on this, regardless of how I feel." He sighed. "I may not like it, but I'm not going to argue with you anymore. All I ask is that you be careful."

Ashley's expression softened. "I will. Besides, we're only here for another week or so, and then we'll be on a plane heading back home."

"Without the pictures we came here for," Grady pointed out, ignoring her glare. "Remember the white tiger? The thing you managed to convince me was worth spending extra time in this sauna of a country for?"

"I also told you that tigers are one of the hardest creatures in the world to photograph in the wild," Ashley reminded him. "If I get even a single shot of a normal Bengal, I'll consider myself lucky."

"You had the chance the other day, but you were off with your stripy friend instead of manning the hide with Simon and Grace."

Ashley shrugged. "Finding Leandra out here is something much more remarkable than finding a tiger, and I intend to make the most of what time

I have with her." She decided to change the subject. "How have you been getting on? Has the scenery been everything Tarun promised?"

Grady began filling her in on his latest works, which included several panoramic shots of the sweeping jungle canopy, taken from higher ground. Happy to put their argument behind her for now, Ashley listened attentively and enjoyed not being mad at Grady anymore.

Leandra couldn't sleep.

All through the night, she'd tossed and turned on her thin sleeping pallet, wishing for some kind of fatigue to steal her away. Restless thoughts haunted her, and she managed only a few hours of light, restless slumber, not nearly enough to satisfy her.

The conversation with Ashley still sounded in her mind, and Leandra wished she could see things as the younger woman did. She wished she could put the past behind her and move on, but it wasn't that simple. She had accepted her mistakes and embraced the guilt that came with that acceptance, but she still owed a debt for the crimes she had committed.

Looking around the dark interior of the cave that formed her current home, Leandra scowled. Four years. Before Ashley had come along, she'd sometimes wondered how long her exile had lasted. Those four years seemed like half a lifetime, but during that time she had never given much thought to the world she'd left behind. Now, things were changing.

Ashley.

The young woman had shattered the perfect isolation of Leandra's existence, bringing the sounds of laughter and conversation into what had been a silent world. Each day, Leandra yearned more and more for the simple human contact Ashley gave, apparently without a thought. Leandra felt herself wishing she could move on and continue her life.

Four years! she screamed silently. *I've been out here for four years! I gave up everything. My money, the comforts of my life, even my humanity. Isn't that enough?* Leandra folded her legs under her and sat staring into nothing, the words raging inside her.

"I want to go home," she admitted in a low whisper. She sighed longingly. "If only there were a home to go back to."

The truth was she wanted to go home with Ashley. She wanted to be part of the life described to her by the young woman: the nice home, the loving family, the caring friends. Leandra didn't want to give up her connection to Ashley. She wanted to remain close to her. During the day, she could feel her attraction intensify until her heart ached with the strength of it. The sensation was strange to Leandra, an odd mix of unfamiliar emotional wants and very familiar physical desires. Lying awake all night, she wondered how she could show Ashley just how much she meant to her.

The answer came easily to mind, but Leandra wrestled against it. She was uncertain about revealing what she considered to be a sacred trust to a woman she'd known scarcely a week. The arguments flew back and forth inside her head.

How do you know you can trust her with something like this?

She wouldn't betray me. If I show her, she'll understand how important it is that it remains a secret.

But why take the risk? You can't be sure.

It would mean a lot to her. It would show her how much I trust and care for her.

This isn't about caring. You're not thinking with your head, that's the problem.

What?

Come on! Four years of celibacy, after a lifetime of debauchery, and now some cute little blonde wanders by and catches your eye. Face it, you've got an itch you want her to scratch.

Leandra blushed. It's not like that.

Isn't it?

No. I like her. She's not like any of the others. I care about her.

So you're willing to betray your most sacred trust? Why?

Leandra's lips quirked. "It would make her happy," she whispered. "I'd do anything to make her smile, and this means a lot to her."

It puts her in danger.

"I'll keep her safe."

Even if you show her, it doesn't mean she'll ever see you as anything more than just a friend.

Leandra got to her feet, stretching as she made her way to the mouth of the cave. Her gaze went toward the distant camp she couldn't see. "I don't care," she said softly. "I want to show her, and I'm going to."

Leaving behind her doubts and fears, Leandra hurried down the mountain, her passage as silent as the night itself. Without bothering to question her decision, she headed off to get Ashley, already excited by the prospect of sharing her secret.

CHAPTER 3

And what shoulder, and what art,
Could twist the sinews of thy heart?
And when thy heart began to beat,
What dread hand? and what dread feet?

—"The Tyger" by William Blake

ASHLEY WAS STARTLED AWAKE WHEN something pressed hard against her mouth, her eyes flashing open with momentary panic at the feeling of being smothered. She calmed quickly when she found intense, cobalt eyes staring down at her and saw the familiar mane of tangled, ebony braids silhouetted against the dim, predawn light. As soon as she relaxed, the hand covering her mouth was removed and she sat up, pulling the sleeping bag tighter against her chest, self-conscious despite the fact that the darkness hid her nudity somewhat.

"Leandra? What are you doing here?" Ashley glanced to the side, where the phosphorescent glow of her wristwatch revealed the early hour. "It's not even four o'clock," she exclaimed, annoyed at the interruption to her sleep.

"Shhh." Leandra put a finger to her lips, her eyes darting around. "Be quiet. You'll wake the others."

"So?" Noticing the strange look in her friend's eyes, Ashley sat up straighter. "Is something wrong?" she asked, her annoyance replaced with concern. "Are you okay?"

"Fine. I just need you to come with me now."

"Why?"

Leandra shook her head. "I can't say. You just have to trust me. Please?"

Ashley studied the tension in Leandra's dimly visible features, and her natural curiosity was piqued by this decidedly unusual visit. "You can't say where we're going?"

Again, Leandra shook her head. "We need to hurry."

"It can't wait until morning?"

"No. Please, I promise, if you just come with me now, it'll be worth it for you."

Ashley pushed her disheveled hair from her face. "How long will we be gone?"

"All day."

"I'll have to tell Grady. He'll be worried."

"No!" Leandra's eyes flashed in the darkness like quicksilver. "The others can't know where we're going."

Ashley hesitated, knowing what would happen if she took off without telling her partner. "Look," she reasoned, "if Grady wakes up and finds me gone, he'll get Tarun and come looking for me. Can I at least leave a note?"

Leandra considered, then nodded in concession. "Fine. But be quick. I'll meet you outside." With that, she turned and disappeared silently into the shadows outside.

Left alone, Ashley quickly got dressed and pulled on her hiking boots. Tearing a blank page from her notebook, she scribbled a quick message for Grady, explaining that she was with Leandra and that she would return when she was ready. Since she didn't know for sure how long she would be gone, Ashley made certain that the note made it clear she would be safe, and that she didn't want Grady trying to come "rescue" her. Leaving the note placed prominently on her sleeping bag, she grabbed her camera and ventured out into the darkness.

Wandering to the edge of the jungle, it didn't take long for Ashley to rejoin her friend. Leandra moved through the night with liquid grace, silent as a wraith. The full moon revealed the shadowy stripes across her form, faded now but still effective camouflage, and her steely eyes flicked to the camera around Ashley's neck. Her lips pursed in consideration, and Ashley saw indecision in the expressive face.

"I can leave it," she offered, her curiosity now fully wakened.

Leandra tilted her head to the side, then waved her hand. "It's okay. But promise me that any photos you take stay private. You won't use them for your magazine, only for yourself and those you trust."

"I promise," Ashley agreed without hesitation, realizing that whatever Leandra wanted to show her must be very special, to warrant this kind of secrecy.

84

"Come," Leandra gestured to the jungle, indicating a narrow trail mostly hidden by dense foliage. "It's a long hike to where we need to get to, and we have to hurry."

"Is it safe?" Ashley eyed the darkness with proper caution, knowing that this was hunting time for the jungle predators.

Leandra smiled mysteriously. "Just stay close to me," she whispered. "Nothing will bother us."

Together, the two women made their way through the forest. Ashley followed close behind the dim figure of her friend and tried not to trip over the exposed roots and fallen tree limbs that crossed the path. Again, she found herself wishing for even half the stealth and ease of motion displayed by the taller woman, and not a little envious of how easily Leandra moved over the often deceptive terrain. As the sun started to lighten the horizon to a rosy hue, the way became easier and Leandra quickened the pace. It wasn't long before Ashley was asking for a break, already tired and starting to feel a little grumpy despite the exciting adventure. She hated being woken before she was ready, and her body was protesting the early start to the day.

"Where are we going?" she grumbled when they paused to rest a few minutes. "Can you at least give me a clue?"

"A secret place," Leandra replied shortly. She stood impatiently, looking into the shadowy darkness and listening to the animal calls all around them. "We have to hurry. Come on."

Ashley groaned and rolled her eyes. Her calves were killing her. "When I get home, I'm joining a gym."

By the time the sun peeked over the distant mountains, Ashley was breathing hard and rubbing a stitch in her side. They were now farther from the camp than they'd ever been together, and Ashley looked around curiously as Leandra slowed their pace and signaled for absolute silence. The jungle was especially dense here; the dew hung heavy in the air, and everything smelled moist and earthy.

Leandra knelt to study a vague print in the soil, then smiled and waved for Ashley to join her on the ground. She looked seriously into Ashley's wide dark eyes, leaning close to whisper in her ear. "Do you trust me?"

Ashley nodded immediately. "Of course."

"With your life?"

Something in her tone made Ashley pause before she answered, and she considered gravely before nodding again. "With my life."

"Promise me that this stays a secret," Leandra whispered.

"I promise." Ashley wasn't sure what this was about, but her nerves were tingling with excitement and she gave her word easily.

"Good." Leandra got on all fours and motioned for Ashley to mimic her. Feeling slightly ridiculous, she did so. "Do exactly what I say, when I say it," Leandra instructed softly. "Don't run. Don't make any threatening gestures or sharp movements. You'll be safe with me just as long as you don't panic."

At that moment, Ashley noticed for the first time how strangely silent the jungle had become—the humid air crackled with a breathless sense of danger and tension. Although the jungle was never truly quiet, the birds and other animals seemed oddly reluctant to make noise here. Her skin prickled, as Leandra led the way farther into the dense undergrowth, on her hands and knees. Heart racing, Ashley followed close behind, not wanting to lose the protection of her friend's proximity.

After a few minutes of crawling through the ferns and foliage, Leandra stopped in a small clearing. Ashley watched, fascinated, as Leandra sniffed the air thoroughly, then made two short, stuttering coughing sounds: the same noises she had made when the two had first met.

Much to Ashley's surprise, there came an identical reply from the jungle. A reply that was followed by something far more terrifying: the sound of a throaty, ominous growl so powerful and deep it put Leandra's imitation to shame.

Ashley froze, feeling the strange sensation of her stomach turning to water as a cold shiver ran through her body. Rare fear flooded her senses, as she watched the leaves of the undergrowth tremble and then part, revealing ice-blue eyes set in a blunt, feline face.

Eyes that immediately passed over Leandra and settled on her with dangerous intent.

There were few times in Ashley's life that she had been afraid. Truly afraid, that was. The kind of fear that makes the skin shiver with cold sweat, the heart leap into the throat. Feeling the weight of that burning gaze settle on her, seeing the long, pearly white teeth gleam extra-large in the early light, Ashley couldn't recall a time in her hazardous career when she'd been more terrified.

For thousands of years, tigers had been revered and honored by people all over the world. Their strength, ferocity, and sheer power had earned them a place in history and mythology that extended far beyond the lands of India and China. Creatures of fierce beauty, tigers had long been deified as symbols of courage and strength. Humanity's fascination with the great jungle cats had, over time, resulted in their near-extinction from zealous hunters, and even though laws had been passed to protect them, the law couldn't stop the demand for them.

Now, watching the great beast stalking slowly closer, Ashley understood why tigers had earned the fear and admiration of a hundred generations of people.

The cat was huge. It stood about four feet high at the shoulder and was probably about eight feet long from its nose to the tip of its quivering tail. It took a moment for Ashley to absorb that this tiger was unusual—where the thick fur should have been colored a tawny orange, instead, stripes of rich, chocolate brown marked a solid white coat. But when the growl turned into a savage roar, Ashley wouldn't have cared if the cat was bright pink with blue polka dots. Only with an effort did she retain control of her bladder as the beast drew nearer, sniffing at the air and apparently not liking what it smelled.

But as the cat approached, Leandra moved quickly to position herself between Ashley and the white tiger, her own actions perfectly feline as she again made the strange coughing sound. Turning slightly, she glanced back at Ashley.

"Don't look her in the eyes," she ordered in a low undertone. "She'll take it as a challenge."

As soon as the instructions penetrated the cloud of fear, Ashley cast her eyes submissively at the ground before the giant predator, trusting that Leandra knew what she was doing. Flicking occasional glances at the striped woman, she watched the subtle interactions that were occurring between her and the wary beast.

The tigress stopped in front of Leandra, sniffing at her curiously and with definite recognition. She bared her teeth again, this time not in a snarl, but almost as though tasting the tall woman's scent. A low, rumbling growl that no longer seemed threatening emanated from deep in the tiger's chest. Leandra crawled forward slowly, dipping her head and exposing her neck. To Ashley's astonishment, the tigress responded by nuzzling her, butting her head against Leandra's in a manner identical to what she'd expect from an affectionate house cat. Leandra responded in kind, closely replicating the noises the tigress made and returning the nuzzling and head-butts before moving back to Ashley's side. The tigress watched, then approached slowly, still wary and growling slightly. Leandra laid a calming hand on Ashley's arm and offered her a reassuring smile.

"Trust me," she whispered. "Just stay still until she gets used to you. She won't harm you with me here."

Ashley nodded to show she understood, but as the great cat drew closer, until Ashley could smell the rank scent of her breath, it became harder and harder not to leap up and run from the clearing as fast as she could. Leandra was making strange sounds again, sounds Ashley guessed were intended to explain that she was a friend, not dinner. The tigress sniffed at her, ears twitching. Ashley forced herself to remain completely still as a tongue with the texture of sandpaper swiped the side of her face, then she smiled with relief as the cat nudged her with her blunt face in a gesture of apparent acceptance. Leandra also smiled, watching the first meeting between her old friend and her new one.

Apparently satisfied that Ashley was no threat, the white tigress ambled back to the edge of the clearing and settled herself down on her haunches, panting a little in the heat, which was increasing as the sun warmed the jungle. Leandra patted a still-trembling Ashley on the shoulder. "You did well," she said.

"Thanks." Ashley was overcoming her fear, now that the shock was fading. She stared at the tigress in awe, marveling at how close she was to the great cat. She wiped at her face where she'd been licked, then turned her head and regarded Leandra with amazement. "This is one of your friends, I take it?"

"Sort of. Her name is Shar-Ranjana." There was a momentary pause before Leandra added in hesitant tones, "She's...my sister."

Ashley looked from the tigress back to Leandra curiously. "Sister?"

Leandra shrugged and looked away. "That's how she sees me. And it's how I see her. It's hard to explain, but—"

"No, I understand. You're family to each other." Ashley smiled reassuringly. "It's not so strange, Leandra."

A dark brow rose cautiously. "You think so?"

"Of course." Ashley turned back to gaze at the jungle cat again. "Sometimes, family is something you find, not something you're born into."

"That's true."

As Leandra settled herself more comfortably on the ground, Ashley cast her a narrow-eyed look. "I thought you said there wasn't any white tiger."

"No, *you* said there was no white tiger." Leandra grinned. "I just didn't correct you."

Ashley considered that, utterly enthralled by the magnificent creature sitting not more than fifteen feet from her. "She's beautiful."

"Yes, she is." Leandra regarded Shar-Ranjana with a look that was affectionate, yet sorrowful. "I've known her most of her life. She was just a cub when I first came out here, and she grew up with me being near."

"What about her parents?" asked Ashley. "They must be like her, right? Where are they?"

"They're both dead," Leandra whispered. "So is her brother."

"Oh."

From the look of regret and sorrow on Leandra's face, Ashley wondered if perhaps she was the one responsible for their deaths. She was reassured when her friend added, "Her father was the one who helped keep me alive the first few months I was out here. He was..." Leandra hesitated. "He was very special to me."

"How did he die?"

"Poachers."

Ashley reached out and patted Leandra's shoulder, sensing how important Shar-Ranjana's father must have been to her. "I'm sorry."

Leandra smiled at the gesture of consolation. "Thanks."

Ashley returned her attention to the white tigress, who watched them with lazy interest. "I guess you were right. This surprise certainly is worth the early wake-up call."

Leandra waggled her eyebrows. "Oh, this is only half the surprise."

"Really?"

"Uh huh. The other half should be coming any minute now." No sooner were the words past her lips than the jungle undergrowth behind Shar-Ranjana began to quiver and jump.

Ashley watched nervously, not sure her heart could take the appearance of another tiger. Her concern was replaced with amazed delight as two small, orange, fur-covered forms tumbled into the clearing, stopped their playful wrestling when they caught sight of Leandra, and rushed over to greet her with juvenile enthusiasm. Ashley watched, as Leandra smacked and nuzzled the two tiger cubs playfully, before they turned their attention in her direction. After a few moments of caution and a lot of sniffing and licking, the two apparently decided she was okay and grappled for her attention enthusiastically. Giggling, Ashley sat cross-legged and let the cubs crawl over her, careful to avoid their needle-sharp claws. Aware of the ever-watchful eyes of the resting Shar-Ranjana, she took care to be gentle and didn't protest when they started chewing on her arms.

"They're gorgeous!" Ashley exclaimed. "Ow, be gentle." She carefully disengaged one of the cubs, laughing and petting them both happily.

Leandra crawled over to where the white tigress sat and joined her there, the two watching Ashley play with the cubs. She settled herself against Shar-Ranjana's warm flank, purring with quiet contentment. Ashley focused her camera and started taking photos of her new playmates, giggling and laughing at their antics, as they pawed curiously at the strange device. Shar-Ranjana licked the paint and sweat from Leandra's back as she watched over her cubs. She seemed happy enough to let someone else deal with their energetic exuberance for a while.

Pausing in her play, Ashley looked up and smiled at the sight of Leandra sitting next to the white tigress. The image was almost too perfect: the orange and tawny striped form of the dark-haired woman beside the enormous pale cat, their expressions somehow identical despite the obvious differences in their features. Grinning, she brought her camera up and snapped several shots of the two, intending to have a copy enlarged and framed for her private collection.

"I can't believe this." She cuddled one of the young cubs, stroking its orange fur. "Why aren't these two white, as well?"

"They were fathered by a normal Bengal," Leandra explained. "Shar-Ranjana has to stay in hiding because of the poachers; they're still looking for her. If she's found—by either the rangers or the poachers—she'll be taken from the jungle and kept in a cage. Or worse, she'll be shot and butchered for her parts. A white tiger is worth its weight in gold."

Ashley nodded, understanding how much Leandra was trusting her by sharing this secret. "You didn't have to show me this," she observed. "You could have let me leave without ever telling me; I never would have known."

Leandra shrugged, avoiding her eyes. "I wanted you to see."

Ashley flushed with pleasure at the gesture of such faith. "Thank you," she said. "This really means a lot to me. And you can trust me not to tell. I know Simon and Grace are only trying to protect the tigers, but you're right. They'd want to put her in a zoo or something."

Leandra nodded, her eyes soft and reverent. "That's not where Shar-Ranjana belongs. She's a wild animal. The jungle is her home." With her right hand, Leandra stroked over the great cat's head and tugged gently at her ear. "Nothing so beautiful belongs in a cage," she whispered.

Still in awe of the majesty and power of the great tigress, Ashley could only agree.

The two of them spent several hours with Shar-Ranjana and her cubs, the tigress patiently enduring both Ashley's interest and the rambunctious antics of the youngsters. Fortunately, Ashley had grabbed plenty of film, and she merrily snapped away at the indulgent yet dignified expression on the mother tiger's face as her cubs grabbed at her flanks and tried to play with her.

Ashley was also amazed by the subtle and not-so-subtle interactions that went on between Shar-Ranjana and Leandra. The tigress seemed to treat her human cohort as she would a sibling, the two trading friendly swats and lots of growling and head-rubbing, which Ashley understood was a symbol of acceptance and camaraderie. Leandra also explained that the strange coughing sounds were a signal of contentment and greeting common among the tigers when they were at peace.

As the sun reached its zenith, it started becoming clear that Shar-Ranjana was growing weary of their company and wanted to be left in peace. Ashley knew enough about big cats to recognize her lashing tail and subtly back-turned ears as signs of irritation, so she didn't protest when Leandra suggested she take her final photos before they left.

"I learned tiger-talk the hard way," she added with a wry smile. "Most people think of cats as being fairly aloof, but that's only because so much of their communication is subtle—tiny things like how they move or stand can tell you a lot. And it can be even harder with bigger cats like tigers because they don't purr."

"They don't?"

"Nope. Any cat that roars can't purr; it's always one or the other."

"Huh…I never noticed that before."

"Luckily they all still seem to understand the same basic signals: purring, growling, head-rubbing…all pretty universally understood. And since tigers aren't the only big cats out here, territories tend to overlap and it's important for me to be able to keep track of who's in the area. I've been chased off more than once by a cat who wasn't used to me being around."

Not long after, the great white tigress called her cubs back to her side and led the way back to the denser jungle paths, casting them a last look back over her shoulder before leaving the clearing.

Snapping a final shot of the great cat before she melted back into the dappled shadows, Ashley felt a mixture of sadness and gratitude. She glanced at her companion and found Leandra looking back at her with deep intensity. "Thank you," she said softly. "I really don't know what else to say." She smiled and reached out to squeeze her friend's arm. "That was very special, Leandra."

Leandra stared at Ashley's hand for a few seconds. She looked up to meet her gaze and then smiled. "I'm glad you liked it."

The two watched the jungle undergrowth for long moments in silence, then turned in unison and left the clearing.

"I still can't believe I got that close to a white tiger!" Ashley exclaimed, wearing the same grin she'd sported since they'd left the clearing. "That's got to be a record or something, right? How many people in history do you think could honestly say they've had a white tiger lick their face?"

"Not many," Leandra replied. Ashley was practically vibrating with rapture, and Leandra was happy to bask in the warmth of her enthusiasm. It had felt so good to finally share the secret of Shar-Ranjana with someone who truly appreciated the miracle of the rare cat, and Leandra now wished more than ever that Ashley didn't have to go back to the States. Every time she reminded herself that her friend would be gone in a week, Leandra felt her heart ache with anticipated loss.

She thought back on the last four years—the months that lasted forever, the silence in her head that could not be filled by the noises of the jungle—and feared that, this time, she would surely go insane. How could she go back to the way things had been? Ashley had burst the walls of isolation that had been Leandra's home for so long, and there was no hope of rebuilding them.

Staring helplessly at the young woman walking beside her, enthralled by the light in her eyes and the laughter on her lips, Leandra struggled against the uncertainty that was creeping into her mind. She feared that Ashley would discover her true feelings, and perhaps decide to break off the burgeoning friendship that was swiftly becoming the most important thing in her lonely world.

Always before, she had been assertive with the women she seduced: cool, determined, and assured of success. For the first time, she feared the consequences of rejection, feared she might lose something she couldn't get back. As much as she wanted to bed Ashley—and certain long-dormant parts of her body were aching with the strength of that desire—she put more value on the simple friendship and comfort she found in her continued company.

"Say, I'm kind of hungry." Ashley's voice penetrated Leandra's troubled thoughts. "I don't suppose you'd be willing to feed me? I mean, it was your fault I missed breakfast, after all." Dark, hopeful eyes batted their lashes persuasively at the tall woman.

Leandra's mood lightened. "Sure. I could use a bite myself."

"Great. Lead the way, oh mighty jungle-woman."

Leandra turned their footsteps in the direction of her camp, slipping lightly through the thick foliage. She put aside her troublesome thoughts, concentrating her attention once more on the sounds of the animals around her as they communicated a wealth of information few could interpret.

They walked for several hours, Ashley's strides beginning to slow with fatigue after the long hike. Leandra accommodated her pace, feeling winded herself. She was relieved when they finally reached the flatlands leading up to the mountain where she made her home. Moving along the familiar trails with a relaxed guard, Leandra was so looking forward to taking a well-deserved rest back in her cave—idly wondering what the chances were that she could talk Ashley into trading foot rubs—that she almost missed the subtle alarm bells ringing in her senses.

Something felt amiss.

Leandra froze in her tracks, raising a striped hand to signal a halt. Ashley stumbled to a weary stop beside her, eyes widening as she noticed Leandra's alert posture, and she scanned their surroundings nervously.

"What's wrong?"

"Shhh."

Leandra tilted her face upwards, her entire body intent on the jungle around her. Faint scents still lingered in the air: sweat and leather and the familiar tang of gun oil. Nothing appeared out of place, but Leandra hadn't survived so long out here by taking things for granted. She concentrated on the sounds of the animals, recognizing instantly that something wasn't right. A pregnant sense of expectation lay heavy in the air, the creatures here obviously waiting for something to happen before they called attention to themselves once more. Leandra knew the signs.

Something was hunting close by.

A less experienced human would have missed the barely audible click. A normal person would never have noticed the barely visible glimmer of sunlight off metal. Leandra was far from normal, however, and her reflexes had her moving even before her brain had fully processed the information.

"Get down!"

Throwing herself at the startled woman behind her, Leandra brought them both to the ground, trying to cushion their fall with her body. A second later, the booming *crack!* of a rifle blast shattered the telltale silence, and a fist-sized chunk of timber burst from a nearby tree. Crouched protectively over her winded friend, Leandra's cold eyes scanned the surrounding wilderness with predatory intent, her every pore open and waiting for some kind of motion. Ashley caught her breath and rolled onto her stomach. Wide-eyed and uncertain, she faced the attack with more confusion than fear.

"What was that?"

"A rifle," Leandra whispered. "Stay quiet. I'm not sure where they are."

It was all so clear now. Leandra cursed herself, knowing she should have seen this coming. The untraceable shot from the other day...the air of disquiet and tension which hung over the scene. Leandra realized she'd been lured out into the open, had allowed herself to become the hunted. A poacher was out there, no doubt seeking to eradicate the threat that had plagued the black market animal trade these past four years.

She waited with honed patience for her adversary to make the first mistake. Her hands gripped the twin sets of claws eagerly, every muscle taut and ready to pounce when the moment came.

Fortunately, whoever was out there was either foolish or arrogant. Scarcely a minute had passed before she heard a faint rustling sound and the metallic *snick* of a rifle bolt loading another round. Her eyes instantly pinned the location of the noise—a sheltered patch of undergrowth perfect for an ambush. Pressing Ashley to the ground with a look that told her to stay put, Leandra crawled forward silently, stalking the unseen attacker.

Rising for a moment from the cover of the grass, she ducked as a second shot rang out, kicking up the dust close by. Leandra didn't hesitate, all thoughts of fatigue vanishing with a surge of adrenaline. She sprang forward into the shadows with a savage and very authentic roar. She heard a curse, then detected movement. Without thinking, she ducked the rifle butt that swung at her head. Lashing out with her right hand, claws extended, she found nothing but air and darted forward again. This time she managed to overbalance her adversary, and he stumbled out from his cover. Leandra followed quickly, pausing to study the rugged-looking man who regained his feet with impressive speed.

"Bitch," the man spat. He reversed his hold on the empty rifle, turning it into a club.

Leandra growled low in her throat. She made a quick assessment of her opponent and recognized a veteran of the field; the man held a fighter's stance with confidence. Moving closer, she feinted to the side and then charged him.

He swung the rifle butt at her head. Leandra ducked the swing and smashed the base of her palm into his arm. The weapon flew from his grasp and spun away into the forest, lost. Unperturbed, the poacher quickly drew a large, gleaming knife from a sheath at his side and raised it ominously.

Leandra and the man shifted back and forth, neither willing to make the first move. As they tested one another for signs of weakness, a second man, armed with a makeshift club, appeared from hiding and began to creep closer to Leandra's exposed back.

Ashley jumped up from where she'd landed in the grass and screamed, "Leandra, behind you!" Leandra spun around and lashed out with a clawed hand, keeping the second man at bay. She recognized him—he was the same man she'd rescued Ashley from on the day they'd first met. The first poacher pressed in, trying to take advantage of her distraction. Moments later, her powerful leg caught him in the stomach and kicked him onto his back.

Winded, he gestured toward Ashley. "Get the blonde," he gasped to his cohort.

A wave of panic and fury rolled over Leandra, clouding her vision. "*No!*"

Leandra moved much faster than the enormous, red-bearded man. She ducked his clumsy but forceful swing and darted in behind his guard. Before the man could backpedal or force her to retreat, Leandra struck. Twin sets of claws snapped out, tore across his unprotected belly, then retreated.

Crouching low, Leandra watched the man's look of shock and pain turn to one of dawning comprehension. He clutched at his stomach with trembling hands, desperately trying to hold himself together as he stared back at her in horror. He turned and managed only a few steps back toward the patch of undergrowth, before falling face down on the ground, his life staining the grass deep crimson as it flowed from the mortal wound.

The first poacher had regained his feet and was closing in on her with an expression of grim determination. Leandra turned to face him, tangled braids falling in a dark curtain over her face. She bared her teeth in a snarl, feeling a feral growl rumble up from deep in her chest as she began stalking forward.

Ashley, still struggling to catch up with this sudden turn of events, covered her mouth to stifle a cry as the poacher's knife darted toward Leandra's chest. Leandra narrowly evaded it and sprang forward with a feral hiss. This time, she didn't hesitate. Not bothering with jabs or feints, she lashed out with savage strength and raw fury.

The poacher stumbled backward, trying to put some distance between himself and the furious jungle-woman, but Leandra pressed her assault relentlessly. She blocked a second frantic stab and slapped the steel blade out of her enemy's grip. He managed to respond with a hard backhand,

and Ashley winced and almost ran forward, but Leandra accepted the blow stoically before twisting to the side and jabbing her elbow into his kidney. Again she pressed in, every line of her body radiating anger and lethal intent. Another successful attack drew a neat set of bloody lines across the man's chest, tearing through the cloth of his shirt with wicked ease.

The poacher no longer seemed so confident of victory, and he looked around for a possible weapon. Seeing none, he swung a desperate punch at Leandra's face. She dodged to the side a fraction too late, the blow connecting with her right shoulder.

It was a minor hit, and watching from the sidelines, Ashley fully expected Leandra would shrug it off with little effort. She was horrified when, instead, Leandra clutched her arm and screamed in agony, turning away from her opponent and dropping limply to the ground as though struck by lightning.

Ashley watched in stunned confusion as her friend curled around herself in obvious pain, her right arm somehow paralyzed by the glancing blow. The poacher hesitated for a long moment, clearly every bit as surprised as Ashley felt, then seemed to realize that the advantage was his once more. He lashed out with a sharp kick to Leandra's face, sending her onto her back, still holding her arm against her body. The poacher looked from the trembling woman to the jungle, then to the body of his companion.

By now Ashley had grabbed up a thick tree branch and was running forward, intent on taking over the fight until Leandra recovered from whatever had downed her. The poacher saw her coming; their eyes met, and she felt the cold appraisal of his gaze…felt him weighing the threat she posed, the value of continuing this fight.

Although he could probably have handled Ashley, he must have decided it was time to retreat and lick his wounds. With a curse and a last dark look, he turned and ran back into the cover of the jungle.

Ashley dropped her makeshift weapon when she saw the man flee, not wanting to admit how relieved she was to see him go. Sprinting over to Leandra, she threw herself on the ground beside her and tried to think of something to do that would help. Leandra's eyes were squeezed shut, involuntary tears escaping and running down her face. "Leandra? What's wrong?" Ashley's hands fluttered uncertainly over her friend, reluctant to touch her lest she make things worse. "Is it your shoulder?"

A faint nod. Leandra was calming a little, but she was shaking all over.

"Is it dislocated?" Ashley asked. "I know how to reset it, if you'll just let me look—"

"Don't touch me!"

Ashley's hands withdrew instantly as Leandra recoiled in fear. "I won't hurt you, Leandra, but I need to see what's wrong."

"No. Please. Just give me a minute, and I'll be okay." Leandra struggled into a sitting position, holding her right arm tightly against her body. She gasped and swayed a little, but remained upright.

"What happened?" Ashley wanted to examine the injury, but she respected her friend's desire not to be touched.

Leandra shook her head. "It's nothing. He hit me in a bad spot, that's all." She smiled grimly, the left side of her mouth already swelling from the kick she'd received. "I just need a few moments to rest, then we'll get out of here. No telling when he might decide to come back and finish the job."

Ashley sat beside her friend, still regarding her with concern. She looked over at the body of the second man and shuddered. "What should we do about him?"

"Nothing," Leandra said, scowling. "Let the carrion feeders do their work. The rangers have enough problems without having to deal with burial detail."

Ashley sighed. "Fine." *She killed him because he was coming after me*, her mind acknowledged. She'd heard the desperate tone in her friend's voice when she'd rushed to intercept the poacher, had seen the angry, protective expression on her face. But knowing Leandra was a killer and actually seeing her kill were two very different things. *I must be crazy*, Ashley thought. *How can I be falling for this woman? She kills without remorse, without shame. How can I feel so safe around her when I know what she's capable of?*

The answer came easily to mind as she studied her recovering companion. *Because I know she'd never hurt me. She trusted me enough to show me Shar-Ranjana, even though she's only known me a week. She invited me into her life and spoke with me, after staying silent for four years. She's lived out here as an animal for so long that death is just another part of life for her.*

"All right," Leandra said grimly, struggling to her feet with another gasp of pain. Ashley helped her up. "Let's go."

"Are you sure you're okay?" Clearly, Leandra was still hurting. Ashley was certain that, beneath the faded paint, her face would be pale and drawn.

But Leandra brushed her concern aside. "I'll be fine. It's happened before. Sometimes it takes a while to get better, that's all."

"All right." Ashley watched her friend carefully as they walked, noticing Leandra's tightly clenched jaw and the dizzy, glazed look in her eyes. *One way or another, I need to see that shoulder. She's in pain. How can she expect me to just do nothing?*

Halfway up the mountain to the cave, Leandra was swaying noticeably and had lost the stealth that normally characterized her movements. She tripped over loose stones, and her breath came in short, hard gasps. It was all Ashley could do to keep herself from stopping right there and demanding to inspect the injury, but she knew Leandra would fight her off. She waited until they were safely back at camp before she confronted her.

"Let me see it," she ordered sternly, once Leandra had settled wearily on her sleeping pallet.

Leandra drew away. "There's nothing you can do," she insisted. "I'll be fine if I can just rest." But her eyes betrayed her suffering, and Ashley's face hardened.

"Leandra, I'm not going to just sit here while you're hurting. I have to do something. That punch shouldn't have affected you like that." She crossed her arms over her chest and glared down at her friend. "Let me look."

For a moment, Leandra's face said she wasn't going to cooperate, then she silently nodded and moved to expose her shoulder.

Ashley knelt beside her and gently reached out. She paused when Leandra flinched reflexively, then she very slowly tugged the fur halter away from the injured shoulder. Leandra's face was a stony mask while she struggled to permit the inspection.

Beneath the brief clothing, Leandra's skin remained covered with dusty paint. Ashley ran sensitive fingers over the exposed area, searching for some sign of injury in the bone. Instead, she felt a series of lumps and ridges in the skin itself, and she leaned closer to examine the irregularities in the dim light. Blonde brows contracted in puzzlement, then shot up as understanding dawned.

No longer hidden by clothing, Leandra's shoulder revealed a series of raised scar tissue that ran in a strange pattern along her chest, near her collarbone. A quick check revealed a second set of scars on her back, nearly identical to the ones in the front. Ashley ran her fingertips over the old wounds, hearing a sharp intake of breath as she probed gently.

"What happened here?" she asked quietly.

Leandra gritted her teeth and gave a half shrug with her uninjured shoulder. "Shar-Ranjana's father didn't exactly take an immediate liking to me."

"He what?" Ashley stared at the raised marks and suddenly saw them for what they were: bite marks. Very large bite marks. She gasped. "A tiger did this?"

Leandra nodded. "A long time ago. When I first came here." She shifted a little on the sleeping mat, the memories of that time making her visibly uncomfortable. "It's a long story."

Ashley recognized the signs; this wasn't a topic Leandra wanted to discuss. Still, she could feel the tension in her body, could read it in the taut muscles that refused to relax. Her fingertips probed a little harder, earning a sharp grunt of pain from her friend. "How long ago did this happen?"

"Four years or so." Tears ran down Leandra's cheeks, though her face remained stoic. When she finally met Ashley's gaze, she choked out, "Why won't it stop hurting?"

Ashley offered comfort the best way she knew how. She reached out and gently pulled Leandra into a hug. Leandra tensed at first, but surrendered to the embrace almost instantly. A sob wrenched from deep in her throat, and she let the tears come. With her good hand, she clutched Ashley to her and buried her face in silky hair that smelled of apricot and flowers. "Why won't it stop?" she sobbed, releasing her pain for the first time since she'd received the wounds.

Ashley hugged Leandra tightly, letting her cry. She made soothing noises, trying to comfort the woman as her body was wracked with helpless shudders. When Leandra started to calm, Ashley gently stroked her coarse dreadlocks and wished she could offer more than a shoulder to cry on. "It's all right," she whispered softly. "It'll be okay."

Leandra's sobs eventually weakened and stopped. Ashley could feel sympathetic tears pricking the corners of her own eyes, and when Leandra finally pulled back from their embrace and met her gaze, the suffering was plain in every line of her expression. Clearly embarrassed by her moment of vulnerability, she wiped at her face with her wrist, smearing the intricate paint. "I'm sorry, I shouldn't be—"

Ashley pressed two fingers to Leandra's lips, silencing her. "There's nothing to be sorry for, Leandra," she said reassuringly. "We all need to cry sometimes."

Leandra snuffled a little, then cast her gaze toward the ground. "It's just…" She struggled for a moment. "Sometimes I don't feel it for days, and I start to think maybe it's never going to hurt again. And then something happens. I'll knock it during a hunt or bump it on a tree branch, and it feels just as bad as when it first happened." She touched the scars gently, then lowered her hand. "Why does it still hurt?"

"I don't know." Ashley studied the marks again. "Did the doctors do any surgery?"

"There weren't any doctors. A couple from one of the villages helped me while I was recovering, but…" She half-shrugged again. "I couldn't go to a hospital."

"Well, it's no wonder it still hurts. The muscles and nerves must be all screwed up. My brother-in-law is a physician. He deals with this kind of damage all the time, only usually it comes from sports injuries." She was amazed that Leandra had been able to survive out here with such an injury. "It could probably be fixed," she continued. "But you'd need to go to a hospital and have surgery done."

Leandra smiled grimly. "That's not too likely while I'm living out here, is it?"

"I guess not." Ashley rubbed at the smeared stripes on Leandra's face. "Guess you're going to need to redo your paint job, huh?"

"Yeah." Leandra sighed and lay down on her pallet, looking a good deal more relaxed. "I'll take a bath tomorrow. There's a little waterfall not too far away, farther up around the mountain. I usually go there to clean up and mix the paint."

"Mmm." Ashley forced her mind not to venture into any contemplations involving her friend's naked, wet body. Instead, she decided to turn her thoughts to more pressing concerns. "Who do you think those men were?"

"Poachers." Leandra closed her eyes and blew a lock of hair from her face. "I've listened to some of them over the years. They call me the 'Indian Menace.' Those guys probably decided to get rid of me so they could go after Shar-Ranjana without having to watch their backs. I'm sure there are plenty of people who would pay good money to have me put down."

"Doesn't that bother you?"

"Why should it? I'm quieter, faster, and deadlier than they are. I'll survive. They won't."

Ashley shook her head at Leandra's simple logic. *That's how she's learned things work. Predator, prey. She's the more effective killer, so nothing else matters.* "What if that man comes back with others? Can you dodge a bullet?"

Leandra grinned. "I dodged two today, didn't I?"

Ashley sighed. "Forget it." She looked around the cave. "Do you have a rag or something? Your shoulder might feel better with a cold compress."

Leandra gestured toward the crates at the back of the cave. "Over there."

"Thanks." Ashley rummaged through the stocks of rice, salt, and other staples, before she found a bundle of cloth. Ripping some up, she ventured cautiously to the river at the base of the mountain and returned shortly with a saucepan full of water. After dipping the rags into the cool water, she pressed them against the sore shoulder. Leandra flinched at first, but smiled as the painful heat in her muscles was bled from her by the damp cloth.

"That feels wonderful." A low purr rumbled through her belly and throat. Ashley grinned at the sounds, knowing she was doing something right. *I wonder what it might take to get her really purring, she thought wickedly, picturing a few things she might try.*

This is one kitten I wouldn't mind letting lick my bowl clean.

Instantly, a hot flush burned in her cheeks, and she was grateful Leandra's eyes were closed. *Bad Ashley!* she scolded mentally. *Bad, bad Ashley! Get your mind out of the gutter.*

But as soon as she let her eyes roam down the full length of Leandra's wonderfully exposed form, the prurient thoughts came right back. She licked suddenly dry lips.

Cats like being stroked, right? Her fingers twitched. *Maybe I could just stroke her a little lower... I'm sure she'd like that.* Her eyes flirted with the hem of Leandra's brief skirt. *Then I could slide my fingers up her thighs and around her hips...then maybe down until I reach...*

Ashley's eyes snapped open, and she pulled herself out of her little fantasy with a shake and a shudder. Leandra sensed her movement and glanced up.

"Something wrong?"

"Uh...no, I was just..." Ashley struggled to formulate coherent thought, her eyes eventually finding a lifeline. "I just noticed it's almost afternoon. Grady will probably get worried if I'm not back by sundown, and it'll take me at least two hours to make it back to camp. So..."

"You have to go?"

Ashley almost nodded, but something in those words stopped her. Tired and hurting, her defenses low, Leandra couldn't mask the desperate, longing tone in her voice. After the magical day they had shared, Ashley found the idea of returning to Grady and the others less than appealing. She wanted to hold on to this moment, this connection, just a little longer. "Do you want me to stay?" she asked, very softly.

Leandra looked away, the fingers of her left hand toying with one of her thin braids. "No. Not if it's going to cause problems for you."

Ashley sidled closer. "So...you *do* want me to stay?"

Leandra brought her gaze back to Ashley's. "Yes."

Ashley's heart soared. *To hell with Grady,* she thought. *Like I told him, if I want to spend the whole night with Leandra, he's got nothing to say about it.* "Then I'll stay." She melted at the look of delight on Leandra's face. That look was worth every moment of hassle she was going to get for this little adventure. "After all," she added, smiling, "you did promise you'd feed me, right?"

It took him almost an hour, but at last he caught sight of the flash of sunlight off metal, winking from the underbrush. Jack Corbin grunted with satisfaction and retrieved the rifle he'd lost during his encounter with the ferocious jungle-woman. Checking the weapon carefully, he was pleased to find it in working order. Soon, it was loaded and slung over his shoulder once more.

Stepping out onto the grasslands, the weary poacher regarded the flurry of feathers and bloodied beaks that writhed about on the ground nearby with detached interest. The scavenger birds had been quick to descend and feast on the body of Shaun Duggan, and soon they would have it stripped to the bone. Jack observed the feeding without a flicker of emotion. The loss of his partner had been unfortunate, but certainly not crippling.

He watched for a few more minutes before turning away, his attention drawn to a distant light that glowed from halfway up the nearby mountain range. His quarry had retreated, just as he had, and he knew exactly where she had gone. Still, Jack had no intention of attacking the tiger-woman in her lair. She would have the advantage there and would fight all the harder to defend her home. Better to wait for her to come out into the open where he could get a clear shot and neutralize her advantage of stealth and speed.

The ambush had not gone as he had hoped. The strange woman was cannier than he'd expected, somehow picking up on his presence and evading his shot with impressive agility. Jack didn't like to think he'd underestimated his prey, but in this case, he had to admit he'd assumed too much. The dark-haired woman was even more dangerous than he'd thought, and he knew he'd only escaped death because of a lucky punch.

All had not been in vain, however. He'd discovered two important holes in his quarry's armor. First, the strange weakness that had felled her with such surprising ease. Jack wasn't sure what was wrong with the woman's shoulder, but he guessed it was an old wound of some sort. Regardless, it would serve as an advantage he could exploit in a hand-to-hand fight next time, if things came to that.

Second—and more intriguing—was the young blonde. Jack hadn't been expecting her appearance, and it had jeopardized his original plan. He had noted with interest the desperate tone in the tiger-woman's voice when the blonde was threatened, and his thoughts went to ways he might use her against her friend. Certainly, she might be used as bait to lure the dangerous jungle-woman out into the open.

Ignoring the burning pain of the deep cuts across his chest and the bruises on his body, Jack turned and made his way back to his camp. He would rest and treat his wounds tonight, and tomorrow he would plan his next attack.

As he tramped along the narrow jungle trails, he felt something niggling at the back of his mind, like an itch he couldn't quite scratch. There was something about the strange woman…something beyond her wild appearance and savage nature. Those clear, sapphire-colored eyes and chiseled features had, for a second there, seemed almost familiar.

Shaking his head to rid himself of the disturbing sensation, Jack scowled darkly and looked forward to round two.

Ashley tossed her leaf/plate away and leaned back against the rock behind her with a long, guttural sigh of utter contentment. Across the fire, Leandra nibbled the edges of her own leaf briefly before chewing the bitter foliage and swallowing it.

"Delicious," Ashley pronounced happily.

Leandra nodded but remained quiet. She had taken a mild painkiller from her first-aid kit and seemed more or less recovered from her fight with the poacher.

Their meal had been another simple affair, consisting of rice, root vegetables, and diced chunks of salted venison, all seasoned with a mix of wild herbs. Outside, the sun stained the distant horizon interesting shades of pink and orange, and turned the edges of the clouds deep purple.

"It's going to be dark soon," Leandra noted.

"Mmm-hmm."

"You know, if you want to go back to your own camp, I can take you," she offered, flexing her arm to demonstrate her recovered range of movement. "My shoulder feels much better now. It wouldn't be a problem."

"Actually, I'd rather stay here if it's okay with you." Ashley didn't want to leave Leandra now. If she went back to her tent, she knew she'd lie awake all night worrying about her. She looked at the thin, rough pallet dubiously. "Think there's enough room on that thing for two?"

Leandra's eyes widened "Um…sure, I-I guess, if—" She cleared her throat. "If you want. But, you know, I could sleep on the ground if you need the room."

Ashley smiled, intrigued by Leandra's flustered reaction. *Maybe I could just sleep on top of you.* "Don't be silly, Leandra. We can snuggle up together, and that way we'll both be comfortable. Although…" She chewed her lower lip coyly and watched her friend's reaction carefully. "I usually prefer to sleep in the buff. I don't suppose that's a good idea without a blanket though, huh?"

"N-no, probably not." Leandra's voice sounded noticeably strained, and she seemed unable to meet Ashley's gaze. "It gets cold just before dawn."

Ashley grinned rakishly, pleased at the response. *What's got you so tongue-tied, Jungle Jane?* "Oh well, I can manage for one night, I suppose. Besides, you'll keep me warm, right?"

"Yeah, sure."

"Great."

As the sun began its descent in earnest, the two women moved to the mouth of the cave so they could watch the stars assume their places in the heavens. Here and there a dark hole formed in the sky where clouds hid the sparkling lights. The distant sound of gibbons singing reached them from the forest below, echoing with the strange calls of the night hunters and their prey. Ashley listened to the majestic symphony of the jungle, trying not to dwell on the fact that she'd be leaving this world behind in less than a week.

She turned to the woman sitting silently beside her. "Do you ever miss all the things you gave up when you came out here?" she asked.

Leandra's eyes glowed in the flickering light of the fire, her face an interesting study of shadowed hollows and primitive stripes. "Sometimes," she whispered.

"Do you ever think of going back?"

"Sometimes." Leandra was silent for long moments. "Going back means opening old wounds." She swallowed hard. "I don't know that I've earned the right to leave this place yet."

"Earned the right?" Ashley considered that statement, that choice of phrasing, and felt another piece to the puzzle of Leandra's history fall into place. Understanding dawned, clear and sharp. "This is a punishment, isn't it?" she said, shifting around to face her friend more directly. "You're out here because you're trying to make up for something."

Leandra nodded.

"For being a poacher?"

Silence for a moment. Then the quiet answer. "Not just for that." Leandra's eyes were distant, obviously looking back at the past. "It's difficult to explain."

Ashley heard the unspoken words. *She's never had to explain it to anyone but herself. She convicted herself of whatever crime she thinks she committed. She passed judgment, and she enforced her decision. And the only one she's ever had to answer to is herself.* "You don't have to tell me about it if you don't want to."

Again, silence descended. Leandra sat cross-legged, staring thoughtfully up at the moon. "Can I ask you a question?"

"Of course."

"Why do you like me?"

"What do you mean?"

"Why do you want to be my friend? You've seen what I do, how I live. Why would you want to be friends with a killer?"

Ashley cocked her head to the side. "You're a nice person, Leandra," she said softly. "I admit, I don't really like what you're doing out here, but I can separate it from the person you are. I think you're interesting and loyal, and I don't know why, but I feel really comfortable when I'm with you. Safe." Her eyes turned inquisitive. "Why do you ask?"

Leandra looked away, then said, "I guess I just never thought of myself as being a likeable person."

Her voice was filled with a childlike quality that touched Ashley deeply. She shifted closer. "Why would you think that?"

"Because it's the truth." Leandra paused, then corrected herself. "At least it used to be. I never really had any friends except my younger brother."

"You have a brother?"

A faint nod, coupled with an even fainter smile. "Ricky. I haven't seen him in a long while." She thought for a moment. "Probably seven or eight years. He must think I'm dead." A lone finger traced an idle pattern in the dirt. "I bet he's happier thinking that than knowing the truth."

The bitterness Leandra directed toward herself shocked Ashley. "How can you say that? I'm sure your brother misses you terribly."

"The last thing he told me before I left was that he wished he could be more like me, even for just a moment. That way, he said, he could have had the cold-bloodedness to kill me without feeling any sorrow. I doubt he'd be thrilled to find out I'm still alive."

Ashley was silent, not knowing what to say or what comfort she could offer beyond a compassionate ear. Leandra had turned back to stare out at the darkening jungle, but by the distant, unfocused look in her eyes Ashley knew she was looking beyond the scenery, recalling long-buried memories.

"My dad was in construction," she said, her voice low and even. "We moved around a lot, wherever he found work. It was hard on Ricky and me, having to change schools so often. We were really close growing up, and when I started falling in with the wrong crowd, little brother came along for the ride. I think it was easier for me to set myself up as a bad-girl bitch, rather than make an effort to find real friends. Friends I'd have to leave anyway, as soon as my father found another contract. By eighteen, I was selling drugs to the other kids and helping my 'friends' fence the guns and other shit they stole. Pretty soon, we were getting in trouble for heavier stuff. I made other friends—people who offered me a better cut of the money. People who wanted someone willing to do what she was told without asking questions."

Ashley listened in silence, not speaking for fear that Leandra would stop.

"I was pretty smart. Maybe not academically, but I had a good sense for dealing in the black market. I left home at nineteen and took Ricky with me. He was sixteen. The cops didn't look too hard at him, so we made a good team. I learned quickly, and before long I attracted the attention of the big boys. They hired me as a runner, at first. Then I discovered I had a talent for smuggling and started moving up in the world. I got cocky, and it was only a matter of time before I started treading on the wrong toes.

"Ricky and I worked together for a long time, but over the years, he changed. When his girlfriend overdosed and died, things got strained between us. It was like I was walking forward, and I'd keep drawing lines in the sand for him to cross. Every time, I'd promise that this one would be as far as we'd go; I wouldn't ask for anything more. He followed me every time, until one day, I guess he decided he'd come far enough and couldn't follow me anymore."

Leandra sighed and pushed long fingers into her tangled hair. "We parted on less than friendly terms. I was angry at him for leaving me. I thought we were going to be a team forever. I called him a coward and told him he was gutless for leaving me. He didn't care. And when he was gone, neither did I. About anything. I threw myself into my work, not caring who I pissed off just as long as I got paid. It caught up with me, of course. I screwed over the wrong people, and they decided to make it personal." Leandra blinked rapidly, her eyes wet with unshed tears. "My parents' house was firebombed one Friday night. It burned to the ground, with them inside."

Ashley covered her mouth in horror. "Oh, Leandra! I'm so sorry."

"I never told them what I was doing, but I think they probably had some idea. At the funeral, Ricky blamed me for their deaths. It was my fault, he said. Even though I shrugged him off at the time, I knew he was right."

"No!" Ashley gripped Leandra's shoulder and forced her to meet her gaze. "That's not true. You couldn't have known."

Self-loathing flashed in Leandra's eyes. "Don't you think I know that?" She pulled away. "For the next three years, that's all I told myself. I wasn't the one who threw the firebombs. I didn't mean for them to die. But it doesn't change the fact that if it weren't for me, they'd still be alive. And no matter how much I told myself I didn't care what Ricky said to me, it still hurt, worse than I could deal with. The only way I could handle the pain was to numb myself to everything I was doing.

"After that, I decided I didn't want to work for anyone but myself anymore. I set out on my own, and with the connections I'd made, it wasn't long before I was making more money than ever before. I had it all: I buried myself in power, cash, drugs, sex, and tried to forget how much it all cost me. Soon, the drugs got harder, the sex got rougher, and I didn't care who got hurt because of me. And then, I found a new market to exploit—the black market animal trade.

"It was unbelievable. The demand was high, the risks were low, and the money was incredible. A single bird could bring in tens of thousands of dollars. I started trapping animals in Australia first, then moved to Africa and Asia. Before long, I wanted more, and I went after bigger prey. I liked it. Hunting elephants, rhinos, lions, everything. I wasn't really doing it for the money anymore, but for the pleasure. It made me feel powerful and in control. Dangerous."

Her eyes closed, and Leandra's voice sounded scornful. "I was such an idiot. I thought I was the Great White Hunter reborn. I thought I was top shit. If only I'd known…" She trailed off for a moment. "Then one day, one of my sources heard a rumor from the rangers in India. A safari group had seen something strange in the jungle. Something no one really believed was actually out there. A white tiger."

Leandra took a deep breath and exhaled slowly. "I knew the odds of the rumor being true were slim. I knew it was stupid to even consider going. But the chance, however remote, was too incredible to pass up. I wanted that tiger. Not for the money but for a trophy. Something I could have stuffed and mounted, so I could look at it and tell myself how damn good I was." A painted lip curled derisively. "I left everything and hopped the first flight out here, ready to hunt.

"It took me weeks just to track down where the reports had come from. The Bandhavgarh National Park is pretty well patrolled, but I didn't care. Most poachers went in groups, but I didn't want to share this kill. I came out here alone, four years ago, and I started searching for tracks. I found a few normal tigers, but no sign of the one I wanted. Then, out of the blue, I found fresh markings. A recent kill, with huge paw prints around it. Somehow, I knew this was the one. I followed the tracks, even when they led into denser jungle. I was brash and arrogant, and I deserved exactly what I got."

Ashley saw the slight motion as Leandra rolled her sore shoulder at the memory. "He found you first, huh?"

"I never even saw it coming," Leandra whispered. "One moment I was stalking my prey, and the next, I was flat on the ground with my face in the mud and four hundred pounds of cat pinning me down. I still remember the moment I realized that I'd walked right into a trap. The tiger had been hunting me all along. I struggled, but I could barely move. Then I felt hot breath at my neck...pressure and heat on my back where claws started raking me." Leandra's face was still, but her eyes were alive with remembered terror. A shudder ran through her body, and she hugged herself tight. "I've never felt anything worse than the sensation of those teeth clamping down on my shoulder...the unbelievable power in those jaws as they started biting. I was screaming like a child. My vision flashed on and off, and I could feel the vibrations of a growl going through my arm and neck. I knew I was going to die, and in the moment before I passed out, I was grateful. I knew I deserved to die for everything I'd done. This was my judgment. Final justice. And I remember welcoming the end—the darkness—with every fiber of my being."

Ashley listened wide-eyed to the story, hanging on Leandra's every word. "What happened?"

"I woke up. My shoulder was a throbbing mess of blood, the muscle exposed right down to the bone. I didn't know what was happening or why the tiger hadn't killed me. I looked around and he was sitting there, not ten feet away. Like a statue. Just looking at me, with eyes like ice." The emotion in Leandra's voice changed subtly, the horror of the memories now blending to an expression of wonder. "I can't even begin to describe what happened next. I'm not really sure I understand it myself. But the way he looked at me... It was like he could see every sin I'd ever committed, every hurt I'd inflicted." Her voice became a whisper. "His eyes washed over my soul like a benediction, and it felt as though all the pain I'd tried to numb myself to rushed in to fill the empty places inside. I stared back at him, and I saw an intelligence and understanding there, beyond the animal. And I realized he was going to spare me. Show me a mercy I never would have shown him. I understood it as clearly as if he'd spoken the words." Leandra sighed. "He was so beautiful, so strong and noble. I was filled with shame that I'd ever thought to hunt him. I looked back at what my life had become, and I realized that in all those years, I hadn't done a single thing that I was honestly proud of. If I had died that day, my legacy would have been nothing but the pain and sorrow I had brought to the world."

Leandra was quiet for a moment, and Ashley could plainly see what it was costing her to claw open the faded scars of those memories. "I'd lost a lot of blood," she continued softly. "I wasn't conscious long. But just before I passed out again, something in his eyes changed. I don't know how, but something passed between us, and I realized his mercy came with a price. He didn't kill me, but a part of me died that day. When I next woke up, I was in a hut on the outskirts of a village. I'm still not sure how I got there. The couple who lived there refused to tell me anything. They saw my clothes; they knew what I was. But they didn't turn me in. I think, somehow, they understood that something had changed me. They nursed me back to health, and I left as soon as I could walk again. I came back out here, leaving everything behind—my clothes, my identification, and all my weapons, except for a single knife. I could feel the guilt of every evil thing I'd ever done weighing me down: the death of my parents, the lives I'd destroyed with the drugs and guns I smuggled and sold, the torture of all the animals I'd caged or butchered. And I saw a way to even the scales. A punishment I deserved."

For the first time, Ashley understood what Leandra was doing out here. "You exiled yourself to the jungle, to protect the animals you once hunted."

Leandra nodded. "It felt like the first truly right thing I'd done in my whole life."

The darkness outside had deepened, and the moon illuminated swaths of rippling jungle in shimmering lines of iridescence. Ashley listened to the jungle sounds in the quiet that followed Leandra's words, trying to imagine what it must have been like for her when she first came back here. Still weak from her injury, naked and torn within herself, yet reborn into a savage world to live among creatures equipped by evolution to survive against harsh odds. "How did you manage to live?"

Leandra bowed her head. "I almost didn't. It was hard at first. I'd been such a good hunter before that I thought I'd have no trouble surviving. But I was very wrong. Hunting with a gun is one thing, but the animals out here are always alert. In the beginning, I couldn't get within a hundred feet of an animal without it running. I was hurting, filthy, and wishing I could just die rather than face the life I was choosing. But I didn't give in. I ate whatever food I could find. Sometimes meat that the carrion feeders had abandoned. Sometimes I had to fight them off. The bad food made me sick, and I got weaker.

"Then I found the white tiger again. This time, he didn't attack me. I started following him around, thinking I could eat from his kills after he finished feeding. He tolerated my presence. There was something in the way he looked at me now that said he understood what I was doing, understood the decision I'd made better than I did. Over the days and weeks, I started moving closer and closer to him, and he only occasionally warned me away. I learned from the noises he made and the way he moved to tell what he was thinking. I could sense when he was hungry, angry, annoyed, content. I started to mimic his actions. Soon, I was moving quieter, faster. My hunting improved. The other tigers in the area got used to me, including Shar-Ranjana's mother and brother. I named the great white tiger Shar-Tushar, and we grew to understand and respect one another. When poachers came, I hunted them to protect my new family. It felt good, knowing I was saving the animals. It felt like I was making up for part of my own crimes. I made my outfit from the skin of a young male tiger who died in a territorial dispute with Shar-Tushar. I sneaked into a small village and stole things I needed: a toothbrush, toiletries, things like that."

"But you couldn't grab a hairbrush?" Ashley teased, plucking at one of Leandra's tangled braids.

Leandra grunted. "It wasn't really my first priority. I used to keep my hair tied back in a ponytail, but in this humidity, it started getting frizzy and out of control. Since I only have my fingers for a comb, I braid it as much as I can manage. It's easier to re-tie when it's wet, but I don't do it often." She fingered one of the wiry braids idly. "I didn't care what I looked like; months would go by without me seeing even a trace of other people, and the ranger patrols were easy to avoid. This became my new home.

"I was still learning a lot every day, but I was determined to be every bit as much a tiger as my new family. Painting my skin helped hide me from prey, and I blended in better. I started wandering farther from here, going to the places I knew were favorite hunting sites for poachers. Still, no matter where I went, I never strayed too far." Leandra paused. "In the end though, it didn't matter. I wasn't here when Shar-Tushar needed me the most. Again, I couldn't save my family."

"It wasn't your fault," Ashley said, hearing the self-recrimination in Leandra's tone. "I'm sure you tried to save them."

"I was away to the north at the time," Leandra said. "I came back, and they were all gone. By the time I found them, the poachers had already killed Shar-Tushar, his mate, and his son. I don't know how Shar-Ranjana escaped their notice. There were about fifteen of them, well equipped with Jeeps and radio tracking gear to keep an eye on the rangers. They'd killed leopards, deer, elephants…and my family."

Ashley couldn't stand the look of grief on Leandra's face. "What did you do?"

"The only thing I could do." Leandra's eyes were colder now, her voice gravelly and harsh. "I avenged their deaths."

Ashley shivered at the feral gleam in Leandra's eyes. She could imagine how terrifying the tiger-woman's wrath must have been at that moment.

"I knew I couldn't take on so many while they were alert during the day. So, I waited for night to fall before I moved into their camp. Most of them were asleep." Shaking away the dark memories, Leandra drew a calming breath. "When the rangers found what I'd left of the poachers, I could see the horror on their faces. I knew word of the massacre would get out, and I hoped it would serve as a warning to those who would dare to enter the jungle. I took Shar-Tushar and the others away and buried them deep in the forest. But first, I took the teeth from the two adults and used them to craft these." She held up her clawed hands, and for the first time, Ashley recognized that the claws were actually fangs. Leandra smiled wistfully. "I carry a part of them with me wherever I go, now. And every time I kill, I avenge them a little more.

"After that, I stayed in the area for a while making sure Shar-Ranjana survived. I helped her hunt, and together we survived until she was competent enough to go her own way. I considered staying, but the absence of Shar-Tushar made things seem so empty. I traveled around and hunted the poachers wherever they went, even into the foothills of the Himalayan Mountains." Leandra regarded Ashley with a fond smile that caused her stomach to do a little flip. "I had no idea how long I'd been out here before you showed up. It felt like decades. I hadn't realized how much I'd forgotten of my former life. Even my own name got buried."

Ashley returned the smile in equal measure. "It sounds very lonely," she said softly.

"Yeah, well, you get used to it after a while." Clear cobalt eyes lowered. "But I'm glad you came here. I…" She hesitated. "It feels good to have someone to talk with again."

Ashley absorbed the kind words eagerly, enjoying the warm tingle that coursed through her blood at the intense look she was receiving. "You're welcome." She reached out a hand and gently touched Leandra's shoulder. "I'm glad you trusted me enough to tell me all that," she said softly. "It means a lot to me."

Leandra's nostrils flared, breathing in the scent of the younger woman as her skin burned from the innocent contact. "We should get some sleep," she observed quietly. "Tomorrow will be a busy day."

"Oh?"

"I need to bathe and redo my paint, and there's still a poacher out there somewhere. I'd rather be the hunter than the prey."

"Oh, right." Ashley glanced at Leandra's sleeping pallet. "You don't snore, do you?"

Leandra grinned. "I don't think so. Then again, it's been a long time since anyone's slept close enough to tell me."

"Well, I'm a pretty heavy sleeper anyway." Ashley stood and helped Leandra to her feet. They made their way over to the mat and, after a moment of initial awkwardness, arranged themselves comfortably. Ashley, accustomed to having a pillow, quickly found Leandra's shoulder made a suitable substitute, and she breathed contentedly as she shifted closer. "Is this okay?"

"S-sure."

Ashley couldn't help but make a note of how Leandra's breathing caught in her throat, but after a long moment she felt her relax and timidly return the embrace.

"Great." Ashley wriggled her lower body more firmly into her companion's warmth. She could almost taste the heavy scent that was unique to Leandra: a distinctive combination of moist earth and wild musk that Ashley knew she was growing addicted to. "Will you be able to sleep with me like this?"

Leandra appeared to consider the question seriously. "I don't know. I haven't tried for a long time. I slept with Shar-Ranjana while she was younger, but since then, no one. I should drift off, though. Don't worry about it."

"Okay." Ashley yawned and closed her eyes, feeling safe and relaxed in Leandra's presence. "You'll let me know if I'm annoying you, right?"

"I will." From somewhere deep in Leandra's chest came the vibrating sound of contented purring. "Sweet dreams."

"Mmm...night," Ashley was already half asleep, wrapping her arms tightly around the painted body next to her and pulling them close together. With Leandra's fingers threading gently through her hair and the rhythm of her breathing lulling her senses toward sleep, Ashley's drifting mind began replaying the day's events over. Already the experience of meeting Shar-Ranjana and her cubs had taken on a dreamlike quality, the way such experiences often do.

Ashley's final semi-conscious thought was to hope that her dreams wouldn't decide to explore more erotic territory and accidentally betray her growing attraction.

The next morning, Ashley roused slowly from a refreshing sleep, her senses taking a moment to fully acknowledge her position. There was a moment of disorientation when she felt the unusual sensation of another person beside—and in some places, under—her, but as soon as she remembered where she was, she happily snuggled against her companion.

"Are you awake?" the familiar raspy voice asked softly.

"Mmm." Ashley moaned and shook her head. "Not if it means I have to get up."

Low vibrations shivered through Leandra's body as she chuckled. "Fine." A hand reached up and fingered a strand of her hair. "I guess it won't hurt us to sleep in."

"Good." Ashley cracked an eyelid open and looked up at Leandra's face. "If I weren't here, you'd be out and about already, wouldn't you?"

"If you weren't here, I'd probably have been out hunting through the night, so right now I'd be resting or bathing. During the day, I usually only hunt people, unless I need meat."

"Oh." Ashley chewed her lower lip thoughtfully for a moment. "Tigers like to swim, don't they?"

"Uh huh."

"Do you?"

"Yep." Leandra shifted slightly to better accommodate Ashley lying half on top of her. "It's a good way to cool down during the hotter parts of the day. You'll like this waterfall I go to. It's really secluded, and there are all these overhanging ferns and palms."

"Sounds nice." Ashley yawned and stretched a little, letting her body wake more fully. "You don't have coffee by any chance, do you?"

Leandra shook her head. "Sorry."

"That's okay." Ashley thought for a moment, then asked, "Do you ever miss all those little luxuries? It must be four years since you last had pizza, or chocolate, or beer."

"You get used to it after a while, like anything else. Honestly, I haven't even thought about that stuff much since I came here." She grinned, and added, "I think the thing that was hardest to get used to was the lack of... shall we say, personal companionship."

Ashley almost swallowed her tongue. "Really?"

"Yeah. I didn't actually think about it a whole lot, but my body still got antsy, if you know what I mean. Before, I used sex to relieve tension and to distract me from thinking about anything too hard. It took a while for me to get adjusted to using all my energy for survival, rather than pleasure."

Leandra had an honest, blunt way of talking about herself that Ashley had never experienced before. It was refreshing, in a strange way, and she found it easy to respond in kind. "It's been a while for me too," she admitted. "My job isn't exactly conducive to building a relationship, so…" She trailed off, and grinned rakishly. "It didn't take me long to find ways of keeping myself happy, though."

Leandra returned the grin and drawled, "I bet." When their eyes met, Ashley couldn't help but wonder whether the sparkle in those sapphire eyes might be construed as flirtatious. But then Leandra gave her a pat on the hip and rolled her off to her side, saying "All right, that's enough sleep time. Lots to do today, so we need to get moving."

Ashley grumbled, but followed her tall companion's example by sitting up and stretching. While Leandra went rummaging through her supplies, Ashley moved to the cold ashes in the fire pit, rubbing sleep from her eyes. In the back of her mind, however, she couldn't help but be curious about the way Leandra had ended their brief conversation.

Not much for girl-talk, huh, Jungle Jane? Why is that, when you're so open about everything else? Ashley grinned as she started building a small fire, wanting very much to read more into her friend's behavior than she thought was really there.

After breakfast, which consisted of wild-grain porridge and dried fruit, Leandra took a couple of leather pouches from her supplies and led the way out of the cave. She promised it was only a short hike around the mountain to the waterfall, though she cautioned that the way was difficult and sometimes treacherous. Trudging up a steep slope littered with loose shale, Ashley blew her bangs out of her eyes and readily accepted Leandra's hand when she offered it to help steady her balance. When the trail became too thickly overgrown with creeper vines and brambles, Leandra led the way forward on her hands and knees, encouraging a reluctant Ashley to follow. Ashley uttered a string of colorful curses after setting her hand down on a sharp thorn, wondering as she sucked her palm if it might be better to turn back.

When they reached their destination, however, she was glad she'd stuck with it.

At thirty feet high, the waterfall wasn't as large as some Ashley had seen, but the plunge over dozens of jutting rocks broke the curtain of water into a series of spectacular chains that sprayed iridescent rainbows into the air in all directions. The thundering cascade drove itself hard into a deep pool of clear, emerald water, which streamed lazily away to the south over ranks of boulders. Gigantic tree ferns and majestic palms swept their fronds out over the waters, smaller plants clinging precariously to the rock face of the fall itself, adding color to the mottled browns and greys of the stone. In the canopy above, a riot of brilliantly colored birds squawked and screeched, obviously nesting close to the abundant water supply.

Gazing at the breathtaking sight, Ashley found herself smiling. "It's beautiful."

Leandra looked pleased. "Yes, and it's very private too. Not many of the larger animals can get down here. They usually water either above or below the fall itself. See over there?" She pointed to a chunk of orange rock near the base of the precipice. "That's the stuff I use to mix my paint. Come, I'll show you."

For the next hour, Leandra showed her around the area, demonstrating how she crushed the soft rock into a powder, which she then mixed with animal fat from one of the pouches and water from the stream to create a thick, orange paste. Other rocks yielded white and brown shades, and the two of them mixed paint until Leandra judged she had sufficient quantities to cover her body. She laid the various wooden bowls on a convenient flat rock and reached for the laces of her top.

"You ready for a swim?"

"Sure... I guess." Ashley flushed deep crimson as Leandra casually slipped out of her garments and tossed them next to the paint-filled bowls, then leaned forward to grab a lump of raw soap from the other pouch. With her attraction growing stronger by the hour, it was impossible for Ashley to keep her eyes from wandering over Leandra's toned figure. She stared helplessly for a few seconds at the painted breasts before her gaze dropped lower, journeying over defined abdominal muscles to the thatch of dark hair that lay between those powerful thighs. When Leandra turned and waded out into the pool, Ashley was treated to a perfect view of firm buttocks and a slight swagger that nearly gave her palpitations. Her fingers toyed reluctantly with the hem of her own shirt, as she watched Leandra swim out to the center of the pool, a little envious of her companion's complete lack of abashment or self-consciousness.

She's not shy, I'll give her that. Ashley wished she had that kind of boldness and lack of inhibition. She didn't mind being naked outdoors when she was alone—traveling to remote locations instilled a certain degree of practicality in a person—but Ashley had never been one to go skinny-dipping with others. Deciding on a compromise that would let her maintain at least some sense of modesty, she stripped down to bra and panties and then waded out toward the middle of the chilly pool.

Leandra made no comment beyond a deliciously raised eyebrow in response to the undergarments. Ashley shrugged and blushed. "I didn't bring a suit," she explained diffidently.

Leandra laughed. "I didn't say anything." Diving under the water, she resurfaced next to Ashley and threw her wet and tangled hair back over her shoulder. "But you really don't need to be shy. I mean, it's just us here, right?"

"I know, but..."

Leandra grinned. "You have a nice body, Ashley. You're fit and healthy. You shouldn't be afraid to show that off."

"Hey, it's not like I'm a prude or anything," Ashley defended, wanting to poke her friend in the ribs but thinking better of it. Secretly though, she was flattered by Leandra's assessment. *She thinks I'm attractive! That's a good start.*

"Uh huh." Leandra's playful gaze dropped to where the water lapped at Ashley's cleavage. "No reason you should be," she said, and swam over to a shallower section of the pool, where she started scrubbing herself with the coarse lump of soap. A generous lather formed, coloring orange, then darkening to brown. As the dusty paint washed away into the pool, pale skin was revealed beneath.

Ashley was surprised by how pale Leandra was without the markings. *I guess it makes sense though,* she thought. *After all, the paint must keep her from being exposed to much sunlight.* Still, as Leandra ducked under the water and shook herself vigorously, Ashley couldn't help but find the change in her appearance somewhat curious.

Wet sapphire eyes blinked at her happily, and Leandra flashed a toothy grin as she swept her wild mane of dripping hair from her face. She stood in the shallow water, raising herself above the pool and spreading her arms in a simple display. "What do you think?"

Given permission, Ashley let her eyes wander everywhere. *Delicious!* was her first reaction, but she decided not to give so candid an opinion. "I kind of thought you'd be more tanned," she offered. "You know, to go with the dark hair and all."

Leandra inspected her arms. "That's what I get for being nocturnal, I guess."

"It's funny," Ashley observed. "When I first saw you, I thought you looked really weird. All the paint and the claws and the wild hair. But now, I don't even notice those things. To tell the truth, it's a little weirder seeing you like this."

"The woman beneath the paint, huh?" Leandra lowered herself back into the water once more and swam out into the deeper part of the pool where Ashley was. "It's all me though, regardless of how I look."

"I know." Ashley flashed a playful smirk, then swept her arm along the surface of the water, splashing her companion full in the face. Leandra growled menacingly, but Ashley laughed and repeated her action. Predatory blue eyes locked with mischievous brown for a split second, before both women started pushing water at one another, alternately laughing and cursing. Their voices were swallowed by the thunder of the fall and the cries of the birds that flitted about the treetops.

The two swam and played in the crystalline waters until they grew tired, then waded back to the shore. Ashley dried herself off with her shorts, but Leandra just shook herself like a dog, spraying droplets all over the place. Ashley giggled and raised an arm to ward off the deluge, grinning at her friend, who made no move to reach for her own clothes. Completely at ease with her nakedness, Leandra instead picked up the small bowl containing the orange paste. Stirring the contents with her fingertip, she began drawing a series of lines over her body in a ritual she'd obviously practiced hundreds of times before.

Ashley tugged her shirt on over her damp head, then sat on a rock and watched the process with fascination. Stamping down the desire to focus more heavily on Leandra's tempting breasts, she watched curiously as the jungle-woman slowly spread the paint over her sides, across her ribcage, back, and neck, and down her legs and arms. Switching to the pale white paint, Leandra then proceeded to fill in the exposed areas of her chest, under her arms, and finally along her inner thighs. With confident motions, she blurred the two tones until they merged correctly, giving her an accurate reproduction of a tiger's coloring. When she was satisfied with her work, she stood with arms spread away from her body, face turned to the sun overhead.

"I have to let the first coat dry before I add the stripes," she explained. "I do my face last, since it requires a little more patience and care."

Ashley was amazed at the overall effect. "Do you need any help?"

For a moment, she feared Leandra had caught her overeager tone, and Ashley held her breath a long moment until Leandra gave her a crooked, difficult-to-read smile and said, "Sure, if you'd like. You can do my back. You remember the design, right?"

Ashley nodded quickly, her eyes lighting up at the prospect of being allowed to run her hands over her friend's body without any guilt. When Leandra decided the chalky paint had dried sufficiently, she picked up the bowl that contained the chocolate brown paste and beckoned Ashley over. Cracks appeared in the smooth paint covering her body when she moved, and a few flakes chipped off, but the overall effect wasn't damaged.

As Ashley took the proffered bowl, Leandra pulled her tangled hair over her shoulder and presented her exposed back. Ashley swallowed hard and dipped a finger into the grainy paste, noticing several old scars that were faintly visible beneath the tawny orange paint. She realized after a moment that they were the marks of Shar-Tushar's claws. With infinite care, she drew a thick, tapering line along Leandra's lower ribcage. Encouraged by the approving grunt from her companion, she proceeded to fill in more stripes in a deliberate pattern until Leandra's back was correctly covered. Lost in her work, Ashley continued down until her finger was tracing tantalizingly close to Leandra's backside. When she received no comment or protest, she knelt on the ground and proceeded to apply stripes to the backs of the firm thighs and buttocks, her breath growing a little shallower as she committed every detail of the body before her to memory.

Leandra was standing very still, face tilted up to the sky with her eyes closed, as Ashley painted a tapering line along her upper thigh. Ashley was a little disappointed to note that she wasn't purring. She had completed half of Leandra's left leg before the tall woman moved to assist her. Soon, Leandra was covering her chest in chocolate brown stripes. They worked in silent concert until Leandra's body was properly decorated.

Standing on somewhat shaky legs, Ashley looked up into clear, sapphire eyes that seemed strangely darker than usual. Without a word, she reached for the other bowls and handed them to Leandra. When all that remained was her face, Leandra accommodatingly stepped onto a lower rock so they could stand eye-to-eye. Taking this as consent to continue, Ashley began to gently cover Leandra's features with the paint, carefully rubbing the fine, grainy paste across her friend's high cheekbones. Leandra showed her where to add the paler tones, and before long, Ashley was reaching for the third bowl, ready to paint the tiger mask pattern that had become so familiar to her these last few days.

There was, she considered, tracing fine lines around piercing eyes, something extremely erotic about the whole process of painting Leandra. It was so intimate, so physical. While she applied gently tapering short lines across the dark cheeks, Ashley was conscious of those intense eyes watching her, unblinking. She found her own eyes skipping constantly to Leandra's full lips, feeling the magnetic pull of this woman's allure draw her closer. She wanted to press her own lips against those that she traced with trembling fingers.

And then, before she quite realized it was happening, Ashley found herself fulfilling that desire.

Her eyes closed, and she moaned helplessly as she kissed Leandra with the lightest of touches. The smell of earth and water and musk filled her senses, and her hands drifted away, their task forgotten. For a timeless instant, Ashley lost herself in the sensation of heat against her lips. Then her eyes snapped open suddenly, and she withdrew, flustered and embarrassed.

Leandra's expression was one of surprise and uncertainty; her whole body was frozen, like a startled deer caught in the headlights of an oncoming car. Ashley felt a moment of pure panic lance through her, felt her heart leap into her throat as she realized what she'd done.

"Oh, God!" She clapped a hand over her mouth. "I'm sorry!" Ashley backed away from Leandra, wishing more than anything she could have these last few minutes back to do over again. But what was done was done, she knew, and the stunned look in Leandra's eyes brought cold fear, as Ashley realized that her momentary lapse into fantasy may have just destroyed their friendship. "I didn't mean to...I mean, I shouldn't have done..." Tears pricked at the corners of her eyes. She stood helplessly for several seconds by the water's edge, then turned and fled into the forest without another word.

"Ashley, wait!" Leandra's senses had been momentarily overwhelmed by the kiss which had stunned her into inaction. Now, she shook her head to clear it as she saw Ashley retreat. She started to give chase, then cursed and grabbed for her clothes. Struggling into them, fumbling to get the laces tied, Leandra cursed herself for freezing and for not responding to the kiss. Pushing her tangled hair back over her shoulders, she wondered how to rectify the situation.

She was unaccustomed to dealing with other people's feelings, and her first instinct was to retreat and hide…let this end now, before someone got hurt. But that was something she knew she would never do. In the short time they had known each other, Ashley had come to mean every bit as much to her as Shar-Ranjana; Leandra wasn't about to let her suffer just so she could avoid complicating her life. Taking a few deep breaths to calm herself, she considered her next course of action.

The first thing to do was go after Ashley and make it clear she had done nothing wrong. There was no point in Leandra keeping her feelings private any longer. Whatever had been developing between Ashley and herself during their time together, it went deeper than simple friendship. And based on that kiss, the attraction was certainly mutual. Beyond that, Leandra's plan got a little fuzzy. Letting this happen meant dealing with consequences she wasn't quite ready to think about.

She assumed Ashley would return to her friends at their camp. Fortunately, Leandra knew a shortcut. As she swept aside the brush concealing the overgrown path leading down the steepest part of the slope, she scolded herself wryly under her breath. "Just had to go and fall for the snoopy wildlife photographer, didn't you? Damn it, Ash, why'd you have to be so damn cute?"

Rushing through the jungle, heedless of the branches and vines that whipped at her face and tried to snag her clothes, Ashley felt hot tears burn down her cheeks. *I will not cry, I will not cry, I will not cry.* She repeated the mantra over and over, fighting the despair that made her want to curl into a ball and forget this day had ever happened. Despite those efforts, her eyes continued to stream tears and choking sobs pulled at her throat.

"Stupid, stupid, stupid." She mentally smacked herself with each word. "I'm such an *idiot*!" Just when Leandra had opened up, just as they'd started to share more and more, she'd gone and ruined everything by giving in to her baser desires. "She'll probably never want to talk to me again."

Lost in confusion and self-recrimination, Ashley didn't bother to hope that Leandra might be understanding, or that she might not care. All her thoughts were negative, tainted with the dark tones of depression and despair. The image of Leandra's shocked expression was burned into her memory, and in Ashley's despondent state of mind, quickly developed a fictional twist of distaste and withdrawal.

Without thinking, Ashley made her way down the gravelly, dangerous slope, not caring when she slipped and cut her ankle on a sharp fragment of shale. Tears still blurring her vision, she made it to the base of the mountain and walked as quickly as she could in the direction of her own camp. Right now, all she wanted to do was retreat to her tent, lie down, and tell herself repeatedly how foolish her attraction to Leandra had been.

It was a long way back to the campsite, and in her cloud of dejection, the distance seemed to grow longer. When at last she reached the circle of tents and the small, dead, cooking fire, Ashley was relieved to find that Grady and the others were nowhere in sight. She really didn't feel like dealing with any lectures about how irresponsible it had been to stay with Leandra last night. Snuffling miserably, feeling sticky and dirty even though she'd just bathed, Ashley flung back the flap that led into her tent and stepped inside.

She came to a stunned stop when she was greeted by a familiar pair of sapphire eyes.

There was no point in running away again. She was too damn tired, anyway. She felt ashamed and drained, and shuffled a little, unable to hold Leandra's gaze for more than a moment.

"It's not fair that you can do that," she said, irrationally annoyed at the tall woman's speed.

Leandra stepped closer, and Ashley backed up a pace. "Ashley, we need to talk—"

"No!" Ashley cut her off. "Please, Leandra, I feel stupid enough as it is. Can't you just leave me alone? I'm sorry, all right? I got carried away, and I shouldn't have. You obviously didn't like it, so there's nothing more to talk ab—mmph!"

Leandra's lips silenced her, descending with passion and force. Ashley resisted for a brief moment, but her legs gave out when Leandra's tongue deftly invaded her mouth and played seductively against her own. Firm hands ran from her neck down her back before gripping her butt and pulling her into a fierce embrace. Completely overwhelmed by the sensual assault, Ashley offered no protest, beyond a throaty moan when she felt Leandra's breasts push against her.

The ardent kiss lasted several seconds, but there was no mistaking the tightly coiled passion behind it...a passion which mirrored the emotions stirring within her. When at last the taller woman pulled away, flushed and breathless, it took Ashley several moments to shake herself back to awareness. Leandra's hands, still gripping her butt, held their lower bodies tightly together.

"You took me by surprise," Leandra whispered huskily. "I'm sorry I didn't have time to respond, but I'm not going to let you think for a moment that I didn't want you to do that. Or that I didn't enjoy it very much."

Ashley nearly swooned. "You really mean that?" she asked uncertainly. "You're not just saying it to make me feel better?"

Those stunning eyes grew hooded, darkening with passion. "You need more convincing?"

Leandra's lips descended again, removing any doubt that might have lingered, leaving Ashley gasping. When Leandra withdrew this time, Ashley looked up into her eyes and tried to refocus her shattered senses. "I think we've both got a lot of thinking to do," Leandra whispered, removing her hands from Ashley's backside with a noticeable air of reluctance. "I'll give you some time, okay?"

Dazed, Ashley nodded. "Uh huh."

"Come find me tomorrow. We'll talk then." Leandra placed a last, almost chaste kiss on Ashley's cheek, her eyes promising more, and slowly backed out of the tent.

Ashley watched the tall, striped figure as she disappeared into the jungle. As she turned back to the tent, a slow, incredulous grin worked its way across her mouth. She pumped a fist in the air. "Yesss!"

Despair forgotten, she threw herself down on her sleeping bag and closed her eyes. Thinking could wait, she decided. For now, she wanted to relive the memory of that amazing kiss and dream of what else might be in store for her.

CHAPTER 4

What the hammer? what the chain?
In what furnace was thy brain?
What the anvil? what dread grasp
Dare its deadly terrors clasp?

—"The Tyger" by William Blake

FOR THE REST OF THAT morning, Ashley lay in her tent, eyes closed, smiling dreamily at nothing in particular. From time to time, she would take a deep breath and catch the scent of earth and musk that still lingered in the air, even after Leandra had departed, and she would flush at the memory of her searing kiss. Ashley wondered idly where Grady and the others had gotten to, but she felt no urge to go looking for them. Right now, she was happy to let her thoughts drift lazily and bask in the knowledge that her attraction to Leandra was fully reciprocated.

Of course, now there were about a thousand and one new complications she would have to deal with, sooner or later—complications far beyond those of a typical romantic relationship. A part of Ashley's mind wanted to address these problems right away, but for the time being, she focused on the warm tingles that still traced around her lips. There would be time enough to discuss practical realities with Leandra, and time enough to figure out what this all meant and where they might go from here. Judging from the ardor of their kiss, Leandra was interested in taking this attraction a whole lot further. Ashley smiled. *And that's just fine with me.*

It was late afternoon by the time Grady and the others returned to camp. Ashley was startled out of her dreamy state when she heard their voices approaching. She knew her partner would probably be pissed at her for spending the night out with Leandra, but it took several seconds for her to shift mental gears. Frankly, she wasn't in the mood to deal with Grady. She just wanted to rest and remember every detail of her morning with the enchanting tiger-woman.

When she heard her name being called and the sound of footsteps nearing the tent, she sighed and gave a mental shrug. It was time to do some explaining.

"Ash? Are you in there?"

"Yeah, Grady." She got up and opened the tent flap, stepping out into the sun's last rays and facing her partner with a neutral expression. "Something you wanted?"

Grady visibly collected himself, obviously realizing that blowing his stack wasn't going to get him anywhere.

Folding his arms across his chest, he said in a carefully moderated tone, "I just wanted to make sure you were okay. You didn't come back last night."

"Yeah, I stayed out with Leandra. She hurt herself, and I didn't want to leave her alone out there."

"Oh." A pause. "Is she all right?"

A faint smile curled the corners of Ashley's lips. "She's fine. Thank you for asking."

Grady returned the smile a little more fully. Glancing down, he pointed to Ashley's ankle. "What happened there?"

"Huh?" Ashley looked down and noticed that the cut on her ankle had bled freely. "Oh, I kind of tripped on some loose stones coming back here, that's all. I hadn't even noticed it."

"Yeah, well, a cut like that could turn septic if you don't treat it properly, especially out here."

"I know. I'll take care of it." Ashley studied Grady a moment in silence before she said, "Listen, I'm sorry about running off like that and not telling you. It's just that Leandra wanted to show me something secret, and it couldn't wait until dawn."

"I figured it was something like that," Grady said.

"I wanted to wake you up, but she didn't want you trying to follow or anything. Given your recent behavior, I think her concern was justified."

"Uh huh." Grady pursed his lips. "Well, I hope whatever it was she wanted to show you was worth the worry you cost me."

Ashley grinned and looked down for a second, remembering her wonderful encounter with Shar-Ranjana. "It was, believe me."

"Are you going out with her again tomorrow?"

Only with an effort did Ashley avoid blushing at the thought of what tomorrow might bring, but she managed a fairly indifferent nod. "I guess so."

Grady grunted softly. "Be careful, huh? I don't want to be explaining to the boss-man why I let you get yourself killed out here. He likes you a whole lot more than he likes me, and I doubt he'll take kindly to learning I didn't at least try to keep you safe."

"Okay."

"And make sure you get some disinfectant on that cut. You don't want lockjaw or gangrene or anything like that."

"I will." Ashley hesitated a moment, then stood on tiptoes to drop a soft kiss on Grady's stubble-covered cheek. She grinned at the raised eyebrow she got in return. "Thank you for caring."

"Hey," Grady said, and laid his palm over his heart, "if I don't look after you, who will?"

Ashley mock-punched him, but chuckled. "Give me a minute to get this scratch cleaned up, and I'll give you a hand with dinner."

"Sure."

Ashley went back into the tent as Grady returned to the others, who were waiting by the dead campfire. Sitting on her sleeping bag, she rummaged around in her backpack until her fingers located the compact but well-stocked first-aid kit. She cleaned the small cut on her ankle gently with a cotton swab, and then applied a healthy coating of disinfectant. After covering the entire wound with an adhesive bandage, she joined her friends outside, nodding to a glowering Tarun and receiving curious expressions of interest from Grace and Simon.

Grady and Tarun had put together a basic dinner of stewed meat and vegetables, and though it wasn't all that dissimilar to what she'd eaten last night, the meal couldn't help but taste a little bland without Leandra to share it with.

Simon made polite inquiries about talking to Leandra regarding help finding more tigers, but Ashley's evasive responses were enough to tell him not to get his hopes up. It seemed the two scientists were having a rather disappointing time of it. Their efforts to monitor the tiger population were yielding only minimal success. Still, Ashley knew she could never talk about Shar-Ranjana, no matter how much it would mean to Simon and his assistant. She recognized a sacred trust when she saw it.

Even as she listened to the conversations of her friends, Ashley's mind was still preoccupied by the earlier events of that day. For the most part, she was content to sit silently in the flickering light of the fire, smiling a quiet, wondering smile and shivering a little at the remembered passion of Leandra's embrace.

When everyone had finished their dinner, Ashley offered her services as dishwasher and, with help from Grace, took the small pile of plates and cutlery over to the bucket of water near the perimeter of the camp. She noticed that Grace was watching her with a curious, slightly amused expression.

Even as they worked, Ashley continued noticing her companion's occasional glances, and wondered at the cause. Drying the dishes with a rag, Grace finally raised a curious eyebrow and said, "Ashley?"

"Hmm?"

Grace paused. "I don't want you to think I'm being nosy or anything, and I know we don't really know one another that well, but..."

"No, that's okay. What's on your mind?"

"I just wanted to make sure everything was okay with you. I mean, with you and Leandra."

Ashley sat up a little straighter. "Okay? What do you mean? Why wouldn't it be?"

Grace hesitated again, clearly not wanting to overstep her boundaries. "Well, you've just been really distracted all afternoon, and you've been wearing that goofy smile since you got back." She shrugged and glanced away. "Plus, I saw the handprints on your butt. It doesn't take much guesswork to figure out who put them there."

Ashley felt the blood rush to her face, and quickly twisted around so she could see the back of her shorts. Sure enough, the marks where Leandra had gripped her and pulled her into their embrace were embarrassingly obvious. "I...We didn't do—"

Grace immediately held up her hand. "I'm not judging you or anything like that," she said quickly. "You're a big girl, Ashley, and it's none of my business. I just wanted to make sure you're not being forced into anything, that's all."

Ashley regarded the other woman carefully a moment, but found only genuine concern in her open face. She smiled. "I appreciate that, Grace. Really, I do. But I can assure you, Leandra isn't forcing me into anything at all."

"I didn't really think she was, but I think it's always best to check. You know, just to be safe."

"Thank you. I appreciate that." Ashley nodded toward the campfire, where the three men were talking and laughing. "You think they noticed?"

"I doubt it."

"Good." Ashley didn't think that Grady would be thrilled to hear about her more personal interest in the tiger-woman. "You won't tell them, will you?"

"Of course not. It's none of their business, either." Grace reached for another dish and wiped it with the rag. "You and Leandra have been spending a lot of time together. I guess you've gotten to know her pretty well, huh?"

"Yeah, I have." Ashley finished washing the last plate and handed it to her companion, but made no move to return to the campfire. It actually felt good to talk about Leandra with someone else, to express her thoughts to another person who wouldn't be judgmental. Growing up, Ashley had always appreciated having a sister around to share things with, and she missed that camaraderie whenever her work took her overseas. This whole experience with Leandra was very new, and her thoughts were running helter-skelter through her head in an exciting, confused jumble. Although she'd known Grace only a short while, she rather liked the quiet, introspective zoologist, and decided a little girl-talk wouldn't hurt. "It's surprising, really," she said softly. "Leandra's not the sort of woman I ever pictured myself being attracted to."

Grace finished drying the plates and gave Ashley her full attention. "I can imagine."

"But she's gentle and caring, and I feel so safe when I'm with her." Ashley blew her feathered bangs from her eyes. "All she has to do is look at me sometimes, and my legs go all rubbery. It's stupid to get involved with her, I know, but at this point I'm finding it hard to care."

"Is this the first time you've been attracted to another woman?" Grace asked.

"Attracted, no. But it's the first time I've ever acted on it." Ashley smiled sheepishly. "Believe it or not, I'm not really good at this sort of thing. My relationships tend to run cold pretty quick." She looked off into the jungle, her eyes dreamy. "But it's not like that with Leandra. We went for a swim this morning, and one thing kind of led to another. One minute I was thinking about kissing her...and then POW! I was."

Grace smiled. "It sounds pretty intense."

"It is. Everything about Leandra is intense. And I want more time with her. I need time to give these feelings the chance they deserve." Ashley sighed. "I don't know what I'll do when we have to leave. I'm trying not to think too much about it right now."

Grace gave her a pat of consolation. "She sounds very special to you. To hear Grady talk about her, you'd think she was the devil incarnate or something."

Ashley laughed shortly. "Well, she has a pretty savage side to her personality, too. Living out here as a predator for so long, I guess that's understandable." Her eyes took on a conspiratorial glint. "But to tell the truth, I think that's part of what I find so attractive about her. She's so *animal*, so unrestrained and primal. It's not something I thought I liked, but in Leandra, I think it's sexy as hell."

Grace smirked. "And from the position of those handprints, I'd say she thinks the same about you."

A crimson flush spread over Ashley's face as she nodded. "Seems that way, yeah." She picked up the clean dishes and cutlery and cradled them in her arms. "I guess we'll be talking more about it when I see her tomorrow, but right now, I just want to enjoy this feeling without thinking about the complications." A sudden gust of wind and a distant clap of thunder interrupted her, heralding the coming of a storm, and the two women exchanged glances.

"I hope things work out," Grace said.

Ashley nodded. "Me, too." She gave the other woman a sincere smile. "And thanks for lending a friendly ear."

"Hey, I know what it's like working in a male-dominated environment," Grace said. "Sometimes it's nice to have another woman around to talk with."

A flash of lightning illuminated the distant mountains, and a call from Grady got the two women moving back to the ring of tents. Depositing the dishes inside a small knapsack, Ashley said her good-nights and retreated to her tent just as fat drops of rain began falling from the sky.

Rain pelted down from grey, heavy clouds, drenching the jungle and carving small, muddy rivers through the undergrowth. The night was dark, moon and stars alike hidden by the obstructing clouds. The heat remained, turning Leandra's cave into something more like a sauna than a home. She looked out over the dim landscape from the mouth of the cave, her eyes taking in her hunting grounds with quiet satisfaction.

This was the perfect time to hunt, Leandra knew. The rain was an effective dampener of both sound and scent, and many animals would be sheltering under trees, not as alert for potential predators in the impenetrable dark. But Leandra didn't feel like hunting tonight. The memory of Ashley's hands as they traced striped patterns over her flesh still burned in her mind. The heat of Ashley's lips…the taste of her tongue…

Leandra hugged herself in the darkness. No. There would be no hunting this night.

She kissed me.

She kissed *me*!

Leandra hadn't anticipated this development; hadn't hoped to dream that her attraction to the younger woman might be reciprocated. She certainly hadn't counted on Ashley making the first move. But she had, and now things were changed forever.

New and wonderful feelings overwhelmed Leandra's senses, thoughts and emotions she'd not experienced in many years, if at all. For four years, this jungle had been both her home and her prison. She had struggled against it, had loved and hated it, and in the end, had come to learn a great deal about herself. The jungle was a harsh instructor, and her lessons had often been painful. But now, for the first time in those four years, Leandra found herself able to look beyond the endless ocean of grasslands and forests, and see again the world she'd left behind.

For the first time in those four years, she saw a future that did not involve this savage world of predator and prey.

A future that involved Ashley.

"Ashley." Leandra whispered the name, shivering at the way the simple word affected her. Painted fingers rose to trace painted lips, recalling the kiss and wanting desperately to relive it. Leandra wondered what Ashley was thinking about right now. How did she feel about all this? Her desires were obvious from the way she'd responded. But Leandra had never cared for anyone the way she cared now for the petite blonde. Always before, she had pursued, conquered, and then abandoned her lovers. She didn't want something so transient and insubstantial with Ashley. She wanted a relationship. Something that could comfort her and embrace her, could heal the old wounds that still pained her. Leandra was entering a new world, and a part of her felt as naked and vulnerable as when she'd first returned here after her encounter with Shar-Tushar.

Watching the rain fall, sniffing air thick with moisture and the scent of wet rebirth, Leandra sat silently and waited for the morrow. Things would be clearer in the light, and she could see Ashley once more.

Somehow, this was right. As strong as her fears were, these new desires and emotions were stronger still. And when all was said and done, Leandra knew she had no choice but to put her faith in them, and in the woman who was at the heart of their creation.

After a pleasantly restless sleep, Ashley woke bright and early the next morning to find the day dawning humid and misty after the passage of the storm last night. The campsite was a muddy quagmire, with pools of water settling into shallow depressions everywhere. The jungle dripped and flowed. Ashley, too, was damp with sweat, but nothing could dispel the good spirits that infected her. When her companions emerged grumpily from their tents, they found that Ashley had already coaxed a small campfire to life from the few pieces of dry wood that had escaped the rain. She had also boiled water for coffee and prepared a simple but sustaining breakfast from their dwindling supplies. But with her anticipation of the coming day running feverishly high, there was barely time for the group to offer their thanks before she said her good-byes and headed toward the river, eager to meet with Leandra.

Wandering along the water's edge, she looked around for the tiger-woman but found no sign of her. After half an hour, she was starting to worry that Leandra might not show. But when she reached the small waterfall that she'd explored that first day in the jungle, Ashley's concerns flew away as she spied the familiar striped figure sitting cat-like on a rocky overhang, head bent slightly into the breeze. Her lips spread helplessly into a smile as she approached, and Leandra sensed her presence and turned to face her.

"Hey." Ashley almost bounced her way forward, grinning like an idiot at the smile Leandra graced her with. She came to a stop a few feet from her tall friend, not quite knowing how to greet her after their kiss and feeling a little awkward. Gnawing her lower lip, she shuffled uncertainly, trying to think of something charming to say. "Some storm last night, huh?"

Leandra stepped forward and pulled her into a possessive embrace. Ducking her head, she quickly claimed sweet lips with a hungry kiss, dueling slowly with a soft tongue when Ashley parted her lips and invited her in.

After several seconds of seductive exploration, Leandra broke the kiss and looked down at her. Ashley licked her lips and grinned, pleasantly surprised. "What was that for?"

Leandra shrugged. "You looked like that was the kind of 'good morning' you were hoping for, but weren't certain you were going to get," she explained, running her hands down the crease of the smaller woman's back. "You never have to worry about that, Ashley. I'll never stop wanting to kiss you like that."

Ashley's smile grew so wide it nearly swallowed her ears. "Really?"

"Really," Leandra promised, sealing her words with another long kiss.

Ashley wrapped her arms around Leandra and laid her head on her breast. Feeling the solid, powerful body against her own felt so right, so perfect. However, she knew there were issues that needed addressing before they could continue. "I guess we should talk, huh?"

Leandra's fingers were teasing the soft hairs at the nape of her neck, and when they withdrew a sigh of disappointment almost slipped past Ashley's lips.

"Yeah, we probably should." Taking her by the hand, Leandra led Ashley to the edge of the overhang and helped her settle on a dry rock. Sitting beside her, Leandra offered a nervous smile. "This is kind of awkward, isn't it?"

Ashley nodded. "Yeah, it is." She took a deep breath. "I was up half the night, listening to the storm and thinking about you. About how much you've come to mean to me."

Leandra squeezed Ashley's hand gently. "You mean a lot to me, too."

"I think I made a list of about a hundred different reasons why this is stupid," Ashley admitted. "I know we should just put a stop to it before it goes any further, before we both get hurt." She saw a guarded, fearful expression wash over Leandra's expressive face.

"But I don't care about any of that," she continued. "I really like you, Leandra. More than I can remember liking anyone in my whole life. I don't want to run away from this because it seems like a bad idea, or because it seems too risky. This is all kind of new for me, and I don't really know what your thoughts are, but—"

"I want to keep going," Leandra interrupted, almost desperately. Mahogany eyes caught and held Ashley in a powerful spell, and she swallowed hard. Leandra continued, "I've never met anyone like you, Ashley. I've never felt anything like how I feel around you. It's pretty new for me, too, but I don't want to stop."

"I should warn you now," Ashley said. "I've got a terrible track record with relationships. They never seem to last more than a month or two."

Leandra grinned. "That's okay. I've never really had a relationship. Not one that lasted longer than the next morning, at least."

Ashley glanced away shyly. "I've never actually..." She paused. "With a woman, I mean."

Cobalt eyes widened for a heartbeat, but Leandra's grip on her hand didn't falter. "Are you okay about this then?" she asked softly. "I mean, that I'm a woman?"

Ashley looked up. "Of course. I've always known I've had a level of interest there, I just didn't expect it to happen quite like this, that's all." She hesitated. "I take it you've been with other women before."

"Yes," Leandra said. "It always felt better for me, more comfortable... although if I'm being honest with you, none of my past relationships ever really extended beyond what we shared in bed. But I want you to understand, that's not what this is," she continued in an earnest and deliberate tone.

"I'm not taking this lightly, Ashley. You're not just some casual plaything for me. I don't want to treat you the way I've treated others in my life. I care too much for you."

Tears pricked the corners of Ashley's eyes at the sincerity in Leandra's words. "I feel the same way."

They both knew there was more to be said, but neither wanted to broach the subject of Ashley's rapidly approaching departure, nor the matter of Leandra's unorthodox lifestyle. It was enough, for now, that they were together and committed to pursuing whatever bond was drawing them closer.

"So..." Ashley raised an eyebrow. "Where do we go from here?"

"Where would you like to go?"

"Well..." Ashley blushed and glanced away to the river. "I thought the kissing was a really good place to start."

Leandra's eyes danced playfully. "Did you, now?"

"Uh huh." Ashley leaned forward, tilting her head to the side and accepting her companion's lips with a happy little mew of pleasure. Strong arms wound their way around her body, and she quickly responded in kind, shuddering at the sensation of Leandra's heated body pressing so close against her own. Future concerns were set aside without hesitation, and in some remote part of her brain, Ashley realized one of the simple truths about this primal world that had been Leandra's home for so long.

In the jungle, life was only ever a single moment. And if that moment was right, nothing else mattered.

They spent the day in pleasant companionship, neither of them caring about the showers that rained down from time to time or the steamy heat that left sweat beaded on their bodies. Leandra took Ashley out to a remote area and, from the safety of the branches of a towering tree, showed her where a young male leopard made his home. Ashley smiled with delight at every new secret she was shown, and with their relationship growing more personal now, Leandra was only too happy to share every wonder she had discovered throughout the park.

Their day was interspersed with frequent caresses and kisses, and by the time the sun was coloring the edges of the horizon with painted hues of purple and crimson, Leandra couldn't help but chuckle at the telltale streaks of orange and white paint covering Ashley's face.

Only when dusk had given over to dark did they part. With familiar ease, Leandra led the way back to the outskirts of Ashley's camp, then stood uncertainly beside her.

"You could always stay the night with me, you know," she suggested in a throaty, hopeful whisper.

Ashley traced her fingers down the length of Leandra's jaw, and Leandra leaned into the touch eagerly. "I'd like that," Ashley said earnestly. "But I should really stay here. I know Grady worries about me, and I've barely spent any time with the others lately." She sucked in a deep breath. "As tempting as the alternatives are, and believe me—" her voice deepened and her eyes darkened "—I'm finding them very tempting right now, I have to put in a little work time."

Leandra lowered her head in acceptance. "I understand." Standing on tiptoes, Ashley gave the striped woman a final kiss, then accepted a little help cleaning the marks from her face. "I'll see you tomorrow, okay?"

"Okay."

They parted with many backward glances from Ashley, and even after she was out of sight, Leandra stood staring after her for many long moments. A part of her wanted desperately to follow. Sighing, she circled the camp instead and climbed stealthily into one of the giant trees just outside the perimeter, where she settled down on a comfortable limb. From her perch, Leandra watched Ashley join her companions for dinner. A slight, longing smile curved her lips. She continued to watch from the tree, thinking about how her life was changing, until the moon hung high in the night sky. Then, knowing she would need sleep for the day ahead, she leapt silently to the ground and returned to her cave, recognizing for the first time in a long while just how lonely her home seemed.

Even before the sun rose the next morning, Ashley was awake in her bedroll, urging the dawn on anxiously from the warm darkness of her tent. Deciding it was never going to move quickly enough for her liking, she shuffled out of her sleeping bag and ventured outside. Again, she prepared a campfire and sipped a steaming cup of coffee while eating the leftovers from last night that she scrounged from the food knapsack. She greeted her companions cheerfully, then left before they could try convincing her to spend the day in the hide with them. Wandering down along the river, she kept her every pore open and alert for Leandra's presence.

So focused were her thoughts on the enigmatic jungle-woman that when a large hand grabbed her from behind, clamped firmly over her mouth, and pulled her back against a muscular body, Ashley didn't struggle at first, figuring Leandra had surprised her. But when she heard the jangle of steel against leather and caught the scent of unfamiliar sweat, her eyes widened. Something cold and sharp pressed against her throat, and stale-smelling breath tickled the fine hairs behind her ears.

"Just behave yourself, girly," a voice muttered, "and I might let you live through this."

The poacher!

The momentary shock vanished, replaced instantly with anger. Ashley was small and lightweight, but she was far from weak. She didn't give in easily. Going limp in her captor's arms, she pretended to be paralyzed with fear. The man cursed under his breath and shifted his footing to better support her, which forced him to relax the pressure on the knife he held to her throat. As soon as she felt the steel edge waver, she lifted her right foot and drove it with all her strength down and into the man's unprotected shin. The poacher grunted in pain and loosened his hold.

Ashley capitalized instantly. Twisting slightly, she slammed an elbow into his side. She was about to go for the groin—a strike that might have ensured her escape—but he recovered too quickly. With a hard pull on her body, he spun her around and then landed a dizzying backhand across her face. Ashley's vision went white, and stars flashed before her eyes. She doubled over when a fist punched her in the stomach and knocked the breath from her lungs.

The poacher grabbed her again, and his knife dug painfully into her throat in a silent, but clear threat. "Feisty little thing, ain't you?" he grunted. "But I'll let that one go. Any more though, and that tiger-freak bitch will be following a blood trail to your body. Understand?"

Ashley gasped for air. Her face felt numb from the blow, but she managed a weak nod.

"Good." Her captor dragged the knife down her body to the edge of her tank top. Ashley tensed as the cool steel edge traced down her belly. She struggled not to flex away from the touch, but the man didn't cut her. Instead, he swiftly sliced a thin strip from the material. Holding up the scrap, he nodded, pleased.

"What do you want with me?" Ashley asked. "My friends will know I'm gone. They'll call the rangers."

"Maybe." He began walking Ashley into the jungle. "But those idiots couldn't find me if they tried. And right now, I'm only interested in one particular friend of yours. I think she'll be pretty desperate to get you back, too."

Ashley tensed. "You mean—"

"That's right. That tiger-freak has been making a nuisance of herself for way too long. It's time she was put down. Permanently."

Ashley snorted in defiance. "What makes you think you can take her? She's been hunting poachers like you for years."

"True." The man tangled his fingers in Ashley's hair and pulled it sharply, wrenching an involuntary cry from her. "But I have the advantage now." He leaned closer, and Ashley recoiled in disgust.

"We're going cat-hunting," he whispered, "and I have a feeling you're the perfect little mouse to use for bait."

Tightening his grip on her hair, he pushed Ashley in front of him and forced their way deeper into the jungle. Wincing in pain, Ashley whispered a silent prayer to any deities who cared to listen, asking them to keep Leandra safe.

Leandra grew concerned after waiting for Ashley by the river in vain for almost an hour. Confused, she stealthily made her way to her friend's camp, thinking perhaps she had been delayed by her companions, but there was no sign of trouble or concern among the others. A feeling of disquiet ran like a chill up her spine. Something was wrong.

Returning to the river, she searched the ground for tracks, and found them fresh and clear in the mud left by the recent rainfall. Her eyes widened when she found a second set of footprints, made by heavy army boots, large enough to fit a man. Leandra lifted her head and sniffed. The air still carried the scent of sweat and steel.

She followed the tracks swiftly, her entire posture and demeanor switching instantly to that of the jungle predator as she slipped through the shadows. It took her only a few moments to find further evidence that something terrible had happened. Pinned to the trunk of a tree by a slender hunting dagger was a torn scrap of cloth. Snatching the material down, Leandra brought it to her nose and breathed in Ashley's familiar scent. A low rumble sounded deep in Leandra's chest as she realized what had happened.

Bait.

The poacher had discerned a weakness and was now intent on exploiting it by using Ashley to lure her into the open.

For a moment, pure rage filled her senses, making her want to just charge in and slash to pieces the man who had dared to threaten Ashley. But Leandra hadn't survived so long out here without learning the merits of restraint. She took a calming breath and focused her energy into a tight, controlled ball, thinking carefully how best to execute an effective rescue. Tigers hunted their prey with stealth and cunning. If they charged too soon, their quarry would bolt; too late, and they might miss their opportunity. Leandra had spent years watching and learning from the great jungle cats. They had taught her control—and infinite patience.

The two sets of tracks were easy to follow. Leandra moved cautiously, not wanting to stumble into an ambush and ruin any chance of rescuing Ashley. When the trail turned back toward the river, it became clear what her adversary was thinking. As the trees thinned and gave way to the stony ground that preceded the water's edge, Leandra saw she had judged correctly. Crouching down in the shadows, her body held tense against the soaked earth, she studied the man standing a hundred feet away on the same rocky outcropping she herself had sat by just yesterday.

The man stood, alert and watchful, his rifle held in the crook of his arm and ready to use. His other hand was wrapped tightly in Ashley's blonde hair, and from the wince that pulled at her pretty face now and again, it was clear to Leandra that he wasn't being gentle. The poacher held Ashley at arm's length, facing the edge of the precipice. His intent was easily deduced.

If Leandra attempted any kind of frontal assault, he had only to give Ashley a quick shove and she would fall into the rocky waters below.

Leandra assessed the situation swiftly, studying the surrounding jungle to determine how she might use the natural environment to her advantage. She had already rejected a direct confrontation. The ground between her and the man was open, completely bereft of any kind of cover. He would have all the time in the world to take aim with his rifle and shoot her down, no matter how swiftly she ran or how well she dodged. Stealth would avail her little, which was obviously why he had chosen this place. Undeterred, she shifted her attention to the precipice itself, smiling as a plan formed in her mind.

The edge of the drop was sheer, but below, the jungle encroached right down to the water's edge. Leandra moved wraithlike along the edge of the tree line, circling her quarry's position until she had worked her way to the base of the cliff. Looking up, she was pleased to see that the rock wall before her provided numerous cracks and outcroppings that would make acceptable handholds. The poacher was paying no attention to what lay behind him, obviously dismissing the cliff as unclimbable. Leandra realized this was another reason he had chosen this particular location. He thought to force a frontal assault by reducing the range of directions from which she could attack.

Leandra's smile became a feral grin; he was underestimating her abilities again, and she intended to take advantage of that mistake.

Slowly, wary of any sound or scent that might signal she'd been mistaken in her assumptions, Leandra crept from the jungle cover and slipped into the knee-deep waters. The hiss of the nearby waterfall effectively masked any noise, and after tucking the claws into the hem of her skirt, she reached for the first handhold. Tugging a few times to ensure the rock wasn't loose, she hoisted herself upwards, testing for and finding a solid foothold before reaching for another grip, higher up.

The climb was difficult, but not nearly as impossible as the poacher apparently had assumed. Leandra's fingers were toughened from years of constant struggle against her environment, but they were aching by the time she neared the top of the precipice. Thick vines twisted across the rock face here and there, at times providing a helpful grip, but more often proving an obstacle to her ascent. Spray from the fall made sections of the rock slippery with green moss, forcing a more difficult hunt to find purchase. Still, Leandra kept her mind focused on the task at hand, determined not to let Ashley be harmed.

When she drew closer to the top of the precipice, she could make out words from above, and she smiled when she heard the angry tone of her friend. Leandra finally gained the lip of the cliff and secured solid footholds which would enable her to spring quickly up and onto level ground. Holding herself as close to the sheer rock wall as possible, she waited, listening for the perfect moment to strike.

At the top of the cliff above the river, unaware of the striped figure steadily drawing nearer, Ashley glared at the man pulling her hair. "You're a dead man, you know," she said coldly. "I've seen what she does to guys like you. It's not pretty."

The poacher gave her hair an extra twist. "I respect her abilities, girly, and I'm not taking any chances this time." He surveyed the broad stretch of open rock that lay before them, barren and devoid of shelter. "If she wants you back, she'll have to give herself up sooner or later."

Ashley snorted derisively and pulled at the hand that gripped her—not because she hoped to escape, just to demonstrate her defiance. She was conscious of the drop behind her, already having judged her chances of surviving a fall as about fifty-fifty. If she hit a submerged rock, it was all over, but if she was lucky enough to land in a deeper patch of water, she'd almost certainly be okay. Still, she wasn't too keen on testing the odds just yet. "What makes you think she'll care that you've got me?"

"I saw the way she reacted the last time you were in danger," he said, glancing at her smugly. "She dropped everything and ran to protect you. I've seen hunting dogs do that to protect their masters. It's the same thing. She's got an animal's loyalty, and I'm gonna use it to put her down."

Ashley couldn't help but smile inwardly at that assessment, knowing it to be true. *She will protect me, she thought. Just like when Grady grabbed me. She'll save me even it means risking her own life to do it.*

"Why?" she demanded out loud. "What do you care about her? Why not just leave her alone?"

Again, he eyed her smugly. "I think you know why. It's the same reason you're out here in this godforsaken jungle." He glanced pointedly to the camera still strapped about Ashley's neck. "White gold. We're both here to shoot it, just in slightly different ways." He leaned closer, his breath hot against her cheek. "Believe it or not, we're a lot alike, you and I. The only difference is, you carry a camera and I carry a gun."

"We're nothing alike!" Ashley spat. "And you can forget about the white tiger. It doesn't exist."

"What?"

Ashley smirked triumphantly, pleased at the sudden change in her captor's attitude. "That's right. It's just some bullshit rumor. A tourist got a look at Leandra and thought she was a white tiger." She laughed at his angry surprise, not caring that his hand gripped tighter at her hair. If she was going to die, the least she could do was protect Shar-Ranjana. "Even if you kill Leandra, you'll be walking out of here empty-handed, and probably with every ranger in the park hot on your trail."

The poacher glared at her furiously for a long moment, weighing her words, and she was elated to see the plain frustration written all over his face. But then his frustration dissolved as he latched onto something more interesting. "Leandra? That's her name, is it? Leandra?"

Ashley's smile faltered uncertainly, and she wished she hadn't let that slip. For some reason, just sharing Leandra's name with this man seemed like a betrayal of trust. Her lips tightened stubbornly, but her captor yanked hard on her hair, his eyes threatening worse. Ashley gasped in pain, clawing futilely at the hand that gripped her. "Yes."

"Leandra?" The poacher looked toward the jungle, his eyes lost in thought. "Leandra Thornton?"

Before Ashley even had time to think about refusing to answer, a striped form leapt from out of nowhere and crouched for a split second at the very edge of the precipice. The poacher sensed the movement and swung around, bringing his rifle to bear. Ashley gave a startled cry—half joyous, half afraid—as Leandra darted forward with the speed of a striking cobra and grabbed for the barrel of the gun, yanking it skyward. There was another blur of movement as she lashed out with her free hand, and Ashley heard a grunt of pain from the poacher as his weapon flew over the cliff. At almost precisely the same instant, Leandra twisted to the side and landed a vicious kick to her adversary's ribcage, and his grip on Ashley's hair loosened. Before she knew it, Leandra had pulled Ashley protectively behind her and out of harm's way.

The man recovered quickly, however, pulling a second knife from a sheath and brandishing it. He couldn't see when Leandra's hands disappeared behind her back, reappearing a second later gripping her claws. With her hands clenched into fists, the bone claws extended between her fingers, their edges rough but wickedly sharp.

Knowing she would likely be more of a distraction than an aid in this fight, Ashley retreated a few paces from the edge of the precipice, as Leandra squared off against her opponent. She stayed close, however, ready to jump in if an opportunity presented itself.

Leandra studied the man before her more carefully. "You know who I am, huh?" She smirked. "I thought most people would have forgotten by now."

"Not likely," the man returned. "I used to hear stories about you all the time. In fact, there was a time I was actually looking forward to meeting you. But then you went and pulled a Houdini, disappearing off the face of the Earth." He brandished the knife to warn her back, studying her with greater interest now. "Everyone always wondered what happened to you."

"Well, now you know." Leandra paced along the edge of the cliff, balancing gracefully, without a thought to the drop behind her.

"I'm surprised no one managed to put it together," he continued. "You vanish, and then a year later the 'Indian Menace' starts picking us off, one by one. Kind of a coincidence, don't you think?"

Blue eyes narrowed. "I just gave everyone what they deserved," she said softly, a low growl rumbling deep in her chest. "But you have me at a disadvantage. You know who I am, but..." She raised a dark brow.

The poacher smiled thinly. "My name is Corbin. Jack Corbin."

Leandra burrowed through the names that had lain, unused, in the deepest parts of her memory. After a moment, she found the right one. "I know that name," she said. "You're the man who led the expedition into Garamba Park about six years ago—the one who almost wiped out the white rhinos there." The man bowed slightly in acknowledgement. Leandra's growl grew louder. "You're a butcher," she stated coldly.

"No more so than you were," Jack sneered.

"Perhaps." Leandra couldn't refute her own actions, but her determination to repent escalated. "But now I hunt the hunters. And you know what?" She grinned, showing sharp canines. "I'm better at this than I ever was at poaching."

The steel blade flickered in the sun's feeble rays. "We'll see."

The two circled, eyes locked together, watching for signs of weakness or intent to strike. Finally, Jack feinted high with his knife, drawing Leandra forward before aiming a strike at her right shoulder. Leandra had anticipated that her opponent would attempt to hit her there, trying to earn himself a swift victory. She easily twisted to the side, dodged back, then leapt forward, her claws snapping out in twin arcs. Jack retreated momentarily, then pushed in again. He slashed repeatedly, keeping Leandra from making a move and forcing her to the very edge of the cliff face. She was unbothered by her precarious position and paced along the precipice with the agility of a tightrope walker. Jack snarled and pressed the attack, trying to force her over, but Leandra ducked and rolled out of the way, skillfully avoiding the silver flash of steel.

Jack was breathing hard after only a few minutes of fighting, but he was pleased to note that the tiger-woman was panting slightly too. The jungle humidity sapped strength quickly, and Jack knew it was best to finish things as soon as possible. He hadn't wanted to take on the formidable woman in hand-to-hand combat, but again his plans had been disrupted. Knowing he needed to neutralize Leandra's advantage of speed, Jack rushed the dark-haired woman and grappled for her arms. Leandra snarled as she saw what he intended, but couldn't move aside in time to avoid being trapped against the drop behind her. Jack grabbed each of her wrists and tried to push her backward, but Leandra resisted. Bone claws raked against the poacher's arms, but Jack ignored the pain, sensing victory. With every muscle in his forearms and neck straining to press his momentary advantage, he edged them closer to the brink of the precipice. Leandra growled and fought to hold her ground.

"I may not get my white tiger," Jack grunted, "but at least I'll be able to say I killed the Indian Menace."

Leandra hissed, baring pearly white teeth, the muscles in her shoulder burning as they absorbed ever more strain. "Better men than you have thought the same thing," she snarled.

Ashley watched breathlessly, as Leandra fought against Corbin. Feeling helpless standing on the sidelines, she scanned around for a weapon of some sort and spied a short length of branch lying among the stones. Not in any position to be picky, she grabbed it and held it like she would a baseball bat.

Studying the two wary combatants, Ashley immediately recognized that Leandra was far swifter and more agile than her enemy, and probably matched the burly poacher in terms of strength and endurance. Still, Jack Corbin had only to land a single hit to the weakened muscles in Leandra's shoulder, and victory would most likely be his. Ashley knew the odds were uncertain, and she was prepared to defend her friend should she be needed.

Watching the two wrestle for control, Ashley wondered if this was the right time to jump in. Jack was focused entirely on his struggle; she could sneak up behind him and club him on the back of the head. But just as she started creeping forward to help her friend, Leandra made her move.

The end was almost blindingly fast. Leandra twisted her arm and managed to slip free from Corbin's grasp. A moment was all she needed. With a primal roar of triumph, she lashed out with her claws, raking them in a savage uppercut across Jack Corbin's face. Shocked, Jack lost his control. Before he could recover, Leandra spun them both around and used her shoulder to deliver a hard push to Jack's chest. The poacher swore furiously for a second, his anger making him slow to realize that his feet were teetering over a long drop. He wavered a moment on the edge, still gripping Leandra with one hand. With a strangled cry, he toppled from his perch...

...taking Leandra with him.

"No!" Time slowed to a crawl. Ashley stared, horrified, as Jack used the last of his strength to drag Leandra over the edge after him. She saw a look of momentary panic and concern flash through Leandra's wide eyes. Ashley's legs froze, ignoring for a heartbeat all her orders to move forward.

By the time she rushed to help, Leandra had fallen, disappearing over the ledge without a sound.

"*No!* Leandra!" Ashley dashed to the edge of the cliff, tears already streaming down her face. For a moment, the fear was overwhelming and she couldn't even process the terrible events. This couldn't happen! Not now…not ever! Ashley threw herself down on the rocky ground and peered into the churning waters below. Through her blurred vision, she saw no sign of either Jack or Leandra. A sob was wrenched from the depths of her being, and she felt a burning pain fill her heart. The crushing reality of the situation broke over her, and the hope that this was all some terrible nightmare vanished.

In that moment, the jungle seemed silent for the first time since she'd arrived.

Then, like a miracle, a familiar raspy voice called up from below. "Ashley?"

Ashley's eyes shot open, tears forgotten. "Leandra?"

A barely audible grunt. "Can you give me a hand? I've hurt my stupid leg."

Ashley made a noise that was half sob, half cry, and peered over the edge again. There, dangling from one of the thick vines that wrapped across the face of the cliff, was Leandra. Her face was sweaty and creased into a grimace of pain, but she was alive.

"Hang on, Leandra! I'll get something to throw down." Ashley scrambled away, wiping her face and feeling such a sense of relief flood through her body that it made her physically weak. She looked around, half in a daze, and her eyes latched onto a thick, rope-like vine hanging not far away. She grabbed it and tore it free from its roots with desperate strength. Dragging the length back with her to the edge, she tied one end around her body, tossed the other end down toward Leandra, and planted her feet firmly. "Can you climb up?"

Leandra paused. "Yeah, I think so. You got the other end?"

"I got it."

"Okay."

Ashley braced herself as the vine pulled at her, then redoubled her efforts to stand firm as she took the weight from Leandra's body. After several agonizing minutes, a painted, slightly bloody hand appeared over the edge of the crag, still stubbornly holding the claws. Ashley immediately grabbed for it and helped Leandra up to safety, struggling when the heavier woman almost pulled her over. As soon as she was certain Leandra was sitting solidly on the ground, out of harm's way, Ashley untied the rope from her waist. She threw her arms around the striped woman and clutched her desperately close.

"I thought you were gone," she cried. "I thought—"

"Shhh. It's okay. I'm fine now." Fingers combed reassuringly through her tangled hair, and Ashley pressed herself harder still against Leandra, shaking with the strength of her relief. It was several moments before she managed to regain her composure enough to draw away and look up into soft, sapphire eyes.

"Don't you ever scare me like that again, you hear me?" she said hoarsely.

Leandra smiled and wiped away the tear marks with her thumbs. "I promise." The two sat silently a long while, just soaking in each other's presence, before Leandra winced and shifted her position. "I think we should get back to the cave," she observed, looking down at her left thigh. "I got banged up a bit when I grabbed the vine."

Ashley snuffled and followed her gaze, gasping when she saw a wicked gash. "Oh, my God!" She reached out to help, but withdrew when Leandra flinched. "You're right, Leandra. That needs a bandage."

"And probably a few stitches, too," Leandra said, frowning. "I have everything I need in my supplies. Can you help me up?"

"Of course." Ashley got to her feet and helped Leandra stand. The tall woman was limping quite severely, blood flowing sluggishly down her leg from the wound, and Ashley didn't even ask if she could help. She simply grabbed Leandra's arm and wrapped it around her neck, supporting some of her weight as they began making their way toward the cave.

Leandra smiled and accepted her assistance without comment.

Some distance downstream, a trembling hand emerged from the swift-flowing river and grabbed for a half-submerged log.

Gasping for breath, Jack pulled himself onto the lifeline, his body aching and weak. His right leg was broken. He could feel the splintered bones grinding against each other, bringing flashing stars to his vision. He suspected that at least two ribs were cracked; his breathing came in harsh and painful gasps. Blood still flowed from the deep gashes scored across his face by the tiger-woman's claws. It ran into his eyes and matted his dripping hair. Still, he managed to haul his body free from the chill, mountain-fed waters before collapsing on the muddy bank. Broken. Bleeding.

Alive.

Jack had been a hunter all his life. He was a shrewd and ruthless businessman, and although it didn't happen often, he knew when he was beaten. This hunt was worthless now. He was in no condition to carry the fight any further and wouldn't be for some time. It was going to be a struggle just to make it out of the jungle in one piece, especially if he didn't get to safe ground before the night hunters detected his presence.

There was no white tiger. The photographer's words rang true in his head. While he was willing to deal with the dangerous tiger-bitch if it meant there was a reward for his efforts, he wasn't the type to pursue a personal grudge. Not until he was fit enough to do so, at least.

Cursing under his breath, Jack accepted defeat. It was time to cut his losses and leave this place.

Ashley watched with a slight grimace as Leandra drew a sharp needle through her skin one final time and tugged the surgical thread tight, pulling together the ragged edges of her torn flesh. She passed a small pair of scissors to the wounded woman, who used them to cut the suture after she'd tied it off.

Leandra flexed her leg slowly, testing it. "Hmm." She grunted softly in satisfaction. "Seems okay."

"It'll need to be cleaned with disinfectant," Ashley pointed out, rummaging through Leandra's first-aid kit until she found the appropriate bottle and a few cotton swabs. She also found a neatly rolled bandage and set it down in front of her. "Here, stretch out your leg and I'll wrap it."

Leandra dutifully complied, closing her eyes with a contented smile and allowing Ashley to wash away the blood and begin cleaning the wound with the antibacterial liquid. Ashley noticed numerous minor cuts and abrasions on her patient's hands and forearms, and she suspected there were several nasty bruises hidden under all the striped body paint. She applied gentle pressure to a swollen area above Leandra's right hip and heard her breath catch.

"How are you feeling?" she asked.

"It's not too bad now," Leandra said with only a slight grimace. "The cut burns a bit and I ache all over, but it could have been a lot worse. Gonna hurt like hell tomorrow, especially if you don't let me outside to stretch my muscles."

Ashley couldn't help but grin at that. "Don't worry, I'll take you out for some exercise if you behave yourself today. You need to take it easy." Her expression turned more serious, and she glanced up at Leandra as she worked. "Do you think he's dead?" she asked softly.

"I didn't see a body. Did you?"

Ashley shook her head, reliving the awful moment when Leandra and the poacher had disappeared over the cliff edge. "No."

"Then maybe not." But Leandra barely shifted her position. "I should probably go check."

Ashley remained silent, glancing up only when she saw that Leandra was making no move to return to the hunt. "Do you have to?"

"He could still do a lot more damage if he survived. I don't like the thought of him making it back to civilization; there are plenty of people out there who'd be very interested in hearing about our encounter." But she still didn't move, and when Ashley met her gaze, she gave her a relaxed, reassuring smile.

"But no, I don't have to go."

"Good," Ashley whispered, returning to her gentle ministrations.

Tending to her patient, Ashley couldn't help but allow her eyes to roam along the firm contours of Leandra's upper thigh. The hem of Leandra's short tiger-fur skirt ran high up her legs, leaving a lot to admire as Ashley cleaned the neatly sutured cut. Without realizing it, her work slowed as her point of focus drifted to more interesting things than first aid, and her breathing grew increasingly shallower. Ashley licked her lips as her fingers roamed unconsciously over the painted flesh before her. The drama of that morning faded from mind, as her blood ran feverishly through her body and the beating of her heart intensified.

Ashley's fingers caressed ever higher, wandering almost to the edge of Leandra's skirt before she shook herself a little and ordered her hands to behave. Picking up the bandage, she began wrapping it tightly around her friend's leg. Her eyes continued their explorations, and the cave seemed to be growing warmer.

"Would you like to see more?"

"Huh?" Startled out of a lustful reverie, Ashley glanced up to find Leandra studying her with a slightly bemused—but encouraging—expression.

"Would you like to see more?" Leandra repeated. "I could take off the skirt if you want me to. You know you only have to ask."

Ashley flushed bright red, caught totally off guard by the frank question, and more so by the heat in Leandra's gaze. She lowered her eyes and quickly turned her attention back to bandaging Leandra's leg. "Oh no, that's…not necessary." *Jeez, Ashley. Get your mind out of the gutter, here.*

But Leandra was now grinning broadly. "You don't have to be embarrassed about it," she said, her voice a low, rumbling purr. "It's natural to get excited by the person you're attracted to. I know I'd find it very arousing if you were naked."

Ashley felt her cheeks burn even hotter, but before she could look away, Leandra leaned closer to her, still giving her that wickedly inviting grin. "I wouldn't mind showing you more, if you'd like."

Ashley was silent for several moments, struggling to rein in a libido that was awakening with a ravenous appetite for the first time in many years. Leandra's husky voice was having a powerful effect on her body, and she wasn't certain how to respond to such an unreservedly sexual suggestion. Shaking herself, she glanced up at the striped face of her friend shyly. "You're a lot different from anyone I've ever been involved with before. I just…" She struggled to find the words to explain. "It's not just that you're…well, you know, a woman. None of the guys I've dated have ever really been all that outgoing with this stuff. You're a lot more open than they ever were. You know, kind of to the point, I guess. Do you understand?"

Leandra held her gaze intently, nodding. "Does it bother you?"

"Well, not bother, exactly." Ashley lowered her head coyly. "It's just different for me. I'm not used to it, that's all."

"Do you like it?"

Ashley thought a moment, and gave an almost imperceptible nod. "It's kind of nice, I guess."

"So, would you like me to take off the skirt?"

Ashley met the seductive pull of those clear sapphire eyes that were darkening with hungry fires, and she couldn't help but laugh. "Let's keep it on for now, shall we? Maintain at least a little mystery for later on."

"Mystery? Ashley, you've already seen me naked. You helped paint me, or have you forgotten so quickly?"

"How could I forget?" Ashley voice rasped. She cleared her throat, shaking herself free of a delicious fantasy that skipped teasingly across her mind. "But, um… I still think we should save something for later on. Okay?"

"Absolutely."

"Great." Ashley dropped her gaze back to the leg she was working on, finished up with the bandage, and secured the loose end with a butterfly clip. When she was done, she shyly let her hands continue wandering along the painted leg, exploring over Leandra's calves down to her thickly callused feet. Leandra made no signs of disapproval, accepting the intimate attention without a word of comment, so Ashley continued for several delicious moments in silence.

Part of her wished Leandra would return the caresses, aching for more intimate contact, but beneath her excitement she could not deny there was some definite nervousness, too. Not enough to make her want to stop; even these simple touches excited her in a way she'd never experienced, stirring a deep ache in the pit of her belly. It was the first time she'd ever touched another woman so intimately—even if it was just a leg—and the experience sent anticipatory tingles racing over every inch of her skin. She watched Leandra watching her through slitted eyes, that lazy, sensuous smile curving her lips, and wondered what the evening would bring.

Ashley stayed with Leandra in the cave for the rest of the day, leaving only briefly to fetch water from the nearby stream. Leandra's supplies were sufficient to provide them both with a satisfying lunch, and Ashley filled the time with more talk about her life and family. Leandra seemed content to lie on her pallet and let herself be pampered. The cut on her leg showed no signs of retaining heat and didn't seem likely to turn septic, but Ashley kept a close eye on it all the same.

For her part, Ashley enjoyed tending to the injured woman's needs almost as much as Leandra seemed to enjoy being tended to. But although she kept up a constant rain of chatter, most of Ashley's mind was preoccupied with ponderings of a more lustful nature, chiefly centered on her companion's earlier offer. The more Ashley considered Leandra's words, the more intrigued she became by the possibilities.

She said all I have to do is ask. And she wasn't bluffing, either. If I'd said yes, she'd be sitting there naked right now, letting me look at her all I want.

Ashley's mental meanderings pursued that line of thought to the next obvious point. *She'd probably let me touch her if I wanted to.*

And kiss her. And…

All of a sudden, the fantasies and never-to-be scenarios that Ashley had only ever entertained in her imagination took on a more serious quality. *I bet she'd let me do anything I wanted,* she mused, the very thought of how far she might take such liberty making her shiver with arousal. Flicking glances at the striped woman lying languidly on the pallet across the cave, Ashley's eyes narrowed to predatory slits.

"The sun's going down," Leandra observed. "It'll be dark soon. If you'd like I can walk you back to your camp; my leg feels much better."

The corners of Ashley's lips curved into a seductive smile. "What if I'd rather stay here tonight?" she asked softly, her voice sounding almost as husky as Leandra's. She was pleased to see Leandra sit up a little straighter, feeling a delicious burst of heat sweep through her, settling between her thighs. Wide cobalt eyes met her own, and Ashley didn't try to mask where her thoughts were taking her.

"If that's what you want, I'd like that very much."

Ashley's smile grew wider, and she abandoned her seat by the fire to crawl closer to where Leandra lay. Her eyes scanned slowly over every inch of the tall woman's frame, from the wild, unkempt hair to the elegant, chiseled features, down over planes of toned, painted muscle and golden skin. The light from the fire flickered over Leandra's body like a bronze caress, running primitive shadows over every intriguing dip and hollow. Her eyes were as clear as shards of tundra ice, yet they projected a heat that struck Ashley to her core.

"Leandra?"

"Yes?"

Ashley swallowed, for a moment unsure whether or not she could actually ask the question she wanted to. But looking at the sensuous, exotic creature lying before her, she rallied her courage. "Would you mind taking off your top?"

Leandra sat very still for several heartbeats, then without a word, she reached for the laces that held the brief scrap of tiger fur closed over her breasts. Ashley watched, hardly breathing, as Leandra slowly pulled the cord free and shrugged the garment from her shoulders. The firelight washed over her painted, naked torso, and Ashley let herself stare, her fingers twitching eagerly.

Leandra sat patiently, letting her look, but eventually she held out a hand in invitation. "You can come closer if you'd like."

Ashley didn't even hesitate, accepting the offered hand and crawling forward until her knees brushed against the edges of the coarse sleeping mat. Her attention wandered back and forth between Leandra's exposed breasts and her flashing eyes, and she slowly leaned closer until her lips brushed against those of the striped woman. With a quiet whimper, Ashley let her tongue glide forth to stroke lightly against Leandra's lips. The kiss deepened quickly, and she trembled when she felt Leandra's naked breasts press against her chest. With a cautious hand, she began tracing a path along the other woman's collarbone, feeling a low, purring vibration rumble through the sensitive skin. Breaking the kiss, Ashley looked down and watched her fingers as they wandered over the slightly faded stripes, shaking noticeably as they drew closer to Leandra's full breasts.

Leandra's breaths were coming in ragged, shallow gasps as she gave Ashley free rein to explore her. But just as Ashley's fingers began to descend lower, Leandra caught her gaze and held it.

"Are you sure?"

Ashley sucked on her lower lip, then nodded shyly. "I want you," she breathed softly.

"There's no rush. We don't have to do anything if you're not ready." Leandra paused, clearly picking up on the nervousness that warred against Ashley's hunger. "I don't want you to regret a single moment of the time we spend together."

Ashley absorbed the gentle concern in Leandra's eyes and felt her love for the woman deepen further. "I could never regret anything I do with you, Leandra," she whispered. "And I want this. I want it so much."

A visible shiver raced down Leandra's body, making her muscles dance. "Me too."

Reassured, Ashley let her fingers continue their southward journey. Her excitement grew to dizzying heights when she traced around Leandra's nipples and felt the effect her touch was having. Ashley had imagined touching another woman in this way many times, but the reality was so much better than any of her fantasies had ever been. Leandra's body was so soft and smooth, even covered in the thin, dusty paint, and Ashley found herself becoming lost in every new curve she discovered. She smiled shakily at the cobalt eyes that watched her, unblinking.

"I, um… I'm not really sure how to do this," she admitted.

"Just follow your instincts," Leandra advised, her voice husky. "Touch me the way you like to be touched."

Ashley returned her attention to what her hands were doing, unable to stop her smile from turning rakish. *That should be easy enough,* she thought. *I've got plenty of experience in that department.*

Gently at first, then with greater confidence, Ashley caressed Leandra's chest, her fingers running in long strokes over the defined ribcage, before returning to tease and torment rock-hard nipples. "You're so soft," she murmured in awe. Listening to Leandra's breathing as it went ragged, Ashley learned which areas elicited the strongest responses, and her touches grew steadily bolder. Before long, her eyes drifted down to the brief skirt that wrapped about Leandra's waist, her fingers craving new territory to explore.

Seeing where her focus was shifting, Leandra unlaced the skirt and lifted herself off the pallet, letting the cloth slide away and exposing herself completely. Enthralled, Ashley stared at the vision before her, hands trembling noticeably as they rested on Leandra's abdomen. Glancing up at the dark-haired woman, she received a nod and a reassuring smile. Taking that as permission to continue, Ashley shifted closer and let her fingers roam ever lower.

She could smell the musky scent of Leandra's desire, and her mouth watered at the thought that she was the one to inspire such arousal. As her fingers began to move hesitantly toward Leandra's center, Ashley's lips descended upon the woman lying under her, kissing her ardently and feeling her respond with equal passion. Ashley let go her fears and caution as she fed from Leandra's mouth, for the first time in her life allowing carnal desires to completely consume her. Her hunger redoubled and she groaned excitedly, as Leandra's hands began to tug urgently at her own clothes. Breaking contact momentarily, Ashley stripped as quickly as she could, all sense of modesty abandoned to the urgency of the moment. She paused a moment once she was naked, enjoying the way Leandra's eyes roved appreciatively over her lithe figure, before returning her lips to their feast. This time she claimed Leandra's throat, sucking forcefully at her thunderous pulse-point while her hands moved feverishly along the curve of her hips, tracing inward.

As soon as her slender fingers grazed Leandra's center, her hips surged eagerly forward, seeking more. Ashley took her time, however, her touches straying for long minutes over trembling inner thighs and stomach before returning to where Leandra's need was greatest.

Hot, wet lips forged a trail down Leandra's collarbone, then dipped lower to snare each nipple in turn. Ashley was completely caught up in the passion of the moment, more aroused than she'd ever been in her entire life. She pulled lightly at sensitized flesh with her teeth, then, hearing the way Leandra responded, bit harder. Leandra convulsed. Ashley's fingers finally sought out liquid heat and began a slow, steady massage. She broke contact and looked down at the body writhing beneath her, breathless with desire as her fingers flowed through Leandra's slick folds.

Leandra was biting her lower lip, her powerful body entirely at the mercy of Ashley's caresses. She twisted and squirmed on the pallet, staring up at Ashley with glazed, desperate eyes. "Oh, God! Harder, please! Harder!" Leandra gasped, and when Ashley complied she clawed at the ground and rolled her hips in urgent, rising ecstasy.

Ashley was stunned at the heat that enveloped her fingers. Leandra felt like liquid silk, and she eagerly set about satisfying her new lover. Though she'd never touched another woman intimately, Ashley had a lot of experience keeping herself happy, and she applied that expertise to this new situation. From the way Leandra's body pulsed around her fingers and the increasingly desperate edge to her cries and moans of pleasure, Ashley decided she was doing okay.

Unfortunately—but certainly understandably—it was quickly apparent that four years of abstinence had taken a toll on Leandra, for all too soon Ashley felt the first spasms of climax begin tightening around her fingers. Though she had intended this to be a slow, protracted exploration, not wanting to rush the experience, Ashley was too lost in the carnal moment to slow down. Instead, she responded by slipping a third finger in beside the two already thrusting into Leandra's core. Instantly, every muscle in Leandra's body snapped taut, straining beneath her rippling skin, and she released a pealing cry of unrestrained ecstasy.

Ashley continued thrusting into Leandra's clenching sex, keeping her at the highest point of climax for at least half a minute before Leandra collapsed, gasping, back onto the sleeping pallet.

Ashley smiled as she slowly withdrew her fingers from their warm nest, feeling the fading orgasmic spasms grip at her pleasantly. An expression of dazed wonder graced her features as she looked at Leandra's sweat-streaked body and face, and her heart almost stopped when sated, sapphire eyes turned on her with radiant joy.

"Thank you," Leandra whispered, struggling to catch her breath after the quick but stunning orgasm. "God, that was…" She grinned, shaking her head. "Incredible."

Ashley's smile turned into a full-fledged grin, her eyes positively glowing in the firelight. "Really?"

Leandra nodded sincerely. "Really."

"Huh." Ashley settled herself beside the striped form of her new lover. "I don't think I've ever been described as 'incredible' before," she mused aloud. "At least, not in this particular department."

Leandra matched her grin. "Well, I think you're incredible in all departments," she purred seductively, her stunning eyes roving hungrily over Ashley's nakedness in excited anticipation. "And if you'll give me a minute or two to recover, I'll be sure to thank you properly."

Ashley shivered at the husky promise. Propping herself up on one elbow, she continued running her eyes over Leandra's powerful frame, feeling the heat radiating from her lover's body. Her fingers still glistened with her lover's essence, and after making sure Leandra's eyes were closed, Ashley lifted the fingers to her lips and took a guilty lick. She marveled at the exotic flavor, finding it very much to her liking, and proceeded to consume the remainder. When her fingers were clean, Ashley's eyes returned to feast upon Leandra's nakedness once more.

Thinking back to all the dream-lovers who had populated her fantasies over the years, Ashley couldn't believe the characteristics that had been common to them all. What the hell was I thinking? Sophisticated? Cultured?

They've got nothing on Leandra. Simply put, Leandra was the epitome of animal sensuality. Savage nobility coupled with primeval strength and passion, all packed into an agile, six-foot-something body that fairly radiated carnal sexuality. Ashley's eyes glowed as the fires in them sparked anew, and she reached out to begin a second exploration.

Cobalt eyes flew open instantly. "Oh, no you don't!"

Ashley gave a startled yelp as powerful yet gentle fingers wrapped around her wrists and pushed her back. Leandra twisted about, pinning her to the sleeping mat and bringing their faces together. "It's my turn now," she growled, pressing her uninjured thigh against Ashley's heated center. Ashley shuddered, her eyelids fluttering, as Leandra began a slow grind.

Painted hands released their hold on her captured wrists and stroked down Ashley's arms, tickling the sensitive skin behind her elbow, making her giggle and squirm. Ashley arched her back as Leandra brought her attention down to her breasts. Nimble fingers sought her stiffened nipples and began to pinch and roll them gently, then with greater urgency as her excitement became more vocal.

Lying on her back on the rough pallet, Ashley whimpered at the attentions her body was receiving. She wasn't a hundred percent sure what to expect from Leandra, but she was certainly enjoying the ride so far. No one had ever touched her with this kind of almost frenzied passion, and the young woman found herself getting wetter at the thought of what might lie in store for her. When Leandra kissed her ardently, she responded with a matching hunger, her tongue fighting an erotic duel for dominance against her lover's. She surrendered control readily, however, the moment she felt Leandra's right hand quest southwards.

Leandra's lips abandoned the kiss to trail a scorching path down her slender neck, and Ashley tilted her head back to encourage her. Lips and tongue explored a path from her shoulder down along her collarbone, then lower until they encountered the tempting swell of her breasts. Ashley stifled a moan as a serpentine tongue lashed and teased her nipple, sending ripples of pleasure all through her body. Then she stiffened, feeling those long fingers begin to play promisingly through the damp curls above her center. A single fingertip began tracing tight circles just above her throbbing clitoris.

Giving Ashley's right nipple a final sucking kiss, Leandra looked up at her breathlessly, sapphire eyes ablaze with ravenous need. "Let me taste you," she gasped. "Please?"

Ashley hesitated.

"You'll like it, I promise." Leandra dipped down to slide her tongue persuasively up Ashley's inner thigh, making her writhe in anticipation. "Please, Ashley?"

Ashley bit her lower lip, considering, then nodded.

Leandra wasted no time laying a wet line of kisses and licks down Ashley's lower body, tracing patterns with her tongue along sensitized skin and moving ever closer to the source of heat between her legs.

Ashley lay back and closed her eyes, focusing on the sensations generated by Leandra's ministrations. She blushed in reflex as her partner settled between her legs, and she felt the cool air caress her intimately, making her fully aware of how exposed and open she was. This was a pleasure Ashley had never experienced before, something none of her previous lovers had offered and she'd never found the courage to ask for. She'd often fantasized how this might feel, and it appeared she was finally about to find out.

Warm air flowed across her sensitized sex, and Ashley tensed, then relaxed as Leandra blew against her again. The first touch of Leandra's tongue ran along the inside of her left thigh, and Ashley trembled as her core pulsed anxiously. She could feel how wet she was, how ready. This kind of patient foreplay was new to her, and her hands grasped the edges of the sleeping mat tightly as she forced her body to lie still, while Leandra's tongue played havoc with her already overloaded libido.

The teasing licks continued for long minutes, as Ashley squirmed longingly, and then became more purposeful. Leandra's lips and tongue abandoned Ashley's thighs and began a more serious exploration of her velvet folds. Ashley's hips bucked hard against the erotic assault, and she cried out when Leandra's tongue flicked her hard nub repeatedly, then returned to the long, slow strokes that swiftly began to drive her to the edge. Her hands grabbed for Leandra's hair, pulling her closer as she convulsed. "Oh, fuck!" Ashley gasped, white lights exploded behind her eyelids as the most unbelievable sensations ripped through her.

Leandra grinned up at her, fingers poised teasingly against her entrance. "You like?"

"Yes! God, please, Leandra, don't stop!" Ashley clutched desperately at Leandra's head, seeking an anchor as her body thrust forward, completely out of her control.

"Would you like more?"

Ashley almost sobbed when she felt the firmer touch of Leandra's fingers slide tauntingly against her wetness. "Yes!" Her hips surged upwards, pleading. "Inside! Please, Leandra! Inside now!"

Leandra complied, pushing into Ashley slowly. The feeling was so exquisite, Ashley feared she wouldn't be able to endure more than a few seconds before climax took her. But Leandra seemed aware of her hair-trigger sensitivity, moving at a languorous pace and using only the lightest, most teasing touches of her tongue. Ashley continued to whimper and plead, lost in a landscape of ascending ecstasy. But every time she felt herself drawing closer to the edge, Leandra would respond by slowing her ministrations until she calmed, keeping her hovering constantly at the brink of orgasm.

Still, the patient lovemaking could only continue for so long before Ashley's body reached the limit of its endurance. The first pulse of climax stiffened her muscles and made her breath catch in her throat. Leandra responded, curling her fingers and thrusting with greater speed and purpose. Ashley looked down just in time to catch the hungry smile on her new lover's face, then Leandra sealed her lips over her clitoris and began sucking fervently.

Ashley screamed as her body stiffened, crying out words that only vaguely resembled Leandra's name as the waves of her climax pounded through her sweat-slicked frame. The pleasure was more overwhelming than any she'd experienced before, and Leandra refused to let it die away quickly, lashing her tongue with the speed of a hummingbird's wings against the tiny bundle of nerve endings at the crown of her sex. But eventually, she could endure no more of the shattering pleasure and collapsed weakly back to the ground, panting for breath as she pushed at Leandra's head.

"No more," she begged. "God, I can't take any more."

Leandra planted a final loving kiss on Ashley's sex, sending a last delicious spasm through her, before stretching out full length beside her and slipping an arm beneath her waist. "Was that to your liking, my lady?" she asked impishly.

Ashley blew her damp bangs from her eyes and laughed, snuggling up to her new lover. "I'll say. I'm still tingling everywhere! That was phenomenal."

"Good." Leandra leaned down, and Ashley didn't hesitate to meet her kiss, moaning when she felt gentle teeth nip at her lower lip. "I'm glad I could make you feel good."

Ashley gazed up into eyes that sparkled in the dying light of the neglected fire. She wrapped her arms around Leandra and pulled their bodies into a tight embrace. "You make me feel wonderful every moment we're together," she whispered. "Thank you."

"You're *very* welcome."

"Mmm."

The two lay as one on the pallet, sated and warmed by the flickering glow of the dying fire. But Leandra's body made an extremely comfortable pillow, and the quiet rhythm of her heartbeat worked as well as a lullaby on Ashley. It wasn't long before her eyelids fluttered, then closed, and her breathing deepened as she drifted off, exhausted.

Leandra lay awake in the darkness for a long time, content to simply watch Ashley sleep, one hand playing gently through her fine, pale hair. The sounds from outside continued to speak their mysterious knowledge to her, but Leandra felt distanced from that world of hunter and prey, wrapped up in a new world of peace and love she'd never hoped to find.

In that moment, Leandra knew there was no way she could ever live without these feelings...no way she could ever fully return to the solitary world of the jungle predator.

Sometime later that night, Leandra woke from a dreamless sleep, her body slightly chilled. Her internal clock told her there were still several hours until dawn, and the night air carried a cold bite. She immediately sensed the absence of her bedmate and sat up, stretching her injured leg stiffly as she looked around.

Ashley was sitting at the mouth of the cave, head propped on her folded hands, looking out over the forests and plains below. She'd donned her shirt and shorts to ward off the chill, but Leandra's sensitive ears still detected shivers in each breath the young woman took. Shafts of light beamed down through the thin cloud cover, illuminating Ashley's features and casting her hair into a radiant halo. As Leandra rose and padded silently over to her, she noticed the pensive expression that marked her features.

"Hey."

Brown eyes that looked almost like smoky quartz in the moonlight glanced up. Ashley smiled. "Hey."

"You okay?"

"Of course." Ashley patted the ground next to her invitingly, and Leandra knelt beside her. Together they watched the shifting shadows of the clouds for a few minutes in silence before Leandra spoke.

"You don't regret anything, do you?"

Ashley immediately shook her head, reaching out to take her hand and bring it to her lips. "Of course not. I told you, Leandra, I could never regret the time we've spent together." She paused, adding with a roguish grin, "And I could certainly never regret doing *that* with you."

Leandra smiled, eyeing her curiously. "You just look a little sad, that's all."

"Not sad. Just thinking," Ashley said. "Today's going to be my last full day out here. We leave tomorrow morning."

Now Leandra understood. She shifted on the ground and stretched out her wounded leg to relieve the pressure on the stitches. "I know."

"It's so close. I've been trying so hard not to think about it, you know? I don't..." Ashley trailed off, seeming unable for a long moment to find words to express her feelings. "I didn't want to spoil what was happening between us by bringing it up, but after last night, I know I can't avoid it anymore."

Leandra had been deliberately avoiding thinking too much about Ashley's imminent departure as well, and about the changes she was going to have to make if she intended to keep the young woman in her life. Glancing at Ashley quickly, Leandra found herself caught by an intensity there she'd not expected.

"Ask me to stay," Ashley whispered.

"What?"

"Ask me to stay, Leandra. Just ask, and I'll do it."

Leandra stared, thrown totally for a loop by Ashley's words. She shook her head. "I can't. I mean, *you* can't. Ashley, you have a home, a family. You can't just—"

"I will." Ashley sat up straighter and faced Leandra directly. "If you ask me to, I will."

"Ashley—"

"No." Ashley shook her head angrily. "I don't want to leave you, Leandra. It's not fair! I can't just walk away from this, not now." Ashley paused and lowered her head, but Leandra saw teardrops threatening to fall. "I want to be with you. I want to wake up every morning and know you'll be waking right beside me. I've never felt this way about anyone in my whole life, Leandra, but I know that what we have together doesn't come along very often. If I walk away now, if I just try to forget all the time I've shared with you, I know the chances are I'll never get to feel this way again. Ever." She snuffled. "And I don't want that to happen."

Leandra gazed into the dark eyes of her friend and lover, seeing the unshed tears and touched deeply by Ashley's words. "I don't want to forget you either, Ashley," she whispered. "But I can't ask you to live in this world with me. I don't want to be the one who takes you from your family, your work. I know how much you love doing what you do."

"But I love *you* more!"

Leandra was silent as she took in Ashley's fierce words of devotion, then she smiled incredulously. "You do?"

"Yes." Ashley reached out and clasped Leandra's striped hands in her own. "I love you more than anyone in the world, Leandra, and I can't lose you now that I've finally found you."

That was all she needed to hear, Leandra realized. Any doubts about her feelings for Ashley disappeared in a heartbeat. "Well," she offered, "when you leave here, I could always just come along with you."

"What? You mean, back to the States?"

"If you want me to."

For a second, Ashley's face filled with excitement, but then she paused. Leandra knew her well enough to see Ashley was forcing herself to think practically. "Leandra, I can't ask you to do that."

"Why not?"

"I just can't, that's all. I mean, you have friends here. What about Shar-Ranjana? What about the other tigers you protect?"

"There will always be poachers, Ashley. Just because I leave here doesn't mean I have to stop helping these animals. As for Shar-Ranjana..." She shrugged sadly. "Just being here doesn't mean I could save her forever. After all, I wasn't able to save her family. But she's smart. She stays hidden in the remote parts of the park, and the rangers do their job fairly well." She tilted her head to the side, then added, "Besides, if Corbin survived, he'll leave the jungle believing there is no white tiger, thanks to you."

"Maybe he didn't believe me."

"He did. I could see it in his face when we fought—he was angry at wasting his time on a useless hunt. If he gets out of here, the word will spread and every poacher in the region will think the rumors are just lies. Shar-Ranjana will be as safe as she can be in this place, and it won't much matter if I stay or leave."

"But—"

Leandra halted any further arguments by pressing her fingers gently against Ashley's lips. "I *want* to leave here," she whispered with absolute certainty. "I'm ready. I want to be a part of your life." Ashley stilled, meeting her steady gaze hesitantly. "Do you remember what you said to me about letting go of the past?" Leandra asked.

Ashley nodded.

"You were right. I can't let the person I used to be stop me from becoming someone better. I'm ready to face the future now, as long as I do it with you by my side."

Cautious hope spread like a sunrise across Ashley's face. "So you're sure about this? It's a pretty big change, leaving the jungle to rejoin civilization. What if it doesn't work out?"

"Then we'll deal with it when the time comes." Leandra glanced away, her eyes wandering to the jungle that had been her home for the last four years. "I don't have any money," she said hesitantly, acknowledging the difficulties of what they were proposing. "At least not with me, but—"

"Oh, Leandra, that doesn't matter. You can stay with me. I have a big house with plenty of space. As long as you don't mind a little extra company, that is. My niece, Casey, spends a lot of time there when I'm home." She leaned forward and planted a quick kiss on Leandra's painted cheek. "I don't care how rich you are, or what you do. Just as long as you're with me."

"It's not going to be easy," Leandra warned gently. "I've been out here a long time. My head might need some time to adjust." She studied her own striped flesh in the moonlight, embarrassed at even having to bring these points to light.

"We'll take it slow," Ashley promised. "You can have all the time you need."

Leandra's eyes were shy as she glanced up through the curtain of her tangled hair. "Thank you."

Ashley's forehead creased. "I can cover your plane ticket, but I don't know about a passport or—"

"That's okay," Leandra interrupted, already having thought ahead. "I buried all that stuff when I first came back here. It might take a while—I never thought I'd need it again—but I think I could find it."

"Really? Oh, God, I can just imagine what my sister will think when she sees you. Or my parents, for that matter. My family's pretty used to hearing about my misadventures, so it takes a lot to surprise them." Her eyes sparkled with mischief. "So...when can we get started?"

Leandra's eyes gleamed. "In the morning. We'll take a quick bath, then I'll start putting my things together and saying my good-byes. If you can arrange the rest, I'll be ready to leave by tomorrow."

"Excellent." Ashley chuckled aloud, threw her arms around Leandra's neck, and hugged her tightly. "I can't believe this! I mean, I wasn't even willing to hope you'd want to come with me." Her grin was impossibly wide. "This is going to be so perfect, Leandra, I promise. You and me, together."

Leandra purred at the very thought. "Forever."

"Forever." Ashley claimed her lips in an ardent kiss, curling up against Leandra when they finally parted. "I can't wait."

"Mmm." Leandra was silent for a long moment, feeling the warmth of the younger woman's body against her own. "Ashley?"

"Yeah?"

Leandra's eyes darkened. "Have you ever wondered what it's like to make love under a waterfall?"

She felt a shiver run through Ashley's slender frame, and knew it had nothing to do with the chill of the predawn air. "Um, not really."

Leandra's voice dropped to a throaty rumble. "Would you like to find out?"

Mahogany eyes instantly darkened. "Are you offering to show me?"

"I most certainly am."

"It's still dark outside," Ashley observed coyly.

"Well, I guess we'll have to keep ourselves busy until the sun comes up." Leandra rose with feline grace and offered her hand to her lover. "Won't we?"

Ashley quickly accepted the offered hand, stripping off her clothes as Leandra led the way back to the sleeping mat.

"She's *what?*"

Ashley faced an incredulous Grady without flinching, having prepared herself for this little speech. She and Leandra had passed an extremely satisfying morning, spent mostly under and around the private waterfall, engaging in long sessions of lovemaking that only left Ashley wanting more. When their passions had been sated—if only for the moment—she had returned to her own camp, so she could prepare for their departure the following day.

Leandra had promised that she would be there early the next morning, ready to leave. Ashley didn't know for sure what preparations the jungle-woman was making, but she respected that they needed to be made alone. For now, Ashley had to deal with her side of things.

"I told you, Grady, Leandra's coming with us," she repeated calmly, keeping her voice level and even. "What's so difficult to understand?"

"Ashley..." Grady's jaw worked. For a moment, he couldn't decide which words to form first. "Are you joking? I mean, why would you even... You can't just..." He shook his head, turning red as he tried to form a coherent sentence.

Ashley watched her vexed partner with a faintly amused smile. "I can. I have. It's all taken care of. She'll be here in the morning."

"Will she talk with us?" Simon stepped forward, obviously nervous about interrupting the tense exchange. "It wouldn't have to be much, just a few little pieces of information, you know? Anything that might help us."

Ashley smiled reassuringly at the pleasant, balding man. "I'm sure she'll be happy to answer a few questions, just as long as you're nice about it. Don't try to push her on personal stuff."

Simon nodded his head vigorously. "Of course. I wouldn't dream of being intrusive."

"Just remember, she's not used to being around people, okay? She'll probably be a bit edgy until she gets the hang of social interaction again."

"Edgy?" Grady gestured wildly with his arms. "This woman is a *killer*, Ashley, or have you conveniently forgotten that fact? How do you know she won't snap and try to kill us all?" He glanced over to Tarun, but the Indian guide held up his hands, unwilling to get involved.

"Leandra's perfectly safe," Ashley insisted. "She's a little rough around the edges, but she's very gentle at heart. Just because she's a danger to the poachers doesn't make her a danger to me, or to us."

"This is crazy." Grady continued to fume. "Why on Earth would you want to drag her back with us? This is so unlike you, Ashley." That comment earned him a very amused raised eyebrow. "Okay, scratch that. This is exactly like you. But it's still stupid."

"What's so stupid about it?" Ashley demanded, planting her hands on her hips. "The fact that Leandra wants to rejoin a society she hasn't seen in four years, or that I'm willing to help her?" Steel shone in her eyes. "Tell me, Mister Judgmental, what do you think I should do? Turn my back on her? Just leave her out here so she can slowly go insane?"

Grady studied his feet. "That's not what I'm saying."

"Isn't it?"

"No. I just think you're rushing into things, that's all. I mean, you've only known this woman for a short time, for God's sake."

"I know enough about her to realize that Leandra's a wonderful, loving, and gentle person," Ashley stated firmly. "I'm not going to abandon her. She deserves the chance to live a normal life."

"Think about that for a moment. Where's she going to stay when we get back to the States? How will she survive?"

"Simple. She'll stay with me, and I'll support her until she gets back on her feet."

"You'll do *what*?"

"It's my decision, Grady, not yours." Ashley took two steps closer to her partner, her posture stern and strong. "Leandra's going to be a part of my life from now on. You'd better get used to that fact quickly, or I'm afraid we won't be able to work together in the future. And I don't want that."

"I can't believe this, Ash. How can you even... Wait a minute." Grady seemed to catch up with her statement, and his eyes narrowed. "A part of your life? What exactly do you mean by that?"

"I mean Leandra and I are going to be together a lot from now on," she said softly. "You're a smart man, Grady. You figure it out."

There was a long period of awkward silence while everyone in the camp looked anywhere but at the two partners.

Grady blinked in surprised, clearly struggling to process this latest information. "So you and she are…"

Ashley nodded. "Is that a problem?"

"Well no, not a problem, I just…" Grady cleared his throat and looked away, clearly not knowing how to take this. "I didn't know you…" He waved his hand.

"Neither did I."

Grady considered. "This explains a lot, I guess. At least I know now why you're spending so many nights with her."

Ashley flushed a little angrily at her partner's tone. "What we do together is none of your business," she stated. "The fact remains that when we leave here, we're taking her with us. She had a few things to do before we leave—saying good-byes and getting her stuff together—but she promised to be here in the morning."

Grady still looked stunned by Ashley's sudden coming out. "What about a plane ticket?"

Ashley relaxed a bit at her partner's concession. "We'll have time to get an extra one for her. Don't worry about anything. I'll cover her fare." She paused, eyeing him sternly. "You don't have to like this, Grady, "but if you really are my friend, you'll at least make an effort to be civil to her. Okay?"

Grady gave a long-suffering sigh, but he nodded. "Fine."

"Good. Now, if you'll excuse me," Ashley said as she met the gazes of the others, each in turn, "I have some things of my own to get straightened out before we head off. Give a yell when dinner's ready." So saying, she marched purposefully toward her own tent. In her peripheral vision, she noticed Simon lean closer to Grace and heard him say in a loud whisper, "I wonder…"

Grace raised an eyebrow. "About what?"

"About who exactly a woman living out here all alone would have to say good-bye to."

169

In a remote part of the park, far from the trails and tracks left by the rangers and tourists, Leandra stood before a neat row of three tall stones that lay half-buried in the earth. Sitting at her side like a giant ivory statue, Shar-Ranjana watched her with an air of primitive understanding. Here, as nowhere else in the jungle, the animals were silent. Here, nowhere else, sound seemed out of place. Even the trees seemed reluctant to disturb the tranquility, and made only hushed murmurs in even the strongest winds.

Leandra smiled down at the great white tigress, tears already pricking at the corners of her eyes. Shar-Ranjana nuzzled her hip affectionately, sniffing with distaste at the unfamiliar scents that clung to her human sibling. Gone was the intricate pattern of stripes that had covered Leandra's powerful frame. Gone were the tiger-fur top and skirt. In their place, Leandra wore a sleeveless khaki shirt and loose cotton trousers cinched at the waist with a leather belt. Her feet were still bare. She'd tried to wear her boots, but found them restrictive and uncomfortable. The clothes felt strange against her body, yet at the same time struck chords of familiarity deep inside. She'd taken them from a poacher more than a year ago, stashing them with her supplies to be used as rags. She'd never seriously considered the possibility that she would ever actually wear them.

Then again, she'd never thought to leave this place.

Leandra sighed and reached out, running her hand along the cool surface of each stone in turn. Remembered images of Shar-Tushar, his mate, and his son flashed before her eyes, and with them, memories of the night she'd brought their bodies here to bury. The night she'd lost her family all over again. Grief, regret, and longing rolled over Leandra, but where the anger had been, there was now only a sense of peace. She knew her decision was right.

"I thought this place would be my home forever," she said softly. "I thought I'd live out here until the jungle killed me." Her eyes went to the largest of the three stones, and she smiled sadly. "I thought that was the reason you let me live, all those years ago. So I could pay for the lives I'd destroyed by giving up my own. But I was wrong, wasn't I? You let me live so I could learn from what I'd been. So that one day, maybe, I could forgive myself and find my place in the world again." Her smile grew wistful. "Well, it took a while, but I did it."

Leandra felt Shar-Ranjana nudge her again, and she scratched the great cat fondly between her ears. "I think you would have liked Ashley," she continued. "She's gentle, kind, and beautiful, and she loves me." Leandra shook her head in wonder. "I don't know why, or how. But I can see it in her eyes and feel it in her touch. I know that I want to be near that forever."

Tears were falling freely now, blurring her vision. Leandra sniffled and wiped her nose. "I'll never forget you," she promised hoarsely. "And I'll never forget the debt I owe. There are other ways for me to make up for what I was, ways that will still let me be a part of Ashley's life. But I promise, you'll always be a part of me…forever."

From the pocket of the shirt, Leandra produced a short length of plaited hair, tied at both ends with strong leather twine. One third of the plait was dark and thick, taken from one of her own braids. Another was made from Ashley's pale tresses. The third was a marriage of the two, twisted together to form a single strand. Laying a soft kiss on the token, Leandra placed it solemnly on the ground before the stone marker.

"I'll come back someday," she whispered, her throat closing over the words as she choked back a sob. "This isn't really good-bye. But I have to go, and I won't be around so much anymore, so you'll have to watch over Shar-Ranjana for me." One hand burrowed into the thick fur of the tigress, clutching with desperate strength. Shar-Ranjana, seeming to understand the needs of her companion, accepted the rough treatment without issue. Leandra lowered her head a moment, letting a tangled curtain of hair cover her face as she composed herself. Taking a deep breath and releasing it slowly, she looked up through her messy braids at the stone.

"I know I've said it a thousand times before," she whispered, "and I know you understand. But I need to say it one last time. I'm sorry." Bitter tears stung her eyes, and Leandra's jaw trembled. "I'm sorry I couldn't protect you when it mattered the most. I'm sorry you had to die." She lowered her head again, listening to the strange silence and feeling the spirit of the great white cat soothe her grief with his presence.

For a long time, Leandra knelt before the three graves in silence, unmoving, feeling the warmth of Shar-Ranjana beside her. Then, standing, she turned and walked away.

Leaving behind the heart of one life, to begin another.

CHAPTER 5

When the stars threw down their spears,
And water'd heaven with their tears,
Did he smile his work to see?
Did he who made the Lamb make thee?

—"The Tyger" by William Blake

WITH AN EXAGGERATED GRUNT, ASHLEY tossed the neatly rolled
bundle that moments ago had been her tent into the back of the ranger
Jeep, along with the rest of her supplies. Flashing a quick smile toward
the men who were helping load the camping gear, she took a moment to
wipe the sweat from her face with her forearm. It was another steamy day
in the Indian wilds, and she was feeling sticky and bedraggled already, her
loose tank top clinging annoyingly to her lithe frame. As much as she was
going to miss India, Ashley was now really looking forward to getting back
home, where she planned on taking a nice long shower, preferably one that
included a certain tall, drop-dead gorgeous jungle-woman.

A jungle-woman who was, she noticed, running late.

Ashley didn't want to get all nervous—didn't want to focus on the
nagging sense of fear that had been growing in her all morning—but
Leandra had promised to be here early, and so far, she hadn't put in an
appearance. The gear was almost all loaded. Grady was accepting a little
help from one of the burly rangers to lift the final heavy chest containing
their more fragile camera equipment. As Ashley watched, the two men
carefully set their burden on the back seat of the second of three Jeeps that
had arrived at first light. The campsite was empty now, the scattered ashes
and scorched earth from their campfire the only lingering evidence of their

presence here. As her companions began claiming their seats for the ride out, Ashley felt their eyes all turn to focus on her. She frowned and cast her gaze at the jungle, willing Leandra to appear.

"We can't wait forever, Ash," Grady stated in a matter-of-fact tone. "The plane'll leave whether we're on it or not."

"She'll be here," Ashley insisted. "She promised."

"Then where is she?" Grady hesitated, clearly not wanting to test her temper by pushing the issue. After a few moments, the silence grew too heavy. "Look, maybe she changed her mind. Maybe she's—"

"She's coming." Ashley pinned her partner with a determined glare, her lips pulling into a stern line, as she set her hands firmly on her hips. "Leandra wouldn't lie to me about wanting to leave here, and even if she did, she wouldn't let me go without at least saying good-bye. She'll be here."

Grady didn't argue, though Ashley thought she heard a quiet, exasperated sigh when he turned away and made a subtle gesture to Tarun indicating they were going to need a little longer. Tarun shrugged, and went to explain the situation to the impatient but curious rangers.

Turning back to the jungle, Ashley tried to keep her stomach from tying itself into knots as she scanned for any sign of Leandra. *She will be here,* she insisted silently, gnawing at her lower lip in a nervous habit. *And if she doesn't come, I'm not leaving. I don't care about the consequences, I'm not letting her get away with chickening out at the last moment.*

Standing in the deeper shadows of the undergrowth, Leandra observed the group of people gathered around a trio of fully loaded Jeeps parked in the clearing. She could tell, even from a distance, that Ashley was getting worried she wasn't going to show up, and felt a pang of regret for her slow start this morning. She would have liked to be able to place the blame on a need to pack or prepare for their departure, but the truth was far simpler—even after saying her farewells, it was difficult to leave this place.

"Well... No need to keep a lady waiting," she whispered under her breath, steeling herself for the journey to come. Stepping from the concealing shadows, Leandra made her way toward the party, letting her hands brush against the lush foliage along the way.

The moment she caught sight of her, Ashley's entire expression shifted in a heartbeat from tense and edgy to glowing and relieved. She glanced back to the group waiting behind her and called, "See, I told you!" before rushing forward to greet her.

Ashley stopped a few paces from her, staring at the changes in her appearance. After running her gaze up and down Leandra's frame, she gave a low whistle of approval. "Very nice!"

Leandra rolled her eyes and chuckled. "Thanks." Without the paint and primal markings, her pale skin glistened under a fine layer of sweat in the Indian humidity. She'd pulled her long braided hair back into a thick ponytail, revealing her classic, angular features and highlighting her stunning eyes. After seeing the picture on her passport, taken almost five years ago, Leandra had realized just how much her appearance had changed during her jungle exile.

"You look so…" Ashley trailed off. "I mean, it's weird to see you without all the stripes and stuff."

"I can't very well walk out of here wearing tiger-fur clothes and carrying claws, can I?" Leandra plucked at her new clothes awkwardly. "I feel kind of naked without them, to tell the truth. And I couldn't stand the shoes, so…"

"That's okay, you don't have to wear them if you don't want to. Maybe sandals would be more comfortable?" Noticing a small rucksack slung over Leandra's shoulder, she cocked an eyebrow. "What's in there?"

"Just a few mementos. My clothes, my claws, and my passport and identification." Leandra looked chagrined. "I hope they don't ask too many questions at the airport. I look a bit different now than when I came here."

"I'm sure we'll manage. But will you be able to get tiger claws onto the plane? Isn't that illegal?"

Leandra's smile turned into a roguish grin. "You're forgetting, my love, what I used to be. Just because I'm not a smuggler anymore doesn't mean I've forgotten how to do it. Believe me, customs won't find them."

"I'm not going to ask any questions," Ashley said, and laughed. "Just don't get caught. I don't want them shipping you off to jail just when I'm about to get you home."

Leandra ducked down to plant a soft kiss on Ashley's lips. "Don't worry. I'll be fine." Straightening, she turned her attention to the three vehicles and their waiting occupants. She took a deep breath. "Guess it's time to go, huh?"

"Yep." Ashley took Leandra's hand in her own, clearly sensing her anxiety. "It's okay to be nervous, Leandra, but they won't hurt you. They're all very nice people."

"Will you be sitting next to me?"

"Uh huh, it's all been arranged. I'll be right with you the whole way. It's a long trip. I know it won't be easy for you, but you can relax when it's all over."

Leandra swallowed nervously, then looked seriously into Ashley's frank gaze. "I haven't had to be a human for a long time," she whispered, uncertain how to express her fears properly. "I don't know how I'll react."

"I understand," Ashley said in a calming tone. "We'll take it slow, just like I said. Don't worry, Leandra. You'll do fine, I'm sure of it."

Leandra trusted the absolute confidence she saw in the expressive eyes of the younger woman. "Okay then. Let's get this over with."

Hands clasped together, the two women approached the Jeeps. Leandra's nostrils twitched as she caught the unfamiliar scents of steel and gas and rubber—scents she'd never really noticed before her exile but which now seemed almost overwhelming. As she met each set of curious eyes in turn, Leandra realized just how sharp her senses had grown. She could almost detect each person's individual scent, could hear every rustle of plastic and cloth. Reaching the first Jeep, she smiled tentatively at the people watching her with interest and, she noted, not a little caution.

As they drew alongside the first mud-tracked vehicle, Ashley released her hand and waved her companions closer. "Leandra, I'd like you to meet our guide, Tarun." Leandra met the man's cool, appraising gaze and offered a nod. "And this is Simon Reynolds, our zoologist, and his assistant, Grace Stirling. They'll be joining us on the flight back to the States."

Leandra nodded politely, her eyes still shy. "Nice to meet you both." Her voice was quiet and raspy, but Simon bobbed his head in return and offered a broad, excited smile.

"We've heard a lot about you from Ashley," he said enthusiastically, holding out his hand. Leandra recoiled slightly, and Simon quickly withdrew, his smile faltering. But he plunged ahead. "Um... I was wondering if perhaps on the ride out, you might be willing to answer a few questions? Nothing big, just a few things about the tigers, if that would be okay? I mean, it's a rather unique situation, meeting someone like yourself with such an intimate understanding of the cats. I don't want to be a bother, especially since this is probably very stressful for you, but perhaps…" He produced a somewhat owlish expression of hopeful anticipation, and Leandra couldn't help but smile.

"I think that would be okay."

"Excellent!" Simon's eyes lit up with excitement, and he squeezed his slender form against the far side of the back seat to make room. "Please sit here, if you don't mind?"

With a quick glance toward the rangers and the occupants of the other two Jeeps, Leandra leapt gracefully in beside Simon, crouching on the vinyl seat in a tense, feline posture that was more comfortable to her than sitting normally. Ashley shot her a wry grin and climbed in after her.

Leandra started slightly when the vehicle's engine roared to life, but she settled down when Ashley laid a comforting hand on her knee. As they began the drive out of the park, Leandra managed to distract herself by concentrating on answering Simon's questions about the habits of the tigers she'd observed—their favorite locations, social interactions, and so on. Still, it took every ounce of willpower she possessed to sit still inside the lurching, mechanical beast as it made its clumsy way through the jungle along one of the more worn tracks. Leandra tried not to think about the fact that, very soon, she would be surrounded by hundreds, maybe even thousands, of people. And that she would have to endure a torturous, extremely long plane ride that would take her halfway around the world before she could relax. As she talked, she thought about the various intricacies of human social interaction that she'd all but abandoned during her life out here; little niceties that had once been second nature, but which served no purpose in the jungle and had therefore been discarded.

Why do humans have to be so much more complicated than other animals? Why do they… Why do we have to place so much importance on so many things that don't matter? As she considered all the changes she was going to have to adjust to, Leandra felt herself becoming overwhelmed. She felt exposed and vulnerable without the shadows of the jungle around her, without the tawny stripes that had been her protection for so long. *What the hell am I thinking? I must be out of my mind! I can't do this. Why am I even trying?*

Only when she looked to the side and found dark, sympathetic eyes gazing back at her did Leandra's mind grow calm. Ashley's quiet smile and comforting presence eased her fears and gave her the courage to face the challenges that lay ahead.

Smiling in return, Leandra focused her attention back on Simon.

That's why I'm doing this, she thought peacefully. *For her. For the way she makes me feel. As long as I know that she'll be with me—every time I turn around, every time I wake up, every time I make a mistake, or feel like it's all too hard—as long as I can see that love in her eyes, this is worth whatever hardships it costs.*

And as the jungle began to give way to the first signs of rural life, Leandra concentrated on the feel of Ashley's hand as it gently stroked her leg. She was willing to ignore the rest of the world just to enjoy the solace of her lover's touch.

"Look, Leandra, I'm not arguing that it was unprofessional for the stewardess to be hitting on you like that, okay? I'm just saying you could have simply asked her politely to remove her hand, instead of growling at her."

"It worked, didn't it?" Leandra gave Ashley a most rakish grin, her eyes glinting wickedly. "She took her hand off my thigh so fast you'd think I had the plague, and she didn't bother me for the rest of the flight."

Ashley did a bad job of trying to hold on to a stern expression. "Yeah, well, she didn't seem to notice me glaring daggers at her, even though I was sitting right next to you. I swear, if she'd come sidling up one more time with her 'Just let me know if there's anything else I can do to make your flight more enjoyable,' she might have found my teeth marks in her hand."

"Maybe we should just be grateful it didn't come to that," Leandra said, a little bemused by Ashley's possessive tone.

"Well, we're almost home now…another ten minutes or so. I don't know about you, but I'm looking forward to kicking my shoes off, lying down on the couch, and spending the next twenty-four hours imitating moss."

"Mmm…sounds good to me." Gazing out the window of the taxi as it cruised along quiet, neatly groomed streets of the Vermont suburbs, Leandra observed her new surroundings with interest. She had been having nightmare flashes of busy city streets and a suffocating throng of people (even though she was well aware that Ashley didn't live in a city), but what she could see looked quite pleasant. Before long, they ventured into pleasant woodlands, with only a few houses spaced every now and then along the route.

The trip had been every bit as difficult as she'd anticipated, despite the fact that it was—almost miraculously—disaster free. No one had questioned her somewhat dated passport. No one had searched her luggage and found the concealed tiger parts. The plane ride had been quiet and uneventful, with the minor exception of the overly friendly young stewardess and her lingering hands. Leandra had even managed a few minutes of restless sleep on the long flight, although the seats felt strange against her body and the air smelled stale and cloying. International travel was stressful even under ideal circumstances, and Leandra was looking forward to being alone again with the one woman she felt truly comfortable around.

Soon enough, they reached their destination. The cab pulled over to the curb outside a sprawling, two-story, brick-veneer house set among the trees of a tranquil forest. As Ashley thanked the driver and handed over a few bills, Leandra exited the vehicle with a sigh of relief. It was going to take a while to get used to things like cars again, she acknowledged, stretching her arms above her head and grunting. The tension and stress of the journey back to civilization made her right shoulder ache, and the pain was making her a little grumpy. Her mood brightened quickly, though, as soon as she reminded herself it was all over now.

Her new surroundings cheered her, too. In every direction, tall maple and aspens spread their branches high into the air, sheltering smaller saplings and underbrush beneath their boughs. Although it was a far cry from the humid jungle and sprawling grass plains that had been her home in India, Leandra felt a good deal more comfortable just being in a natural setting. There was a sense of safety to be found in the gently shifting shadows of the trees, and she took a moment to listen to the unfamiliar birdcalls that filled the air before turning her attention to studying the house itself.

The gardens leading up to the house looked somewhat wild and overgrown, but Leandra realized quickly that they had been purposely nurtured to appear that way. The garden suited the forest setting perfectly—not trying to bring order to the scene, but rather, complementing it with a harmonious design that probably required very little maintenance. The house continued this embrace of the natural world, sporting many large-paned windows and even a few stained-glass designs of kingfishers and other birds.

The cab pulled away, and Ashley joined her, the younger woman lifting her heavy backpack and fumbling for a set of keys.

"Home, sweet home," Ashley said in a warm voice. "Come on, I'll show you around."

Leandra followed her along a twisting rock pathway that ran up a few steps to the front entrance of the house. Ashley unlocked the door and knocked it open with her hip, gesturing for Leandra to precede her inside. Leandra accepted the invitation, looking around with great interest at what was to be her new home.

The first thing that struck her was the sense of openness and space. The many huge windows allowed natural light to flow in from outside, and Leandra appreciated the feeling of freedom it created. Hardwood floors covered by a few Indian-style rugs shone in the sunlight, and the interior walls were dotted with dozens of framed photographs, each a spectacular shot of one animal or another. In the center of the room was a sunken sitting area, with a large screen television and a comfortable-looking sectional couch. An archway to the right led into a neatly arranged dining area and kitchen, and a closed door on the left led to what Leandra assumed was a bedroom. A set of stairs ran up the far wall, giving access to the second floor of the house. Numerous indoor plants set tastefully around the room continued the natural theme. The air smelled clean and fresh, and Leandra felt her tensions drift farther away.

Ashley dumped her backpack on the hardwood floor and blew her bangs from her eyes. "What do you think?"

"I think I should have looked more seriously at pursuing a career in photography," Leandra said, genuinely impressed. "How can you afford a place like this?"

"A combination of raw talent, good luck, and generous parents." Laughing a little, Ashley took Leandra's hand in hers and guided her around the sunken living room. "I get paid well for my work, but that's not how it is for most photographers. I just happen to be one of the best in my field." Leading Leandra over to the far wall, she pointed out a number of plaques and framed awards displayed proudly beside pictures of various animals. "See? When you get this much praise, your talent comes at a much higher price."

Leandra leaned forward and studied the awards, reading the elegant words of glowing approbation from Ashley's peers. "I'm impressed."

"Yeah, well…" Ashley shuffled her feet unassumingly. "Like I said, part of it is just having luck on your side."

Leandra gestured to the many photographs hanging on the walls. "Did you take all these?"

"Uh huh. They're my favorites. The best of the best."

"They're magnificent." Leandra wandered around, pausing to study a fantastic underwater shot of a humpback whale and her calf. "You're more than lucky, Ashley. This is pure talent."

Ashley blushed at the praise. "Thank you."

"Still, this house must have cost a fortune, especially for someone as young as you to be able to afford."

"My parents helped me," Ashley admitted. "They live nearby, and I guess they were willing to support me a bit if it meant keeping me close to them, at least when I'm not traveling. They did the same for my sister, who lives a few minutes up the road."

Leandra nodded, still looking around. "No pets?"

"Only Melanie." Ashley pointed to a cabinet that was recessed in the right wall of the living room. Wandering over to investigate, Leandra's eyes searched among the rocks and tree branches inside until she made out the shiny, serpentine body within. Looking closer, she saw a pale, slightly dusky-colored snake with a head that looked as though it had been dipped in black ink.

"A black-headed python," Leandra identified quickly. "These only live in Australia."

"Yep. I was over there a few years ago, and I fell in love with them. I almost strained my wrist filling out all the licensing paperwork to get a permit, and she wasn't the cheapest pet I could have got, but it was worth it."

Leandra watched the sleepy reptile. "I thought you'd have more animals. I mean, you spend all your life around them."

"Yeah, I do," Ashley agreed. "And I'd love to get a dog or something, but my life's not exactly suited to having a lot of pets. Melanie doesn't need that much care, so she doesn't mind my not being around much. My niece, Casey, absolutely adores her, so she takes care of feeding and cleaning duties when I'm overseas."

"I see."

Ashley held out her hand. "Come on, I'll show you the rest. My bedroom's upstairs."

Leandra grinned at the mischievous twinkle in her lover's eyes and accepted the offered hand happily. "Lead on."

Ashley led her through the dining room and kitchen, pointing to a closed door as they passed it. "That's Casey's room," she explained. "She spends a lot of time here, so I gave her some space of her own."

A short hallway led to a study, filled wall to wall with overflowing bookcases, and beyond that was a spacious bathroom. Leandra smiled at the thought of taking a shower using water that wasn't icy cold. She decided that was one of the first things she was going to do, as soon as she'd seen the rest of the house.

Upstairs, she was shown a second, rather empty bedroom, as well as a sunroom that led out to a wraparound balcony. Finally, Ashley pushed open the last door and pulled Leandra into what was obviously her own bedroom. It contained a large, neatly made bed, a dresser, wardrobe, and all the other usual bedroom furnishings. A doorway to the side led into an adjacent bathroom, and another led outside to the balcony. Leandra lifted her head and sniffed as her sharpened senses detected the scent of her lover in the air.

Ashley spread her arms out to encompass the room. "I hope you like it. If you need some space of your own for a while, you're welcome to use the other bedroom, but..." she gave a shy smile. "There's plenty of space in here."

Leandra hesitated, a little overwhelmed by the changes in her life this past day and night had brought about. Accustomed to living among creatures that placed great importance on possession of their own territory, she had a lot of respect for personal boundaries. "I don't want to crowd you, Ashley. It's enough for you to offer me a place to stay in your home."

"I don't mind," Ashley quickly reassured her. "It's a big bed after all, and it would be such a waste for me to have to sleep alone on it now that you're here to keep me company."

Leandra saw only sincerity in the younger woman's face. "Okay, then." she agreed. "If you don't mind."

"I practically insist." Ashley wrapped her arms around Leandra's waist and pulled her close. "I didn't drag you halfway around the world just to have you sleep in another room. I want you as close to me as I can get you."

Leandra bent down and kissed her. This kind of affection was still new for her, but she was quickly accepting the way her body craved contact with Ashley. "Can I talk you into sharing a shower with me?" she purred. "I could use a change of clothes."

"Mmm, I don't know." Ashley grinned, and her eyes narrowed to seductive slits. "Are you going to make it worth my while?"

Leandra almost growled. "I think we could come to an arrangement."

"Okay." Ashley stepped back and released her hold on Leandra. "Just give me a minute. I should call my sister and tell her I'm back. Why don't you look around a little and make yourself comfortable? You know, rummage through the wardrobe, open a few drawers, stuff like that. Maybe you can find something of mine to wear." She ran her eyes appreciatively over Leandra's long, muscular form. "I think we're going to have to take you shopping, though. Can't have you running around naked for too long."

Leandra cocked an eyebrow saucily. "You can have me any way you want me," she husked throatily. "Anytime."

Ashley threw her a smoky, lustful grin. "That sounds like the kind of offer I can live with." For a moment she leaned nearer, not quite pressing the warmth of her skin against Leandra's body. Before their lips could meet, however, she teasingly withdrew. "Later. Let's get settled in first."

Leandra watched her lover exit the room and enjoyed the extra little swagger Ashley threw in for her benefit, then she took a deep breath and looked around. Deciding to do exactly as Ashley had suggested, she opened the wardrobe. Inside, the clothes were organized into neat sections, and Leandra began to search for something that might fit her larger frame. She found a sleep shirt and a pair of sweatpants that would have positively swamped her smaller lover, and threw them on the bed. As she closed the wardrobe door, she caught sight of her reflection in the mirror on the dresser. She paused and studied the face looking back at her.

It had been four years since she had seen her reflection so clearly; the rippling surface of water ponds in the jungle couldn't match the clarity of the glass mirror. Those four years had taken their toll, she thought, running her fingertips over her face. Her skin was pale from being covered by mud and paint, and there were a few more lines creasing the corners of her eyes and mouth. Her hair, once her proudest feature besides her electric-blue eyes, now framed her face in a mass of tangled snarls. Although she'd always kept herself in shape, life as a jungle predator had equipped Leandra with a body built for endurance, speed, and sheer power. Whipcord muscles rippled along her arms, thighs, and stomach. Leandra stood straighter in front of the mirror and flexed the enhanced muscles.

"Not too bad," she whispered, eyeing herself critically. "Not too bad at all."

Leandra had lost any sense of self-image during her exile—it hadn't mattered how she looked, since no one who saw her during that time lived long enough to offer any compliments—but it was nice to know that she was still attractive. It mattered more to her now that she had Ashley in her life.

Turning away from the mirror, Leandra padded around the room, her footsteps as silent as they'd ever been. She studied the few ornaments that rested on the bedside table and the dresser, seeing photographs of people she guessed were Ashley's family members. Stepping around the bed, she ran her hands along the quilt, luxuriating in the soft, feathery sensation after having slept on the ground for so long. Wandering around the room, she took a tour outside onto the balcony and looked around at the view of tranquil forests and placid gardens.

Should be fun to explore, she thought, looking forward to learning more about her new environment. Although Ashley's home was very nice, and she had no doubts that she would be comfortable here, Leandra knew it would take a long time before she could fully break free of the desire to return to the protective embrace of the forest shadows. *Four years alone in the jungle can't help but leave a mark,* she idly observed. *It'll be in my blood forever. I just hope Ashley can understand that.*

Returning to the bedroom, Leandra sat on the bed, thinking. After a moment or two, her eyes wandered to the bedside table, and she gave in to the temptation to snoop a little. Pulling open the drawer and peeking inside, she studied the contents curiously. A wrinkled, obviously much-loved romance novel, a small box of mints, an appointment diary, and finally...

Leandra's eyes widened slightly, and her lips formed a wicked grin. "Well, well, well, what have we here?" She reached in and pulled out the smooth, cylindrical plastic device that lay at the very back of the drawer. "I guess Little Miss Innocent's not so pure after all." Her sensitive ears picked up the sound of footsteps approaching, and she raised one dark brow devilishly as she held up her find.

Ashley entered, talking. "Well, I hope you don't mind, but my sister wants to come over for a visit. She hasn't seen me in a few months, so I said she could drop b—Eeek!" Ashley's eyes grew wide as saucers, and her face colored with an instant blush when she saw what Leandra was holding.

Leandra grinned and waved the vibrator at her lover. "You should have told me I was going to have some competition."

"Where did you…" Ashley sprang forward and grabbed for the plastic device. "Give me that!"

"Why?" Leandra used her longer arms to good advantage, keeping her find out of Ashley's reach. "Are you going to give me a private demonstration? I think I'd like that."

"Leandra." Ashley tried to wrestle Leandra's arm down, but couldn't manage it. "Give it here."

"Oh, come on. Didn't your mother ever teach you to share your toys?" Leandra pouted and began retreating toward the bathroom with Ashley stalking her every pace, emerald eyes narrowed to menacing slits.

"Leandra…" Ashley stepped closer.

"I guess a girl needs something to keep her happy on those lonely nights, right?"

"Hey, I've gone without a boyfriend for a long time now," Ashley defended. "I have normal appetites that need to be satisfied, just like everyone else."

Leandra purred. "I know." She backed up a few steps, feeling the cooler air of the tiled bathroom behind her. "You want to take that shower now?" Long, tapered fingers caressed the length of the plastic shaft seductively.

Ashley paused, her face glowing with a crimson blush, as she considered Leandra's proposal. "Give it back first."

"Why?" Leandra teased, sensing the younger woman's rising desire. "I was thinking maybe we could play a little."

Mahogany eyes widened. "What do you mean?"

"Well…" Leandra considered, studying the vibrator thoughtfully. "It's just a suggestion, but I wouldn't mind letting you…watch me."

Ashley's lips were parted, her breathing accelerated. "I don't know…"

"It'll be fun," Leandra promised in a husky whisper. "We can make it an 'active audience participation' kind of thing, if you'd like." She began unbuttoning her shirt with her left hand, enjoying the look of naked lust that immediately bloomed in Ashley's eyes. "You know, I haven't had a hot shower in four years." Leandra slipped the khaki shirt from her shoulders, exposing her naked chest. "It'd be a terrible shame if I had to do this all by myself." Ashley's eyes darkened to a smoky hue, as Leandra turned around and entered the small bathroom.

Behind her there was a moment of silence, then a quiet, "Well, we don't want that." Leandra struggled not to laugh at the sound of clothes being shed with frantic haste; clearly Ashley didn't want the show to start without her.

Sometime later, a flushed, tousled, but extremely satisfied Ashley emerged from upstairs, still toweling her hair dry. After the shower, which had involved a comprehensive and thoroughly enjoyable demonstration of her "plastic friend," Ashley had spent nearly fifteen minutes using a comb and plenty of conditioner to work out the worst of Leandra's hair tangles. She had left her lover to get dressed while she went in search of something to eat.

Wandering into the kitchen, Ashley began to rummage through poorly stocked cupboards, hoping to find a packet of cookies or something that hadn't expired during her overseas trip.

"Hey, sis, what's up?"

Startled, Ashley whirled around, almost slamming the cupboard door on her fingers. Cursing, she glared at the intruder.

"Jesus Christ, Evie! Can't you knock on the door or something, next time?"

Evelyn gave her an unrepentant grin and swept her into a warm hug. "It's not often I get to take you by surprise, Ash. And for your information, I did knock. You didn't answer, so I figured you were in the shower or something and let myself in. It's great to have you back." Ending the hug,

Evelyn held Ashley by the shoulders and ran her eyes shrewdly down her body. Ashley knew she was looking for signs of injury; it wasn't uncommon for her to return from these trips covered in insect bites, nasty scratches, and sometimes worse. "Well, you don't look too bad for someone who spent the last few weeks roughing it. How was India? Did you bring anything back with you? You know Casey's going to kill you if you didn't get her that singing bowl she was asking about."

Ashley glanced at the stairs. "Well, I didn't get to go shopping as much as I wanted to. Things got a little hectic toward the end. But yeah, I did get to bring one really interesting surprise back with me."

"Really? What?"

At that point Leandra's husky voice called from upstairs. "Hey, Ashley? If you can't find anything in the kitchen, I've got something up here you could nibble on."

Evelyn looked from the stairway to Ashley—who was struggling to keep a rising blush at bay—then back again. "Who's that?"

Ashley shrugged sheepishly. "That's my surprise."

Evelyn raised an eyebrow, but before she could ask for more elaboration, Leandra appeared at the bottom of the stairway. The clothes she'd borrowed from Ashley fit her a little snugly, and her hair and body were still dripping with water, making the clothes cling to every impressive curve of her six-foot-something frame. When Ashley saw her lover, she rolled her eyes at the water pooling around her feet. *I guess she's forgotten about towels and stuff, too.*

Leandra stopped uncertainly when she saw Evelyn. "Oh. I didn't hear the door…" She gave Ashley an apologetic look and stepped closer to her.

"Evie, I'd like you to meet Leandra." Ashley quickly made introductions. "Leandra, this is my sister, Evelyn."

Leandra smiled shyly. "Nice to meet you."

"Likewise." Evelyn studied the tall, dripping woman curiously a moment, then turned her questioning eyes back to Ashley.

"Leandra's going to be staying with me," Ashley explained, reaching out a hand to pull her lover closer.

"I see."

Leandra squeezed Ashley's hand lightly, but her eyes darted hopefully to the door. "I was actually thinking I might take a look around outside, if that's okay. I'm sure you two have a lot of catching up to do."

"Sure." Ashley understood that Leandra was giving her some space and also that she needed some herself. "Just don't go climbing too many trees or rolling around in any mud patches. I just got you clean, and I'd like to keep you that way for a while."

Leandra made a face. "I know." She glanced at Evelyn, then leaned down to give Ashley a quick kiss, taking the opportunity to whisper, "I love you," into her ear. She then turned and offered a nod to the watching Evelyn. "Ashley's told me a lot about you. It's nice to finally meet you in person."

"Well, I look forward to getting to know you better, Leandra."

Leandra smiled, then headed for the door with silent footsteps.

"Leandra?" Ashley called just as she reached for the handle.

"Mmm?"

"If you see anyone out there, try not to growl at them," Ashley said with a touch of humor. "Remember, we have to live with these people, okay?"

Sapphire eyes glinted playfully. "Don't worry, I'll be good." Leandra gave her lover a quick wink before disappearing outside.

Ashley watched the door close, then turned back to face her sister. Evelyn raised an eyebrow at her, and she shuffled somewhat awkwardly. "Um... That was Leandra."

"So I see." Evelyn was obviously trying to hide a shit-eating grin.

Ashley had been subconsciously preparing for this conversation, knowing it was coming, but Evelyn's surprise visit had caught her off guard. "You know, I could use some coffee. You want a cup? I think I have some in here." She began to rummage through the cupboards again.

"Sounds good." Evelyn claimed one of the barstools and rested her arms on the breakfast counter, continuing to watch her with an amused smile. It was rare for Ashley to get flustered, and her sister was clearly enjoying it. "So, let me see if I understand this." She cleared her throat. "You went to India on a shoot, and you brought home a woman? What's the matter, couldn't find anything good in the souvenir shops?"

"It's a long story."

"Oh, I'll bet. I can't wait to hear it."

Ashley set the kettle on to boil and occupied herself with preparing two cups. She glanced at Evelyn a few times, trying to gauge her reaction. Thankfully, she found no trace of persecution or distaste being aimed toward her. She took a deep breath and exhaled slowly. "I don't really know where to start."

"You two are involved, right?"

Ashley nodded.

"I see." Evelyn was silent for a moment, studying her with a neutral expression. "You never told me you were interested in women."

Ashley shrugged awkwardly. "Well, you know me. I'm not really comfortable talking about that sort of stuff. And I guess you could say Leandra's kind of a first for me, in more ways than one."

"Ah. Well, she seems nice. A little quiet, maybe."

"When you get to know her better, you'll understand why that is."

Evelyn cocked her head. "What was that bit about her growling at the neighbors?"

"Believe me, it was a valid warning." The kettle boiled, and Ashley added steaming water to the cups along with instant coffee and sugar. She handed one cup to her sister and left the other on the counter. "Wait here a minute, I'll get something that might help explain better."

She raced upstairs and returned a moment later carrying a small paper folder. Reaching in, she drew out a couple of Polaroid's and handed them to her sister.

Evelyn took the pictures and studied them curiously. "What's this?"

"That's Leandra, before I got her back here," Ashley explained. Evelyn's eyes narrowed in confusion. Each photograph showed Leandra dressed in her striped tiger-fur outfit, her body painted up like a Halloween costume. The jungle filled in the background, vines and palms obscuring the scene. Even in the still picture, Leandra managed to convey at least a sense of the savage, primal energy that so characterized her in the jungle. "Why is she dressed like that?"

"It's how she looked. She lived alone in the jungle for the last four years. I was pretty much the first person she talked to in that whole time, expect for the tigers."

Evelyn's eyes widened. "You're kidding."

"Nope." Ashley reached for her coffee and took a sip. "It's hard to believe, but she had been living as a tiger all that time. She can hunt like they do, move like they do. She can even talk like they do. She's absolutely amazing to watch in action."

"But why? I mean, what was she doing out there?"

"She had her reasons." Ashley hesitated, not comfortable sharing the secrets of Leandra's life, even with her own sister. "I guess life hit her badly, and she needed some time to get herself together again."

Evelyn studied the pictures again with new appreciation, shaking her head in amazement. "How the hell did you hook up with her?"

"When we went out there, we happened to set up camp in her hunting ground." Ashley climbed onto the barstool next to her sister. "She was curious about us and came snooping round one night. She scared the heck out of me, I'll tell you. Then, one morning I was out by the river, and I got in some trouble. I surprised a poacher, and Leandra came along and scared him off. She disappeared before I could say much, but that night, I saw her campfire. You know me, I couldn't let well enough alone. The next morning, I went looking for her, wanting to say thank you, and we just kind of clicked."

"That's unbelievable. I mean, I'm used to you coming home from these trips with some good stories, but this is pretty wild even by your scale."

"I know." Ashley grinned. "She was really lonely out there, so we started spending time together. She showed me everything she knew, shared all her secrets with me. We really fit together well, and the more I got to know her, the more I liked her. I couldn't really help it. I fell for her—hard." She chuckled a little sheepishly. "Imagine my surprise when I found out she felt the same way."

"Well..." Evelyn gave the photograph a last look and handed it back. "She's easy on the eyes, I'll give you that. And I guess she can't be any worse than that last guy you dated. What was his name? Steve?"

"Ugh, don't remind me." Ashley made a face. "Leandra's nothing like anyone I've ever been involved with."

"So, I guess this is pretty serious then, huh?"

"She came halfway around the world just to be here with me," Ashley said, "and if she hadn't, I would have stayed in the jungle to be with her. She left her whole world behind for me, and I know that wasn't easy for her. So yeah, it's about as serious as it gets."

"Well, I'm happy for you, sis." Evelyn leaned over and gave her another hug. "She must love you a lot to give up everything just to stay by your side."

"Thanks." Ashley felt an unrealized tension ease from her shoulders. She was grateful she had her sister's support, knowing it would help smooth the way when it came time to tell their parents. "That means a lot to me."

Evelyn pulled away from the embrace, her eyes dropping to Ashley's neck and chest. She grinned mischievously. "And all of a sudden, those marks are looking less like insect bites and more like love bites."

Ashley blushed and tried futilely to pull her shirt over the light bruises. "Yeah, well...Leandra gets pretty intense sometimes."

Evelyn waggled her eyebrows, clearly enjoying this rare display of discomfort. "I'll bet. What are you planning on telling Mom and Dad? I take it they don't know you're back?"

"No, I was going to wait a bit before I called them." Ashley rubbed her eyes and took another sip of coffee. "I need some time to rest after the flight and also let Leandra get settled in. Coming back to civilization has to be a serious culture shock for her."

"Uh huh. Maybe it would help if I talked to them first? Just to give them a heads up, explain things a little so they have some time to get used to the idea?"

"You can if you like," Ashley said, her expression stern. "But Leandra's here to stay, no matter how they feel about it. It's not like I can send her back there. I love her, and that's just something they'll have to accept."

"Okay, but this is pretty big news, Ash," Evelyn pointed out patiently. "Mom and Dad don't freak out easily, but this is going to be a bit of a shock. I think it'll go better if you don't just spring Leandra on them."

Ashley considered that and had to agree her sister was right; she wanted her parents to like Leandra, and that was more likely to happen if they had a moment to get used to the idea before they met her. "I'll call them tomorrow night," she said. "If you want to go over there and explain the situation before that, I don't mind."

Evelyn smiled agreeably. "No problem." Swallowing the last of her coffee, she dropped the cup off in the sink. "Casey's going to go nuts."

Ashley snorted. "Trust me, Evie, I think she'll get along just fine with Leandra." Casey had never really gotten along well with any of her past romances. The somewhat rebellious seventeen-year-old treated her aunt more like an older sister. They were close to the same age, both determined to do what they wanted in life regardless of the opinions of others, and they spent a lot of time together.

Casey sometimes got a bit possessive whenever Ashley had a boyfriend. Still, for some reason, Ashley didn't foresee any troubles regarding Leandra. It was just a feeling she had, but somehow, she knew the two would mesh well.

"She'll be home from school in about an hour," Evelyn said. "I should warn you, she's been waiting for you to get back for the past two weeks, and none too patiently at that. Will it be okay if she comes around tonight?"

"Sure, no problem. You want me to feed her?"

Evelyn glanced at the bare cupboards wryly. "I think I'd better do that. Looks like you need to do some shopping."

"Yeah. I'll take a trip into town tomorrow and restock. Leandra needs some new clothes, and I should stop in at work and process some film." She put the Polaroid's back in their folder. "Just wait until you see some of the other shots I got. You won't believe them, they're so amazing."

"I can't wait." Evelyn glanced at the oven clock. "I'd better head off," she said with a sigh. "Sorry it's such a brief welcome home, but I should have started cooking dinner an hour ago. I'll stop by as soon as I get some spare time, okay? I'm looking forward to getting to know your new friend a bit better." She wrapped Ashley in a final farewell hug. "You're not planning any more trips for a while, right?"

"I hope not." Ashley returned the hug tightly. "It's good to be home again. I've missed having someone to talk to about everything."

"We'll sit down and have a proper talk soon, I promise. I want to hear all the details about your latest adventure." Evelyn's eyes sparkled playfully. "Even the juicy ones."

Ashley blushed and gave her sister a gentle shove. "I'm not the type to kiss and tell."

"Yeah, well I've been a staid, old married mother for nearly eighteen years, young lady, so the least you can do is give me a few interesting tidbits." Evelyn waved. "I'll see you later, Ash."

"Yeah, see you."

Ashley watched through the window, as her sister got in her car and drove off. She was glad her older sibling had been so understanding. Although she had told herself she didn't care what her family thought of Leandra, she now realized that deep down, she still wanted their approval. She had been very successful in her professional choices, and her parents were justly proud of her efforts. Now, she wanted them to love and accept Leandra the same way she did, and a part of her feared they wouldn't be willing or able to embrace this latest development in her life.

Ashley headed upstairs to retrieve her shoes so she could go looking for her lover in the forest. She smiled at the trail of water Leandra had left after her shower, shaking her head with fond indulgence.

"We've got some re-education to do, Jungle Jane." Ashley knew that getting Leandra back to civilization wasn't going to instantly tame the wild instincts that had developed these last four years. The tiger-woman would require a lot of patience and understanding in the weeks ahead, and Ashley had no illusions about this being some kind of fairytale romance where everything was always easy. It was going to take hard work and endless compassion in order for their budding relationship to survive.

Still, Ashley was never one to back down from a challenge. She had faith in the strength of her love for Leandra, and almost looked forward to the challenges they were going to face in the coming days.

Later that evening, Leandra sat on the floor of the sunken living room, her back propped against the lounge, legs stretched out across the comfortable Indian rug before her. Ashley sat on the lounge, one leg thrown over each of Leandra's shoulders, playing idly with a few cords of tangled ebony hair. A couple of empty dinner plates sat on the coffee table, only one of which had any cutlery on it, since Leandra still preferred eating with her hands. The television was on, and images of colorful cartoon characters played across the screen to the quiet sounds of accompanying music. They watched the Road Runner evade yet another wildly improbable scheme cooked up by Wile E. Coyote, and Ashley enjoyed the sweet smile that lifted the corners of Leandra's lips.

"It's nice to know some things don't change," Leandra remarked huskily. "Television seems just as inane as I remember it."

"I think they're kind of cute," Ashley said, watching the ever-persistent Coyote plummet off a cliff. "You know he'll never catch the Road Runner, and that makes it funny when he fails. And he never gives up. That's a good message."

Leandra grunted and began stroking Ashley's bare feet softly. "I'm exhausted."

"Me too." Ashley wriggled her toes and gave a sleepy, encouraging moan. "Jet lag plus stress equals one massive energy drain. We'll get some sleep soon."

Leandra was silent for a few moments before she asked. "What are we doing tomorrow?"

"I thought we'd go into town and do some shopping. You can't be comfortable wearing clothes that are five sizes too small for you."

Leandra glanced back at her with heat in her eyes, a shiver-inducing purr rumbling from deep in her chest. "You could always take them off me."

Ashley blushed. "I could, but I think that'd be a bit much for when Casey stops by."

Leandra's expression changed, and the purring grew silent. "Oh, right. I'd forgotten about that."

Ashley shifted around on the couch so she could give Leandra's shoulder a comforting squeeze. "You don't need to worry, Leandra. Casey doesn't bite."

"I know, it's just…" Leandra struggled for a moment, looking around at the furnishings with a wistful expression. "I haven't had to socialize with anyone in so long, it's hard to remember how to act. In the jungle, things were so much simpler. The rules were clearer. Here, things are so much more complex."

"You'll get the hang of it again soon," Ashley said. "There's no reason to rush anything. We'll take it as slow as you want." She paused, and then added, "Tomorrow is Saturday. We can go to one of the quieter places to look for clothes, if you like. It'll be fine, you'll see."

"What about money?"

"I don't mind paying our expenses."

"Ashley, I can't just expect you to support me forever," Leandra insisted. "That's not fair to either of us."

Ashley couldn't deny that had their positions been reversed, she would feel the same way. Leandra had lived in a world where the only person she could rely on was herself; expecting her to sacrifice her independence wasn't reasonable. "Okay, I suppose I can understand that. But this has been a big move for you, Leandra. You need to take some time to settle in, and worrying about money isn't going to help. If it makes you feel better to pay me back later, fine, but I want to do what I can to make this easier for you."

"I know, and I appreciate it. But I've been giving this some thought since I first decided to leave, and I might have at least a temporary solution."

"Oh?"

Leandra shifted around so she could face her directly. "Before I went to India, I was pretty well off. I had an expensive apartment in New York and a lot of assets."

"But you've been gone for four years," Ashley pointed out. "Whatever was in the apartment probably got sold for back rent."

"Maybe. But I had money stashed in several overseas accounts that no one could have touched. There were a few storage houses holding my stuff, too. They would have been paid automatically. It might take a while, but I know all the details are in my head somewhere. If I have some time, I can remember them. The money would be more than enough to pay my way, at least until I figure out a way to earn my keep."

Ashley considered this idea and smiled. "Okay then, if that would make you feel better."

"It would." Leandra turned back around and pulled Ashley's legs tighter against her chest. "You know, I'd forgotten how much importance people place on money," she whispered after a period of silence. "It's kind of ironic, in a way. I spent so much of my life trying to accumulate as much wealth and power as I could, just like most people do, thinking it gave me greater control over my life. But four years in the jungle have a way of changing your priorities, showing you what's really important. The control I thought I had was just an illusion, and all the money in the world couldn't have saved me if Shar-Tushar had decided to take my life." She smiled. "When you strip it all away—the money, the home, the secure little world where you're in charge of everything you see and touch and desire—when it's all gone, you start to understand just how little control you actually have. I hadn't really thought about it until now, but it's kind of liberating to live as an animal. So much simpler. Hunt, eat, sleep." She cast a saucy glance behind her. "Mate."

Ashley smiled slightly. "You're going to miss that world, aren't you?"

"Would I be a terrible person if I said yes?"

"Of course not."

Leandra's lips pressed into a firm line. "Have you ever heard about how some people who have been in prison a long time start to fear their freedom?"

"Institutionalization? Yeah."

"I can understand that," Leandra said in a soft voice. "The jungle was my prison, my punishment. I hated it so much, sometimes. But in a way, I loved it just as intensely. I understood the jungle world; even though sometimes it hurt me, I learned a lot about myself from experiencing life the way I did." She regarded Ashley seriously. "But at the end of the day, I'm glad you came along before it became too late for me to leave my prison."

Ashley felt the full force of Leandra's love and affection hit her as she looked into those burning sapphire eyes, but before she could think of anything to say in response, there was a knock on the door. Both women glanced up, then turned to each other.

"That'll be Casey," Ashley said.

Leandra disentangled herself and stood up, then offered a hand to help Ashley to her feet. "I think I'll take a look around outside. Maybe climb that great big oak tree out there."

"You don't have to go, Leandra." The knocking was repeated, and Ashley went to answer. "Casey's going to want to meet you sooner or later, so you might as well—" She turned back around but found the living room empty. Leandra had vanished, swift and silent as a dark zephyr. Ashley turned back to the front door. "Damn, that woman moves fast," she muttered. "I'm going to have to get a bell or something to tie around her neck."

Sitting in the branches of the ancient, gnarled oak tree that dominated the backyard of Ashley's home, Leandra closed her eyes and listened peacefully to the sounds of the night animals. Things were a good deal quieter in this sedate forest than they were in the steamy depths of the Indian jungle, but Leandra could detect subtle calls and cries others might ignore. Her hearing was finely tuned to pick up the minutest details, and to her, the sounds told a dramatic story of hunter and prey.

My first night back in civilization. I can already tell I'm going to be spending a lot of time in this tree.

The tree was huge, its branches sweeping close to the ground and providing easy holds for climbing. Leandra had positioned herself among the topmost branches of the great tree, hidden from below by the dense foliage. She felt safe here. Comfortable. Although she wasn't exactly afraid of meeting the rest of Ashley's family, she could admit to a little private nervousness. She'd lost her own family a long time ago, and all the different interactions and familial relations were strange to her. Leandra wondered if she'd ever really feel at ease in this world.

I fit in with the tigers better than I do with my own species, she thought sadly.

A noise from below made her tense, and she shifted on her perch to listen as footsteps made their way closer to the base of the oak. Sniffing the air, she detected an unfamiliar scent. *Not Ashley,* she concluded, as the sound of someone climbing up toward her grew louder, Leandra remained crouching there silently in the shadows, her senses picking up the smells of leather, perfume, and youth.

Moments later, a hand reached up and wrapped around the thick branch on which Leandra was sitting. A second joined it, and soon a young girl pulled herself up onto the perch, giving a slight grunt. Taking a second to look around in the light of the waning full moon, she spied Leandra sitting against the bole of the tree and smiled briefly.

"Hi."

"Hello."

The girl settled herself somewhat awkwardly on the branch, then studied Leandra curiously. "I'm Casey, Ashley's niece."

Leandra smiled a quiet smile. "It's nice to meet you, Casey."

"Yeah."

Leandra was a little amused at the young girl's posture and attitude. Years spent among unpredictable and often savage jungle cats had given her a lot of experience reading expression and body language, and right now she had the distinct impression that Casey was sizing her up against a very critical scale. *Well,* she thought. *Can't avoid this forever, I suppose.*

From what Leandra could see in the shifting moonlight, Casey looked to be right at the rebellious part of her adolescence. She was about Ashley's size, and slender as a reed, but she held herself with an almost aggressive confidence that Leandra recognized from her lover. The left side of her face was framed by light blonde hair, while the right was shadowed by bright green locks. Several metal loops sparkled along the rim of each ear, and a single elegant ring hooked through her left nostril. Dark eye shadow made her emerald eyes seem almost disconcertingly bright, and she wore torn denim jeans and a black T-shirt sporting a picture of what Leandra guessed was some rock band. Looking at Casey, Leandra flashed on an image of what Ashley might have looked like at seventeen.

Casey performed her own assessment, running shrewd eyes up and down Leandra's curled-up form. When she was finished, she regarded her with a flicker of reluctant interest. "Ash said you were going to be living with her."

Leandra nodded. "That's right."

"So you're her girlfriend now?"

"I suppose I am," Leandra said. *I've never been anyone's "girlfriend" before.* "Is that a problem?"

Casey shrugged. "Doesn't matter to me. Ash never told me she liked chicks, but I'm not surprised." She paused. "I doubt there's anything she could do that'd surprise me anymore."

"I bet."

"Do you love her?"

Leandra was momentarily taken aback by the bluntness of the question, but she appreciated the sharp challenge in the teenager's eyes. "I love her more than I can put into words," she said, not breaking eye contact. "I'd rather die than live without her in my life."

Casey held Leandra's gaze a long moment, reading her sincerity. Then she nodded, apparently satisfied. "Most of the guys she dated before avoided that question. They hemmed and hawed and talked about devotion and companionship, but they couldn't actually say the words."

"You don't need to worry about that, Casey. I could say them a thousand times a day, and I'd mean them every bit as much as I do right now."

"Good." Casey was silent for a long while, then she gestured to Leandra's hair. "I like your braids. Must take ages to do."

"A while, yeah. It's a lot easier when I don't have to do it by myself." Leandra fingered one of the neat cords hanging over her shoulder; Ashley had insisted on giving her hair a thorough brushing, after which she diligently retied the dozens of thin braids. "I like the nose ring. Kind of goes with the bright-green hair."

"Thanks." Casey smiled fully, and her resemblance to Ashley was suddenly a lot stronger. "My mom about had a fit when I got it done. I want to get my tongue pierced too, but she said not until I'm eighteen." There was a pause. "Ash said you used to live in the jungle with the tigers. Is that true?"

Leandra inclined her head slightly. "For four years."

"What was it like?"

"Lonely. But I learned a lot from them."

"Really? Like what?"

Casey's expression now held definite curiosity and interest. Leandra felt herself warming to her lover's niece, and she relaxed her posture slightly. "Like how to move without making noise, for one thing. How to track by scent. I could smell you coming when you were still on the ground."

"Yeah?" Casey's eyes widened a little.

"Yeah." Leandra hesitated, knowing this girl was an important part of her lover's life, and now, by extension, her own. "I could teach you, if you wanted to learn."

"That sounds pretty cool. When?"

"Anytime you like."

"Tomorrow?"

"Okay. I'm going shopping with Ashley in the morning, but if you'd like, we could go walking after that and I'll show you some stuff."

"Cool." Casey grinned brilliantly, her eyes lighting up her entire face. "You know…" She shifted closer to Leandra. "Ash never had great taste in guys. Most of her boyfriends were jerks. They didn't like it when she tried to stand up for herself, or when she had to travel all the time." She paused, studying Leandra in the moonlight. "It's nice to know she has better taste in girls."

Leandra raised a brow in amusement, her lips quirking into a half-grin. "Thank you."

"Welcome." Casey looked around at the dark forest. "Were you hiding out here because of me?"

This time Leandra couldn't help herself, and she laughed at the young girl's brashness. "Sort of," she admitted. "You haven't seen your aunt in a long time, and from listening to her talk about you, I know how close the two of you are. I didn't want to get in the way of you catching up."

Casey gave Leandra an approving, friendly look. "Most of Ash's boyfriends hated having me around all the time. You don't have to wait out here if you don't want to."

"It's okay. I like the nighttime, and it's interesting just listening to the different animals."

"Yeah, well, you can do that some other night." Casey repositioned herself on the bough, preparing to climb down the massive tree. She fixed Leandra with a stern gaze. "Come on. You and Ash can tell me all about how you two got together."

Leandra considered, then nodded. "Fine." Rising from her seat, the former jungle-woman glanced at the ground below for a second, and then sprang into the air. With the agility of a trapeze artist, she grabbed for a lower branch, then another, moving down the limbs of the oak with fluid speed until she landed soundlessly on the ground.

Casey watched wide-eyed, then scampered down the usual way. When she reached the base of the tree, she stared at Leandra in awe. "Wow! You're like a circus person. How'd you do that?"

Leandra shrugged modestly. "Four years in the jungle. You learn a lot of things."

Casey stared a moment longer, then grabbed Leandra by the hand and started dragging her toward the house. "You and me are going to get along just fine, Tiger Tarzan," she said confidently.

Leandra grinned and followed her lover's niece inside.

After the stress of the last two days—Leandra leaving behind her jungle home, traveling halfway around the world, and then enduring a rather late night with Ashley and Casey—Ashley was unsurprised when the midday sun found Leandra still deep in restorative sleep. It had been close to midnight by the time Ashley had tugged her taller partner upstairs to bed, and they had both been so drawn with fatigue that they hadn't even bothered getting undressed, but had simply fallen into bed and pulled the covers over their weary bodies before drifting off almost immediately.

Now, with her eyes still closed and the last misty tendrils of a pleasant dream still tempting her back to sleep, Ashley relished the feel of the warm, powerful body pressed against her. One of her arms was curled possessively around Leandra's waist, and at some point during the night, she had thrown a leg over her lover's hip. Twisting around slightly, careful not to wake her bedmate, Ashley glanced at the alarm clock that rested on the bedside table and groaned.

We've slept half the day away. Studying Leandra's face at close range, Ashley noticed the beginnings of dark circles under her eyes.

I guess she needed the rest. We both did.

Ashley knew she could only let her partner sleep a little longer; there was a lot to do today. Not only did she need to go clothes shopping, but she needed to call in at the magazine so she could begin processing film. Her boss would probably want to rant at her a little, but she wasn't too worried about that. Joseph Harding was a shrewd man, and he knew talent well enough to recognize how important Ashley was to his business. In the last few years, her pictures had managed to increase sales by a significant margin, so he wouldn't complain too much about her late return. Still, she was going to have a lot of work to do in the next few weeks. She needed to select which shots to use and which to discard, coordinate with Grady to find the best scenic spreads to complement her pictures, and set up arrangements for her next assignment.

It was going to be a busy time, especially with the changes in her personal life.

Fortunately, Leandra woke not too much later, blinking sleepily and giving her waist a long, affectionate squeeze. "Morning."

"Good morning." Ashley twisted to look up at the fuzzy eyes and tangled hair of her lover. "Did you sleep well?"

Leandra stretched, a purr rumbled in her chest. "Wonderfully," she rasped throatily.

"The bed didn't feel too strange, did it? I mean, you're used to sleeping on the ground."

"Are you kidding? This is the softest thing I've slept on in four years." Leandra gave her a soft, loving smile. "I adapt quickly, especially when I have such great incentive." She glanced down at Ashley's fully clothed body, held tight against her own. Ashley lifted herself up and laid a kiss on Leandra's lips, earning a muffled chuckle. "That's not really the best way to motivate me to get up, if that's what you were hoping."

The two snuggled for a few more minutes, exchanging light caresses that hinted at something deeper, before Ashley reluctantly reminded herself that they couldn't spend all day lazing around…tempting as the thought was. After she got them moving, they enjoyed a light breakfast of toast and coffee while discussing their plans for the day. Fortunately, Casey stopped by for a visit and invited herself along for the ride, so Ashley took advantage of her presence to speed things up a bit.

They decided that Ashley would drive them all into town, where she would leave Casey and Leandra to go shopping while she checked in at work. Casey agreed readily, constantly flicking glances at Leandra. *She's hooked,* Ashley thought, amused. *I'm finally involved with someone she can relate to, someone interesting and exciting.* Casey liked things that were different and unpredictable, which was one of the traits that had cemented her bond with Ashley. Leandra had lived a shady life as a poacher and smuggler, then spent four years living with giant jungle cats. She was about as different and unpredictable as a person could be. Small wonder that Casey was fascinated by her.

The town of Silver Falls was about a quarter hour's drive from Ashley's house. Quiet, serene, and untroubled, the town was supported year-round by tourists who came to visit the beautiful forests that bordered the mountains to the north. Driving along the winding road that led into town, Ashley glanced at her partner, sitting next to her in the passenger seat, trying to gauge her mood. Leandra's face was tense and her eyes fixed straight ahead. Her breathing was somewhat hurried.

Reaching out a hand, Ashley patted her on the thigh. "You okay?"

Leandra nodded shortly. "Fine."

"Will you be all right with Casey? I can come with you if you want me to."

"No, I can manage. I wasn't really much of a big shopper before I went to India, but how bad can it really be?"

"The shops should be pretty quiet," Casey put in, perhaps sensing Leandra's nerves. "Most people around here prefer to go camping or stuff on the weekends. We'll be okay, Leandra, trust me."

Leandra nodded again, looking out the car window at the neatly spaced shops and houses that lined the streets.

Ashley pulled over near one of the department stores and let Leandra and Casey out of the car. Winding down the window, she handed her lover a plastic card. "That's my savings account," she explained. "Casey knows the pass code, so just use it to buy whatever you like." Leandra opened her mouth to protest, but Ashley insisted. "I want you to at least have clothes that fit you properly, Leandra. You can pay me back later if you want to, but don't argue with me now."

Leandra pocketed the card. "Fine."

"We'll meet back here in an hour, okay? And Casey?" Ashley eyed her niece sternly. Casey had been caught shoplifting a few times this last year, and had more recently developed quite an acid tongue that she liked to exercise against shop assistants. "You behave yourself. I don't want you making things harder for Leandra than they already are."

Casey rolled her eyes and shifted her feet. "I won't smart-mouth anyone," she promised sullenly. "And I'll make sure we stay out of trouble." Glancing aside, she shot Leandra a crooked grin.

Ashley saw the look, and frowned. She glared at Leandra. "And you play nice with the people, too. No growling, no snarling, and no destroying the merchandise."

Leandra smiled. "I'll try to restrain myself."

Ashley looked from one set of eyes to the other, and satisfied they were going to behave themselves, blew a quick kiss to Leandra and pulled away from the curb. *One hour,* she thought as she glanced in the rearview mirror. *How much trouble could they possibly find in an hour?*

The moment Ashley pulled away from the curb, Casey took Leandra's hand in her own and began pulling her toward the automatic doors leading into the department store. "Come on. Let's go spend some of Ash's money."

Following somewhat more hesitantly after her enthusiastic guide, Leandra flinched as they entered the store and were caught under the glare of the bright fluorescent lighting. She looked around, taking stock of her environment in a single glance as she had trained herself to do during her exile. Only a few groups of people wandered the aisles, their voices mixing with the sound of classical music played through invisible speakers. The air was filled overwhelmingly with conflicting smells—disinfectant, perfume, and the subtle scent of pressed and cleaned fabric. Leandra felt exposed in the artificial light and had to restrain the urge to flee. The survival instincts she'd honed in the jungle had instilled in her a natural inclination to stay hidden in the background. As she followed Casey to the displays of women's clothing, her eyes darted around with penetrating intensity and she concentrated on blending in with the other shoppers.

Her guide, however, did not seem to have any such concerns. Casey strode purposefully down the aisles, chin lifted, wearing a slightly amused smirk. The other shoppers didn't even glance at Leandra, but a few of them stared at the young teenager from the corners of their eyes. Casey's bright-green hair, aggressively assertive demeanor, and leather-and-denim clothing made her stand out in the neatly ordered store, and she seemed to enjoy the attention.

"So, what do you want to look at?" she asked, as they reached their destination. "I don't see you as the dress-wearing sort. Am I right?"

Leandra's gaze swept the immediate area. "Let's stick with jeans and T-shirts for now, okay?"

"Sure thing." Casey led them to racks of variously arranged cotton shirts and began to pick through them. "Any preference for color?"

"No, I don't think so." Leandra eyed the clothing curiously.

"Been a long time since you had a choice, huh?"

"Yeah, it has."

"You'll probably want to check out the shoe department, too." Casey glanced meaningfully at Leandra's bare feet. "You step on some broken glass or something, and you'll be hobbling for a while."

"I doubt it." Leandra lifted one foot and showed the girl her callused soles. "My feet are pretty tough. I can walk over sharp rocks and thorns, and they don't hurt me. It's more comfortable like this."

Casey shrugged. "All right, they're your feet."

Sorting through the racks, Casey helped her select three T-shirts, two pairs of jeans, and a pair of sweatpants. Leandra didn't bother trying the clothes on; she simply held them against her body to determine their fit, confident she'd be able to live with any minor faults. As they wandered through the women's fashion section, she noticed a store security officer discreetly tailing them.

"Looks like they've decided we're the suspicious types," she noted to her companion.

Casey glanced over at the neatly dressed man and rolled her eyes. "That's what you get when you're a teenager. Every shop I go to these days, they always look at me like I'm about to club them with a sack of pennies or something." She stared at the detective for several moments, waiting for him to realize he'd been spotted, then turned away and deliberately ignored his presence. "Come on."

Leandra smiled as her younger companion led them into the lingerie section. Glancing behind, she noticed the in-store detective had decided not to pursue them any farther. Looking around at the various lacy undergarments, Leandra's interest in shopping rose a few notches, and she slowed her strides accordingly.

Casey stopped when she realized she was alone. "Need something here, too?"

"I guess so." Leandra reached out to run her fingers along the satin cloth of a fringed teddy, and a slight smile twitched the corners of her lips upwards. "It might be nice to have something special to wear…something Ashley might like."

"You mean something she might like to see you in?"

"Yeah." Leandra glanced back at the girl curiously; Casey was watching her with a difficult to read expression. "Is there something wrong with wanting to look good for the woman I love?"

"Of course not." Casey hesitated. "It's just a little weird to be talking about Ash like that, that's all."

"Because she's your aunt, or because I'm a woman?"

"Ash is a lot more than just my aunt," Casey explained. "She's my best friend. I mean, I don't really think of her as 'Auntie Ashley,' you know? She's just…my friend. It's weird talking about her like this because…" Casey sucked on her lower lip. "Ash doesn't really *do* much in this particular field, if you know what I mean. She never has. I always just figured she put most of her passion into her work rather than, you know, into the bedroom."

Leandra grinned. "You think she's a prude?"

"I didn't say that." Casey held up a hand in protest. "And just so you know, Ash hates that word. It's just…"

"I can tell you right now, Casey, that Ashley is as passionate and energetic a lover as she is a photographer," Leandra said, her eyes sparkling playfully. "Where do you think I got these bruises on my neck?"

Casey hastily averted her gaze when Leandra pulled her collar to the side to show off a faded bruise just above her shoulder. "You can spare me the details," she said wryly, turning her attention back to the racks of lingerie.

The two browsed along the aisle in silence for a time, before Casey checked a glance at the taller woman. "Leandra?"

"Hmm?"

"Can I ask you a personal question?"

"Sure."

"What's it like? Being with a woman, I mean?"

Leandra stopped looking at the lacy undergarments and gave the teenager her full attention. "Are you asking in general, or…?"

Casey blushed. "Yeah, general is good. I mean…" She paused, considering. "We're doing sex-ed in school right now, and one of the girls asked about that stuff. The teacher got all nervous and said he couldn't answer because it wasn't part of the material he'd been given. It was pretty stupid, I thought. We're there to learn about this stuff, but it's not much good to anyone who happens to be gay, is it?"

"I guess they don't want to have to think about it," Leandra said, shaking her head a little. "Some things never change."

"Yeah. Like I said, pretty stupid. So I was just kind of curious, you know?"

"I understand." Leandra thought for a moment, wondering what she should say. She'd never had to justify, defend, or explain her sexual orientation before. No one had dared say anything about it during her years as a smuggler, and it hadn't been an issue during her exile. "I don't know what I can tell you. I've never been with a man before, so I can't really compare it to anything."

"You've always known you liked girls?"

"I figured it out fairly young, yeah."

"What did your parents think?"

"I never told them." Leandra was silent for a moment, sadly remembering the faces of her mother and father. "I didn't tell them about a lot of things in my life. But my brother knew I was gay, and it was never a problem for him. He admired me a lot when we were younger, and I doubt he cared much who I was sleeping with."

"Hmm." Casey listened attentively, then she remarked in a deliberately casual tone of voice, "I've thought about it. You know, about being with another girl. I guess it might be cool." She caught Leandra's glance, and laughed a touch self-consciously. "Don't get me wrong or nothing, okay? I like guys just fine. But say I was out somewhere, and a good-looking girl started coming on to me. I'd probably go along with it. No point in limiting my experiences, right?"

"Sure."

Casey absently fingered the cloth of a lacy nightgown. "I've never told anyone that," she murmured. "Not even Ash, and I tell her pretty much everything."

Leandra saw a slight wavering in Casey's confident shell. "I understand, and I won't tell anyone if you don't want me to." Shar-Ranjana leapt to mind. "Believe me, I know the importance of keeping secrets."

"Thanks." Casey gave her a grateful smile, then turned back to the clothing hanging on the racks. Her smile turned into a rakish grin as she spotted something interesting. "What about this?" She pulled out a satin slip patterned with tiger stripes and held it against Leandra's upper body. "Perfect!"

Leandra rolled her eyes, took the slip, and hung it back on the rack. "Ashley's already seen me in more tiger stripes than she could count, and she can have me in the real thing anytime she wants. I think something different would be better. Something sexy, that she'd appreciate."

"Okay, how about this?" Casey pulled down another article and held it up.

Leandra laughed at the imitation-leather bustier with its silver inlaid chains. "I think that might be a little on the kinky side, don't you?"

"You never know. It might be just what she needs to broaden her horizons." Casey waggled her eyebrows saucily, looking Leandra up and down and taking knowing measure of her strong, predatory aura. "I'm betting it wouldn't be the first time you'd worn something like this, huh?"

Leandra lifted a single brow in amusement. "Maybe."

"Well then, no harm in introducing Ash to something new. She might like it."

Leandra had to admit the idea gave her a tingle. Memories of nights spent with former lovers rose in her mind, and she imagined sharing such erotic delights with the woman who had won her heart. After a moment of delicious fantasy, however, she shook her head. "I think we should find a middle ground for starters. Something a little tamer." She scanned the arranged undergarments. "Maybe this." She pulled out an elegant black satin slip and panty set and held it against her body. "This is nice."

Casey pursed her lips, considering. "I guess."

Leandra smiled, already knowing how she was going to thank Ashley for buying her the clothes. "Trust me. With some appropriate lighting and a romantic setting, this'll be just the thing."

The teenager groaned and covered her ears. "Something tells me I'm going to be putting up with a whole lot of make-out sessions now that you're around."

"Hey, I can't help it. Ashley's gorgeous, and she's a great kisser."

"Yeah, well, save the lovey-dovey crap for when I'm not around, if you can control yourself." Casey laughed. "If I have to think of what you two get up to when you're alone, it'll scar me for life."

Leandra laughed as well, and added the lingerie to the other clothes. So far, she liked Casey a lot. Even before her stay in the jungle, Leandra had never had an easy time making friends, and it was nice to meet someone besides Ashley with whom she could feel comfortable. "Come on, let's finish this up and see if we can find something to eat before Ashley picks us up."

"I've been in this business for twenty years, Richards, and in that time I've had to put up with a whole lot of crap from stuck-up, know-it-all photographers just like you, who thought their talent put them above the rules. You were supposed to be back here, assignment completed, two weeks ago. You had no right to rush off like that into the jungle without first consulting me."

Across his desk, Ashley blinked innocently at the man berating her, a slight, unconcerned smile on her lips. Joseph Harding, editor-in-chief of the popular magazine Wild Planet, was a bear of a man. Standing easily six feet tall and weighing at least two hundred and thirty pounds, he towered over Ashley. Beneath his full beard, Mr. Harding's face was bright red, and his neck was swallowed up by his broad shoulders, which made him look somewhat like an oversized bulldog. But Ashley knew her boss's bark was far worse than his bite. She had worked for Wild Planet for years now, and this wasn't the first time her antics had landed her in hot water. She waited with a patient, expectant expression for him to cool down.

It didn't take long.

Glaring down at her, Harding's expression became exasperated when his words failed to shake Ashley's calm. He took a deep breath and looked again at the selection of sample shots she had laid out for him to consider, scowling deeply. The scowl was a good thing, Ashley knew; Harding liked to keep his employees humble, but he could recognize quality work when he saw it. "If it weren't for your damn luck, Richards, I'd have fired you a thousand times before today."

"Luck's all well and good, Mr. Harding, but you're looking at talent, plain and simple," Ashley stated calmly. "And as for taking off without notice, I tried to get in contact with you, and your secretary told me you were unavailable."

"So, you shouldn't have gone."

"In which case, you'd be tearing me up right now for missing one of the greatest opportunities ever to come along." Ashley regarded her boss sternly. "You know as well as I do that even the chance—however remote—of shooting a white tiger in the wild was worth the risk and the delay. And even though I didn't find it, I wasn't wasting my time or your money." She gestured to the still slides, images she knew were well above her already high standard, thanks to Leandra's assistance. "The rest are just as good, maybe better. I don't see what the problem is."

Harding looked from the slides back to Ashley, the scowl never leaving his face "Fine," he conceded after a moment. "Get the rest of this stuff developed and sorted, and we'll let this go. Again."

Ashley gave him her most charming smile. "Thank you." Rising from her seat, she turned and walked out the office door, glad to get the minor confrontation out of the way.

Wandering through the sprawling office complex that was the hub of the nature magazine, Ashley exchanged brief pleasantries with her co-workers. She was well liked by her colleagues, with the exception of a few fellow photographers who were jealous of her talent and good fortune. Still, Ashley's easygoing temperament, quick wit, and good humor made her popular around the offices.

Pushing open a door marked *Studio—PRIVATE*, Ashley found herself in a large, professionally lit room that was designed to revolve around a single stage set against the far wall. Several people milled about in the studio, and Ashley looked around until she found the face she was looking for. When she spotted a tall, slender man wearing thick-lensed glasses, she again summoned her most charming, persuasive smile and headed over.

"Hey, James!" she called as she approached. "Can you spare a minute?"

James Grosser glanced up from his work, his face lighting up when he saw who was calling him. He nodded quickly. "Sure, Ash. I heard you were back. Did you have a good trip?"

"It was amazing, thanks. I got some really awesome shots." It was well known that James had a crush on her, and Ashley wasn't above using his infatuation to her own advantage. James was a likeable enough fellow—the shy, quiet, bookish type—and Ashley found his adoration kind of cute.

She knew he would never summon the courage to actually ask her out, which saved her from having to reject him, but she made a point of giving the young man a kind word and a friendly smile every now and then. And Ashley knew James was the perfect person to ask for help in her current mission.

"Listen, I was wondering if you could do me a really big favor?" she asked.

James nodded with such vigor she feared he might suffer whiplash. "Of course! You know you can ask me for anything. What can I do for you?"

"I need to get a little time in one of the processing labs. It'll only be a few minutes, I promise, but I have some personal shots I need to handle by myself."

James nodded. "Sure, I think I can work something out. Studio Four should be clear for most of tomorrow, but if you need some film processed, you know I'd be happy to do it for you."

"That's okay, I'd really rather take care of these prints myself. I took a few shots out there I'm keeping just for my collection."

"Ah, keeping the good stuff to yourself, huh? No problem. I'll, uh… work out a time for you and let you know."

"Thank you." Ashley patted him on the shoulder. "I really appreciate it."

He bobbed his head. "Anytime, Ash."

"I'll see you later." Ashley gave him a last grateful smile, then turned and exited the studio. She needed time in the labs to develop the pictures of Leandra and Shar-Ranjana in private, and this was the best way to guarantee that no one would interrupt her. She had it in mind to hang a print of the great white tigress in her bedroom, thinking that Leandra would appreciate having a reminder of her feline sister that she could look at every morning.

Pleased with the accomplishments of the day thus far, Ashley headed to her workstation to catch up on whatever needed doing. She wanted to get everything done as quickly as possible, knowing that Leandra might start getting more nervous if she was late. Ashley said a silent prayer to any gods who might be listening, hoping they would keep Leandra and her guide safe and out of trouble.

I'd better hurry with this stuff, she thought. *Putting those two together for too long can't be a good thing. A rebellious teenager and a woman who's been living like a giant cat for four years... Yep, better do whatever I have to do and get back to them as soon as I can.*

Ashley replaced the cordless phone on its wall mount and ran her fingers through her hair in frustration. "Damn it."

After stopping in at work, Ashley had taken time to do some grocery shopping, making sure to include a few special treats she thought Leandra might appreciate. When she returned to pick up Leandra and Casey, she found them waiting for her outside the store. Leandra looked a good deal more at ease than when she'd dropped her off, and it appeared from their shared smiles that she and Casey had bonded quickly.

After they'd returned home, Leandra had taken Casey for a walk in the forest to demonstrate some of the skills she'd acquired from her association with the great striped cats, while Ashley packed away the fresh food. It was late afternoon by the time Ashley drove her niece home. When she'd returned, she decided to make the promised phone call to her parents before starting dinner.

The subsequent conversation had been somewhat tense. Ashley guessed that Evelyn had informed their parents of Leandra's presence and also of her involvement with Ashley. It had been awkward, but Ashley managed to skirt the issue for the most part, wanting a little time to get settled before she confronted her folks about the changes she was making in her life. Still, even pleading fatigue hadn't been enough to get her mom to completely drop the case, and Ashley had been cornered into agreeing to a dinner visit on Wednesday night.

Sighing, Ashley closed her eyes and hoped the dinner would go well. It wasn't so much that she was worried what her parents might think of Leandra, although that was certainly part of it. Rather, she was concerned for how their judgment and possible rejection would affect Leandra. Ashley knew her lover didn't want their relationship to cause problems between her and her family.

"Hey, Ashley?" Leandra's voice called from upstairs. "Could you come up here for a minute? I've got something for you."

"Might as well give her some warning about Wednesday," Ashley muttered. She climbed wearily up the stairs and pushed open the door to her bedroom. "Leandra? What did you want to—" Ashley's voice choked off, her brain unable to complete her sequence of thought, when she saw the vision before her.

The bedroom was lit by the soft glow of several candles, which were positioned on the dresser and bedside tables. Soft music played in the background, and the air was sweet with the scent of perfumed wax. But it was the sight of Leandra that stole Ashley's breath. Her lover lay on the bed, clad in a black satin slip and lace panties that hugged every curve of her toned, powerful body. Sapphire eyes glinted in the candlelight, and a seductive smile greeted Ashley when she finally pulled her eyes away from their feast of flesh and form.

"I thought we'd skip dinner for a while," Leandra said, her voice dripping with raw animal lust. "Unless you're hungry now?"

Ashley took a step closer to the goddess reclining on her bed, her eyelids growing hooded. "Oh, I'm hungry now all right." She licked her lips.

"Excellent." Leandra shifted on the bed to better display her new lingerie. Her fingertips traced a path from her collar to her cleavage, finally tugging at the satin cloth covering her ribcage. Ashley's gaze followed them helplessly. "You like it?"

Ashley nodded immediately, all thoughts of family and problematic dinner invitations vanishing. "Very much so."

"I bought it to say thank you, for everything you've done for me. For giving me back my life. For understanding me the way you do." Leandra rose to a crouching position, and Ashley stepped closer, until their faces were almost touching. "Thank you, Ashley. Thank you for loving me."

Ashley's response was swift and passionate. She crushed her lips against Leandra's, her tongue wasting no time gaining access to the other woman's mouth. Leandra's hands reached out and began working at the buttons on Ashley's jeans. As soon as they were off, Ashley pushed Leandra onto her back and straddled her, breathing hard as she pinned her lover to the bed and ground her center firmly against a well-muscled abdomen. Dizzy from the sudden rush of arousal, she pressed a series of heated kisses over Leandra's lips and chest.

Breaking away breathlessly, Leandra smiled up at her. "I'm glad you like it."

Ashley groaned, her eyes and hands wandering over Leandra's scarcely veiled body. "God, I think it's the sexiest thing I've ever seen," she gasped, her voice thick with hunger. The heat in her belly flared into a sudden bonfire, and Ashley marveled at how Leandra could inspire her passion so easily. "You have no idea what you do to me."

"So tell me." Leandra's hands slipped sinuously around Ashley's slender waist and held her tight, steadying the rocking motion of her hips "Tell me."

Ashley paused, uncertain. "Tell you what?"

"I want to know how you feel…what you want." Leandra's sultry eyes regarded her earnestly. "You've told me everything else, but now I want to hear about your fantasies. About every erotic dream you've ever had, no matter how silly you think it is. I want to bring you all the pleasure I possibly can."

Ashley blushed. "You want me to tell you about my fantasies?"

"Uh huh." Leandra's lips curled into a slinky smile. "Tell me yours, and I'll tell you mine."

Ashley hesitated, still fully caught up in the moment, but uncertain. No one had ever asked her about these things before, and she'd never had much desire to share those types of fantasies with anyone before. But Leandra wasn't like any lover she'd ever experienced. She gave her a slight smile. "Well, some of my fantasies you've already fulfilled."

"Oh? Like what?"

"Like the shower." Ashley's voice was low and shy, but her eyes radiated heat like glowing embers. "And maybe the waterfall, too."

"Are there any other things you'd like to try?" Leandra asked in a smoky tone. "Anything you'd like me to do, or that you'd like to do to me?"

Ashley felt her cheeks glow hotter, and Leandra grinned like a Cheshire cat. "Tell me."

"Well, it's not really a fantasy, as such, it's just something I think about sometimes."

"I'll do anything you ask, Ashley. Anything."

Ashley saw a whole world of erotic possibilities open up with that word. She leaned close to Leandra's neck and whispered, "Would you growl for me?"

Both of Leandra's eyebrows shot up. "What?"

Ashley hesitated. "You know, that growly, rumbly noise you make. The one that vibrates through your chest." Her hands traced the undersides of Leandra's breasts, feeling her ribcage expand and contract as she breathed.

"You want to hear me growl?"

Ashley's blush intensified at the amused curiosity in Leandra's tone. "Forget it. It's silly, I know, but I just—ulp!" Ashley almost bit her tongue in surprise as Leandra twisted beneath her and easily rolled on top of her. In a second, Ashley found herself pressed hard into the soft mattress by Leandra's powerful frame. She tensed reflexively, but relaxed when a low, rumbling growl rolled over her senses, the vibrations sending shock waves to her core. The sound was the very essence of Leandra's animal side: primal, carnal, and deeply arousing.

Leandra dipped her face down and nuzzled at her neck. "That turns you on, doesn't it?"

Ashley struggled for breath, unable to fight her body's reaction. She nodded, exhilarated by the sound Leandra made and the predatory gleam in her crystalline eyes. "It's silly, isn't it?"

"Not if you like it." The growl continued deep in Leandra's throat even while she spoke. Hot lips pressed against Ashley's neck, and she laughed and squirmed when she felt teeth nip gently at her skin. Leandra tugged at the hem of her shirt, pulling it up her body, and Ashley moved to accommodate her. Leandra quickly divested her of shirt and bra, then gripped her wrists lightly and spread her arms wide. "This is going to take a long time," she purred. "I want you to keep your arms exactly where they are. Can you do that?"

Ashley whimpered slightly as she felt the heat of Leandra's right thigh press against her highly sensitized center, but she managed a quick nod.

"If you touch me, I'll stop," Leandra warned softly. "Are you sure you can behave yourself, or should I tie your hands to the bedposts?"

"Oh, God." Ashley squirmed, her arousal reaching an almost overwhelming level. The idea of being tied up, completely at her lover's mercy, was extremely appealing at that moment, but Ashley sensed Leandra wanted her to do this with willpower alone, and decided to take the harder road. "I can behave," she whispered.

"Excellent." Soft lips planted a trail of kisses down Ashley's throat and between her breasts. "When I'm done, I promise you can do anything to me that you want. For now, let me show you how much I love you."

Leandra released Ashley's wrists and began exploring her body, running feather-light touches down her arms, teasing her breasts until they ached for a firmer touch, then skirting downwards along her ribcage to her outer thighs. Leandra followed this path with her lips and tongue, seeking out the most sensitive regions of Ashley's body and tormenting her with tantalizing caresses that stoked the embers of her passion to even greater heat.

Ashley struggled against the urge to put her hands on Leandra's head so she could guide her movements, grabbing for the bed sheets to resist the temptation. No lover had ever sparked her ardor the way Leandra did. There was never any awkward fumbling with Leandra, no need for directions or instructions. Her touch was confident and knowledgeable. She seemed to know every erogenous zone in the body she was tantalizing, including some Ashley hadn't known existed. Ashley panted as Leandra's mouth moved nearer to the center of her need, a fine sheen of sweat already glistening over her skin and making her glow in the candlelight.

Settling between her eagerly spread thighs, Leandra paused a long moment to gaze at Ashley's most intimate flesh, smiling a carnal, hungry smile. She dipped her head forward and swiped her tongue slowly up through her slick, satiny folds. Ashley bucked her hips, a needful squeak escaping her throat as she stared down into the watching eyes of her lover. Leandra used the tip of her tongue to trace the outer lips of Ashley's sex, one hand pressing her into the sheets to hold her steady, the other tickling a path up her inner right leg.

Ashley moaned and whimpered, her jaw clenched tight with the effort it took to control her need to touch Leandra. Pleasure rushed through her body, and she cried out in delight when she felt two fingers slowly penetrate her core. Her cry of pleasure became a growl of frustration when she found her lover's grip on her waist prevented her from controlling the rhythm of their lovemaking, and she felt, more than heard, a deep chuckle.

"Patience," Leandra said softly, pausing in her efforts. "Just relax. I know what I'm doing."

Ashley struggled for breath, as she willed herself to give Leandra total control over her body. A moment later, she felt the silken sensation of her lover's tongue against her clitoris, and the deliciously long fingers resumed their thrusting. Soon the first tingles of climax began to pulse through her blood, and Ashley bit her lip to keep from begging Leandra to go faster.

Leandra must have heard the ragged edge in her breathing, because she paused for a long moment looking up at her as she teetered at the edge. Ashley panted, pleading with her eyes, every muscle in her body strained taut in desperate anticipation. Finally, she felt Leandra's lips close around the glistening bundle of nerves that crowned her sex, and her back arched when Leandra began sucking and licking fervently. A spasm tightened her inner muscles around Leandra's thrusting fingers, and she released an explosive cry of ecstasy as climax seized her senses.

Squirming and writhing in unabashed bliss, Ashley maintained just enough presence of mind to keep her hands clasped together tightly above her head, and the struggle not to reach down and pull Leandra's face more forcefully against her sensitized core only made her climax all the more delicious. When the electrifying spasms of ecstasy finally abated, Ashley felt Leandra plant a final wet kiss above her tingling clit as her fingers withdrew.

Dazed and breathless, Ashley attempted to sit up to thank Leandra. But as soon as she began to move her arms, she found them instantly pinned back to the bed, and smoky sapphire eyes regarded her with hungry intent.

"I don't think so," Leandra growled. "I'm a long way from being finished with you, my love. That was just a little something to take the edge off."

"But that—"

Leandra pressed her glistening fingers against Ashley's lips, and the scent of her own arousal filled her senses. "I want to hear you climax again," Leandra whispered heatedly. "I want to feel you shudder and writhe from my touch. And I want to see how many times I can do that to you before your body can't take any more." She pressed Ashley's hands back down against the mattress. "Are you sure you can control yourself?"

Ashley was still dizzy from her first orgasm, and that dizziness increased as she understood Leandra's intentions. She nodded and lay back quietly on the bed, feeling the cool air against her sweat-slicked body. "I can take it." She paused. "Not that I'm complaining or anything, but just how much more were you planning on giving me? I mean, you know…"

Leandra was already working her way back down Ashley's body, trailing her tongue languidly over her sweat-slicked skin. "Let's just say I'm going to make sure it's slow." She gently bit Ashley's right nipple. "Intense." Her teeth moved on to the left nipple. "And utterly satisfying."

Ashley whimpered as she stared up at the ceiling, bracing herself for what she had no doubts would be an extremely thorough ravishing. She was about to become the most satiated woman in the western world.

CHAPTER 6

Tyger! Tyger! burning bright
In the forests of the night,
What immortal hand or eye
Dare frame thy fearful symmetry?

—"The Tyger" by William Blake

THE SOUND OF THE FRONT door opening and slamming shut with a distinctive, vigorous *bang!* heralded the return of Evelyn's wayward daughter. Without looking up, she called out her standard reproach, "Can you try not to bring the house down when you come inside, please?"

"Hey, Mom," Casey greeted brightly. "Sorry. What's for dinner?"

"Tuna casserole." Evelyn glanced up from her work at the kitchen bench, her eyes widening when she caught sight of her daughter. "Casey, could you at least wipe your feet before you come inside? And where are your shoes? Have you been running around out there barefoot?"

"Yep. I was practicing some of the stuff Leandra showed me. She never wears shoes. She says you can move quieter without them." Casey obediently went back and scuffed her bare feet on the welcome mat before she continued inside; Evelyn gave her an approving nod. "Is Dad home yet?" Casey asked.

"No. He called a few minutes ago and said he'd be a half hour late." Evelyn regarded her daughter curiously. "What sort of stuff did Leandra show you?"

"How she moves fast, how she climbs trees and stuff. It's pretty cool. We went out into the forest, and I'd take my eyes off her for a second, and POOF! She'd just disappear. And then I'd look around for her, and she'd be standing right behind me. I didn't even hear her move. She's really quick, too. And she can make all these really cool animal noises, and when she does, the birds and stuff all come around because they think she's one of them. She even showed me how to do tiger noises. Listen." Casey managed to make a fairly decent growling sound. "Pretty cool, huh?"

Evelyn smiled indulgently. "I guess." She started chopping herbs on a wooden board. "So, you like her?"

"Yeah, she's okay."

"Really?" Evelyn raised an eyebrow. Usually, any time Ashley introduced a new love interest, Evelyn would have to listen to an hour-long rant from Casey, listing every reason why the poor man wasn't good enough. She was a little surprised that Leandra was different.

Casey scowled. "She's better than any of those guys Ash went out with. Bunch of stiffs and suits. At least Leandra's got a sense of humor, and she doesn't try to be the Big Man with Ash. They're good together."

"And it doesn't bother you that Ash is, you know, gay?"

Casey snorted and rolled her eyes. "What do I care? If Ash likes girls, that's cool. She could do a whole lot worse than Leandra. She's pretty hot, what with those eyes and the cool braids and stuff."

Evelyn considered as she chopped, hearing the subtle admiration in Casey's tone and knowing that her daughter had found a new idol in Leandra. What kind of influence would the jungle-woman be on her impressionable child? Casey was at a difficult age right now, and Evelyn had always been thankful for the role Ashley played in her life. Evelyn's husband, Jason, often had to work long hours as a physician, and she'd had to raise the headstrong child Casey had developed into more or less on her own. It hadn't been easy. Quick-witted, rebellious, and with a keen intellect that gave rise to an acid tongue, Casey was a source of constant worry for her parents. Fortunately, she had found a kindred spirit in her aunt, and Ashley's influence had helped turn Casey away from dangerous paths she might have otherwise ventured onto. Now, it seemed, she had found another focus for her attention in Leandra, and Evelyn's curiosity about her sister's new partner gained a new perspective in light of how that partner might affect her daughter.

"So, what's she like? I only got to see her for a second before she took off. Is she nice?"

"I wouldn't exactly describe her as 'nice,'" Casey said after a moment of thought. "She seemed a bit nervous while we were shopping, but I guess that's natural. I mean, I can't even begin to imagine what it'd be like to live with tigers for four whole years. It's almost like she's still half-animal. I could see her watching everything around us, as though we were going to be attacked at any moment. But she was okay when we were out in the forest. She really relaxed a lot."

"What did you talk about?"

"Stuff. Mostly Ashley, I guess, and a bit about what it was like living in the jungle." She paused. "I don't think she likes talking about herself much. She just gave bits and pieces of information. But Ash said she used to be a poacher and a smuggler, and she told me not to ask too many questions about her life story."

Evelyn recognized the intense look in her daughter's eyes; Casey had always had a love for all things mysterious and peculiar. If anything didn't quite fit the mold, or left her curious for more details, she would immediately begin to employ a subtle sequence of interrogation techniques until she was satisfied she knew the whole story. It was a trait she had in common with her aunt, but unlike Ashley, Casey had an infinite amount of patience. She could pursue her quest for months if need be, gathering little pieces of information that she would put together until she knew the truth. Leandra was certainly enigmatic enough to garner her interest.

"Well, you should respect her privacy," Evelyn said firmly. "It might take Leandra a while to settle in, and I don't want you doing anything to make it harder for her."

"She doesn't mind me being around," Casey defended. "I think she likes me. In fact, she offered to show me more stuff whenever I wanted, like, after school. If you said it was okay."

Finished chopping the herbs, Evelyn set the knife on the countertop and regarded her daughter with the kind of stern look only a mother can give. "What about your homework?"

Casey rolled her eyes. "What about it? I'm doing okay." Which was true; Casey maintained at least a B average, even though she shied away from any form of study and despite being something of an outcast at school. "Besides, the stuff Leandra's teaching me is useful, too. She's got real life experience. I could learn a lot from her."

Evelyn studied the innocent expression on her child's face for a long moment, knowing full well that Casey was quite capable of lying if it suited her purposes. "If you fall behind in class," she warned, "I'll find out about it, sooner or later."

"I won't."

"Have you asked Ashley if she minds? Maybe she wants some extra private time now she's got Leandra around."

"She won't mind. Besides, if they want to make with the lovey-dovey stuff, they can do it when I'm at school."

Evelyn frowned, considering ways her daughter might use whatever Leandra taught her to further her troublemaking. "We'll talk to your father about it tonight," she allowed.

Casey's face lit up. Clearly, she took this as a sign of imminent victory. "Thanks, Mom."

Evelyn picked up the knife and began to chop vegetables. "Just be sure your grades don't slip, young lady, or I'll slap a curfew on you so fast it'll make your head spin." The threat was somewhat hollow. Evelyn knew her daughter would never respect a curfew if she didn't feel like it, and if it came right down to it, she wasn't sure how to enforce one. After nearly eighteen years as a mother, she was still somewhat uncertain how to handle her headstrong child.

This time, however, Casey didn't argue. She just nodded and gave Evelyn a quick peck on the cheek. "No need. You'll see. Leandra's cool." She headed toward the stairs. "I'll be in my room. Give me a yell when Dad gets home. I want to tell him about the stuff Leandra showed me."

"Okay, Case."

Evelyn watched her daughter race up the stairs, noticing the look of fierce concentration she wore as she tried to move silently. She shook her head ruefully and returned to the preparations for dinner, shuddering a little at the thought of Casey adding stealth tactics, hunting, and other jungle survival skills to her repertoire of chaos.

Leaving her lover passed out on the bed after her marathon ravishing, Leandra padded silently downstairs in search of something to feed Ashley when she awoke. Investigating the cupboards, she found them neatly stocked with various foodstuffs, including pasta, cans of fruit, and an array of condiments she'd not tasted in many years. Leandra frowned as she considered her choices. She couldn't actually cook anything herself, so she decided to check the refrigerator for something simpler. Her eyes immediately locked onto a brown and purple package on the top shelf, and Leandra reached in and pulled out the block of milk chocolate.

"Perfect."

When she returned to the bedroom, her lips curved into a sensuous smile as she detected the strong musk of her lover's scent lingering in the room. Setting the chocolate down on the bedside table, Leandra crawled slowly back into bed and took a moment to gaze lovingly at her nearly comatose lover. Ashley's face was peaceful, if slightly flushed, and her hair fanned out around her in messy tangles. Her lithe body glowed in the low light of the candles that still burned away the darkness, every muscle highlighted under a light sheen of sweat. Gently, Leandra reached out and ran her fingers over the elfin features, smiling when Ashley's eyelids twitched, then parted.

"Hey."

Ashley wriggled on the bed, looking adorably dazed and befuddled as she gazed up at Leandra through sleepy, slit eyes. "Hey. Wh-what happened?" Her voice sounded almost as husky as Leandra's from crying out during their lovemaking.

"You passed out." Leandra grinned, planting a chaste kiss on her lover's lips. "I went downstairs and got something to eat. I figured you'd be hungry." She picked up the chocolate and held it out like a token, pleased when Ashley's eyes lit up instantly.

"Gimme!"

"Uh uh, let me." Leandra undid the paper and foil wrapping, then snapped off a piece of the dark treat. "Open up."

Ashley complied, sighing contentedly as Leandra fed her. "Mmm. God, you're spoiling me."

"I'm enjoying it just as much as you are," Leandra whispered. A fresh fire kindled in her belly when Ashley's tongue accidentally scored along her fingertips as she accepted the last of the chocolate. Her eyes narrowed salaciously as they drifted from Ashley's face, down over her nude body, and she remembered the younger woman's screams of ecstasy that had filled the room not ten minutes ago.

Ashley paused mid-chew, obviously spotting the hungry look in Leandra's eyes. "Leandra…"

"Huh?" Leandra's focus snapped back to Ashley's face. "What?"

"Stop looking at me like that."

Blue eyes blinked innocently. "Like what?"

"You know like what. If I have to go through another ravishing like that again anytime soon, I can tell you right now I won't survive. I'll be sore enough in the morning as it is, after what you did to me."

Leandra grinned rakishly. "I didn't hear any complaints," she purred. "In fact…" She leaned closer and nipped lightly at the skin above Ashley's breast. "I seem to recall that at several points, you were crying out for more."

Ashley shuddered at the sensation of Leandra's teeth against her flesh, but squirmed away. "Oh God, I can't."

"I could be gentle," Leandra whispered persuasively, her fingers beginning a trek down Ashley's body. "I could make it so soft you'd barely feel me there at all."

Ashley groaned, but managed to stop Leandra's advance before it continued past the point of no return. "I can't," she repeated, with breathless regret. "I wish I could, but I really can't take any more."

Leandra stopped and studied her lover. "Okay, I'll behave."

Placing one last kiss to Ashley's cleavage, she pulled back and settled down on the bed beside her. Picking up the momentarily forgotten chocolate, she broke off another piece and popped it into her own mouth. Instantly, her eyes closed in rapture and a loud purr rumbled through her chest. "Mmm."

Ashley sat up a little. "Nice?"

"Mmm-hmm." The sensual flavor of the chocolate exploded against Leandra's taste buds, and she was momentarily overwhelmed.

"I thought you'd like it." Ashley helped herself to another piece. "I got a bunch of other stuff too. It's only fair that I re-introduce you to all the things you missed out on in the jungle." She traced a finger down Leandra's chest, exploring along the edge of the satin slip that still clothed her body. "I wish I had the energy to give you more pleasure than just chocolate, but you kind of wore me out."

Leandra clasped her hand over Ashley's and smiled down at her. "That's okay. You can pay me back in the morning, if you like." Leandra's body was still singing with arousal, but she was content to ignore it for now. During the course of Ashley's ravishing, Leandra had paused at intervals to see to her own pleasure, using such moments to drive her lover almost frenzied with desire as she was forced to watch. It had been, for both of them, the most delicious of tortures. "Tonight was all for you."

Ashley lay back on the bed sheets, wriggling herself against Leandra's body and pulling her arms around her. "You know," she whispered, "I really enjoyed tonight, Leandra. It was..." She paused. "It was something I've never experienced before. No one else ever did all that stuff for me." Mahogany eyes met Leandra's shyly. "I've never really...gone more than one round before, either."

"Well, get used to it, my love," Leandra murmured, leaning down to plant a soft kiss on Ashley's lips. "Ravishing you only once would be such a waste. I could do it a thousand times a day, and still hunger for more."

Ashley blushed and lowered her eyes. "You'd say anything to get me worked up again."

"Can I help it that you're so delicious?" Leandra placed a piece of chocolate between her teeth and fed it to her lover in the midst of a deep kiss, the two parting only when the chocolate had melted between them. Leandra licked Ashley's lips and grinned. "I think we'll have to work a little more on your endurance, though."

Ashley snorted indignantly and pushed her off. "We'll see how well you do, as soon as I get my strength back." Rolling over, she managed to pin Leandra to the bed and grind herself against her. "In the morning, I get to play."

Leandra growled, sending thrills through the sated woman above her. "I'm looking forward to it."

"Mmm." Ashley smiled and ran her hands over Leandra's body for a few more moments before withdrawing. Laying back down on the rumpled sheets, she blew a few errant hairs from her face. "By the way, I called my parents. Before you distracted me, I was going to tell you that we've been invited to dinner on Wednesday. I tried to get out of it, but my mom can be pretty persistent."

"That's okay." Leandra hesitated, not certain how to interpret her lover's tone. "Are you sure I was invited?"

"Oh yeah, quite sure." Ashley grimaced, and the bitterness in her voice became clearer. "She said something along the lines of bringing my 'new guest' over to meet them." She snorted inelegantly. "She couldn't even bring herself to call you my girlfriend. Or partner, or whatever."

Leandra propped herself up on one elbow. "Are you worried about them meeting me? I know I'm not exactly Miss Social Etiquette, but—"

"No, it's nothing like that," Ashley quickly assured her. "I'm not ashamed of you, Leandra, so don't even think that. I love you. I just…" She paused, and Leandra remained silent while she sorted through her thoughts. "I know how my folks sometimes react to things they don't understand or approve of. Like when my sister got pregnant at eighteen. They really flew off the handle at her. They started threatening to never speak to her again, and stuff like that. After a while, they calmed down and were all supportive, but not at first." She met Leandra's gaze earnestly. "I don't want them to say anything that might hurt you, or make you think that you and I shouldn't be together. And it's entirely possible they might do exactly that. They don't like controversy, or anything they don't understand. It might take them a while to accept that we're together, and in the meantime, they might make things uncomfortable for both of us."

Leandra listened carefully, realizing her lover wasn't worried about her not being good enough for her family, but was concerned she might be wounded by their disapproval. "Nothing they could say or do could make me love you any less, Ash," she whispered, stroking the damp, tangled blonde hair. "I want them to at least know who I am. I'm part of your life now, right?"

"Right," Ashley said a little more brightly. "But still, Wednesday doesn't give you a whole lot of time to settle in. You're adjusting to a lot of changes, Leandra. You can't rush that."

"I know." Leandra relaxed back onto the mattress, snuggling her long body against that of her shorter lover. "But I can handle a simple dinner invitation easily enough."

The two lay in silence for a few minutes. Ashley began drawing idle patterns over Leandra's toned abdomen, inspiring a soft, rumbling purr. "I'm glad Casey took so well to you," she said softly. "She can be a little abrasive sometimes, when I start seeing someone new."

"Yeah, I can see that. I like her. She's got a lot of you in her personality." Thinking back on her own life and the experiences which had shaped it, Leandra added, "When I was her age, I was all attitude and arrogance. But she's a good kid, and I can see how much she loves you just from talking with her. She really looks up to you."

"Mmm…And now she can look up to you as well," Ashley murmured. She covered a yawn with the back of her hand, then pulled the rumpled sheets up over their bodies. One arm snaked its way underneath Leandra's waist and pulled her close.

Leandra heard Ashley's breathing deepen, and watched her eyelids flutter, then close. For a moment, she contented herself with simply watching as Ashley abandoned herself to slumber. She memorized every beloved feature, and adoration warmed her heart with an achingly soft burn. She settled her arm more comfortably around Ashley's lithe form, and closed her eyes as well. "Sweet dreams, Ash," she whispered into the blonde tresses that tickled her chin.

Ashley whimpered in her sleep and tightened her hold.

The next few days felt like settling into a surprisingly comfortable domestic rhythm. Ashley was forced to abandon Leandra from time to time, when the duties of her work called her attention away, but Leandra didn't seem to mind. She was apparently spending most of her alone time exploring the surrounding woodlands, gaining familiarity with this new, more temperate environment. Ashley overheard a few tourists and locals commenting that they had heard ominous, growling sounds while hiking the trails around town, and there was some debate over whether it could be a bear or mountain lion. Ashley kept her grin to herself and made a mental note to warn Leandra not to have too much fun playing jungle predator with the hikers.

Casey was a frequent visitor through the week, spending almost every minute she could spare away from studying in the company of Ashley's new houseguest. The two quickly formed a companionable bond, and Ashley was impressed by how patient a tutor Leandra proved to be. Utterly taken with her new friend, Casey struggled without complaint in her quest to toughen the soles of her feet so she could walk barefoot over brambles and sharp rocks. She even tried refusing to wear shoes to school, an action which Evelyn reported had prompted a fresh round of phone calls from her concerned teachers.

Even when Ashley was forced to spend precious hours away from home, seeing to her duties at the office, she was extremely happy. Content for the moment to forget about the Wednesday night appointment with her parents, she delighted in the pleasure of having Leandra with her almost all the time. Having never cohabited in a relationship before, Ashley was pleasantly surprised that she adjusted so well to Leandra's intrusion into her personal space. The two women never argued or disagreed, despite the fact that Leandra still had a long way to go before she was, as Ashley fondly put it, "housetrained." Ashley found it rather adorable that her lover kept forgetting about little things like using bath towels, cutlery, or laundry baskets, and picked up after her without comment, for the most part.

Living together also gave Ashley new insight into her lover. Every day, it seemed, she learned something new about her, as Leandra continued to familiarize herself with the modern world once more. Everyday things— music, books, a well-cooked meal—took on new meaning as Leandra rediscovered them. Comforts that most people took for granted seemed to enchant Leandra each time she experienced them. As Ashley learned more about her partner, her love for Leandra deepened. The days passed, their connection grew stronger and more binding, and they reveled unabashedly in their affection and passion for each other.

In particular, Ashley found herself growing ever more addicted to this new world of sexual freedom. Leandra was, without a doubt, the most uninhibited, passionate, and playful lover she could ever want, and Ashley slowly began to relax as she grew more accustomed to being able to explore her desires fully. She took delight in the discovery that Leandra was such a spontaneous lover; sometimes all the warning she got was a momentary look of animal hunger before Leandra pounced on her and began a frenzied conquest of her body. Their lovemaking ranged from slow and breathtakingly intense to hot and carnal; a raw desire to satisfy their lust for one another. Ashley found it all exciting and intoxicating, and was far too happy to question this newly awakened outgoing attitude in her sexuality.

On Tuesday night, Casey watched with excitement, as Ashley surprised her lover with a special gift: a large, flat object, wrapped in tiger-print paper. Leandra tore away the wrapping and gasped in surprised delight at the framed print of herself and Shar-Ranjana that Ashley had taken in the jungle.

"It's beautiful!" Leandra stared at the image of her tiger-sister, and Ashley saw tears forming at the corners of her eyes. "Thank you so much!"

"You're welcome. I thought you'd like a reminder of her...a tangible connection to your family. We can hang it in the bedroom, and you can see her every morning when you wake up."

Casey, sitting on the lounge opposite the couple, gagged noisily at their open display of affection, then stood up and moved closer to study the print. "What is it?" Her eyes widened when she saw the picture of the pale, striped cat, then she fixed an accusatory glare on Ashley. "Hey! I thought you said there wasn't any white tiger. That's what you told your boss, isn't it?"

"Yes, it is, and as far as anyone else is concerned, this picture doesn't exist." Ashley gestured for Casey to sit. "You have to keep this a secret. Okay, Case? No one else can know about Shar-Ranjana."

"Shar who?"

"Shar-Ranjana," Leandra said. "She was my friend in the jungle, the last of my family. Her existence is a sacred trust for me." She regarded the teenager with a serious expression. "If people know about her, they'll hunt her down and lock her in a cage. Or worse, kill her. I showed Ashley because I trusted her to keep my secret. I hope I can trust you as well."

Casey stared from the picture to Leandra, then back. "You're so close to her," she whispered in awe. "She didn't attack you?"

"She was raised with me being close to her. We were like siblings," Leandra explained. "Will you promise never to tell anyone about this picture, Casey?"

Casey immediately nodded earnestly, and Ashley knew her well enough to recognize how pleased Casey was to be trusted with something so important...included in this secret as an equal to the adults. "I promise." Her sea-green eyes studied the great cat for another moment, then shifted to the image of Leandra, dressed in her tiger fur and striped paint. "You look so different there."

"It was a different world," Leandra said softly. "There were very different rules."

Casey turned toward Ashley. "How close did you get to her?" Ashley smiled, remembering her magical experience in the jungle. "She came right up to me and gave me a good licking. I even got to pet her a bit."

Casey smirked and lifted an eyebrow. "I was talking about the cat."

Ashley rolled her eyes dryly, but felt her color rising nonetheless. "Hardy har har."

Ashley sighed as she pulled her car up outside her parents' stately house. Her expression when she glanced at Leandra was resigned but determined. "Well…this is it. You ready?"

"As I'll ever be." Leandra had been mentally bracing herself for this night all week, and now that the moment had arrived, she was nervous. "Meeting my girlfriend's parents…" She grimaced a little ruefully. "That's not something I ever thought I'd have to go through."

"You'll do fine, Leandra. Don't let them get to you. It's going to take them a while to get used to the idea that you're here to stay, and until then, they might be a little abrasive."

Leandra took a deep breath. "Okay, let's get this over with."

Stepping out of the vehicle, she took a moment to study the house. Although similar in appearance to Ashley's home, it possessed a greater air of structure and discipline. The gardens were neatly groomed and obviously well cared for. There were fewer windows than there were in Ashley's house, and a decorative stone path led around to the rear. As she walked up to the front door, her hand clasped gratefully in Ashley's, Leandra concentrated on keeping her breathing even and controlled, fighting down the urge to escape into the soothing shadows of the forest that lay just across the road.

Ashley pushed a finger against the elegant brass doorbell and was answered by a musical jangle from inside. A moment later, the door was opened by a slender woman of medium height who had sharp blue eyes and blonde hair that was liberally streaked with grey. She smiled delightedly at Ashley and pulled her into a hug.

"Ashley! It's so good to have you back." She held Ashley by her shoulders and studied her face, her smile only growing brighter. "You look fantastic. Evie said you weren't sporting too many new injuries, but sometimes she says that just to spare me the worry."

"It's good to see you too, Mom." Ashley drew back a little from the embrace, and Leandra was caught by the woman's sharp gaze. They smiled a little hesitantly at one another, uncertain of what to say or do. "Mom," Ashley said, "this is Leandra Thornton. Leandra, I'd like you meet my mother, Emily Richards."

Leandra bobbed her head politely. She felt the pull of the forest shadows even more strongly now, and wished she could hide in their protective embrace. "It's nice to meet you."

"Likewise." Emily Richard's eyes ran speculatively down Leandra's frame, her lips pursing slightly. She looked from Leandra to Ashley and smiled a little thinly as she regarded her daughter. "Evelyn mentioned your new friend. I'm looking forward to hearing more about her."

Leandra saw Ashley wince slightly at her mother's dismissive, disapproving tone.

"Why don't you two come inside?" Emily stepped back and waved them in. "Evelyn and Jason should be here soon, and Casey promised she'd come. Dinner's all ready, so we can sit and talk for a few minutes about your trip."

"Thanks." Ashley took Leandra's hand again and led the way into the living room. Leandra took in her surroundings with a quick glance, noting expensive oak furniture neatly arranged throughout the room and framed prints of classic oil paintings on the walls. The air smelled of polish and cinnamon, and the hardwood floor felt cold against her bare feet. In all, this house felt a lot colder and less welcoming than Ashley's happy home.

As they entered the room, a man sitting in one of the plush armchairs put down the newspaper he was reading and stood up, smiling. Ashley returned the smile with one of her own and released Leandra's hand so she could accept his embrace.

"Ashley! How are you, sweetheart? Let me look at you." The man pulled back and ran his eyes over Ashley, then hugged her again. "You look great."

"Thanks, Daddy." Ashley stepped back and regarded her father fondly. "You're not looking so bad yourself."

The man's smile grew even wider, then his eyes swept past his daughter to where Leandra stood, somewhat uncertainly, in the entryway. "You must be Leandra," he said. "I'm Owen, Ashley's father. It's nice to meet you." He held out his hand.

Leandra hesitated only a moment before she stepped forward and shook the offered hand, matching the firmness of his grip. "Nice to meet you, too," she said. "Ashley's told me a lot about you." This was not quite the truth. Leandra knew Ashley's father had first introduced her to photography by buying her a camera for her tenth birthday present, and she knew he had operated a successful real estate agency before retiring a few years ago. Beyond that, Ashley hadn't spoken much about her parents. Still, looking into Owen's intelligent, benevolent eyes and seeing a warmer welcome there than she'd received from Emily Richards, Leandra decided the polite lie couldn't hurt.

"Come sit down, both of you," Owen invited, gesturing to the couch. "Tell me all about India. I remember after your uncle came back from hiking through Nepal, he said the heat was so bad he was sweating out of his eyeballs. We also had some pretty funny and frank discussions about the joys of Delhi belly…bane of travelers everywhere."

Leandra couldn't help but grin as Ashley took her hand and led her over to the couch. She already liked Owen. He had a friendly, fatherly demeanor that eased her nerves a little, and his voice carried the same inviting, easygoing attitude as his daughter's.

Ashley began telling her father about her trip, taking obvious care to gloss over certain details she probably felt would only worry her family, such as their conflict with the poachers. Emily joined them, and Leandra felt the older woman's eyes studying her with curiosity that seemed not exactly hostile, but certainly defensive.

That makes sense, Leandra thought. *I'm her daughter's new lesbian lover, straight out of the jungle. She has every right to be defensive, just like Shar-Ranjana was protective of her cubs. It's a natural instinct for a mother to want to keep her offspring safe from harm, and right now, she sees me as a possible threat.* Sitting quietly, listening as Ashley talked about her jungle adventure, Leandra concentrated on the reassuring pressure of her lover's hand against her own.

Owen listened to his daughter's tale with interest.

"And how did you two meet up?" he inquired, when Ashley paused in her tale. His eyes met Leandra's. "Were you working in the park while Ashley was there, Leandra?"

"Not exactly," Leandra said, uncertain how to explain the nature of her presence in India. She glanced hopefully at Ashley for rescue.

"Leandra was sort of working with the rangers to help control the poachers over there," Ashley quickly improvised, "and to keep track of the tiger populations. We met up one day, kind of by accident, and she offered to help me with my shoots." She squeezed Leandra's hand and gave her an adoring look. "Leandra's an expert tracker, and she's great with animals. We hit it off right from the start."

"I see." He regarded Leandra again curiously. "So, you gave up your job to stay with Ashley?"

Leandra swallowed nervously. "Actually, my job was kind of temporary, and I wanted to be with Ashley more than I wanted to stay in India."

"And what are your plans now?" Emily asked bluntly, her eyes fixed on her daughter. "Evelyn was sketchy about the details, but she made it clear you two are living together."

"That's right." Ashley faced her mother's disapproval without flinching. "Leandra's staying with me."

"And what happens next?" Emily turned her attention to Leandra. "What are your plans for the future, Leandra? Were you thinking to apply for work in the area?"

Leandra stiffened under the assault of the older woman's gaze. "I hadn't thought much about it." She paused, glancing at Ashley. "I guess I'll probably look for something in animal welfare."

"I see. And will you be finding a place of your own after you get back on your feet?"

"Mom." Ashley's tone was a warning and her eyes were slits of steel, but Emily was unperturbed.

"I just think you're moving awfully fast." She gestured to Ashley and Leandra's clasped hands. "I mean, how long have you known each other? What, about a month? Less?" Ashley's face colored, and Emily nodded. "You know the problems you've had in the past, Ashley. Living together could make things much messier down the road."

"Mom, Leandra is not—"

Her response was interrupted—much to Leandra's relief—by the musical jangling of the doorbell. "That'll be Evie." Ashley gave her mother a quick glare, then stood up, pulling Leandra with her. "I'm going to show Leandra the backyard," she declared, then turned and dragged her lover away.

Outside, Leandra took a calming breath and smiled when she heard Ashley do the same. "I'm sorry about my mom," Ashley apologized. "I knew she was going to be like this."

"It's okay. I understand where she's coming from, really. She doesn't know anything about me, and all of a sudden I'm living in your house and sleeping in your bed. Believe me," Leandra said, and grinned wryly, "I've seen enough protective mothers in my lifetime that I don't hold it against her."

Ashley wrapped her arms around Leandra's taller frame and squeezed. "Thanks for being so understanding. Although," she said, with a wicked little grin, "if you want to do a little growling and snarling later on, I promise to look the other way."

Leandra laughed, and kissed the tip of Ashley's nose. "I doubt that'd give them the kind of impression I'm going for."

"Mmm, but it might be good for a laugh."

Grinning, the two women turned and looked out at the backyard. The twilight gloom was lit by several porch lights artfully arranged to display the landscaped garden and pool, and plates of finger food had been set out on a redwood table on the patio. The small lawn was obviously well tended, and a number of tree ferns gave the garden a slightly tropical feel. Leandra smiled. "Nice."

"Yeah. My mom loves to get her hands dirty out here, and she's got a pretty good eye for landscaping. When I was younger, I used to take my camera into the garden during foggy mornings and photograph the spider webs. They were all covered in dew, and the water beads would sparkle like diamonds in the light. It was great."

"I can imagine." Leandra smiled at the mental image of her lover as a child, taking pictures with youthful enthusiasm. "Your dad seems nice."

"Yeah, he's pretty great. He used to be a lot more uptight, but since he retired he's kind of cooled down. I like him more, now that he's not working."

Just then, they were interrupted by a familiar voice. "Hey, you guys! What's up?"

The two women turned to greet the intruder, and Leandra flashed Casey a grin. "Not much. And you?"

"Same old stuff. Some kid at school made a crack about me wanting to go barefoot, so I made a comment about his acne scars, and he got pissed and tried to throw a punch." She laughed shortly. "Unfortunately, he tripped over his own feet and ended up falling flat on his face. I laughed so hard I almost wet my pants."

Ashley rolled her eyes, but Leandra chuckled. Her mirth petered out, however, with the appearance of Evelyn, who was followed by a tall, handsome man with chiseled features and light brown hair. Casey turned when she saw Leandra's focus shift, and grabbed the man's hand, tugging him forward.

"Leandra, this is my dad. Dad, this is Leandra."

The man extended his hand. "Jason Harrid," he said. "Casey's told me a lot about you, Leandra. It's nice to finally be able to put a face to the name."

Leandra shook hands and offered a polite response, feeling a little more confident now that the gestures of introduction and welcome were coming to her more easily. From the time she'd spent with Casey these last few days, Leandra knew Jason Harrid was a devoted father, and the scent lingering on his person helped her remember that he was a physician at the local hospital. His eyes were gentle and friendly, if a little uncertain. That was only to be expected, she knew. Casey had been adopting many of Leandra's mannerisms recently, and in those circumstances, any parent would be curious.

Evelyn gave Leandra a welcoming smile of her own. "Nice to see you again," she said kindly. "How have you been settling in?"

"Very well, thank you. Ashley's been making me very comfortable. In fact, she's been spoiling me pretty thoroughly." She looked toward her lover with wicked humor.

Ashley caught the seductive glimmer in her eyes and cleared her throat, blushing. "I happen to believe you deserve a little spoiling." Beside her, Evelyn smirked, obviously reading the sexual undercurrent that had flashed momentarily between them.

Owen and Emily soon joined the group, each carrying large platters of food that they placed on the table. Dinner was an informal affair, for which Leandra was particularly thankful. Plates and cutlery were brought out, and everyone helped themselves to what was available.

Feeling a definite sense of self-consciousness—after all, this was the first time in four years that she'd dined in even a casually formal setting—Leandra was extra careful as she selected coleslaw, salad, and a few slices of honeyed ham from the table and arranged them on her plate. Reaching for the cutlery, she couldn't deny feeling a momentary pang of longing for the simpler delights of a meal of dried venison and rice served on a bed of leaves.

Ashley stayed near to Leandra as they ate, wanting to be close in case her lover got an attack of nerves, and also to ensure that her family didn't overwhelm her. She recognized the tension in Leandra's eyes, and the way she kept glancing around as though searching for an escape route. Fortunately, Casey was on hand to keep her somewhat distracted, eagerly showing her off to her parents, who were already curious about Ashley's new romance. Ashley was grateful when her father joined them and began making friendly conversation, inquiring further about Leandra's life in India and how she and Ashley had gotten together. Leandra fielded the questions well; her intimacy with the tigers and other animals gave her the kind of knowledge only a true expert could possess, and she managed to sound like a genuine ranger.

Ashley was impressed. She knew this was difficult for Leandra and had envisioned numerous potential disasters that could ruin this night, but her concerns diminished over the next few hours. Leandra came across as being a modest, quiet sort of person with a great love for animals, and the looks she cast toward Ashley were illustration enough of how much she loved her. The Richards family seemed to accept her into their midst, and Ashley gave her father and sister looks of thanks. Glancing aside, however, her expression turned slightly sour when she saw her mother's worried, disapproving eyes watching from across the way.

Leandra was wearing cotton pants and a simple white shirt, comfortable and casual. With her intense eyes and her braided hair pulled back in a thick ponytail, she looked—to Ashley's admittedly biased eyes, at least— ruggedly gorgeous. Her mother, however, clearly had a very different opinion. Although Ashley had always gone her own way in life, her parents always found ways to balance their support of her independence with their desire to stay close as a family. They didn't always like or agree with some of her decisions, but Ashley knew that sooner or later, they'd get used to the idea of her having a girlfriend. Her concern was that Leandra might be hurt in the meanwhile by her mother's initial dismissive attitude.

So when her mother went back inside, Ashley made a subtle gesture for Casey to take her place beside Leandra, then whispered, "I'll be back in a minute," into her lover's ear. Leandra nodded and went back to listening to Owen, who was telling stories of Ashley's many misadventures in her youth.

Ashley found her mother in the kitchen. Emily glanced up when she heard her approach, opening her mouth to speak. Ashley beat her to it.

"I think we need to talk about this."

"About what?"

"About the way you're treating Leandra." Ashley folded her arms across her chest and glowered. "Everyone else is at least making an effort to be nice to her, even Dad, and I remember times when he was less than liberal-minded in his opinions. But you're sitting out there staring daggers at her, without even trying to get to know her. It wouldn't kill you to say something kind, or failing that, to at least stop being so hostile."

Emily rested her hands on the kitchen counter. "You don't understand, Ashley," she said. "This isn't something I ever thought I'd have to deal with. I don't want you getting hurt because of this."

"I'm not going to get hurt, Mom."

"How can you say that?" Emily regarded her with a confused expression. "Ashley, you've never had a relationship last more than a month. Now all of sudden you drag home some woman from India, and let her move in with you! She has no job, no way to support herself, and no place to go if things end badly. How can you possibly say you won't get hurt?"

Hearing her mother's emphasis on the word "woman" made Ashley narrow her eyes. "Are you upset because I'm sleeping with another woman? Is that what this is all about?"

"No!"

"I think it is." Ashley shook her head. "Well, I'm a grown-up now, Mom, and this is what I want. If you can't deal with the fact that I'm a lesbian, that's your problem, not mine. I don't much care if you like me being with Leandra or not. But I do care when your behavior starts to hurt the woman I love."

"Love? Ashley, I don't care who you're sleeping with, be they male or female. If you want to experiment, I think that's great. But you can't honestly tell me you love this woman. You only met her a few weeks ago."

"That's all the time it took." Ashley shook her head again, trying to calm herself down. She didn't want the sound of raised voices to carry outside. "Leandra is the most wonderful, caring, sensitive person in the world, and if you'd spend just five minutes talking with her with an open mind, you'd realize how much she loves me. Do you think this is easy for her? Coming here to meet you, knowing you might not approve of her?"

"Look, I'm sure—"

"Let me tell you, it isn't. She's scared out of her mind right now, and you're making it that much harder for her to relax." Ashley took another calming breath. "Leandra hasn't had an easy life, Mom. It doesn't take much to make her feel guilty, and she punishes herself for every little thing that goes wrong. Being around other people is hard for her, but she's trying to make this work because you're my family, and she knows you're a big part of my life."

"Ash, all I'm saying is that you should be careful," Emily argued insistently. "I've seen you get all excited about a relationship before, only to have it fall apart a few weeks later."

"Leandra's not like anyone else I've ever been involved with. Why can't you see that? She makes me feel complete, loved. She'd sooner jump off a building than hurt me, and she'd die to protect me from harm." Ashley saw her mother's resolve start to weaken in the face of her absolute certainty, and she took a step closer. "Can't you at least give her a chance? She's not half as intimidating as she looks once you start talking with her." She threw in a hopeful little smile. "Please?"

Emily sighed, clearly helpless in the face of Ashley's persuasive appeal. "I suppose."

Ashley's smile was sincere. "Thank you, Mom. It means a lot to me."

"I'm not saying I'm going to like her right away," Emily continued, "and I plan on keeping an eye on her. But I guess I can be a bit more civil to her."

"That's all I'm asking."

Returning to the others, Ashley made a brief stop at the cooler that sat underneath the table and grabbed a couple of beers. Splashing noises from the pool caught her attention, and she smiled when she saw that Casey had changed into her bathing suit and was taking a dip with her parents. Leandra was watching with definite interest from the sidelines, and Ashley wished she'd thought to get a suit for her. Although, she thought, recalling memories of her jungle adventures, there are advantages to going without. Still, she knew how much Leandra loved the water, so she made a mental note to buy Leandra a bathing suit when she next went into town.

"Don't get any ideas about stripping off and jumping in," she teased, reclaiming her seat. "You'd give everyone a heart attack."

Leandra grinned playfully. "Afraid to show me off?"

"No, but I don't think they need to see all the…shall we say, intimate facets of your personality."

Leandra laughed. "Don't worry, I can restrain myself."

"Good. We're not in the jungle anymore." Ashley glanced up in time to see Casey dive into the pool, squealing, then offered her lover one of the bottles she held. "You want something to drink?"

Leandra studied the offering a moment, her eyes filled with a strange emotion Ashley couldn't read, then she shook her head slightly. "No, thanks."

"Are you sure? It might help you relax a little. Take the edge off, you know?"

Leandra leaned closer. "I used drugs and alcohol to numb myself to the world around me," she said softly. "They helped me stop thinking or feeling the things I wanted to avoid. I don't want to take that road again." She smiled, and Ashley felt her heart melt. "I don't want anything to dull the experience of being with you."

Ashley quickly put the beer on the bench beside her, mentally kicking herself for not thinking of this sooner. *She used to be an addict,* she reminded herself. *Of course she wants to avoid the temptation.* "I'm sorry."

"That's okay. I know you were just trying to help." Ashley held up her own bottle. "Do you mind if I drink?" Leandra smiled. "No, go ahead. Just don't get carried away. Remember, you have to drive us home."

"I'll be good." Ashley twisted the lid off the bottle and took a sip, sighing in pleasure as the cool, malty liquid slid down her throat. She was quite partial to the occasional beer and was happy to indulge after her assignment to India. "You know, if you wanted to drive, I'd be happy to let you. You'd be rusty, but the roads are quiet out here. And those old skills never really go away."

"Thanks, but I don't think so."

"Why not? It'd be a good thing to get used to again."

"I can't drive," Leandra admitted. "I never learned how."

Ashley paused as she was about to take another sip and stared at Leandra in shock. "You're kidding."

"Nope."

"You never learned to drive a car? How did you get around?"

"I rode a motorcycle. Just before I left, I'd bought my first Harley. It was pretty great."

"Really? Wow." Ashley felt a flutter in her lower belly, instantly intrigued. She nudged Leandra with her shoulder. "I can just imagine you on a big, black bike," she grinned. "I bet you looked sexy as hell."

Leandra seemed to catch the heat igniting behind her eyes and scooted a little closer. "I put the bike in storage before I left for India. If it's still there, maybe..."

Ashley grinned. Images of herself wrapping her arms around Leandra's leather-clad waist as they drove along an open freeway on a rumbling Harley made her insides shiver. "I'd love to take a ride with you." She gave Leandra a light kiss on the lips, conscious as they parted of her father's eyes watching a little awkwardly from across the yard. She licked her lips and took another sip of beer. "Better not get too frisky right now," she whispered.

Leandra nodded, a slight smile twisting the corners of her mouth. "I guess not. Maybe later?"

Ashley's grin widened devilishly. "Count on it."

The rest of the night was comparatively pleasant. Leandra seemed to notice the change in Emily's attitude, and readily engaged in a more relaxed conversation with the older woman when she approached. Keeping an eye on them, Ashley appreciated that her mother was making an effort to be courteous. Later on, Casey dragged Leandra away into the house, asking to practice some of her jungle-stealth techniques in private, which left Ashley behind to have a little chat with her sister.

"She's pretty impressive," Evelyn remarked, as she sat beside her sister and watched Casey lead Leandra away. "Casey's a hard sell, but your jungle lover has her hooked completely."

"Yeah, they've been getting along really well."

"To tell the truth, I was a little worried when Case started acting so different. You know, the whole no shoes thing, climbing around outside, getting blisters and cuts on her feet." Evelyn sighed. "And every second word out of her mouth was 'Leandra said this' or 'Leandra said that.' I've never seen her take to someone so readily."

"Leandra's a good role model," Ashley said, always ready to defend her partner. "She may be unorthodox, but she's got a strong sense of responsibility, especially when it comes to family."

"I know. I can see that now." Evelyn patted her lightly on the arm. "Casey's been reading a lot about tigers lately, and India, and all sorts of things. She found a documentary on tigers and forced me and Jason to sit down and watch it with her." She smiled a fond, motherly smile. "This last year, with her studies getting more serious, we've been concerned about Casey's direction in life. She seemed so shiftless."

"I thought she wanted to get into graphic design."

Evelyn grimaced. "She gave up on that a week or so after you left. Now, she's been talking about doing animal studies and maybe looking at a future in animal welfare, or something. I don't know how permanent her interest is, but at least she's giving it serious thought. That's a good start, and I'm sure a lot of it has to do with the time she's been spending with your new friend."

"That's Leandra for you," Ashley said. "She can be charming as hell when she wants to be."

"Yes, I see that." Evelyn's eyes narrowed as she leaned forward. "After all, she managed to charm her way past that chastity belt you've been wearing for the last two years, didn't she?"

Ashley's eyes shot open. "Evelyn!"

"What? It's the truth." Her sister smirked unrepentantly. "You haven't had a date since the Dark Ages, Ash. I thought you were heading into the land of spinsterhood. Leandra deserves a medal for getting you back in the game."

"I wasn't—she didn't have to—what?" Ashley spluttered incoherently, while her sister grinned at her. Her cheeks grew hotter, and she took a deep breath as glared at Evelyn. "I had my priorities," she stated primly.

"Sure you did. Priorities that changed quick as a wink as soon as something interesting caught your eye." Evelyn laughed. "I'm sorry, Ash, it's hard not to tease. I mean, you can't bring home Lady Tarzan and expect nothing from me." She sat back in her seat and regarded Ashley more earnestly. "Seriously, I'm happy for you, sis. The last few years, it seemed like you'd stopped looking for someone to share things with. I didn't want you to have to go through life all alone." She smiled. "I guess it just took you a while to figure out what you were looking for, huh?"

Ashley hesitated, wondering if she was being set up for more teasing. Seeing only sincerity in Evelyn's face, she nodded. "I guess so," she said quietly and chuckled. "Who could have guessed that what I was looking for would be hiding in the middle of the Indian jungle?"

Evelyn laughed. "You never could do anything the easy way, Ash."

"Nope."

The two sisters laughed together for a few moments more, then Evelyn quieted and fixed Ashley with a sly expression. "So, seriously, what's it like with her?"

"What's what like?"

"You know." Evelyn waggled her eyebrows suggestively. Ashley's eyes widened as she interpreted her sister's meaning, and her face burned scarlet.

Evelyn grinned. "I bet she's an animal, right?"

Ashley tilted her nose up and assumed an air of modesty that was ruined by her blush. "I'm not telling you anything."

"Oh, come on! Your first foray into the world of Sapphic delights, and you're not going to give me any details? That's not fair, Ash! I've been a married mother for eighteen years. The least you can do is give me a few stories."

"If you want dirty stories, you can find them somewhere else," Ashley said resolutely. "How Leandra and I express our love is none of your business."

Evelyn snorted. "Oh, don't be such a prude," she taunted. Ashley almost took the bait—her sister was well aware how much she hated any insinuation that she was some kind of straitlaced stick-in-the-mud—but stubbornly kept her lips locked tight. Evelyn gave her a poke in the ribs and added, "You know you want to tell me about her, I can see it on your face. Come on, tell me all about it and make us both feel better."

"Uh uh. No way."

For nearly ten minutes, Ashley's modesty kept her from giving up any intimate details, but eventually Evelyn managed to badger her into offering up a few small confessions. By the time Leandra joined them, they were huddled together giggling, and Ashley shot her sister a murderous look when Evelyn opened her mouth to say something. Though Leandra made no comment, it was obvious by her bemused smile that she had surmised the nature of their conversation, and Ashley offered her a sheepish shrug.

Before they left, Ashley made sure to ask her brother-in-law if he would be able to set aside some time at his office to see Leandra. Her shoulder wound was still a constant source of pain, and Ashley wanted to find out if something could be done to repair the damage. Despite his busy schedule, Jason was happy to agree to an appointment and promised to call and arrange something for later the next week.

Driving back along the winding road toward home, Ashley felt a good deal less stressed than she had that morning. "I actually think that went pretty well...right?"

"Yeah, it did. Your parents didn't seem too stand-offish." Leandra gave her a grateful look. "I don't know what you said to your mom, but whatever it was, it worked wonders. She was almost nice to me at the end."

"You noticed that, huh?"

"Oh, very little escapes me." Leandra's eyes glittered playfully. She reached over and ran a finger lightly over Ashley's thigh, causing her breath to catch loudly in her throat. "For example, I saw the way you and your sister were whispering together like a couple of schoolgirls, and the way you shut up as soon as I appeared."

Ashley flushed a little. "So?"

"What were you talking about?"

"Nothing."

"Uh huh." Ashley knew her tone was thoroughly unconvincing, but Leandra just gave her a loving smile. "Did you reassure her that I'm the best lover you've ever had in your life?"

Ashley almost missed a corner as she felt the heat of Leandra's finger trace closer to the apex of her thighs. "Leandra!" She glared at her lover. "You're going to make me have an accident."

Leandra pouted—an expression that seemed oddly adorable as it contrasted with the predatory gleam in her eyes—but moved her hand away. "I'm sorry." She paused and adopted a meek, submissive tone. Blue eyes peered hopefully at Ashley. "I'll behave if I can have a reward when we get back home."

Leandra's uncharacteristic behavior was having an interesting effect on Ashley's libido, and she was growing increasingly distracted. She glanced at her lover curiously, uncertain where she was going with this line of action, but more than willing to play along. "What kind of reward were you hoping for?"

Leandra grinned, her teeth flashing in the lights of a passing car. "Oh, I'm sure you'll think of something appropriate. You have a very creative mind."

Ashley's smile turned roguish as a few decidedly X-rated images burned their way across her imagination. It took a conscious effort for her not to put her foot down harder on the accelerator as the need to get home became suddenly more urgent. The sound of Leandra's purring reached her ears, and she flashed her lover a hungry glance. "I have a few ideas, if you're up for it?"

Leandra's eyes narrowed. "Always."

The next morning, Leandra lay in bed beside a still-sleeping Ashley, as shafts of sunlight crawled across the room through the gaps in the vertical blinds. Outside, the birds had started their morning chorus in earnest, and Leandra listened intently to the lively sounds. The sensation of Ashley's naked body pressed against her own was softly pleasant, and when she breathed deeply, Leandra could still catch the lingering scent of their lovemaking.

She had been awake for about an hour now, lying silently and enjoying the peace of her surroundings. One arm was wrapped around Ashley, and her fingers combed softly through the long, golden hair in a soothing pattern. After four years of waking up before dawn so she could hunt animals as they watered at the streams, Leandra's sleep pattern had been conditioned to an early start. Now that she didn't need to hunt for her food anymore, she spent this time in quiet reflection, soaking up the presence of her lover and thinking about her life and her future.

Coming back to civilization meant that all the energy Leandra had once spent just trying to survive now required a new outlet. She didn't want to become fat and lazy in this new world, and she could see that happening very easily if she didn't find something to keep herself active. She'd never been one to sit around idly, watching television or some such. Before, Leandra had invested the greatest part of her energy in hunting—both for animals and for new conquests in the bedroom. While the idea of spending the bulk of her time ravishing Ashley senseless had its appeal, Leandra knew she was going to have to find something else to do besides being a great lover. With true survivor instincts, she had adjusted quickly to her new environment, and now her thoughts turned to how she should face the future.

Ashley stirred against her, one hand reaching out and unconsciously fondling Leandra's left breast. Leandra smiled, feeling her lover's breath tickle her sensitive skin. Waking with Ashley in her arms had become familiar, and she knew she'd never grow tired of it.

"Are you awake?" asked a sleepy voice from against her side.

Leandra glanced down and smiled at her adorably disheveled lover. "Yeah."

"Mmm." Ashley yawned long and hard, then, seeming to notice where her hand was resting, she gave a final lingering caress and moved her wandering fingers to a more appropriate location on Leandra's abdomen. Shifting slightly on the bed, Ashley molded her body more closely against Leandra's. "You always wake up too early," she mumbled sleepily.

"It's hard to break old habits." Leandra was quiet for a long moment. "I need to get a job."

Ashley's eyes opened wider, and she studied Leandra's face curiously. "You what?"

"I need a job," Leandra repeated. "What your mom said last night was right. I need to start thinking about what comes next."

Ashley sat up in bed. "Are you sure you're ready for that? This is a big transition for you, from jungle to civilization. I don't want you thinking you have to rush things just because my mom made you feel guilty."

"I'm ready. I need this." Leandra regarded Ashley seriously. "I've been thinking about it these past few days," she said softly. "I've always needed to keep myself busy. I've always needed to define myself by my actions. When I was a poacher, I believed in pleasure, profit, and power. I buried myself in that world and hid from the death of my parents and the loss of my brother. I screwed people over without a care because it achieved what I wanted in life. Then, when I lived in the jungle, my beliefs changed. Out there, I believed in survival, atonement, and protecting my family. Hunting the poachers gave me a new reason to live, a new set of boundaries and rules that I understood and followed." She sighed and shrugged. "Now, my life's changed once more, and I feel lost. I need to figure out my place again."

Ashley listened attentively, then nodded slowly in understanding. "What do you believe in now?"

Leandra thought for a moment, then said in a soft, serious tone, "I believe in us." Her lips curved into a sensuous smile. "In our love."

Ashley returned the smile and planted a kiss on the nearest bit of Leandra's skin she could reach. "What else?"

"I don't know." After a moment of silent contemplation, she continued. "I still believe in atoning for all the things I did wrong. I want to continue the good I did in the jungle, protecting the animals I used to exploit."

"Well, there are lots of organizations that do that sort of stuff. You could get in touch with them. I'm sure they can always use another willing hand."

"Maybe." Then Leandra shook her head. "Those types of organizations are spread out, aren't they? I'd have to travel a lot."

"Perhaps, but I have to do a lot of traveling for my job. It's not so bad."

"Yeah, but…" Leandra smiled shyly at her partner. "I was sort of hoping you'd let me tag along with you when you go off adventuring. I could be an assistant, or an advisor, or something. I know how to track animals and where to find them. I think I could be a big help to you."

Ashley's eyes lit up. "That'd be perfect!"

"That way, we wouldn't have to spend so much time apart," Leandra pointed out needlessly. "I mean, if you need some space, I'll understand, but—"

"No," Ashley interrupted, shaking her head as she hugged Leandra close. "I'd really like that. And I'm sure I can convince my boss to let me take you on as an assistant, especially once he sees how helpful you can be." Her expression turned serious. "But you can't just want to follow me around all the time, Leandra. You need to pursue your own goals as well."

"I know." Leandra was silent for a few minutes. "I was a poacher for most of my life. I spent four years living with tigers in the jungle. I understand how the hunters and smugglers operate, where they go, and when they go there. Surely someone can use that knowledge."

"I'm sure they could, but it's up to you to make the first move. They can't accept your help if they don't know you're willing to give it."

"How do I get in touch with them?"

"You've forgotten that we're living in the Information Age. Communication is as easy as pressing a few keys on a computer."

Leandra sat up a little straighter. "Oh?"

"Yeah. It shouldn't be too tough to find a suitable organization on the Internet, and you can send them an e-mail telling them who you are and how you can be of help to them."

Dark brows contracted in confusion. "Internet? E-mail?" The words sounded like gibberish to Leandra.

"Didn't you have a computer before you went to India?"

Leandra shook her head. "They seemed stupid. I didn't care about typing or numbers. Aren't they just overpriced calculators?"

"Not anymore. Technology has moved fast these last four years. Come on. Let's get up, get some breakfast, and then I'll take you on a tour of the information superhighway." She grinned as she threw off the covers. "Time to bring you up-to-date with the future, Jungle Jane."

After breakfast, Ashley took Leandra into her study and introduced her to the sleek, new-looking computer having pride of place on her desk. Leandra watched, curious, as Ashley switched the machine on. Even before her exile to the steamy, Indian jungle, Leandra hadn't cared for complicated gadgets or expensive electronic conveniences. She had preferred to live her life in the world of flesh and blood, where she could exercise complete control over her environment. Four years of living with nothing more technical than a toothbrush had only increased her estrangement from such modern appliances. Now, watching the computer monitor light up with a crisp, colorful illustration of an African rhino against the backdrop of the Serengeti, Leandra was unsure of how this device was supposed to help her.

Ashley fiddled with the mouse and made a few knowledgeable-looking clicks. "We'll just get on the net and see what we can find." After a few moments and some strange noises, which Leandra thought sounded very much as though Ashley's actions had killed the machine, the screen started changing through a few different pictures, finally settling on one. Ashley glanced at Leandra. "We'll need some keywords first," she explained. "Then the computer will look for those words on the net and bring up a list of possibly useful sites. Let's see, how about wildlife protection organizations." She clicked away at the keyboard.

Leandra moved closer to the computer, her curiosity piqued. Ashley indicated the swivel chair beside her. "Sit down. It's not going to bite you."

Unaware her nerves had been showing, Leandra sat hesitantly in the offered chair. She watched in silence while Ashley studied the screen intently, scanning the search results.

"Okay, this looks good. We've got a lot of things here." Mahogany eyes perused the names and brief descriptions carefully. "Here... This one sounds good." Another point and click brought up a new window, with colorful animal illustrations and a whole list of directories. She gestured for Leandra to move closer. "See? If you click on the thing that sounds like what you want, it'll take you to the next page. Like here, we've got info on poachers and poaching control, so we just move the mouse like so and click on it." Like magic, a new window opened, featuring text on poachers. "We use this bar here to scroll down as we read, and this button here takes us back to the last window." Ashley scooted her seat over a little to make room. "Here, give it a try."

Leandra recoiled. "Oh, I don't think that would be a good idea."

"Why not? You won't break it just by touching it. Come on, just put your hand on the mouse and see."

Leandra reached out to place her hand on the mouse. Moving it around, she found that the arrow on the screen moved with the motion of her hand. Her smile grew broader, as she managed to scroll down the page, reading the neatly printed words as she went.

"So, you have all this stuff on your computer already?"

"Not exactly. This is all on the Internet—it's like a big, electronic library that you can access over the phone lines. People make these websites about stuff they like, or businesses create sites for advertising, selling, recruiting—things like that—without having to travel long distances. The Internet has a lot of uses, although some people just think of it as a global pornography source."

Leandra flashed a wicked grin. "Well, that's important, too."

Ashley rolled her eyes. "Anyway, you find a group that looks like they could use your help, and you can even send them a letter to introduce yourself."

Leandra absorbed this revelation and shook her head in wonder. "The world outside the jungle moves so fast," she whispered to herself. "Four years seems like a decade."

"Technology, in particular, has made some pretty rapid progress," Ashley agreed. "Computers go out of date in a year, nowadays."

Leandra eyed the humming machine with new respect. "Could this thing be used to do banking?"

"Sure. Why?"

"Maybe I could check if I still have an active account."

"Well, if you weren't using the Internet for banking before, you'll probably need to speak with the bank directly to set it up." Ashley gently nudged her aside and made a few clicks. "Let's see…What was the name of your bank?"

"It was a little place in Switzerland called Holmes and Grey."

Ashley typed in a search, and the name came up immediately. "Okay, this is it." Opening the new page, she scanned the details and clicked on a link to their contacts, which brought up a list with numerous phone numbers. Ashley identified one with a finger. "Look, they have a dedicated number for international clients. They'll need an account number and password before they can be much help, though."

"I always used the same password for everything, so that shouldn't be a problem. The account number, on the other hand…" Leandra regarded the screen with narrowed eyes, casting back through her memory for details she'd long ago abandoned. "I hated keeping any private info written down, so I made myself memorize this stuff. I had this trick for remembering the numbers by singing them in a song, so if I can just get the first few digits… It's all in my head somewhere, but it could take some time to dig it out."

"No problem. A lot of banks will accept your date of birth or passport number as identification if you've forgotten your account number, but I'm thinking this is the kind of place that won't be so lenient, right?"

"Right." Leandra took a pen and a sheet of paper from the desk and laid them in front of her. "This could take some time."

"Want me to make some coffee?"

"How about orange juice?"

Ashley gave her an indulgent smile; since returning to civilization, Leandra had developed a strong thirst for orange juice, and she guzzled it by the gallon. "Sure. Keep trying, I'll be back in a minute."

It only took Leandra a few minutes of quiet contemplation before she recalled the first four digits of the account number, and with them came the tune she had used to commit them to memory. By the time Ashley returned with two tall glasses filled with juice, Leandra was humming to herself and hurriedly filling in the rest.

Ashley seemed to have no trouble reading her expression as she handed over a full glass. "You got it?"

"Got it!" Leandra confirmed proudly, smacking the pen down on the desk with a big grin. "Should we call now?"

"It's a twenty-four-hour number, so I don't see why not." Ashley retrieved a portable phone handset and dialed the number from the computer screen. When it connected, she handed it to Leandra, who brought it to her ear just in time to hear a tinny, male voice offer a bright, friendly greeting.

"Holmes and Grey Banking Financial Services, this is Jeremy speaking, how may I help this morning?"

"Uh…Hi, I have an account I haven't accessed in a while, but I'd like to set it up for Internet banking."

"Certainly, I can help you with that. Do you have your account number and pass code?"

Leandra read him the details, ignoring Ashley's amused snort when she heard her password was ARTEMIS01. There was a lengthy pause as Jeremy entered her information, and for a moment, she feared she'd recalled the numbers incorrectly. But then he asked a few additional security questions in a slightly more formal tone, and Leandra guessed this was due to the fact the account had been inactive for several years. After she demonstrated she was who she claimed to be, Jeremy's chipper attitude returned in full measure.

"Excellent. Now, do you have access to a computer at the moment? I can get you all set up here and then make sure you're right to go."

Jeremy walked her through the process for setting up her online banking; it proved to be simple enough that even a confessed Luddite like Leandra could manage it. Thanking the helpful Jeremy, she refreshed the screen and hung up the phone, considering the account details with a melancholy smile. "That should help me pay my way for a while."

Ashley's mouth hung open as she stared at the number displayed at the bottom of the screen. "Is that in dollars? *American* dollars?"

"Yep."

"My God, Leandra…you're *rich*!"

Leandra shrugged a little. "I was pretty good at what I did."

Ashley was still staring at the screen. "Leandra, that's *millions*!"

"Looks that way." Leandra regarded the number, her smile transforming into a sad frown. "It cost me more than it was worth," she said quietly. "That's blood money, Ash. It can pay my way now, but more importantly, it can help me make up for some of the things I did." She sighed. "The next time we go into the city, I'll make arrangements to have the money transferred and the account closed."

Ashley laid a comforting hand on her shoulder. "You're a different person now, Leandra. Just the fact that you're willing to make some kind of reparation shows how much you've changed."

"Being sorry for the choices I made won't bring back my parents," she whispered. "It won't bring back all the animals I hunted and killed, either. I left my exile because I love you, and I want us to be together…not because I've made all my amends."

The two regarded one another for a long moment, then Ashley reached into her back pocket and pulled out a crumpled scrap of yellowed notepad. She handed it to Leandra. "Maybe this could give you a place to start."

"What is it?" Leandra studied the handwritten note curiously.

"Before we left the park, I asked our guide, Tarun, for his contact details. He works mostly around the areas you used to patrol, and he has good contacts with both the rangers and the government. Best of all, he knows enough about you to appreciate how useful your experiences as a poacher could be to the people fighting them."

Leandra considered the suggestion. She had been too distracted by her own anxiety on the drive out of the park to recall much about Tarun, who had been mostly silent the entire journey. "You trust him?"

"Well, I'll admit I found his utter lack of curiosity regarding who was killing poachers to be a bit irritating," Ashley admitted with a grin, "but in this case, it only counts in his favor. You wouldn't have to tell him everything about Shar-Ranjana, but he sees the damage done by poachers all the time. I'd say he's trustworthy."

"It would be good to have eyes in the area. now that I can't be there myself to protect her," Leandra added. "You're right, he's a good place to start. But there's more I can do than just help guide the rangers to target hunting sites."

"I figured you'd feel that way, and I've been thinking about that, too." Ashley reached for the mouse and clicked back through several screens. Leandra watched as she brought up a fresh, blank document. "I rub elbows with a lot of people who work for wildlife preservation groups; my work helps bring attention to their cause, so we often move in the same circles. I can think of several people we might reach out to, who'd be sympathetic to your situation. If you write them and tell them your story, I'm sure they'll agree there's a lot to be gained by working with you."

Leandra looked from the screen to her lover and back again. "It's not that easy," she whispered. "I was a criminal, Ash. What if they condemn me?"

"They might, but I doubt it. They need all the help they can get, especially from someone like you." She stood up and gave Leandra's shoulder a comforting squeeze. "Just take a minute to think about what you want to say. We don't have to do anything with the letter, at least not right now, but you'll be taking that first step." Placing a soft kiss on her lover's braided hair, Ashley turned and left the room.

Alone, Leandra regarded the computer monitor with trepidation. Her fingers traced along the edges of the keyboard, as a thousand memories flooded through her mind in ghostly waves. The faces of her parents and her beloved brother. Images of carnage she had been responsible for. The tired, drawn faces of drug addicts and young kids whose lives she'd helped destroy with the narcotics she'd smuggled and sold. Haunting, pain-filled cries of animals as she'd confined them in locked cages, to be shipped all over the world. The memories rushed through her mind so fast, Leandra had to close her eyes to keep them from overwhelming her. When she opened her eyes again, it seemed her whole life had come down to this one moment...to the emotionless, bleak screen of the monitor and its sterile non-judgment.

Leandra took a deep breath, laid her hands on the keyboard, and slowly began to type.

When Ashley poked her head into the study later, she couldn't help but grin at what she saw. Leandra was perched on the swivel chair with her legs tucked under her, one hand on the mouse and the other resting beside the keyboard. The monitor displayed a detailed, intricate map on which dozens of small figures raced around. The computer speakers relayed sounds of battle and cries of victory. As she stepped into the room and circled her lover, Ashley's grin grew wider at the expression of fixed intent Leandra wore—an expression reminiscent of the one she'd worn while hunting in the jungle.

"Hey, you." Ashley raised an eyebrow when Leandra glanced up from her game. "I thought you were writing a letter."

"I did." Leandra turned back to the screen. "I followed the help directions and figured out how to save it. It wasn't so hard. Then I was looking through these disk things and I found this game."

"Warcraft, right? That's Casey's." Ashley stepped closer and watched the miniature soldiers launch another attack. "I'm impressed you figured it out so fast. I could never really get into it. Having fun?"

"Yep. These orc thingies are stupid. I've almost taken them down." The exultant gleam in Leandra's eyes was indication enough that she was completely involved in the game.

"You should be careful," Ashley advised. "These games can be addictive." She paused when her warning elicited no response. "Did the letter turn out okay?"

Leandra's hand stilled on the mouse a moment. "I think so, but I'm open to suggestions. It actually felt a little like I was writing a job application… which I suppose is what it is, huh? Here, take a look."

With a few clicks, Leandra minimized the game and brought up the document. Ashley leaned over her shoulder and scanned the lines on the screen:

To Whom It May Concern,

I am writing to you in the hope that I may be of assistance to you in your wildlife preservation efforts. In particular, I believe I could be of great aid in your fight to curb the black market animal trade.

In a previous life, I made my fortune as a smuggler, poacher, and dealer of exotic animals. I slaughtered entire herds of endangered animals for profit and pleasure. I was responsible for trafficking shipments of rare wildlife to other countries under torturous conditions. And I helped refine the art of smuggling butchered animal parts so the black market trade could continue, despite laws that might otherwise have been effective in their efforts to restrict it. In short, I was one of the people you are trying so hard to exterminate...and it is for this reason that you will find this letter unsigned. I don't wish to appear untrusting, but I understand the disdain you must have for one of my former profession.

Four years ago, something happened which changed my life and forced me to recognize the terrible creature I had become. I was saved—to my way of thinking—by the very animals I would have hunted and killed without mercy. In penance for my crimes, I turned my back on civilization and dedicated myself to protecting the lives I had once sought to exploit. Living among them, I gained a deeper and more personal appreciation for the creatures I had once viewed only as prey. When poachers came, I fought against them in defense of my new family.

Now, however, fate has once again altered the course of my life, and my exile has come to an end. I can no longer live in that solitary world, and so I must seek other ways to atone for my crimes. To that end, I am writing this letter to you, hoping that you will be able to see past the creature I once was and help me continue my path to redemption.

I have a great many skills at my disposal, which I have no doubt would be of great service to your mission. Not only do I understand the methods and means of the poachers you are trying to stop, but I also understand the ways of the animal world. The jungle was my home for four long years, and the animals I lived with were my only family. I know that if you could find it in your heart to look beyond the person I once was, my talents and resources could serve as powerful weapons in your war against the men who are destroying the natural world.

I would dearly like to meet in person to discuss how I might benefit your cause, and anxiously await a response. I hope it will be one of a positive nature.

Sincerely,

"The (Former) Indian Menace"

Ashley gave Leandra's shoulder a gentle squeeze. There was so much sincerity and pain and hope in those words, she only hoped whomever they sent the letter to would find it as moving as she did.

"It's good," Ashley said, her voice catching a little. She cleared her throat. "Really good. We can tailor the wording a little, depending on who we're reaching out to. Like I said, I know a few people we could try contacting. Sending the letter anonymously is a good idea, but we'll need to figure out a way for them to reply that won't expose you until you're ready. I'm thinking a prepaid mobile phone would probably be best."

Leandra lifted an eyebrow, clearly amused. "How very cloak and dagger."

"Hey, I said I *doubt* they'll condemn you, not that I can guarantee it. Not everyone's going to warm up to you the way I did. We play it safe to start with." She was silent in thought for a while, not wanting to overwhelm Leandra with too many issues at once. "You know," she said at last, "we could use the Internet for other things, too. I know we haven't talked about it yet, but there's a chance we could track down your brother. He should at least know you're still alive."

This time, Leandra turned and gave Ashley her full attention; her expression hauntingly vulnerable. "Is that something you...think I should do?"

"I don't know, Leandra, but I definitely think it's something you should consider." Ashley paused. "It's been so many years. Maybe he's thought things through. Maybe he's forgiven you and wants his sister back. Is it fair to let him go on thinking you're dead?"

"Is it really fair for me to open those old wounds again?" Leandra looked away. "I don't know that I could handle his rejection a second time."

"At least you could show him you're trying to make things right and that you're sorry for what happened."

"Maybe." Leandra was still for a long moment, then she turned back to the computer and brought the game back to life. Ashley took that as a sign the conversation was over, and she didn't press any further.

"Just think about it," she said softly, giving her attention back to the game Leandra was winning with brutal, cunning tactics.

The next night, Leandra lay on the couch, her head resting in Ashley's lap while she watched the television through slitted, feline eyes. Casey sat cross-legged nearby, her interest focused intently on the documentary she'd recorded and brought over for Leandra and Ashley to watch—one which featured some admittedly spectacular footage of various wildlife. Ashley was combing her fingers softly through Leandra's braids, and the resulting sound of her purring reflected how utterly relaxed and pampered she was feeling.

Casey rolled her eyes and glared at them. "God, Leandra, can't you keep that noise down? You sound like a fighter jet."

"She can't help it," Ashley said. "It's instinctive for her." Leandra stretched herself out more fully across Ashley's lap and made a conscious effort to tone down the rumbling coming from her chest. This mollified Casey, who turned her attention back to the images on the television screen.

Ashley leaned over and whispered softly in Leandra's ear. "You sound like you're in a good mood."

Leandra glanced up lazily. "Do I?"

"Yes."

"Maybe that's because of all the attention I'm getting right now."

They continued watching the television in silence, Ashley's fingers continuing their relaxing ministrations, then Leandra heard her say in a soft undertone, "This really is working out, isn't it?"

"Yeah, it is." Leandra turned a little and gazed lovingly at her partner. "Better than I thought it would, actually."

Ashley hesitated. "Did you really have a lot of doubts? You know, about being able to make this thing work?"

"I knew there were going to be problems," Leandra acknowledged. "I wasn't sure how much of my humanity had been lost out there. But if you're asking if I doubted our love?" She smiled teasingly. "I wouldn't have come back with you if I had."

Ashley leaned down and pressed her lips to Leandra's forehead. "Thank you."

"You're welcome." Leandra fixed her sleepy eyes back on the screen before her.

Things really were coming together. Leandra could feel herself changing in subtle ways. The edgy instincts that had developed in the jungle were still strong, and she knew they would be a part of her nature forever, but she was finding it easier to deal with them than she had expected. Of course, the true challenges had yet to be faced. Leandra hadn't really ventured into social situations yet, and there were still issues that she knew would have to be confronted at some point: her brother, the animal rights groups, and of course, the suggestion Ashley had made that the torn ligaments and muscles in her shoulder might be repaired with surgery. Leandra had no misconceptions about how difficult things could become down the road, but she had accepted this place as her home now, and she had a new family to love and care for.

After four years in the jungle, Leandra felt like she had finally come home.

ABOUT AMBER JACOBS

Amber Jacobs was born in Adelaide, South Australia, in 1979. She grew up in Victoria, spending most of her adolescent years living in a wildlife shelter and helping care for a motley menagerie of orphaned and injured native animals. After graduating from University with a BA in Communication, Amber worked in a variety of jobs, but has always nurtured her creative energy through her writing and art. She is always working on new stories and ideas that usually incorporate her passion for animals, medieval history, and romance. She hopes to publish more novels in the future.

CONNECT WITH AMBER

Facebook: www.facebook.com/people/Amber-Jacobs/100010392061669

E-Mail: amberj8@hotmail.com

OTHER BOOKS FROM
YLVA PUBLISHING

www.ylva-publishing.com

NIGHTS OF SILK AND SAPPHIRE

Amber Jacobs

ISBN: 978-3-95533-511-3
Length: 309 pages (113,000 words)

Dae is rescued from desert slavers by the mysterious Zafirah Al'Intisar and placed as a prize in the Scion's harem. At first, Dae struggles with desires she has never before experienced, but as love and lust collide these two women slowly forge a bond.

REQUIEM FOR IMMORTALS

Lee Winter

ISBN: 978-3-95533-710-0
Length: 263 pages (86,000 words)

Requiem is a brilliant cellist with a secret. The dispassionate assassin has made an art form out of killing Australia's underworld figures without a thought. One day she's hired to kill a sweet and unassuming innocent. Requiem can't work out why anyone would want her dead—and why she should even care.

SECOND NATURE

2nd revised edition
(The Shape-Shifter Series – Book 1)

Jae

ISBN: 978-3-95533-030-9
Length: 496 pages (146,000 words)

Novelist Jorie Price doesn't believe in the existence of shape-shifting creatures or true love. She leads a solitary life, and the paranormal romances she writes are pure fiction for her. Griffin Westmore knows better—at least about one of these two things. She doesn't believe in love either, but she's one of the not-so-fictional shape-shifters.

FENCED-IN FELIX

(Girl Meets Girl Series – Book 3)

Cheyenne Blue

ISBN: 978-3-95533-706-3
Length: 308 pages (87,000 words)

A tough life in outback Australia means Felix has no time for romance. When the peripatetic Josie asks Felix to board her horse, Flame, Felix is delighted as she'll now see more of Josie. But there's something suspicious about Flame, who bears an uncanny resemblance to a stolen racehorse. Felix is falling hard for Josie, but is Josie all she seems, or is she mixed up in shady dealings?

COMING FROM YLVA PUBLISHING

www.ylva-publishing.com

ROCK AND A HARD PLACE
Andrea Bramhall

Jayden Harris is an expert climber filled with demons after surviving an avalanche. When she and marketing executive Rhian Phillips are forced to work together for a reality show, she expected it to be hard. They both expected things to get rocky—they are facing snow, ice, and a daunting mountain range, after all. But neither of them ever expected the hardest thing would be resisting each other.

THE BRUTAL TRUTH
Lee Winter

Aussie crime reporter Maddie Grey is out of her depth in New York and secretly drawn to her twice-married, powerful media mogul boss, Elena Bartell, who eats failing newspapers for breakfast. As work takes them to Australia, Maddie is goaded into a brief bet—that they will say only the truth to each other. It backfires catastrophically. A lesbian romance about the lies we tell ourselves.

Primal Touch
© 2017 by Amber Jacobs

ISBN: 978-3-95533-858-9

Also available as e-book.

Published by Ylva Publishing, legal entity of Ylva Verlag, e.Kfr.

Ylva Verlag, e.Kfr.
Owner: Astrid Ohletz
Am Kirschgarten 2
65830 Kriftel
Germany

www.ylva-publishing.com

Second revised edition: 2017

Credits
Edited by Zee Ahmad & CK King
Proofread by Paulette Callen
Cover Design and Print Layout by Streetlight Graphics

www.ingramcontent.com/pod-product-compliance
Lightning Source LLC
Chambersburg PA
CBHW031216020726
47499CB00002B/600